Breaking Away

Tonya Muir

Yellow Rose Books
a Division of
RENAISSANCE ALLIANCE PUBLISHING, INC.
Austin, Texas

Copyright © 2000 by Tonya Muir

All rights reserved. No part of this publication may be reproduced, transmitted in any form or by any means, electronic or mechanical, including photocopy, recording, or any information storage and retrieval system, without permission in writing from the publisher.

ISBN 0-9674196-4-6

First Printing 2000

9 8 7 6 5 4 3 2 1

Cover art by Barbara Maclay
Cover design by Mary Draganis

Published by:

Renaissance Alliance Publishing, Inc.
PMB 167, 3421 W. William Cannon Dr. # 131
Austin, Texas 78745

Find us on the World Wide Web at
http://www.rapbooks.com

Printed in the United States of America

Breaking Away

Special Notice

In honor of the many who have courageously fought the battle and won, and in memory of all those we have lost, it is our very great honor and privilege to donate $2.00 from the sale of this book to Unknown Primary Sources Cancer Research. With the permission of the author, and in coordination with Sword and Staff, we give this back to our community in the hope that our small effort will help and one day soon a cure will be found. A special "thank you" goes out to all who help us in this effort.

Dedicated to:

Dawn and Georgia whose tireless work and keen eyes made it better than it was and also taught me a lot. They're also priceless friends. Thank you both, so very much.

My husband Clive who doesn't understand why I write but gives me the time and freedom to do it.

And, finally to those wonderful people who have offered their support not only in my writing but in my health. Words cannot express my gratitude and there is no better support team.

— Tonya

With Faltering Steps

Chapter 1

Lacey Montgomery downshifted the RX-7 with casual skill as she took Exit 19 and followed the signs for Aqueduct Racetrack. *Horse racing*, she thought as she shook her head with mild distaste. Of all the jobs she'd done for her boss, this one had to be the most peculiar.

Waiting for a light to change, Lacey casually flipped a thick black braid over her shoulder and glanced into the rearview mirror to meet her own ice blue eyes as she recalled the conversation with her superior the afternoon before.

"Lacey, get in here," Vincenzo Russo had called in his Italian-accented baritone, bidding his lieutenant into his office in the several million dollar mansion he liked to call a home. She had entered quietly, as was her style, and had observed him and the surroundings with negligent ease, having been in this office countless times before. She'd run her eyes casually over the oak-paneled walls and overflowing bookcases, searching for anything out of the ordinary and finding nothing. Finally, her eyes had rested on Vinnie himself.

He was a large man, just over six foot five with dark hair and dark eyes. His temples had greyed slightly in indication of his forty or so years of existence though he often cited his employees and his family as the real cause. He had pinned her with those dark eyes; caramel-shadowed depths surrounded by tanned skin and handsome features.

"I need you to go to Aqueduct tomorrow to watch morning workouts. The horses aren't doing as well as they should. I need you to find out why." With a wave of his hand, he'd dismissed his most trusted employee and bent back to the papers cluttering his desk.

Without a word, Lacey had nodded and left. Great. She'd done everything from drug runs to illegal arms deals for Vinnie. She'd never batted an eye at murder and torture, serving him loyally for a decade. It seemed odd that she had to go play with horses for a day or more, but she would never question orders from the man.

Briargate Farm was a breeding and racing establishment and was actually one of Vinnie's more legal ventures. The horses themselves were a legitimate business, though it also provided a nice cover for drugs and other illicit endeavors as needs arose. In truth, he had a soft spot for the horses and racing and the social circles the farm permitted him access to.

As a woman who'd tortured and killed many times in the normal duties of her job, it was almost insulting to be sent on a lesser mission. But Vinnie knew that, and would have only sent her if he thought her skills were required for this task and the horses were important enough to him that he wanted her to handle them personally. So she pulled the RX-7 into the trainer's lot, already having received the required passes from the farm itself, and parked as near the entrance as she could.

No amount of warm holiday cheer could have worked its magic past Christmas and into the bitter month following. January had brought with it icy rain and biting winds. This morning's only bright point was the rain hadn't started to fall yet, though the overcast skies threatened such an imminent downpour. Still, the air was unpleasantly cold as the dark woman unfolded her six foot frame from the small sports car

With Faltering Steps

and wrapped her leather trench coat more closely around her. She glanced at her Ray Bans on the passenger seat, deciding the early grey dawn did not require such protection, so she left them where they lay and checked to make sure her Glock was in its shoulder holster. Then, with a deep sigh of icy frosted breath, she made her way through the guarded gate and towards the track, knowing the Briargate horses should be warming up.

She wasn't disappointed as she came to the rail and recognized a short balding man who was thicker through the middle than he probably should have been. He turned grey eyes towards her as she approached and she watched the recognition and alarm flash through his eyes before he held a hand out to her.

"Lacey." He nodded once, gripping her hand firmly. He easily recognized her from business meetings and dinners. No one forgot Vinnie's right hand man if not for her striking eyes and contrasting hair, then for her six feet of intimidating muscular build and often feral look. The stories he'd heard about her inhuman coldness were enough to chill him to the bone despite the heavy barn jacket he wore. He shivered.

"Bob," she said casually, running cool eyes over his stocky frame, allowing her stoic visage to do its work for her. "Vinnie wants to know how the horses are running."

The trainer shrugged one shoulder and turned back to the track with relief when one of the exercise boys called to him.

"Sunnyside is up at the pole, do you want me to join 'im?" the kid asked, standing upright in stirrup irons as he fought a young chestnut colt for his head.

Bob glanced to the horse in question, 5 furlongs out, dancing at a marker but held in check easily. "That girl never listens," Bob muttered, then, more loudly. "Yeah, take Laddie up there and move back a furlong. I want you to breeze 'em the first and then drive 'em for the five. Stay off the rail, that colt's a hugger. Got it?"

"Yeah, Boss." The boy turned his mount and cantered

him up to the bay across the track where the two riders chatted for a moment before pushing back another furlong.

Then chestnut and bay stood shuffling at the marker, each decked out in the barn's colors of blue and red, the bay wearing a hood with blinkers to prevent him from shying. The chestnut was wearing a shadow roll on his nose band to similarly prevent spooking at shadows in front of him across the track.

The riders glanced at each other and then, simultaneously, urged the horses forward down the dirt track. When they passed the first furlong marker, Bob started his stopwatch.

The riders were balanced precariously on the tiny saddles, their bodies raised above the horses' shoulders and necks. Manes whipped at helmets and goggles with the wind. As they came closer, the chestnut edged ahead, long strides eating up the ground easily to pull ahead by a few inches, then half a length.

"Go to the whip, dammit," Bob yelled, his face getting red with his frustration but neither rider did and the bay came behind by a length as they passed the finish line. Bob stopped his watch and glanced over at another man holding a watch.

"Got one oh five on Sunnyside," the other man offered.

"One oh three and four fifths on Laddie," Bob responded with a growl.

Lacey watched all this with mild interest, easily perfecting her air of nonchalance with hands in pockets and dark hair escaping her braid and wisping across leather clad shoulders. She personally didn't care if the horses had broken a land speed record. Actually, she didn't really care about anything except what was wrong and why Vinnie hadn't given her more information on this problem she was supposed to be discovering. It was her job to know all about his drug trades and arms deals but she'd never ventured into his horses outside of their less legal uses.

Ice blue eyes followed Bob casually as he stormed onto the track and grabbed at the bay's bridle, literally pulling the rider to the ground as the horse still circled around them, breathing heavily. The rider landed lightly on her feet and ripped her arm angrily out of the short man's grasp.

He yanked the rider's helmet off and threw it to the ground, revealing blonde hair that fell free to the woman's mid-back. In turn, she pulled off her goggles and retrieved the bay's reins from Bob's hand.

"What are you doing out there? We're not here for a Sunday ride, missy. I said all out and he was loping!" Bob shouted angrily as the rider passed the reins to another helper and watched the horse walk away.

Lacey noticed the smaller woman bristle at the man before her and clench her jaw, but she raised easily to his challenge. "He's not right, Bob. There's something wrong with that colt and he needs to be evaluated before he gets hurt."

"That's my job, not yours. You get on their backs and you don't use your pretty little head for anything except running 'im!" He poked at her shoulder furiously with enough force to actually push the woman back slightly.

"Well if one of us doesn't think, this horse is gonna fall apart before he hits the races. Is that your job? Pull your head outta your ass, Bob, and look at him! He's not right! He's the best-bred horse in this whole goddamned barn and he won't run past a one oh four. Whipping an off horse isn't gonna make him better." The heat fairly emanated from the young woman as she raised her voice in anger, using all of her roughly five foot four inch frame and standing on her toes as well as she poked a finger into the trainer's shoulder in turn.

Bob was fuming, his face beet-red and the sweat on his brow evident.

Lacey observed all this with a small smirk and an interested eye. This girl was full of attitude, and might just have some answers to her questions. Regardless of the reason, she found herself liking the blonde instantly, if only because she'd never much cared for the slimy trainer and enjoyed watching him get his due.

"Get back to the barn, girl, and cool out that colt. If you can't ride 'im, you won't. Is that clear?" the stocky man growled in response, the spittle flying from his lips causing Lacey and the small rider to each wrinkle their noses in reaction.

"Crystal," the young blonde responded coldly and retrieved her helmet and goggles before turning on her booted heel and stomping away to take back the colt from the young boy who'd been walking him.

But Lacey noticed that as soon as her hands touched the reins, her shoulders relaxed and she reached up to pat the bay gently on the face. He ducked his head into her and pushed her chest with evident fondness.

Lacey observed Bob carefully as he came back around to the rail side, maintaining her passive look without effort. "Bring 'em all back, that's it for this morning," the trainer yelled then tossed a glance to the tall dark-haired woman waiting for him. "C'mon to the barn." But the invitation certainly wasn't extended eagerly and Lacey kept her responding grin to herself. She fed off of the fear of Vinnie's little worker bees.

She walked quietly behind him, running a cold hand through wind-tossed bangs before returning it to the warmth of her pocket. Then she extended her stride.

"Who is that girl?" she asked him casually as she caught up to him and they followed the string of colts and fillies towards the Briargate section of the long training barns.

"Only the most annoying rider I have."

"Why keep her?"

Grey eyes met hers briefly but learned nothing from the stoic face beside him. Of all the things he'd heard about Lacey Montgomery, none of them were good. She was a ruthless killer with a quick temper and no tolerance for bad jobs or stupidity and Bob had lost one of his best jockeys to her cruel hands less than a year ago. Vinnie must be worried about something to send her out. "She's good. She knows the horses. She's not a full time rider, she's out here with Sunnyside. She normally works at the farm itself."

Lacey nodded silently and made a mental note to definitely speak with this young woman. She was familiar with the track and the farm, which could only be helpful.

Once at the barn, she deviated from Bob's side and walked down the large cement aisle to find the rider in question. She was at the far side of the barn, stripping the cross-tied colt with expert hands and placing the tack in the nearby tack room.

As Lacey approached she heard the woman's voice, soft now and not filled with anger, murmuring to the bay whose ears flipped back casually from time to time. "It's okay, boy." Her gentle voice floated through the quiet barn easily. "We'll figure it out, I promise."

"Figure what out?" Lacey asked from her position, leaning against a stall door not fifteen feet away from the small rider, left ankle neatly crossing the right, hands stuffed casually in coat pockets. The young blonde nearly jumped out of her skin.

"Saw you with Bob, you one of the Big Man's cronies?" she recovered and looked to the other woman briefly, but long enough for Lacey to see bright green eyes that twinkled slightly with amusement.

"Depends on which Big Man you're referring to," Lacey responded in her typical husky voice but she found herself liking the gutsiness of the young woman before her. She pushed herself away from the door with her elbow and took a step closer to colt and girl.

"Vinnie what's-his-name," she responded waving a hand with a careless gesture then ducking under the colt's neck to sponge off his other side.

"Ah." Lacy nodded with a smirk and a raised eyebrow, which was lost on the busy young rider. "Then, yes, I am a crony."

The woman laughed lightly at Lacey's agreement to that title. "Do you have a name? Or do they just call you Crony Number Six or something like that?"

The dark woman acquiesced, nodding her head slightly. "Lacey Montgomery."

"Rachel Wilson." The blonde ducked back under the horse's neck to offer a soapy wet hand. Lacey knew this was a test of sorts so she accepted the hand easily, ignoring the wet mess dripping from their joined grasp, and noticed that the smaller woman's grip was firm and well-muscled. And that her green eyes were open and honest, if not a bit challenging.

"Can I help you with something?" Rachel asked, hesitating maybe a bit too long with grasped hands and connected eyes before going back to her task by throwing the soapy sponge into a bucket and scooping another sponge from a bucket without soap. Once the colt was rinsed, she grabbed a sweat scraper out of the tack box and set to work on the mahogany hide. She moved the grooming tool quickly over the bay's muscular body and sheets of moisture splattered on the cement floor to steam there in the cold winter air.

Lacey watched her work, impressed by her efficiency and casual nature, moved inexplicably by their brief moment of contact. This was a confident, self-assured woman before her, who wasn't afraid to speak her mind. Rachel glanced to her again as she switched to the colt's other side when the dark woman didn't answer her question.

"Ah, the strong silent type." The blonde nodded knowingly. "That's all right, I'm not." Rachel grinned wryly. "So I can talk enough for both of us. Let me guess." She paused in her work to tap the sweat blatle against her chin and crinkle her brow in thought. "Vinnie whoever thinks his horses aren't running well and sent you to check it out. Now, the question is, how worried is he ... which would presumably be answered by your number in the line of cronies."

Lacey considered the question in stony silence for several long seconds before she felt her amusement get the better of her. "Call me Crony Number Two in charge of business affairs." The dark woman smirked at this young rider before her, giving her more leeway than she'd ever done in such an interview. In fact, at this point her subjects were often bloody and begging.

This was not lost on Rachel, who read the other woman's

stance and eyes carefully, knowing her to be capable of great violence. She tread the line carefully, having too much fun to back off entirely. "Ah." The blonde nodded. "Business affairs. So the horses are losing money?"

"Don't think so. Why don't you let me ask the questions?" Lacey responded with flashing blue eyes and it made Rachel smile, not at all responding to the threat in that glare which surprised and impressed the darker woman.

"Ask away. I'm all ears ... well, not all ears. Sunny has bigger ears than I do but I think, in the end, I'm a better listener. Huh, big boy?" She patted the colt affectionately as she pulled a woolen cooler over him and attached it to the back strap of his halter. Then she moved to settle it over his haunches and clip it around his tail.

Lacey was doing her best to not outright smile at this woman, enjoying her company and easy nature more than she probably should. "You said the colt wasn't running right. What do you mean? Is he lame?"

"Nah." Rachel slipped into the tack room where she exchanged tall leather riding boots for ratty tennis shoes and pulled a canvas barn jacket over her navy turtle neck. "He comes up sound for all the checks. Vet's been to see him several times. But he's not himself. He used to love to run, but now it's like pulling teeth to get him into stride. And he doesn't fight to win. He's listless, depressed maybe."

"Bloodwork?"

"Nothing unusual, high white counts. See how he's standing?" the rider asked, indicating the colt with a wave of her hand.

The dark woman shrugged, he looked okay to her.

"His feet are spread kinda wide, like he's trying to keep his balance. When he moves he stumbles more than I think he should. We tried a bunch of different shoes on him but it's the same."

"Off his feed?"

Rachel cocked her head the other woman's direction, surprised at her exhibited knowledge of horses. "Yeah. A little. He's lost some weight. His coat's not in as good condition as it should be for his feed and level of exercise."

"Is he the only one?"

The blonde unhooked Sunny's cross-ties and attached a lead shank to his stud chain, then jostled it slightly to let him know it was there. "C'mon, Sun," she said softly to him and started leading him down the barn aisle. Lacey fell into step beside the smaller woman, hands in pockets, head tilted slightly to look at her.

"No. Not really. The barn's been kinda off lately in general. There's a filly we sent back last week, she was here in training and started acting the same. Took her home and she fell down on a morning exercise, it took three people to get her standing and then she kind of acted drunk. She ran great last year."

They left the barn and started out towards a large barren area where others were leading horses decked out just like Sunnyside. "There's a Slew colt who's just being broken and he managed to get hung up in the starting gate at the farm. He stumbled on the way out and ripped the hell out of his saddle and now they're retraining him to the gate. He's behind anyway, shoulda been starting in the Spring this year but he can't even look at the gate without falling apart so they'll probably have to sell him. Plus, he has the other symptoms, too. Off his feed, listless, clumsy," she continued easily, only occasionally glancing to her silent chaperon.

"Slew colt? What does that mean?"

Rachel cast her companion a somewhat humorous look. Apparently cronies didn't need to know much about this part of the business. "Seattle Slew. Won the Triple Crown in '77. His lines go back to Bold Ruler?" She watched the woman for any hint of recognition. "Bold Ruler was Secretariat's sire."

"Ah." The dark head nodded. There was a name she knew.

Rachel smiled, everyone knew Secretariat. As the '73 Triple Crown winner, he was the first in twenty-five years to claim that title. He'd run the Derby in under two minutes and won the Preakness by thirty-one lengths. The young rider had a framed poster of that victory on her apartment wall.

"Not worth the money and effort to retrain him if he misses this year?" the dark woman asked.

Rachel inclined her head slightly. "Well, Seattle Slew is a broodmare sire."

"What does that mean?"

"His daughters make great broodmares but his sons aren't normally spectacular. Cigar is out of one of his daughters."

"So, this colt may not have had much promise anyway." Lacey nodded her understanding.

"Ah ha!" Rachel beamed. "Good to know you're not all beauty and no brains." *Oh my God, did I just flirt with this woman?*

Lacey did her best to ignore the comment and the somewhat shocked expression on the younger woman's face. "So what happens?"

Rachel glanced at her briefly, recovering from her moment of insanity and searching the other woman's well-planed features and concentrated look. "Nothing. We sell him as a prospect, hope they look at his bloodlines and his flat run and not ask to see him in the gate. It's poor business for future deals, but ..." She shrugged, letting her voice trail off.

The blue eyes flashed towards her but Rachel had already redirected her own gaze to watch the horse ahead of her who was giving his walker a little trouble. "Is that legal?"

Rachel delivered her own raised eyebrow smirk at this question. "Legal? What do you care about legalities, Crony Number Two? How do you make your money, Miss Black-Leather-Trench Coat?" But the harshness of her words was lightened by the sparkle in her eyes. *I think either I am flirting with her or I've lost my mind because there's no doubt she's a murderer.*

And Lacey found herself smiling back even though she'd

punched people for less than that. "You always speak so frankly?"

Rachel glanced at her companion again and her expression softened slightly. "Sorry. I'm not normally quite so abrasive," she admitted with a self-deprecating grin. "Don't know what got into me." For the first time since they'd met, Lacey saw something close to doubt pass over the fair woman's features. "It's been a rough morning, a rough couple of days. And I guess I knew they'd be sending someone like you to get rid of me. So I thought I'd go out with a bang." The smile she offered this time was apologetic.

"Get rid of you?" Lacey asked slowly, quirking an eyebrow. "I'm not here to off you, lady. I'm just asking questions."

To which Rachel responded appropriately and laughed again. "No, no. I meant there's a lot of stuff going down and I'm about the most verbal person they have at the barn or here. Figured if they needed a scapegoat ... I'd be the best they could find. Easy to fire ... not kill." There were moments of silence between them. "I hope," the blonde deadpanned.

Lacey considered this as they walked along in silence for a few more strides. "So, being verbally abrasive with me helps you how, exactly?"

Rachel flashed a full-fledged smile to the taller woman. "Well, you know, brave and smart aren't the same things. I figured I'd go down with a fight. I like to live on the edge." *Though this fire I'm playing with now may be too hot for me.*

Lacey smiled, the simple move making her dark features light up and her eyes shine brighter. "Okay, let's try this again." She stopped and Rachel pulled Sunnyside to a halt as well. "I'm Lacey Montgomery. Here to do a little research for my boss and find out why his horses aren't doing as well as they were." She removed her warm hand from her pocket and extended it to the smaller woman.

The rider switched Sunny's lead line to her left hand so she could shake with her right, smiling as she did so. "So who'd ya piss off to get that crappy assignment?" But she laughed when she got a raised eyebrow from the other woman. "Right, new beginning. Sorry. Rachel Wilson, rider and barn rat, pleased to meet you."

"Now ... what's the deal with Bob? You two don't seem to be fans of each other."

Rachel resumed walking and shrugged her shoulders. "Bob's an asshole. He knows a lot about horses and how to condition them and train them, but he doesn't like them. Good money, good social ladder. But he'll run a horse to death for the quick win and not care about its future. I don't agree with that."

"So why do you work for him?"

"Tricky question on two different levels. Truth is I work for the farm manager, though I'm equally unimpressed with him, and on loan to Bob. Sunny's their up-and-coming star but he does better for me than the exercise boys. So I come out and work him here, then go back to the farm and do what I was hired to do ... care for the broodmares and foals."

"And what's the second level?" Lacey asked, blue eyes leaving her companion's profile to travel their surroundings: populated with horses and people glowing orange as sun broke through grey clouds. They'd walked in silence for several minutes before Lacey realized her question hadn't been answered. "Rachel?"

Green eyes glanced her way and something inexplicable flashed across them as she considered her answer, then she turned away and absently ran a hand under the colt's cooler along his neck. "Well, I guess the more accurate question would be 'why am I working for Briargate when it's run by criminals and I disagree with everything they do for the horses.'"

More silence. Lacey couldn't explain her interest in this young woman whose depth and charisma were intriguing her to no end. She felt an urge to know her better and a twinge of regret at the look that crossed her companion's features. "Well?"

She was answered with a shrug of shoulders and the tilt of a blonde head. "I'm ... uh ... not comfortable answering that question."

Lacey nodded and dropped the subject, knowing already that she'd be headed to Vinnie's offices and rummaging through his personnel files as soon as she left here.

"I gotta put him up and get back to Briargate," Rachel said to fill the void. She offered the woman beside her a slight smile. "Sorry about earlier."

Lacey shrugged her shoulders. "No need to apologize, right? Maybe I'll see you around."

"Yeah, later." She turned the colt to walk him back to the barn, but glanced over her shoulder twice to see the dark woman's retreating back. She hoped she would see her again, liking the woman's husky voice and striking eyes.

Chapter 2

Lacey glanced at the clock on the mantle. It was just past 11:00 p.m. and she'd been up since well before dawn to go to Aqueduct. Now she sat on the large leather couch in her own home, reading from the detailed personnel files she'd gotten at Vinnie's. Being a paranoid man, Vinnie had thorough checks done on everyone who worked for him.

She'd also questioned Vinnie more thoroughly about his motives and realized the man was genuinely concerned about the horses. Sunnyside was one of his favorites and he had big plans for the stunning colt including campaigning overseas and then returning to stud. The lame filly Rachel mentioned was nice but nothing spectacular, same with the other colt. So now she concentrated on the personnel files she'd pulled.

Lacey found quickly what the rider had been hiding.

Young Rachel Wilson grew up in rural New York, just outside of Rochester, until her father died when she was in high school. A few short months later, Rachel and her sister became dependents of an aunt and uncle, apparently the mother's brother, when the mother committed suicide. The bare bones factual account had no details on the death or the suicide.

The girls were apparently living in a questionable household at that point. This was evidenced by repeated calls to social services by teachers to investigate bruises on their bodies and markedly withdrawn personalities. When Rachel turned seventeen, she dropped out of school and ran away from home, dragging her younger sister with her to live in New York City. Her employment history for this time showed minimum wage work in restaurants and hotels. There was no address so the girls must have been living in shelters or on the street.

Rachel also had a criminal record. This part of the file had come from the DA's office, immediately alerting the dark-haired reader to Rachel's association with them. At twenty-one, she'd been convicted of robbery, having turned states evidence against her associates to reduce her sentence from manslaughter.

There was a signed affidavit that outlined the events, from Rachel's point of view, of that fateful night. Her actual offense had been driving the getaway car at a convenience store burglary. When she'd gone into the store, after her comrades had been inside too long, she'd seen what they had done and the bloody bodies that were left. The DA's report identified the victims as a cashier and two customers. The young woman had talked her partners in crime into surrendering when the police came, receiving a gunshot wound to her stomach for her troubles. The written account indicated it had been transcribed from a recording of a live interview. It was complete with pauses, hesitations, and stuttering words. The discussion had not been an easy one for the young woman. During this interview in the hospital, Rachel was told that Leslie Ann Wilson was killed at the scene when stray bullets from the store shot her as she waited in the car.

According to the accompanying DA's report, Rachel had never had a weapon and her true crime had been in aiding and abetting what was supposed to be armed robbery. So the dealing had been quick and easy, the sentence reduced to seven years in addition to time served, eligible for parole at three. Parole had been granted and the young blonde had been tossed back on the street. She'd been out of prison for two years now and working at Briargate for just under that.

The only family on record for Rachel Wilson was the aunt and uncle, and an eight-year-old daughter who lived with someone in Rochester. Interesting.

Lacey considered this information carefully, setting aside the factual accounting of Rachel's life as she again pictured the young blonde woman in her mind. She worked for a criminal because she had a criminal record herself, which really didn't make her shine as hirable on the open job market. Vinnie had a way of overlooking those kinds of things.

The other woman's history of violence paled in comparison with her own. It was only her ties to Vinnie and their discreet cover-ups which prevented the dark woman from spending her life in prison and she already knew she'd be spending eternity in hell. But the value of human life was not one of the things she pondered late at night. Nor did she think about her own inclination towards violence and bloodshed. It had become such a part of who she was that she no longer questioned it. She couldn't picture the small-statured woman as a criminal, though. And she certainly couldn't picture her serving time.

Something about those green eyes and that brash smile had captured Lacey's interest and it was this curiosity that had her in her car at just before midnight and headed towards Briargate nearly an hour away. She now knew the factual recital of the young rider's life but she wondered at the emotions behind the printed words. She wanted to know how Rachel Wilson ticked and what she thought. Surely she hadn't misinterpreted the banter and the easy nature, surely the young blonde was equally captivated. And, of course, she wanted to know more about the horses and their poor running. Didn't she?

By the time she arrived, the farm was dark except for the broodmare barn. She knew from her research and her questioning of the farm manager that this is where she'd find Rachel Wilson. Lacey walked down the wide cement aisle towards the center office and opened the door slowly to see Rachel leaping to her feet and blinking at her sleepily. When the dark woman glanced down, she was greeted by a red-masked face and ice blue eyes.

"Woo woooo," the four-legged beast offered her happily, doing a full-bodied wag with ears flattened against skull and neck. Lacey recognized the dog to be a Siberian Husky. It wasn't large, maybe forty pounds, with red and white fur patterned typically across back and shoulders. From what little Lacey knew about the breed, she realized they were normally outgoing and friendly and very rarely made any kind of guard dog. If the image before her was any indication, her memory was correct.

"Hey," Rachel said sleepily, running a tired hand through bedraggled blonde hair. "C'mon in and close the door. Cuz if she gets out we'll be chasing her for hours and that's just not on my list of things to do this morning."

"She a runner?" Lacey asked as she stepped inside and pulled the door shut behind her.

"Almost all huskies are. She's no exception."

The dark woman nodded and reached down to stroke the dog's soft fur, laughing when she twisted her body around the woman's legs like a cat and continued her verbal serenade. "So shy and reserved," Lacey commented.

"Yeah, that's her. A regular wallflower." Rachel watched the woman pet her dog for awhile longer before raising her eyes. "To what do I owe this late night visit?" *Not that I mind, really.*

Lacey hesitated because that was indeed the question and here she was without a good answer. So instead, she responded, "Frank said you were on mare watch at nights. Said I could probably find you in the office if I needed to speak with you again."

Rachel nodded, recognizing the name of the farm manager. "Here I am, loading up on caffeine and watching monitors." The younger woman picked up her mug of coffee again and took a sip, gesturing to Lacey. "Want a cup? It's only fair that you catch up since I'm on my second pot." She grinned ruefully and Lacey found herself returning the grin for no better reason than she liked this woman.

"Sure. Count me in. Is that the dog's excuse, too?"

"Her? Goodness no," Rachel snorted as she pulled a new mug out from the cupboard over the sink. "That's a natural high. Though I'd pay good money for that kind of love of life."

The dog in question danced behind Lacey gleefully, following her all the way across the office to retrieve her cup. The tall woman poured in some sugar and cream before moving to the small couch and letting her eyes slide along the half dozen monitors set up on the coffee table. The dog jumped up next to her to settle a masked head in her lap and look up at her adoringly. "What's her name?"

"Karma," Rachel responded and the dog rolled eyes towards her owner in response before turning her gaze back to the woman she was using as a pillow. With a shake of her head, Rachel spoke more loudly. "Karma, get down you idiot," for which she just got a huge dog sigh.

Lacey laughed and shrugged. "I don't mind," and rested a hand on the dog's shoulder to show that she really didn't mind. Karma flashed her eyes in Rachel's direction as if to brag about her success. "How many mares are due?" Lacey motioned to the monitors in front of her.

"The barn's full of 'em. About twenty. But we're watching five mares and one injury tonight."

"Why the injury? Do you always watch lame horses?"

"No. This filly's a bit sensitive. Whenever we change her routine or feed she gets colicky on us. She hurt herself this morning so they moved her from the training barn over here so I can keep an eye on her. I mean, I'm up all night anyway." Rachel moved to sit beside the darker woman on the couch, realizing fully that her question concerning the late night trip hadn't been answered.

She let her eyes roam casually over her visitor, noticing she still wore the black leather trench coat. When their eyes met slowly, she had to look away because of the flush warming her skin. Though having come to terms with her attraction to women years ago, Rachel normally wasn't quite as flustered as she was now in Lacey's presence.

Lacey smiled at the blush and turned away as well, her fingers playing idly in the soft red fur beneath her hand, because she felt it too. That was the real reason she'd come, she knew. She'd felt it this morning when they'd first met and wanted to see if it was real. At the very least it was mutual. *Great, I'm attracted to Pippi Longstocking. Where does that leave me?*

They each sipped their coffee quietly until Lacey finally broke the silence. "I know why you work for us," the dark woman blurted. Beating around the bush had never been her strong point. She had a lot of respect for people who came right out and spoke their minds so she tried her best to do the same.

Rachel glanced at her briefly, not missing that this woman easily included herself with the organized crime who signed her paycheck, before rising to her feet again and pacing across the room. "I knew you could find out. Did Frank tell you?"

"No, he didn't say a word. Vinnie keeps personnel records and I read yours."

The blonde head nodded slightly and met Lacey's eyes again. "How much do you know?"

"Not much," the dark woman allowed carefully, watching the rider closely to determine when she'd gone too far. "Just the facts. Death of your parents, living with relatives, conviction, time served."

"That's more than anyone else knows." The blonde turned away again to fiddle with the coffee makings. She organized the small containers unconsciously, lining them up behind the sink. "I'm not proud of it."

"I see that," the older woman acknowledged, able to read the regret in her companion's shoulder-slumped posture. "Is there more to the story? Something else you'd like to tell me?"

Rachel considered these words for a very long moment and realized, much to her own shock, that she did want to talk to this person. She glanced back across the room, observing the lanky woman, dressed casually in jeans and a denim button-down shirt, Nike high tops completing the aloof look. Her dark hair was pulled back into a loose braid that fell behind her and blended into the black leather coat. Rachel sighed deeply, turned her attention back to the sink where she now opened the overhead cabinets and started rearranging the contents. "I didn't know they were going to kill anyone. I didn't even know they were really armed. Bunch of punks, ya know? Met 'em on the streets and they had these grandiose ideas of getting what life owed us. Whatever. Life owed us nothing, we were street rats. We left the world that had threatened us because we weren't brave enough to stand up to it. We thought it would be easier to be on our own."

She paused for a long moment but the dark woman said nothing to fill the silence.

"So they had this silly plan to heist some quick cash at a convenience store," she continued at last. "I thought it was the dumbest thing I'd ever heard. I mean, stores like that are so used to punks that the doors are marked like yardsticks and cameras are mounted everywhere. Their money is kept in safes and minimal cash is in the drawers. I knew these things. I argued them. But Leslie was sleeping with one of the guys and she begged me to help. They just needed a driver. She said if I didn't go with them, she could drive. And when I knew she was going with or without me, the decision was easy enough. I'd taken care of her for nearly three years by that point, she was my responsibility."

"So you went along," Lacey urged gently.

"Left my daughter with some waitress at the hotel where I was working at the time and away we went. I didn't see Molly again until we were in court and the foster parents brought her and stood in the hall with her when they escorted me by. It was nice of them, I needed to see her."

"What about Leslie?" The dark woman knew she was on thin ice here. But for some reason she didn't understand, she wanted to hear everything. She wanted to help shoulder the burden the young woman had been carrying for years.

"You know what happened." The green eyes flashed away from their mundane task of organizing sugar packets. They reflected annoyance and fear.

"How did you find out?" Lacey pushed a little harder, sensing that the young rider did want to tell the whole story.

Rachel turned back to her task, fingers now numbly pushing around coffee filters. "After surgery. I was in recovery. They'd pronounced Leslie in the car so she didn't come to the hospital when I did. The nurses and doctors hadn't been thrilled to treat me when they found out how I'd been shot: in a robbery mishap. I could hear them complaining and making derogatory comments. I was angry because I needed them to fix me so I could find Leslie and take care of her. And for my daughter. When I found out the truth, there was never a question as to what I would do. I felt no loyalty towards those assholes. They'd killed three people plus my sister. And shot me. They deserved the life sentences they got."

The small office nearly rang with the ensuing silence.

"It took a lot of courage to do that," Lacey said at last, her dark voice gentle.

The smaller woman barked a laugh, closed the cupboard doors. "First time in my life I showed any. I ran away from everything else or evaded it ... or found the short cut. And that night, instead of driving away with Leslie in the car, safe and alive, I walked in there and faced the devil himself. I've had better ideas in my life."

"You brought them to justice," her companion pointed out, slightly amazed that she gave a damn about justice given her personal employment.

"Coulda done that a bunch of different ways. I should have gotten my sister to safety first." Finally the evasive emerald eyes now watched the woman across the room. "I'll never make a mistake like that again."

"Leslie asked you to go in there, didn't she?" Lacey realized, already able to tell that the small woman before her had been strongly influenced by her younger sibling's desires.

She shrugged. "So what? I didn't have to listen."

"But you did. Because you loved her and she was worried. You were going to round up the other guys and get them out of there, get Leslie's boyfriend back."

"That was the plan. Not a good one in retrospect."

"Hindsight is always twenty-twenty, Rachel," the dark-haired woman allowed softly. "You can't kick yourself for decisions you made then. You were working off of limited information, you made the best decision you could."

The silence strung out between them and when Rachel met the ice blue eyes she would have found cold just the day before, she saw a gentleness she could hardly believe. She tilted her head, acknowledging the other woman's offered compassion. Then she rolled her shoulders slightly, realizing they did feel a little lighter.

"Why didn't you tell me? Surely you know I've done worse?"

Rachel half smiled, turned away again. She'd, of course, known that anyone who admitted to being Vinnie Russo's Crony Number Two was well accustomed to violence and killing. "Why would I? I don't even know you. Just because you enjoy a life of crime does not mean it's my cup of tea. You're some random dark woman who wants to know all the barn's secrets. Why would I have spilled mine as well? In fact, I can't believe I told you now."

"Good point," Lacey murmured, on all counts. "So tell me all of the barn's secrets." She made a valiant effort to lighten the mood and change the subject.

It appeared her young companion was more than ready to take the diversion. "You tell me. You know some of them, I'm sure. Why did that filly fall down on the track last week?"

Lacey considered this for a very long moment before deciding to answer the question. "I really don't know. Vinnie's worried about the horses ... apparently he has a soft spot for them. He thinks something shady's going on."

Rachel took in this information silently.

"Do you know a barn hand by the name of Oz?"

Anxious eyes flashed her direction and caught Lacey by surprise. "Yeah?"

"Why does that name worry you, Rachel?"

She laughed softly, setting her mug back down on the counter to twist her hands together nervously. "Sometimes he comes here at night and ... bothers me. I thought maybe you were him when the door first opened."

"Bothers you?" Lacey felt a fury rise in her belly. "How?"

She shrugged it off. "He hasn't been back since I started bringing Karma to spend the nights with me. He's afraid of her."

Lacey glanced down at the sleeping dog and then raised a questioning eyebrow to the blonde across the room.

"Hey, don't look a gift horse in the mouth, I say. Why do you ask if I know him?"

"Spoke to him today. He seemed kind of evasive."

Rachel raised her head to meet ice blue eyes across the room, "That lame filly I told you about this morning?" She waited for the dark head to nod. "She was his ... like Sunny's mine. We all have certain horses we handle." She was silent for a moment, putting two and two together rather quickly. "He had a colt last year that suddenly started acting differently."

"Like Sunny and the others are now?"

"Yeah. They sold him to some German guy and shipped him there to be put at stud. We never found out what was wrong but he apparently did fine once he got there."

Lacey nodded slowly.

"Where were the drugs?" Rachel blurted, suddenly worried. "Did they put them in him? Did they kill him when he got there?"

"No, no drugs," Lacey promised softly. "Honestly, there are a lot cheaper and more efficient ways to ship drugs than using horses."

"That's good ... I guess." The blonde managed a confused smile. "What do you use them for then? What happens to the horses?"

Lacey met the searching emerald eyes and tried her best to put forth a reassuring smile. "There really is nothing, Rachel. The horses are legitimate. Occasionally, Vinnie uses them to close a business deal or to meet someone promising but, for the most part, the horses are just ... horses. A hobby."

Several long moments of silence hung between them until Lacey broke it. "Did you know that Wheatridge wants to buy Sunny?"

"No." Rachel's voice was tired.

"I think he's been made to run poorly so that he'll be for sale."

Rachel nodded but was silent for many long moments as she absorbed the last few minutes of conversation and her unprecedented confession. Then, with a sigh, "Wow, I feel enlightened. What great news. Did you come here just to cheer me up, Crony Number Two? Cuz it ain't working."

"No, sorry." Lacey smiled gently. "I didn't intend to tell you all this. Who would be working for Wheatridge?"

"You haven't told me anything," Rachel pointed out quietly, shaking her head. "Hell if I know. I didn't even know there was anything going on here, really. Just a string of bad luck, I thought. So I sure as hell don't know who would be giving away secrets. You really think Wheatridge did something to Sunny?"

"Maybe." The dark woman shrugged.

"Why am I so blind?" she groaned and was vaguely surprised at the gentle laugh across from her.

"Because I get the feeling you like to be optimistic."

"Shit load of good it does me." Then she seemed to consider something carefully before lifting her chin. "If you're looking for leaks, I'd start with Oz. And he has a friend he hangs out with named Benny, but Benny works the stallions."

"Any stallion trouble?"

"I'm not over there much so I don't know."

Lacey nodded and stared thoughtfully at the fur under her hand before she glanced back up at the emerald eyes watching her from the desk. "Can I have another cup of coffee?" she requested, not quite ready to leave.

Rachel sat for a long time, part of her wanting to send this darkness away and the rest of her intrigued by it. "Come with me to check the mares and then we'll have another cup," the blonde suggested as she gained her feet and started towards the door.

"I thought that's what the monitors were for," Lacey said but she pushed the dog gently to the ground and stood anyway.

"Still have to look at them. A camera doesn't show everything." She opened the door for her companion while pointing a finger at the dog that followed on the dark woman's heels. "You, wait," she commanded.

Karma gave her owner a startled look before launching into another round of vocal assaults. "Rooooo. Arrrrrrrr."

"I'm not kidding, girl," Rachel said in her sternest voice and was answered by more noise and a swinging of the dog's head from side to side as blue eyes rolled.

"What's she doing?" Lacey asked quietly from her position in the barn aisle, peeking around Rachel to watch the dog's antics.

"She's telling me off."

"That's pretty funny," the dark woman chuckled.

Rachel pushed the door closed and made sure it latched before turning her attention to her companion. "Oh sure, you laugh but you don't live with her." But the young woman was smiling fondly as she spoke.

They walked side by side down the barn aisle, Lacey staying outside when the blonde entered certain stalls and spoke to the inhabitants in a soothing voice. Before too long they were back in the office and pouring more coffee.

"So you do this every day? You're up for morning workouts and then stay awake all night?"

"Mmmm," Rachel agreed, sitting on the couch again and patting its surface for Karma to join her. It didn't take much prompting. "I usually try to sleep a little in the afternoon but I didn't get a chance to today. It's only for a couple of months, really, and then the mares are re-bred and I get to be up more normal hours to concentrate on working the foals that don't go back to their own farms."

Lacey sat on the other side of the dog who greeted her eagerly, thumping a fluffy tail on the couch's cheap upholstery. Ice blue eyes met gentle emerald for very long moments, warming each woman immediately as they read the clear emotions. Finally, Lacey smiled and stood. "I gotta go." Chicken, she admonished herself.

"Some place to be at two in the morning?" Rachel teased and was rewarded with a smirk and one wryly raised eyebrow. But the eyes that had revealed so much moments before were now shuttered and showed none of the emotions the young woman had seen. Instead they were cold and lifeless.

Rachel tilted her head slightly at this transformation and saw a look of sadness cross Lacey's features.

"Sorry ... I just ..." She faltered, not willing to reveal too much to the probing gaze before her. She'd spent years closing herself off from others and living in her world of darkness and death. Rachel was the first person in a long time to chink at that well-placed armor. And she wasn't even trying. She felt bad that the young woman had poured her heart out tonight and she, in turn, was merely taking that and running without any sort of recompense. "I'll see you around, Rachel. We'll get to the bottom of this."

Chapter 3

Two mornings later, Rachel stood in the barn aisle at Aqueduct, wrapping Sunny's legs in heavy cotton bandages. The bay shook his head, tossing the stud chain up and catching it easily in his teeth, seemingly unconcerned at this turn of events.

In contrast to the colt, the young blonde occasionally wiped at wet eyes with her sleeve. The colt's performance had continued to decline and a new rider had been put up for this morning's workout. The exercise boy had been willing to go to his whip as Bob had instructed and Rachel could still see the welts on the bright bay hide. Sunny was being sent home.

She was furious at Bob, the exercise boy, and Lacey. *Where did that come from?* she wondered idly, but it was true. She'd felt a fierce attraction for the woman, had known it was returned, but hadn't heard from her or seen her since that night in the broodmare barn when she'd revealed so much of herself. Probably running scared, she mused. A woman like her doesn't need my emotional baggage.

"C'mon, Sun," Rachel whispered to the colt as she fit a head protector over his ears and then fastened on a bright blue stable sheet with the farm's red lettering on the side.

Bob watched silently as the young rider led the colt outside the barn and to a waiting horse trailer. She tossed the lead line over his withers and gave him a pat on the rump and the colt loaded easily, stepping up into the three horse slant without hesitation. She followed him to attach the trailer tie and take his lead shank off, then she pushed the slant wall into place and secured it before hopping out and closing the back trailer door.

"Rachel," Bob called from the doorway to the barn but just got an evil glare of glittering green eyes.

"Shove it up your ass, Bob," she muttered, not projecting her voice but hoping he heard it anyway.

Then she was driving the Ford diesel out of the race track grounds and towards the highway that would take them back to Briargate farms.

She unloaded the colt nearly forty-five minutes later and led him silently into his waiting stall in the training barn. There she unwrapped his legs and removed the halter and head protector, but left his sheet on him. She was latching his stall when Oz walked by.

"Hey, baby," he said in his creepy southern drawl. "Looks like your baby boy has come back to me."

"Not to you, Oz. Shari's gonna get him." Rachel turned to face the young man.

"No, I got 'im," Oz sneered. "Frank wants some sense knocked into this boy and the job is mine. Unless you want to give me some more favors and I'll spare him."

That was about all that Rachel could take and she snapped. She threw down the items in her arms and launched her compact body at the lanky man in front of her, landing a solid punch before he recovered from the initial shock and returned the punch in kind. Then Rachel jumped on him, forcing him to the ground, straddling his hips and wrapping her fists in his shirt front.

His only response was taunting laughter. "Oooh, this is just right, baby. Like it was the first time ... move your hips a little to the left, baby."

The young blonde started pummeling him in the jaw and face, oblivious to his words and her own surroundings at this point, growling fiercely to him throughout her assault. She was shocked to suddenly feel an arm wrapped securely around her waist and more than shocked when she was lifted bodily from the man below her. She squirmed against this hold until she heard a dark husky voice.

"Easy, Raich, easy," Lacey breathed into the younger woman's ear as she placed her feet securely on the ground.

"Lesbian slut," Oz sneered as he gained his feet and Rachel lunged again but was held securely in place by the taller woman.

"Get the fuck outta here, you shit," Lacey growled, the anger evident in her look and her stance. "Or I'll rip you limb from limb. Ya think I can't do it?"

Oz knew she could do it. He knew who this woman was and what she was capable of. So he scrambled to his feet and fled the barn, leaving the two women standing in the empty aisle.

Slowly, Lacey released her hold on the young woman and watched her closely as she trembled all over with anger and frustration.

"God dammit," she screamed at last, spinning away from the dark woman and kicking a nearby tack trunk with all her might. "Fuck him and his fucking attitude." There were tears in her eyes. "Damn it." Rachel remained quiet for several long moments before turning to Lacey. "What the hell are you doing here?"

Lacey quirked her lips into a half smirk as the assault turned in her direction. "Can I ask what started this?" She gestured with one hand toward Oz's departure route.

Rachel took a deep breath, expelled it slowly, then ran a tired hand through blonde hair. Then she pointed silently to the stall in front of them.

Lacey glanced at the young woman before advancing a step and peeking over the half door. "Sunnyside Up," she read from the embroidered blanket. "Aw, Rachel, what happened?" she asked with sincere regret.

"Bob put up someone else this morning and he whipped the shit out of him. Of course he didn't run any better. Bob pulled him from the string and sent him back here for Oz to fix."

"Why not you? He's yours."

"He's mine only in a pinch. I usually only deal with the foals and weanlings. And I'm an extra rider when they need it."

Slowly, the tall woman tried to assess the slight form in front of her, wondering if she should broach the subject on the tip of her tongue. Lacey decided to go for broke. "I heard Oz say some things, Rachel. About you being on him like the first time ..." Her voice trailed off as she watched the blonde tense up. "Wanna talk about it?"

"Go back to your drugs and guns, Crony Number Two," she muttered softly, trying to hurt the dark woman, intent on forcing her away. She didn't want the pain her already deep feelings for this mysterious woman would inevitably bring. She'd given up her darkest secret only nights before and had gotten nothing for her heartbreak. "I got enough problems without your on again, off again compassion. You come in here like some damned knight in shining armor and you want to know my whole life. You already know most of it. Who the hell are you anyway?" She started to stomp away, moving away from Lacey, attraction be damned.

"Rachel," the dark woman called, causing her companion to stop in her tracks but not turn around. "I guess I'm more used to investigating than revealing. I want to know you better ... for me, not for Vinnie or for Briargate. I've read the records but it's all paper and facts ... I wanna know who Rachel Wilson really is."

"Why?" she asked still without turning.

Lacey took a deep breath, ran nimble fingers through her dark bangs. And decided, once again, to spill it. "Cuz there's something about you that just pulls me ... and I want to know what that is. Because I swear to God I've never felt it before. You feel it too, I know you do." *Look at me, Rachel. I'm pouring my heart out to you like I've never done in my life.* "What do you want to know, Raich? Anything." *God, am I pleading to her?*

The blonde turned slowly, wiping at tear streaked cheeks with an already soaking sleeve. She tilted her head in consideration before smiling meekly. "Just how tall are you anyway?"

Lacey laughed with relief. "Six feet even." More silence as they watched each other from several yards apart. "C'mon. Let's go have some coffee. My treat."

Rachel nodded solemnly and waited for Lacey to come even with her before turning and walking beside the dark-haired woman out of the barn.

****

"Sprite." Rachel nodded to the woman behind the counter.

Lacey cast her companion an odd look. "I thought you were loading up on caffeine these days?"

"Unh unh." The blonde shook her head. "It's too early yet, I still have to take a nap this afternoon."

They sat quietly at a corner table, each fiddling silently with her cup until Rachel, unable to stay silent any longer, began to talk about the horses. She told the dark woman which mares had foaled since she'd been gone and what they'd had. Told her about the lame filly and Sunnyside.

"What were you doing yesterday?" the blonde ventured after nearly an hour of idle chatter. "Can you tell me?"

Sapphire eyes met emerald as the dark-haired woman shook her head slowly. "Better if I don't."

"How ... look," the young rider sighed softly. "I ... I like you. You know that right? And I'm thinking that you ... probably ... play on my team as well." She used the euphemism with a wry grin.

"Good team." Lacey nodded, raising her eyebrows. "Wouldn't play for another." She didn't know how she still managed to be surprised at the young woman's candor.

"Okay ... but how can ... we," said with pale hands

motioning between the two of them, "go any further if one of us, meaning you, Crony Number Two, can't tell the other one of us, me, anything?"

"Ah." Lacey nodded, meeting bright green eyes before glancing away to study something infinitely less interesting, like the wallpaper across the room. "That would be a problem. Because, see, I kinda like you and I'm afraid that if you know what I know ... you'd be in danger."

"Are you in danger?"

Her eyes flashed back into the inquisitive gaze for just a moment. "Yeah. But it's my choice."

"Can I choose? Or are you going to do that for me?"

Lacey's lips twitched very slightly. "Well, we're here aren't we?" *This is a big step for me, Rachel.*

As if the young blonde could read her companion's mind, she leaned away from the table slightly. "You need me to back off a little? Are you uncomfortable?"

The nod was barely noticeable.

"But you are willing to try?"

Another very slight nod.

"That's good, Lacey. I can live with that." Rachel grinned, all tenseness from the morning seeming to disappear when faced with the remote chance of knowing this dark woman better. "Now, can I talk you into driving me to Aqueduct so I can pick up my Jeep?"

"That I can do."

****

Lacey watched the young blonde climb into her white Jeep Wrangler and pull out of the lot before leaving as well and heading back into the city proper to speak with Vinnie.

She used the hour or more of driving to consider her feelings for this woman. She wanted, on some level, to walk away and never come back because the small woman couldn't know what she was getting into. Rachel Wilson had an open mind and a love of life, though she denied it. She was honest and good, loving animals and people with abandon. Her smile welcomed Lacey from the darkness she'd known her whole life into the light the other woman held against all odds.

The last relationship Lacey had been in was nearly four years ago. It had ended badly, her lover of nearly six months having decided that she wanted in on the organized crime action. She'd gotten in too deep, too fast, and quite frankly wasn't cut out for it anyway.

She mentally shrugged off the haunting recollection, not willing to think about the dark past when her present contemplations were so centered on the fair young rider. It hadn't been love, she'd known that then and she knew it now. It was convenience and good sex and loneliness needing an outlet. But it was an eye-opening experience.

She'd had her occasional flings since then but mostly one-night-stands or nameless faces whom she'd forgotten by morning. Rachel was different. She pounded closed fists on the black leather steering wheel, growling to the dashboard. How could she make sure that this time was different? Aside from not starting anything at all ... because her heart simply wasn't into considering that option.

****

Rachel, on another level, was questioning her own sanity when she returned to her apartment and took Karma for a quick walk. How in the hell had she fallen for this woman who was so unlike her, so dark and dangerous?

But she'd had occasional glimpses into a heart that was good. Into a soul that had some love left to give. In the way Lacey had listened to her story in the office, had touched her arm as they walked, had pulled her off of Oz and then held her steady. God, it had felt good.

And no one had called her Raich since Leslie. No one. But then again, no one had stood up for her since Leslie either, she grinned ruefully to herself, sitting on the couch and hugging Karma to her.

What now? I don't know her world, but I have an idea

and I don't care. Which is more frightening than anything because I should.

"Everyone has a soul mate," her mother had said mere hours before committing suicide. "And that half of their soul is why they live and breathe, Rachel. It's everything in the world. Everything. It lasts for eternity."

I hope to God you were right, Mama. Because you sure chose to test that theory to its fullest extent. You taught me to see the good in people. You taught me to put my heart on the line. I think it's time I tested your theory myself.

Chapter 4

The scrawny man was tied securely to the chair, his eyes wide and frightened but he'd finally stopped whining. Thank God, Lacey thought.

"What do you know about Wheatridge, Oz?" she asked again, obviously growing tired of this escapade. When she was answered by more blinking silence, she backhanded his already swollen face then grabbed his shirt collar and pressed her nose within an inch of his.

"Look, ya little shit. I don't much like you anyway and we certainly don't need you to continue this investigation. So you can talk or die, I really don't give a damn which you do."

Blink.

With a fierce growl, Lacey shoved him and the chair back before spinning to the other man in the small room who had, until this point, been standing in the corner watching silently. "Kill him," pointing to Oz with one long finger, "and clean it up."

"Wait!" Lacey's hand was already twisting the cold metal doorknob. She stopped but didn't face him.

"There's a guy at Wheatridge who's trying to get some of

our horses. Don't know what he wants 'em for. But I get a cut ... if we help."

"Why does he want certain horses?" Lacey turned on him, letting her glittering blue eyes convey her seriousness.

"I told you, I don't know. They tell me which ones and then ... then I ... give 'em something. I make 'em sellable." His nasally voice was pleading.

Lacey stood watching him for a very long time. "Who's the guy at Wheatridge?"

"I don't know! I swear to God." Smack. And then for good measure, Lacey grasped his middle finger and twisted it until the bones crunched inside her fist. He screamed at the pain. "He leaves an envelope and money at my apartment. I've never seen him!"

"Are you working with anyone at Briargate?"

"No, no," he said quickly, fear in his eyes. "Just me."

The dark woman, with bone-chilling calmness, withdrew several paces to survey the sniveling mess before her. Instead of pursuing the issue with the horses and Wheatridge, she could only think of one more question. She glanced at her companion, knew he was listening, before turning her gaze back to Oz. "What did you do to Rachel Wilson?"

The words shocked everyone in the room, even herself, actually, because though she'd been thinking it, she really shouldn't have asked it. She silently cursed herself for her lack of professionalism.

"What?" Oz stared at her, crinkling a sweat-glazed brow.

In for a penny, in for a pound, she sighed. "You heard me, asshole. Rachel Wilson."

"She attacked me!" he yelled indignantly. "You saw it, you were there! You had to pull that bitch offa me!"

Lacey lunged forward, grabbed his other middle finger and gave him the fiercest look he'd ever seen.

"No!" he screamed. "No, okay ... okay." Her grip relaxed slightly. "I ... uh ... made a deal with her. About that dumb colt she loves so much. I was gonna hurt him for

Wheatridge because they wanted him to be put up for sale ..." His voice trailed off and she tightened her grip again, twisting his finger slightly. "But I told her I'd spare him ... if she ... she had sex with me."

Lacey felt her stomach drop and tasted the bitterness of hatred in her mouth.

"But she chickened out ... in the end ... and I wouldn't let her back out."

"You raped her?" Lacey growled, the sound of it being so feral that Oz just blinked at her for several seconds.

"No ... uh ... it was a deal. That's all. That I wouldn't hurt him. A deal's a deal."

"But, the colt, he's still not right? Wheatridge still wants to buy him?"

The sleazy face before her widened into a grin. "I didn't say I would keep my part of the deal." He sounded so damn smug.

"What did you do to him?"

Silence.

With two quick punches, Lacey broke his nose and two ribs. "What did you do?"

He blinked at her stupidly even as he choked on the blood trickling down his throat. She gave him a few more well-placed blows and asked him again. It was evident after she shattered his cheekbone that he wouldn't be talking.

Lacey kicked the chair over backwards to send his howling body to a painful impact on the cement floor. She turned to her companion. "I'm done with him. Kill him." Then she turned to the sobbing man and gave him one more withering glance before looking away. She left the room with all the grace of a prowling panther.

Lacey looked at the clock on her dashboard, not yet noon. So she pulled out her cell phone and Rachel's personnel file, dialing quickly.

"Hello?"

"Rachel? It's Lacey." The dark woman expertly steered the sports car one handed along the New York City streets.

"Hey." The voice on the other end softened and it

caused Lacey to smile slightly.

"Hey, yourself," said gently, then, more abruptly, "Do you think someone could have given Sunnyside an injection of some kind?"

"I'm great, Lacey. So good to hear from you. How are you doing?" Rachel spoke sarcastically.

"Rachel." There was a hint of warning in the darker woman's voice but the smile that edged it took away any bite that may have been there.

"Not likely. Blood work's been done on him several times and most drugs would have been picked up. He's getting progressively worse so continuous injections would have been evident."

"How else could someone have given him something? Feed?"

She was answered by thoughtful silence. "Maybe. But he's not eating well, he's losing weight."

The husky voice on the end of the phone line seemed to breathe deeply. "Raich, if you were going to feed a horse something to poison him, how would you do it? Is there an easy way?"

"Poison him!" Rachel squeaked.

"Yeah."

"Is the poison tasteless, odorless?" the blonde asked after overcoming her initial shock.

"Let's say yes."

"Did you talk to Oz? Is that how you know this?" Her voice sounded a little bewildered.

"We questioned him, yes."

"Did he tell you how?"

"Would I be asking you?" the husky voice teased gently.

"Good point," Rachel acceded. "If it's not in his grain, we'll assume it would be too hard to put on hay." She paused for a long moment, considering. Grain would be too tricky anyway because he'd have to either personally feed the horse or slip in afterwards and put it in. "Mineral blocks!"

"What?"

"Mineral blocks. Each horse has its own ... in the stall.

Sunny's been chewing on his like it's damn candy."

"Can you get to Briargate and switch out Sunnyside's block? Plus the others: the fillies and the colt who got hung up in the starting gate."

"Yeah, of course."

"I'm going to confirm that and then I'll meet you there. You may want to call a vet out."

"Lacey?" Rachel's voice became soft. "Is he gonna die?"

"I don't know, Raich. We'll do what we can. I'll see you there in a bit." She ended the call with a quick jab of her finger.

****

Rachel stared at the phone in her hand for nearly thirty seconds before hanging it up. Her association with this dark-haired blue-eyed woman was getting weirder and weirder by the moment. Oh, by the way, kid, that guy you hate so much is poisoning your favorite horse. Cool.

"Karma," she called, already grabbing the dog's leash off of the doorknob. Her call was answered by the sound of paws hitting the ground and tags jingling as the dog came out of Rachel's bedroom.

"Wooo."

"Yeah, yeah, yeah. Can you not argue with me just this once? I don't know how long I'll be at the farm."

With Karma belted into the front passenger seat, Rachel took every short cut she could and went twenty miles an hour over the speed limit to arrive at Briargate in record time.

"Wait here," she said calmly to Karma while unzipping the passenger window in the Jeep's soft top and checking to make sure the dog was attached securely to the seatbelt by her harness. "Good girl." And she turned and ran from the lot, ignoring Karma's expressed complaints.

Rachel sprinted to the training barn first and slid to a stop in front of Sunny's stall. The colt casually pushed his head over the stall door and whickered eagerly at her.

"Hey, buddy. Hi, my boy," the young blonde whispered, slipping into his stall with him and hugging him soundly around the neck. "Oh, thank God." Then she released him to push his curious nose away from her and run hands along his body, under the blanket, down his legs. Of course he looked the same, she chastised herself. He's been this way for weeks now, standing in his odd spread-legged way. He stomped one foot impatiently as she paid him no further attention and instead grabbed his half-eaten mineral block and left his stall.

Then she retrieved the others Lacey had suggested, carrying all four brick sized blocks with her to the broodmare barn office and called the vet. Rachel went back to her Jeep to disengage Karma and lead her to the office where she tied the young dog to the couch, and propped the door open to wait.

Moments later, Lacey came into the room and Rachel realized that the woman's presence immediately calmed her. She smiled tightly by way of greeting and pointed to the small stack of red mineral blocks, while talking on the phone to the barn manager and explaining that there could possibly be tainted blocks for four horses.

"There may be more," Lacey interjected as she went over to try and quiet Karma. "Hi, baby," she said softly to the dog, sitting on the couch and allowing herself to be mugged and kissed.

"Maybe more. We'll have to check it out when you get here." A pause as she raised eyebrows at the dark woman across the room and received a nod. "Vet's on his way. See you soon."

She hung up and walked over to the couch, bending down to her knees to scratch Karma behind the ears. Rachel looked up and met an ice blue gaze.

"You okay?" Lacey asked gently, reaching out to rest a hand on the younger woman's shoulder which was now just above the couch's seat. "You're trembling."

"I'm worried for him," she whispered as the intensity of the sapphire gaze became too much and she had to look away. She shrugged one shoulder, laughed self-deprecatingly. "Silly, I know. He's a horse."

"Not silly, Raich. Don't think that," the woman said gently. A moment hung between them as the young blonde felt the heat of Lacey's hand on her shoulder, but absorbed it with head bent and closed eyes, still stroking Karma's soft ears. "C'mon," Lacey said at last. "Let's go check on the other horses."

"Right." The young woman bounced fully upright so quickly it startled both Lacey and Karma. Two sets of blue eyes studied her closely and she smiled at them. "Let's start in the training barn."

The rest of the afternoon was spent pulling blood on horses and having the vet evaluate them. They'd isolated three other horses based on their behavior and the mostly devoured mineral blocks. Lacey left just before dark when the vet said they'd know nothing more for several days at least.

The dark-haired woman had taken a big step upon her departure. She smiled gently at her young blonde friend before stepping forward to hug her and place a warm kiss on the wind-cooled cheek. Then she mumbled something about calling Rachel tomorrow and abruptly climbed into her little sports car and sped away.

****

Lacey Montgomery left her house later that same evening, dressed in black jeans, a black turtleneck, and her customary black leather trench coat. Her weapons consisted of a Glock, a Sig Sauer, and two knives and were all concealed by the length of her coat. She left the sports car snugly in its space in the garage and chose instead a black Jeep Grand Cherokee parked in the farthest spot of the garage.

She ran a tired trembling hand through her bangs as she made her way first to Vinnie's then, later, she would collect her helpers and go to her previously scheduled meeting. She drummed her fingers impatiently on the steering wheel, the nervous tension completely new to her. Just a month ago her hands wouldn't have trembled, she wouldn't have felt apprehensive, and she had no clue how to deal with this new facet of herself.

Her mind wasn't on tonight's drug pickup and she blamed the strange mess with Oz and the horses. But, the truth of it was, she was occupied with a certain blonde-haired green-eyed young rider. Her mind kept spinning back to the warmth and smell of the young woman. Simply thinking of Rachel caused a flipping feeling in Lacey's stomach that she couldn't shake.

"What the hell have I gotten myself into?" she murmured to the surrounding darkness, revving the V-8 to merge with highway traffic.

****

In addition to the broodmares, Rachel's rounds included the horses who'd had the tainted blocks removed that day and found no change in their appearance. Then the young rider decided to pull all of the mineral blocks, just in case, and piled them in a wheelbarrow as she walked through the barns. She returned her confiscated bounty to the broodmare barn office where Karma still waited for her.

Rachel was glad she didn't run into Oz and, in fact, realized she hadn't seen the gangly man since Lacey'd said she'd questioned him about the horses. She hoped he was gone for good.

Feeling like she'd done the best she could for now, she pulled a sandwich and salad out of the small dorm-style refrigerator and prepared a fresh pot of coffee.

"You know, I may have lost my mind," she said softly to the eager blue eyes that watched her every move as she emptied a plastic condiment packet of salad dressing. "I can't stop thinking about her."

"Arrr," Karma answered and began running through every trick she knew in weak attempts for food tidbits.

"You like her, doncha?"

Karma was in the middle of rollover.

"I know you do. How can she be ... who she is? And still ... still be so caring? When she touches me, or those eyes. Ugh." The young blonde tossed her head back in frustration, completely ignorant to Karma's playing dead. "What am I gonna do? We're okay by ourselves ... we don't need someone else ..."

The red Siberian leapt to her feet, tired of waiting to be noticed, and sat primly on the linoleum, waving a paw at her owner.

"But I think I do need her, Karma. It kinda scares me." She licked her fingers clean of dressing and picked up the sandwich before leaving the small kitchen area to sit on the couch in front of the myriad of monitors. "You're shameless," she intoned to those hopeful blue eyes on the way by.

****

"Not right," Lacey muttered. Then more loudly. "Rico. This isn't right. Get over here."

They stood several hundred feet from a dark underpass. She'd been accompanied by three other men and a second black sedan. One young man ran to her now. He pushed unruly blond bangs out of blue eyes before he smiled at her weakly.

"Wipe the mug, Rico. This isn't good."

He cleared his throat. "What's wrong. His car is up there." He started to point but his arm was smacked down by a powerful swipe of Lacey's hand.

"Amateurs," she growled. "Who sent the kid?" Her voice was exasperated as she questioned the two men standing on her other side but they simply grinned at her. She knew Rico'd been sent specifically with her because she could handle the rookies. She didn't like them but she could keep them alive and show them a lot. Which is exactly why she had called him over from his hindmost position in the group.

"That car is a grey Ford Taurus," she explained impatiently. "Al doesn't drive a Ford Taurus. He drives a black BMW. And he always has a follow car."

"Oh."

"Whaddya think, Bernard?" This question was directed to one of the other men.

"Sent someone else, Lace?" a heavy-set man ventured, having learned from years of working with this woman that you should be more afraid to mistakenly consider her questions rhetorical than answer them.

"Not Kalzar. He only works with certain people."

"Think Al got busted?"

"I think he got jumped."

"Couldn't he have just bought a new car? And not wanted company?" Rico offered. Lacey glanced from the teenager to the large man who'd been speaking and lifted an eyebrow. Rico got a firm swat in the back of his head for his comment and Lacey grinned her thanks to the other man who simply shrugged.

Suddenly, the Taurus began moving, gaining speed as it came under the bridge. All four of Vinnie's men scrambled over the nearest sedan and drew weapons as the driver of the Taurus swerved towards them. A dark tinted window rolled down to reveal the muzzle of an AK 47 peeking sleekly into the poorly lit night.

"Here we go, boys," Lacey yelled in her own version of fire at will and her team discharged their weapons immediately. The Taurus lost two windows and had several pocks in the body panels. They may have even lost a passenger before the limping grey vehicle passed them and drove easily into the darkness beyond as if reclaiming a lair where it could curl up and lick its wounds. "Everyone?!" Lacey shouted, standing slowly and leveling her weapon at the retreating vehicle.

"All good, Lace," one of the men responded after hauling Rico to his trembling legs.

"Fuck!" the dark woman growled, slamming her fists into hood of the car. "Bernard, call Tony and get a team over to Al's bakery. Fuck it all, we're going to check out Kalzar."

Both men stood away from her and eyed her carefully. Rico tried to touch her back but he caught the dark waves of anger rolling off the woman next to him and he backed away.

****

After a thankfully uneventful night, Rachel and Karma stumbled into the apartment. The young blonde hit the blinking button on the answering machine on the stand by the door.

"Hey, beautiful. It's Lacey."

The young woman smiled, both at the compliment and at the thought that a woman with a voice like that would have to identify herself.

"I wanted to take you to dinner tomorrow before your shift, but I have to take care of some business. Don't know how long, but I'll call you as soon as I can. Later."

Rachel crawled into bed feeling decidedly warmer despite the early morning chill.

****

Lacey broke into the old building with negligent ease. Rico was hot on her heels, which annoyed the hell out of her, but she was too interested in being quiet to snap at the kid ... again. She could see the shadows of her other two partners coming in through the back door before it registered that she shouldn't be able to see them.

She'd been in this old deli before and there should be a wall between the front room and the back. Only now there was a nice jagged hole and the glass deli counters were shattered and laying around on the linoleum floor. Surprisingly, there was no stench of spoiled meats and cheeses. No scent of bodies. And the front door hadn't appeared to be damaged in any way.

Quietly the small group prowled the ground level floor and then climbed to the living quarters, which seemed untouched. Then they made their way downstairs again. Treading their way carefully back through the kitchen, the team walked into the large refrigerator at their dark leader's bidding. There they pried away shelves, bloodying their fingers and giving Lacey funny looks.

Until their effort revealed a half door.

"How'd ya know?" Rico asked, his whispered voice full of awe.

"I'm psychic." Lacey grinned. "One of my many super talents. Stick around, kid, and it may rub off."

"No, really," the young man said, not even buying her reasoning for a split second which made Lacey smile wider.

"Where I woulda put it." She shrugged. They made quick work of the door and were immediately assaulted with gut wrenching smells. Rico gagged behind her but everyone else just kept moving down the darkened stairs.

"Lace?" Bernard said softly when they reached the floor. The other team member, a tall and lanky black man in his forties, moved around his larger companion to squint into the darkness around them.

"They shoved the bodies down here," Lacey responded quietly, hoping her voice would have a calming effect on her team. "Turn on the lights and count 'em up. We should have Kalzar, his wife, his brother, three kids. Look for the drugs or the money ... but I'm sure they're gone."

Chapter 5

Lacey took Karma for a walk around the apartment complex while Rachel showered. The dog's normal exuberance did little to lighten her mood as she recalled the previous hours of heartbreak and torture. She couldn't shake the haunting images of her young friend sitting in the straw of the stall, hugging a bloody and lifeless body to her.

The crony had shown up in the middle of the afternoon, her mind still reeling with the visions of last night's slaughter, to find out the progress on the tainted mineral blocks. She'd also hoped to see Rachel and talk to her about dinner. What she'd found instead was a strangely calm and confident young woman calling vets. The primary veterinarian had been called and said he was already working an emergency but would be there as soon as possible. Not believing him, back up vets had been called instead. In the end, all were too late.

The two women had done everything to save mare and foal but both had been lost in the wee hours of the morning after nearly a twelve hour battle. The foal's nose had been locked below the mare's pelvic bone, one knee bent there as well, and Rachel had reached inside to right Mother Nature's wrong. Slender arms protected with long plastic gloves had pushed at the foal, suffering through contractions, until she pulled one foot out, followed by another, then a small nose. But the foal had slipped back and Rachel had to fight again, both she and the mare exhausted. The second time the foal came, one small struggling hoof ruptured the mare's canal, causing blood to pour everywhere, covering the young attendant.

She fought for the foal, but the mare had stopped pushing from exhaustion and pain, and though the foal's head and neck were exposed, big round eyes blinking at all who watched, its chest was constricted in the canal, the umbilical cord apparently pinched. Lacey had helped the best she could, never having done anything like this. The two women had pulled steadily on the foal's front legs to try and extricate it from its smothering prison. But they were too slow in pulling him out; he died right in front of them.

Rachel had tried CPR once the colt was lying bloody and wet on the ground but it was unsuccessful. So, she'd been forced to turn her attention to the dying mare.

The first vet arrived just in time to see what Lacey would always remember: the mare, dead and bloody lying on the floor of the stall, the foal limp and lifeless lying near her hind feet. Rachel had been wrapped around the foal's body and was pleading its forgiveness. She blamed herself for her lack of skill and ability to prevent the tragedy.

It wasn't until the vet's arrival and the barn manager's assumption of control that Lacey had been able to lead the weary woman away from the barn and pack her gently into the waiting sports car. Rachel had objected to the ride, insisting she could take the Jeep home, not wanting to get blood on Lacey's leather seats, but the dark woman had been tenacious and, in the end, Rachel had complied, quietly giving directions to her apartment.

Lacey had gently shoved Rachel to the shower, ushering her quickly past the accident Karma had had on the kitchen floor. The blonde apologized to her pet, insisting that Lacey not be mad with the dog as she'd been left unattended for far too long to be able to help it. The dark woman cleaned up the mess wordlessly and clipped a leash to the dog's collar.

Now, as she let herself back into the apartment using Rachel's key, she heard the shower had stopped running. She unhooked the leash and released a bouncing Karma who flew down the hallway in search of her mistress. Lacey followed and they found Rachel seated silently on the bed, dressed comfortably in T-shirt and flannel boxer shorts, her hair still wet and tangled, framing her tired face.

Lacey smiled softly and leaned against the doorjamb to watch this woman she'd started to know as a friend and whom she wanted to know as something more. It had been a week since they'd talked in the early morning hours about Rachel's past and she'd felt them growing steadily closer every time they met again.

"Get some sleep," the tall woman suggested now, her dark husky voice carrying easily across the room. "Do you mind if I shower, too?"

Rachel was already moving off the bed. "Course not, let me get you some—"

She stopped mid-sentence when Lacey moved forward and pushed her gently to the mattress. "I can find towels, you lay down," the dark woman insisted.

Green eyes watched her intently before she nodded and settled down. Karma immediately curled up on the bed, pressed solidly against Rachel's legs.

Lacey emerged from the shower to find that Rachel had left out a T-shirt and shorts for her as well and she smirked lightly at the thought that anything that would fit the smaller woman couldn't possibly be suitable for her larger frame. But she found the young woman's tastes went for extra large everything and she was able to slip into them easily. She took the offering of comfortable clothes as an invitation to stay, which she wanted desperately. She peeked in on her young friend's sleeping form before padding to the couch.

She lay a towel over the decorative pillow to protect it somewhat from her still wet tresses, then pulled a folded blanket from a nearby chair and settled comfortably into cushioned softness. Sleep quickly found her, though the dreams were filled with images of blood and frustration and, for the first time in a long time, she mourned the passing of a life. Ironic that it should be an animal she'd tried to welcome into the world and not the many humans she'd assisted out of it.

Some time later, how much later or what time of day was unclear to the dark woman, she felt her cover pulled away from her body. She blinked into the dim room to see Rachel crawling under the blanket with her, laying her length against the dark woman. Green eyes met her ice blue ones in a question, asking permission to lay here with her, to touch her and feel her.

Without a word, Lacey pressed herself farther into the back of the couch and opened her arms in invitation. A shy smile rewarded her as the young blonde crawled into her arms and snuggled her face into the dark woman's neck, breathing in the smell of her own shampoo and soap. Her arms at first were timidly tucked between them as Lacey settled the blanket around them, then, slowly, uncurling one to wrap it around the woman in front of her, draped comfortably over ribs to rest between broad back and couch cushions.

Then Lacey touched her lips to the temple by her cheek, rubbed the young woman's back tenderly, and settled back to sleep, lulled there by deep breaths and a warm body.

Lacey opened her eyes to see sunlight sliding through closed blinds and igniting dust motes in its path to the carpet. She blinked at the image several times before moving her attention elsewhere and realizing that sometime during their sleep, both women had moved.

Now she lay on her back with the small blonde covering her very intimately, legs entwined easily with her own. Rachel's head rested on her collarbone and one arm had ducked under the dark woman's shirt and lay along bared ribs to circle her shoulder. Lacey's own arms were wrapped tightly around her companion, keeping the smaller woman snug against her. And Karma lay quietly at their feet on the long couch, gazing at them with tired blue eyes before closing them again and tucking her nose under her tail.

Lacey smiled, moved one arm from her tight hold to run gentle fingers through her companion's tangled hair. With her other arm, she felt the deep intake of breath associated with waking before green eyes opened briefly and closed again. She watched as the fair skin began to redden as Rachel blushed when realizing their intimate positions.

"'Morning, sleepy," Lacey murmured softly, tilting her head forward to brush a kiss on the other woman's forehead. Rachel squirmed slightly until the tall woman tightened her grip. "Relax, Raich. It's okay. Are you comfortable?"

"Yeah," came the whispered response.

"Good. Then stay right where you are because I'm comfortable, too."

The young blonde sighed, then relaxed her body against the other woman's. Until she realized her hand was under her companion's shirt and she began to withdraw it.

"Stay put," Lacey mock growled. "Better," when the movement stopped. She continued to silently use her fingers to untangle the long blonde hair and felt the warmth in her body grow as she came to fully realize how much she enjoyed feeling this small body resting on hers.

Rachel must have felt it, too, because after many long minutes of her companion's gentle caresses, she pushed herself away slightly to turn her head and meet blue eyes. Silently, they watched each other as if each were waiting for the other to do something.

Never being one to like silences, it was Rachel who broke the spell. "Thank you ... for taking care of me. And Karma."

Her words were greeted with a smile and sparkling blue eyes. "My pleasure." No kidding, her body screamed.

Then the blonde head tilted forward very slowly to touch her lips to the woman beneath her, tentatively at first. Lacey held back, letting this smaller woman set the pace, her senses reeling as a hesitant tongue reached out to trace her lips, parting gently to reach in and touch her tongue before withdrawing. The dark-haired woman felt the passion rising in her and fought every urge to devour the tender mouth above her. She opened her eyes to meet the green before her and knew Rachel must have easily read her dilated-pupil look of desire.

Instead of frightening the blonde, though, it gave her courage. She pressed her lips more firmly to Lacey's. Her tongue sought entrance with more abandon this time and her hand moved from under Lacey's shoulder to slide tantalizingly along ribs.

Soon they were kissing deeply, mouths hungrily searching, tongues exploring new depths and tastes until their fingers joined in the search by mapping out the other's body. Rachel slid her hand up to very hesitantly stroke the outside of her companion's breast, fingertips gentle and probing. Lacey responded by reaching under the young woman's shirt to splay large hands across muscular back.

Then they were gasping for air and pushing against each other's hips, mouths barely breaking apart to breathe. For several long minutes they used hands and tongues to touch the other, Rachel still lying firmly atop her companion. Lacey nudged her knee between Rachel's, bringing her thigh firmly to the other woman's center, pressing against the flannel shorts and feeling the young blonde's wetness through the thin fabric. She moved her hands from Rachel's back to her bottom where she cupped the cheeks in large calloused hands and held her steady while grinding her thigh rhythmically against Rachel.

The young woman broke their kiss to arch her head back and slide hands from under her companion's shirt to frame the tan face before her. "Ungh ..." she protested vaguely. "No, Lacey ..."

The dark woman slowed her sensual assault, relaxing her hold slightly. "Do you want me to stop, Raich," she whispered, her own voice strained with passion.

Green eyes flicked open briefly and any further protests were nullified both by the intensity of emotions in the jade depths and the continued pressing of hips against thigh.

"No ... I ... ungh." Her eyes closed again. "So much ..." she whispered.

"Let it go," Lacey murmured in her companion's ear, tightening her hold again and renewing her efforts to bring the young woman to release. "I've got you, Raich." She leaned forward to nip Rachel's earlobe before moving away to seek the other woman's lips again.

The overwhelming sensations left Rachel speechless as she practically devoured the mouth before her, seeking, plunging, moaning. Then she moved her own leg up to match her partner's and felt the jolt of contact rush through the body she held.

Their grinding was almost frantic as they came closer and closer to the edge until Rachel disengaged from the mouth before her to groan out her release. Her body jerked with the orgasm, sending Lacey over right behind her. The dark woman leaned forward to moan into the young blonde's shoulder, her own body thrusting against the other for several more beats before resting back on the couch where it twitched occasionally as she relived the moments before.

Without warning, Rachel shoved against the body below her, struggling out of strong arms as she covered her face with her hands and stumbled her way to the bathroom. Lacey lay on her back, completely dazed, her body still throbbing from their shared passion, before she leapt to her feet and followed the smaller woman.

"Raich, honey?" she asked softly, her forehead pressed against the closed door. "What is it?"

She heard the distinct sound of retching and blinked back tears. "Rachel? I'm sorry ... I didn't mean to take advantage of you. Oh God, Raich?"

"I'm okay. I need to be alone," the blonde replied softly, voice only slightly muffled by the cheap door.

"No." Lacey slid down to the floor, kneeling now with head and hand on the cool white painted wood. "I won't leave you like this. Tell me what's wrong. I thought ... God, I'm sorry." There were tears on her cheeks and she wiped at them angrily, surprising herself with the previously never felt emotions warring through her body. The last thing she'd wanted to do was scare this young woman. She'd taken too much too soon.

"No, no. It's not you ... it's me. I ... thought I was ready and my body was ... but my mind ..." She trailed off. "It's me. Not you, Lacey. Never you ..." Her words were broken by a sob.

"I'm coming in," Lacey announced, not giving her partner a chance to argue as she opened the door and slid the few feet to wrap the trembling woman in her arms. "I'm so sorry, sweetheart," the dark woman cooed, pulling Rachel into her lap and rocking her there. "I knew about Oz. I knew what had happened. I just didn't think about how you needed me to be ... us to be."

Rachel slowly leaned up and wrapped her arms around the other woman's neck. "You knew about Oz?" she asked after several long minutes of just absorbing the nearness of the other woman. "How?"

"I asked him," Lacey said simply. "I knew there was something between the two of you."

"When you asked him about the horses?"

"Yeah," quiet agreement. She turned the woman slightly so she was cradled in her lap, arms no longer wrapped around the neck but now moving to embrace Lacey's middle.

"It was my fault. I made the stupid deal with him. But he was so repulsive to me that I went back on it ... when he already had me naked beneath him."

"Not your fault, Raich. No means no, I don't care who or when. He took you against your will and that's rape."

"No!" The small body jerked upright. "No. It wasn't like that. It wasn't. He didn't rape me. It was a deal ... and I changed my mind."

"And he had sex with you anyway. That's rape."

"No," she whimpered softly. "I wanted him to. I thought it would protect Sunny. I asked him to."

Lacey leaned her head affectionately against the other woman's, knowing this argument was getting her absolutely nowhere. Karma's tags jingled softly as she came in to find the two women sitting on the floor. She stood quietly in the doorway, tilting her head, flashing expressive blue eyes to both women before edging forward and placing a paw on Rachel's exposed leg.

"C'mere," Lacey said softly, reaching out to pull the dog into her companion's lap. Rachel hugged Karma close and pressed her face into the warm fur.

"Raich, you're wrong about you and Oz. I don't know how to convince you. But I am sorry that I let my body take control. It shouldn't have been like that. It should have been gentle and romantic the first time with us. I should have respected your history. I knew how vulnerable you were after last night, how drained. I should have taken that into account. Because it's not just your body I'm falling for. I want to know all of you. I want you to trust me and ... and taking advantage of you was not the way to do that."

"You didn't take advantage." The young blonde's voice was muffled. "You didn't. My body reacted, too. I wanted you too ... but ..."

"But what, honey," Lacey whispered, caressing the smaller woman's back with one hand, petting the resting dog with the other.

"But ... sex ... has never been right for me. It's always been someone else's idea or with someone I didn't care about. And I didn't want it to be that way with you. I wanted to know you before that ... but I crawled under the covers with you. And I kissed you ... I started it. But things just happened so fast and I realized, when it was over, that I'd done it on purpose. I wanted you ... I wanted you to wipe away the feelings and the anger ... and Oz. And I took advantage of the fact that you were kind and you cared." She took a deep breath. "I was so ashamed because the one person in my life ... the one chance I had of doing it right ... and I blew it."

Lacey just sat for several long seconds, completely shocked by the murmured words. "Well," she said at last, clearing her throat. "Let's start with the basics. You did not take advantage of me, Rachel. And ... and ... no one in my entire life has ever cared if they did or not. I wanted you to kiss me, I wanted to make love with you. It could have been more romantic, I would have liked to make it more ... special. I do care for you, Raich. Very much. My being with you has not been about getting you in bed. Don't be ashamed. But making love with me is not going to change what's happened to you before. We need to deal with that, too."

The blonde head nodded glumly.

"I rushed you. Forgive me for that," Lacey whispered into her companion's ear. "Please."

Rachel nodded again. "Forgive me for running out on you? And for being sick?"

"Why were you sick? Did it remind you somehow-"

"No." The young woman finally looked up to meet her partner's sapphire eyes. "No, I just ... I was embarrassed and nervous ... and I get sick to my stomach when I'm nervous. It was nothing you did." She grinned sheepishly, glanced away briefly to concentrate on Karma's soft fur. "I liked what you did. I've never ... felt that kind of ... of passion before." She looked up again. "I knew that I liked women better, I've known that for a long time. But it's still never been like that."

Lacey smiled and squeezed the woman to her tightly. "I promise, not again until you're ready. Okay?"

Rachel nodded slowly, relaxing into the warmth surrounding her. "I don't deserve you," she whispered softly.

Lacey closed her eyes, feeling the tears well up immediately. "You deserve so much more. I'm the one who doesn't deserve someone like you."

"How can you ..." The gentle voice trailed off.

"What?" Lacey asked guardedly, her muscles tensing at what she imagined the question to be.

The young blonde took a deep breath and, despite her best judgment, asked the question. "How can someone like you ... kill other people? I know you must. I know you hurt Oz." The body beneath hers was suddenly rigid. "You're the kindest, warmest, gentlest person I know," she continued.

Lacey took a deep breath. "I'm only that way with you, Rachel. You bring out the best of me. I don't want you ever to know the other person that I am."

"I can't even believe you are that other person."

"Believe it," Lacey growled softly. "Believe everything you hear about me because it's true. I think once you learn who I really am ... you won't want to be anywhere near me."

Rachel shook her head. "Nothing you could tell me would change my mind," she said with conviction.

"I'm not so sure about that," Lacey whispered, her own heart breaking. All the things she'd done, all the harm she caused, she never thought about it past that moment. And now she would do anything to take it back if it would assure her future with this woman.

"I am." Green eyes met hers and her hands left Karma to frame the dark woman's face and brush at wayward tears. "I am," she repeated.

"You want to know who I am?"

"I do."

"Fine." The tall woman pushed Karma off of them and stood quickly. She pulled the blonde with her and righted her on her feet, her motions suddenly quick and angry. "Fine," better to end this charade now. "Get dressed. I'll show you who I am." Rachel blinked at her for a moment, startled by her actions but not afraid. She shrugged and headed out of the bathroom toward her bedroom.

****

Twenty minutes later they were flying down the freeway, Karma tucked comfortably into the hatch back, panting through the glass at all the cars she could see. Lacey hadn't said a word since telling her young companion to get dressed. Her features had turned dark as she prepared herself for this rejection.

You want to know who Lacey Montgomery is? I can show you some stuff that will make you sick all over again. And then I'll bring you back to your safe apartment with your safe dog and your job of bringing life into this not-so-safe world.

But the eyes that glanced at her profile weren't particularly worried, the young blonde even reached out to rest her hand on Lacey's arm for a moment.

More than anything, the dark woman was angry with herself for allowing their frantic session just an hour before. This young woman had the right to know what she was getting into before they'd been intimate. She deserved the entire picture. She was sure that once Rachel knew the truth, she'd be telling her next lover about yet another poor sexual experience.

It was nearly forty-five minutes later before Lacey was maneuvering the sports car into a three car garage and killing the ignition. She hit the garage door button before opening the car doors to eliminate any chance of Karma escaping. Rachel noticed this thoughtful move and smiled at her friend, but got no response from the dark woman.

Moments later they were entering the house through the connecting door to the kitchen, Karma jumping around excitedly on the end of her leash.

"Let her go," Lacey said quietly. "She'll be fine here."

"Do you have any pets?" Rachel asked, concerned for the safety of any other animals, especially small potential prey animals.

"No."

"Must be lonely," the blonde muttered as she unhooked the leash and watched Karma take off through the kitchen, tail wagging and nose busily sniffing anything and everything.

Lacey smirked slightly at the woman's comment before shaking her head. "C'mon."

"Do I get a tour?"

Lacey stopped and turned so quickly that Rachel ran into her before backing off a few steps. "Look, Rachel. I think it's best that you just hear about me ... about the bad me, about my job. Because there's no sense in you getting any more attached before you decide to leave."

Rachel stood quietly for several long seconds, head tilted slightly and brow wrinkled. "Would you knock off the tough broad act, Lacey? I want to know all of you. The good and the bad." Her voice was slightly demanding and got her a double raised eyebrows look from her companion. "Attached? What does that mean anyway? Like you're some stray I may want to keep?"

"You asked for it. Just remember that." She turned quickly and led the young woman through an expensively decorated dining room, arriving at a spiral staircase.

"Karma," Rachel called, eyeing the valuable furniture warily, as she mounted the stairs behind the dark woman. She wished she'd kept the dog on a leash.

"Leave her be," Lacey instructed. "She's fine."

"Lacey, that couch costs more than everything I own put together. A lot more." She stopped halfway up the spiral staircase and pointed through the arched doorway into what appeared to be a living room.

"She can shit on that couch for all I care. C'mon."

"Well," Rachel raised her eyebrows and grinned, "let's hope it doesn't come to that."

Her host led her down along a hallway, which had rooms on one side but overlooked the lower level on the other before wrapping around to have windows on one wall. Rachel looked out of the large tinted glass panes to see fields and forest in the setting sun. "It's beautiful, Lace," she said softly.

The dark woman stopped to turn to her companion and then look out into the woods she knew so well. She nodded mutely. That was the only reason she bought this house: the fact that it was surrounded by fields and forests and not other houses. That had been very important to her. "In here," she said after a moment, leading her young friend into her office and showing her to the large desk.

Rachel sat quietly in the chair that had been pulled out for her. It was deep burgundy leather and faced a large oak desk. On one end of the desk was a personal computer, the rest was clean except for some scribbled notes and closed folders. Lacey tossed a green file folder in front of her.

"Read this."

"What is it?" Rachel asked as she started to open it but a large tan hand held it closed.

"Please wait until I'm gone." Blue eyes turned to her. "It's my copy of my personnel folder. What Vinnie keeps on me."

"You have a copy?"

"I can get a copy of everyone's." She shrugged.

"Where are you going?"

"For a run. Wait for me and I'll take you home. Or if you need to go, you can call a cab, there's some cash over there." She pointed to a filing cabinet across the room.

"I'll be here. Take Karma, she loves to run," Rachel suggested. "Just keep her on her leash."

"Raich, look. I know you think this is no big deal. You think this information won't change your mind. But the truth is you'll probably want to leave before I get back. And that'll be hard without Karma."

The young blonde shrugged, clearly not bothered by anything this dark woman told her. "Look at it this way. The cab won't like Karma anyway. So if I'm gone before you come back, you know where I live."

Silence.

"She's good company, Lacey. And I really think you need company right now."

Lacey raised both eyebrows and wondered at how easily this young woman read her. Finally, she nodded her assent before turning and walking to her bedroom where she changed into sweats and running shoes. Then she located the leash where Rachel had left in on the kitchen counter and called for Karma who came eagerly and wooed at the prospect of a walk.

The dog ran excitedly beside her as she left the front of the house to go around to a footpath she often used for running. The young Siberian took three or four leaps to every one of Lacey's in an attempt to rid herself of excess energy, singing and hopping and dancing the entire time. Lacey couldn't help but smile at the red dog's antics.

Back in the office, Rachel finally opened the folder as she heard the front door close. Lacey Ann Montgomery, she read on the first page, finding out her age and place of birth. Then she moved into the more detailed information about her family. The second of three children, her mother had killed her father in a drunken rage when Lacey and her two brothers were still under ten. But the mother had claimed self-defense and was actually, after an extended trial and time spent in public care, able to get her children back and raise them.

Several years later, Lacey and her younger brother were picked up for running drugs. The kids were tried as juveniles, spent some time in a home, and were returned to their mother. During this time, their older brother had been shot and killed while breaking and entering.

The years advanced, showing gang affiliation for both children, several trips to juvenile detention for offenses such as robberies, possession of drugs and firearms, and auto theft. But when Lacey turned eighteen, the official records stopped and Rachel set aside those sheets of information to begin reading about the woman Lacy Montgomery had become.

Lacey took a hill at full force, feet pounding, chest aching with the cold February chill. Karma had calmed down considerably during the run, somewhat shocked that they were still going and losing her enthusiasm for the adventure, but not her inborn drive to continue. Now she ran in long loping strides, head and tail parallel to the ground, tongue lolling out to the side. Occasionally she glanced at her companion with questioning blue eyes.

"Good girl, Karma," Lacey commented in her now familiar dark voice and the simple words seemed to add more spring to the Siberian's stride.

The rest of Lacey's file read almost like a resume, starting with her early work for Vinnie's father, which was mostly as a runner for information. Or a tool to distract opponents with the young woman's body. Then, later, as she learned more about the operation and organized crime, she became his personal protector and hit man.

There were some detailed examples of her handiwork, of her ability to cold-heartedly torture men and women. Some pictures of her jobs. There was a thorough accounting of the jobs she'd been asked to do in her decade for Vinnie's family, complete with avenging her boss's death and then working for his son.

The material went on and on in sickening detail, gave dates and places and times. And she knew not only was she holding the life of the woman she was coming to love but she was also holding Vinnie's insurance against her loyalty. Even more sobering was the fact that Lacey had handed all of this to her, even though the blonde could have taken this evidence to the police with sure results. Some of the pictures were of Lacey actually working people over; some were of her killing.

Rachel didn't read the entire file, didn't really need to. She closed the folder quietly and pushed it away from her, absolutely sickened by what she'had seen. But not surprised. She'd known the dark person Lacey must be to do her job. Knew the countless lives she must have taken. She was still inexplicably attracted to this woman. The raven-haired friend who had guarded her and held her. Who talked softly and understood Rachel's fears and compassion. Having the proof of what she already knew didn't change that.

So the young woman rose to unsteady feet and found her way to a bathroom where she was sick for the second time that day. Then she glanced at her watch to realize that Lacey had been gone for almost two hours and it was now completely dark outside. She caught herself worrying before she remembered whom this woman was and realized she was completely capable of taking care of herself.

Rachel made her way down the spiral staircase and started a fire in the hearth in the living room, using wood and starter logs that were already piled nearby. Having accomplished that, she smiled at the gently licking flames before making her way back through the immaculate house to the kitchen where she started rummaging through cupboards and realized suddenly how very hungry she was.

She was adding fresh cut vegetables to boiling pasta when she heard the front door open, followed immediately by clicking nails on hardwood floor as Karma came sliding into the kitchen to stand panting in front of her mistress. Rachel smiled slightly as she bent over to peek in the oven at the baking chicken breasts.

Lacey followed the dog slowly, stood quietly in the entranceway, somewhat shocked at the young woman's presence, moreso that she was casually cooking their dinner. She didn't say a word as she watched Rachel pull a bowl out of the cupboard and show it to the dark-haired woman.

"Can I give her water in this?"

Lacey nodded dumbly.

She filled the bowl and set it on the floor on a dish towel, watching Karma fondly as she eagerly lapped at the water. Then the young blonde moved to pull bottled water from the fridge and place it into Lacey's trembling hand. It was now that she looked at her companion for the first time and noticed that her hair was absolutely wet with sweat and her clothes were soaked. Blue eyes flashed back at her fearfully and Rachel wondered that such a woman could be afraid of her or her reactions.

"Goodness, how far did you run?"

The dark woman shrugged one shoulder, uncapping the bottle with nervous hands and taking several swallows before wiping at her mouth with an already wet sleeve.

"Well, you have enough time for a shower. Then we'll have some dinner."

"And then I'll take you home," Lacey said softly.

Green eyes met blue for a very long moment, interrupted only by the sound of Karma pushing around the now empty bowl. "Only if you want me to leave. I called off of work tonight. I ... couldn't go in after last night."

The dark woman worked her jaw uneasily. "Didn't you read it?" she asked at last. "That's why I brought you here."

Rachel nodded. "I read it. Or parts of it ... got kinda

repetitious after awhile." She shrugged her shoulders casually. "I knew what you were before, Lacey. I could guess at what you did to become Crony Number Two. But I see more of you than that stupid file. There's nothing in there about your warmth and compassion."

"That's because no one else has ever seen that in me," her companion whispered, breaking eye contact to refill Karma's bowl and return it to the floor.

"Go shower," Rachel ordered gently, making a show of wrinkling her nose. "Go on."

The dark woman started to walk away towards another set of stairs leading upwards before turning around and meeting green eyes. "Will you really still be here when I get out?" she asked with uncustomary awkwardness and a bit of hope.

"Of course I will be. I promise. Go ahead," Rachel assured easily. She couldn't explain her effortless acceptance of the woman before her, but neither could she explain the intense need to be with her, know her better. So she took both mysteries in stride and offered her companion an encouraging smile.

The table was set when Lacey returned, her wet hair slicked back from her face to fall in a mass between her shoulder blades. Ice blue eyes surveyed the kitchen table curiously before she walked around it to step through the threshold into the screened in patio. There she found Rachel sitting in a well-cushioned chair, casually flipping through a magazine. Karma was sprawled out on the floor, still panting, but raised her head and thumped her tail against the Astroturf floor covering upon seeing her dark-haired running partner.

Rachel turned, smiled at her. Lacey couldn't help but smile back.

"You hungry?" the young blonde asked as she stood and set the magazine down.

The dark head bobbed in agreement. The taller woman backed out the doorway to give her companion room to step through but Karma decided to stay where she was in the cool night air.

Lacey closed the door to just a crack in case Karma wanted to come join them later, before taking a seat at the table.

They ate quietly, relaxed and comfortable. Though Rachel noticed Lacey's continued glances her direction.

"What happened to your brother and mother?" Rachel asked suddenly, catching her dark-haired companion completely off guard. She stopped mid-chew, glancing around as if looking for a way out, before finishing and swallowing.

"Umm," she started slowly, blue eyes looking a bit bewildered.

"You don't have to tell me, Lacey," her companion offered, reaching a hand across the table to lay it on the other woman's forearm.

"No ... it's okay. I actually don't know. When I left to work for the Russo family, I tried to bring Jeremy with me. But he wouldn't come. He had some mother worship thing going on ... didn't see her for what she was. But I had to leave. So I did."

"You've never gone back?"

Dark hair swung slightly when Lacey shook her head, stabbing at a broccoli stalk. "No. I kind of try not to live in the past. You know ... just do something and go. Don't pay attention to what the impact will be. Don't plan for the future, don't get caught up in history."

"Do you wonder?"

There was silence except for the clank of fork tines chasing around a slice of carrot. Then sapphire eyes flashed up. She shrugged. "Sure. Sometimes. I loved the little guy. I raised him, pretty much. But she was a charming woman and she had him fooled."

Rachel nodded slowly, offered her friend a small smile before turning her attention back to her meal. "Was she mean? I mean ... did she hurt you?"

"A couple of times. Mostly we were runners for her, though. Small time drug dealer. We were kids, couldn't be tried as adults and could get into the school yard without trouble."

"How about your father?" Rachel asked gently, perfectly aware she was prodding where she shouldn't be. But the dark woman had done the same to her previously so she felt a certain amount of freedom.

Lacey shrugged half-heartedly. "He was kinda heavy-handed. Drunk a lot, on drugs a lot. They were poor dealers, really: using the materials. No profit in that. We were there when she killed him. Social services never knew that we had seen it. She had us all lie so that we could go back to her."

"Was it really self-defense?"

"No. He was ... abusive, but our lives weren't in danger," Lacey said flatly, taking a quick few bites that finished her meal. "I'm done," she announced as she stood and made her way across the kitchen. And Rachel knew she was referring to the conversation as well as dinner.

"Me too," the young blonde agreed, also rising. She tried to elbow her friend away from the sink but Lacey chuckled.

"No. I'll do dishes. You cooked. It's only fair." The two women wrestled for sink space a little longer before Rachel gave in and stepped away.

"Go sit by the fire. I'll only be a minute."

She was dozing on the deep pile rug in front of the fireplace when Lacey came out and sat next to her. The dark woman tentatively reached a hand out and began to stroke the blonde hair. Rachel's eyes opened.

"Mmmm. Sorry. What time is it?"

Lacey glanced to her watch. "A little after nine."

"The night is young," Rachel murmured sleepily and Lacey laughed softly.

"Yeah. I can take you home, Raich ... if you'd rather?" The young blonde rolled from her side to her back to gaze at her companion, trying to read behind the shadows in those sapphire eyes but not having much luck at all.

"Do you want me to go, Lacey?" Cuz you're going to have to tell me to leave. I like it here."

"What about Karma? She hasn't eaten yet today, has she?"

"No." The young woman wiped at her tired eyes with partially curled fists. "But I can just chop up some chicken for her, and some vegetables. It's what she normally eats."

"No dog food?"

"Do you know what they put in dog food?" Rachel wrinkled her nose.

"Horses?" Lacey grinned evilly and the younger woman poked out just the tip of her tongue.

"Among other things. It's the stuff that's too bad to go into bologna and hot dogs. I wouldn't eat it, can't expect her to."

Lacey smiled, smoothed the other woman's brow with long gentle fingers. "She's spoiled."

Rachel returned the smile and shrugged her shoulders. "She's an only child."

Silence hung between them for several long moments before Lacey decided to broach the subject. "You have a daughter."

Rachel nodded. "Molly. She lives in Rochester with one of my high school teachers. She quit teaching, has some foster kids. I want her back once I'm more financially secure. But I was convicted when she was two, she needed a home. I get to visit her all the time."

"How often do you see her?" Lacey murmured softly, still continuing to smooth the young woman's brow.

"A few weeks in the summer. Usually a weekend a month, depending on her school. Spring break"

"She's eight?"

"Yeah." Green eyes grew slightly misty. "She's beautiful. Blonde hair, blue eyes. She's very special, Helen's done right by her. We get along well, Helen has always been honest with her and never denied me seeing her."

"Who's the father?" Lacey asked hesitantly, wondering how the young woman would tell her if she'd pushed too far.

"A guy I met here not too long after I'd run away from home. Just some guy. Like I said, sex never meant much. I dunno ... condom broke. But I love her."

"I can tell." The dark-haired woman grinned gently. "I'd like to meet her."

"I'd like that, too," Rachel whispered softly, returning her partner's smile.

Lacey stood and offered her hands to her companion who took them willingly and was pulled quickly to her feet. "How about this. We take care of Karma. Then we go upstairs and watch a movie?"

"You want me to stay?" Rachel asked pointedly, wanting to hear the other woman's decision.

"Yeah," Lacey said softly. "I'd like that a lot."

The young blonde smiled gently as she reached out and stroked her companion's forearm. Then she led the way into the kitchen, sporting the world's goofiest grin.

In the end, Lacey watched the last hour of the movie on her own because Rachel had long since let her blinking eyes finally stay closed. The dark woman glanced from the ending credits to the sleeping woman in her arms. They lay sprawled on her king bed, supported by pillows, resting on the down comforter. Rachel was on her side, facing the television across the room. Her head rested on Lacey's shoulder and one arm was casually draped across her abdomen. Sometime after the small woman had fallen asleep, she'd also possessively moved her leg across her companion's thighs.

Lacey watched her now, smoothing the golden hair away from her sleeping features with the utmost of care. "You are beautiful," she whispered tenderly, kissing the woman's forehead. "And I don't know why you stayed ... but thank you."

The pale face smiled gently and green eyes fluttered open. "Ya big softy," she murmured and Lacey blushed slightly but smiled at her anyway, moving her knuckles along the other woman's fair cheek.

"Shhh," the dark-haired woman whispered. "Don't tell anyone."

Rachel grinned, reaching up to capture the large tan

hand and place a kiss on the knuckles. "Secret's safe with me."

"You ready for bed?" her companion's voice was husky and traveled right down Rachel's spine in gentle vibration.

"Aren't we there already?" she answered, her mouth suddenly dry.

"Why are you answering my questions with questions?" Lacey teased and was rewarded with a soft laugh.

"How was the movie?" Green eyes sparkled with humor.

The dark woman shrugged negligently. "The company was better."

"Let me take Karma out again," Rachel said, pushing lazily away from the other woman's warmth. The movement caused the Siberian Husky to hop down from her comfortable position at the foot of the bed.

"Maybe I need a doggy door," Lacey said absently as she also rose from the bed, brushing her black hair away from her face.

"Nah, cuz then you'd need a fence, too."

"What kind of fence?" Lacey asked as she followed woman and dog out of the room and down the hallway to the spiral staircase.

"You in the market?" Rachel teased. "Privacy fence is best. Some day I want a house with a big yard for her. Nice tall fence."

"Do they jump?"

"Huskies are escape artists, too. Some can climb a fence, dig under it, jump over it. Even open gates. They're a little too smart for their own good."

They arrived in the kitchen and Rachel picked up Karma's leash from the countertop. "So, they escape, run away, and are full of energy?"

Rachel nodded, grinning at her friend.

"Why own one?" Lacey asked but she was smiling, she'd already been taken by this dog's charm.

Rachel turned back to Karma and held up the leash, which launched the Siberian's vocal assault of howls and woos. "Look at that face, Lacey," the young blonde cooed which only encouraged Karma's efforts.

"Put a leash on that dog and get this over with, woman," Lacey growled playfully.

They walked quietly along the footpath Lacey had run earlier in the evening, following the circle of light from the flashlight in the dark woman's hand.

"It's so quiet here," Rachel whispered, her warm breath fogging in the cold night air. She tucked herself farther into the down jacket Lacey had lent her. It practically swallowed her whole. "Are we still in New York?" She asked jokingly.

"Pretty sure." Lacey nodded with the barest hint of a wry smirk.

The young blonde leaned her head back to stare at the stars which shone brighter here than where she lived. "Nice."

"Mmmm," the dark woman agreed, following her companion's gaze and thought the stars were more beautiful when she saw them as Rachel did. "Are ya done, pooch? It's getting cold out here."

Lacey showed her young friend into an upstairs guest room. She turned back the bed and made sure there were clean towels in the attached bathroom. The dark woman handed her companion a t-shirt and cotton shorts before turning to leave the room.

Rachel grabbed her arm as she turned, causing her to stop in her motion. Then she stood on her tiptoes and placed a very gentle kiss on Lacey's lips. "G'night," she whispered.

"Night," the tall woman replied, reaching a hand up to push back golden hair. "I'll see you in the morning."

"Do you have to work tomorrow?"

Lacey raised an eyebrow and focused away for just a moment before nodding. "Yeah," she said meeting the emerald green eyes. "In the evening. But we can have breakfast somewhere then I'll take you to the barn so you can get your Jeep. I want to see if we can find anything out about the blood work or salt blocks. Shoulda heard something by now."

"Sounds good. Sleep well, Lace."

"You too." Lacey kissed the younger woman again, lingering there a moment, before leaving the room.

****

Lacey awoke with a start, immediately reaching over to the nightstand and picking up her Glock, releasing the safety and cocking it. She heard a loud gasp in the darkness and recognized the timbre of it.

"Shhh, shh, Raich," Lacey whispered, sliding the safety on and putting the gun back down quickly. "It's okay. I didn't know it was you."

The young blonde stood quietly in the doorway, holding one hand out in front of her awkwardly while the other rested over her pounding heart. Never sneak up on a hitman. Really, how hard is that to figure out?

"C'mere," the dark woman said softly, pulling back the covers and patting the bed next to her. Karma flew into the room and hopped on the bed. "Not you, pooch," Lacey laughed, pushing the dog to the foot of the bed to make room for Rachel as she lay down. Then she took the young blonde in her arms, hugging her tenderly, and feeling her heart still hammering,

"I'm sorry, Raich. I didn't mean to scare you," the dark woman whispered huskily, rubbing her companion's back firmly.

"M'okay," Rachel murmured, her face tucked into the other woman's neck. "Just wanted to be with you."

Lacey smiled and continued to rub the small woman's back until she felt the heartbeat slow. Then she heard her breathing even out as she reclaimed sleep.

But sleep was a long way off for the dark-haired woman as her eyes traveled from the blonde in her arms to the curled up dog at the end of the bed. Then, slowly, ice blue eyes looked at the moonlight glinting off the barrel of her Glock. It could have been bad. That was careless.

Chapter 6

Lacey watched red-orange light crawl across the hardwood floor in her bedroom, then chase across the white comforter cover to finally play over the pale features of the woman in her arms. She moved her hand slightly to cup around her companion's face and protect the still closed eyes from the growing sunlight. Rachel moved slightly in her sleep, squeezing the other woman tightly for a brief moment and then releasing her.

Karma blinked up at Lacey from her position at the foot of the bed, then opened her mouth in a doggy grin and began crawling up the mattress to poke the dark-haired woman with a very cold wet nose.

"No, no, Karma," Lacey laughed softly and pushed at the dog but it didn't work as the red furred beast suddenly jumped up to all four feet and smacked the awake woman with a paw. Then lunged forward and swiped at her face with a long tongue. "Agh," Lacey growled which only incited the dog further and, before long, Karma was play bowing and wooing while bouncing around the bed. Then Rachel was awake, blinking into the sunlight.

"Your stupid dog," Lacey groaned, sliding out from

under her companion to dive across the bed and scoop up the hapless dog in her arms. Karma struggled until her freedom was granted and then she was off the bed in a flash. Her nails echoed on hard wood floor as the dog flew out of the room and down the hallway, Lacey hot on her trail.

Rachel lay in bed for a few more moments, somewhat dazed by her rude awakening and the game of chase currently being acted out on the upper level of the house. Karma was making consistent growling and wooing noises while her pursuer was muttering under her breath.

Then, next she knew, both ran back into the bedroom, over the bed, and into the large attached bathroom. Rachel crawled to the end of the bed to lean over and watch them in the bathroom.

"Now you're cornered, ya little beast," Lacey growled, slowly closing in on Karma who stood near the end of the room by the large bathtub. Her entire body was tense, tail up, nose twitching as blue eyes regarded her attacker. And just as Lacey was ready to swoop down and grab the dog, Karma leapt straight into the air and used Lacey's bent over back as a platform, jumping off of her and out of the bathroom door to leap on the bed. Then she sat casually, tail thumping on the messed up covers, tongue lolling in a pant.

Rachel lay on her back now, laughing so hard she could barely breathe and Lacey returned to the room and watched her young companion fondly.

"Oh my God," the young blonde cried, wiping at teary eyes. "Are you okay?" this directed to the dark-haired woman standing over her.

She got a wry grin and two raised eyebrows for her question. "You sound so concerned."

"I am, I'm sorry," Rachel managed to say through more laughing. "I've never seen her use a person as a jungle gym before."

"I'm flattered, Raich," the dark woman teased before bending over her companion and tickling her ribs.

"Agh! No." The young blonde squirmed, laughing all the harder. Then strong arms picked her up and flipped her over so she lay across Lacey's left shoulder, facing the woman's lower back. "Hey, hey." She squirmed some more and wrapped her arms around Lacey's waist. "Put me down you big bully!"

Lacey carried her down the stairs and to the formal living room, Karma bouncing and cheering her every step of the way. Then she knelt and lay the woman on her back on the carpet in front of the cold fireplace. Green eyes sparkled up at her but before the blonde had a chance to speak, Lacey closed her mouth over soft lips.

She kissed her deeply, tongue pushing between lips to play in the soft moistness she found there. Rachel stopped squirming instantly to reach her arms around the neck above her and pull the woman closer. Karma lost interest rather quickly in this new game and trotted away.

They spent several long minutes of being lost in sensations as they explored each other with mouths and gentle fingers. Lacey pulled the young woman to a sitting position and then into her lap where fair legs wrapped solidly around the dark woman's waist. Lacey tilted the blonde's face back to kiss the neck she exposed. Rachel groaned, moving her hands down Lacey's front, trailing tantalizingly over breasts before sliding bravely under the waistband of the loose shorts she wore to find crisp curls. Then lower to feel for moisture.

Lacey jumped at the contact, nipped at the other woman's neck and moaned, pressing herself into the probing fingers.

"Unh unh," the dark woman said at last, when she regained her composure. She reached down and pulled Rachel's hands away. "Easy," she whispered as much to herself as the woman straddling her lap. Then she touched her forehead to Rachel's, taking deep breaths to calm herself and blinking blue eyes into her companion's green.

"Yes," the blonde whispered, pressing her hips forward and fighting for her hands. "Lace," she groaned quietly.

Lacey leaned forward to press the young woman back to the hearth rug, kissing her again but still holding her hands.

When Rachel relaxed her leg hold around Lacey's waist, the dark-haired woman took the opportunity to pull away and out from between fair legs.

Rachel moaned in protest but the moans were drowned out by the mouth covering hers. "Lace," she said again, breathing the word into the other woman's lips.

"Lay still," the dark woman whispered, pushing herself up and away from her young friend but keeping her hands pinned just next to the blonde hair fanning across the rug. "Don't move." Lacey met emerald depths filled with staggering amounts of desire. She smiled gently. Trust me. The words remained unspoken but understood between them.

Rachel's pale eyelashes flicked against her cheek as she blinked then relaxed, no longer straining against the hands that held her. Lacey released her hold, smoothing large palms down her arms to her shoulder, over breasts to stomach.

"Okay," the tall woman said softly, taking a deep breath, flashing her friend another grin. "You be very still ... and quiet. Can you do that?"

Rachel nodded, smiling back at the woman above her. She was rewarded by another deep kiss. Then Lacey very slowly began to run her hands along the other woman's body over her clothing. Her fingers traveled delicately along the insides of her companion's legs, running over her pubic area tenderly, up her stomach, in between breasts. All the while she continued her assault on lips and face.

After several more minutes of gentle caresses, Rachel was moaning again, her body arching into the fleeting touches but denied any further pressure. "You're not supposed to move, Raich," Lacey teased gently, letting her fingers continue to dance along the other woman's skin.

"I'm trying," was the groaned response from the woman beneath her.

The dark-haired woman grinned, kissed the young blonde. "Or talk."

"Slave driver."

"You love it."

Green eyes flashed open and met blue for a very long moment, suddenly serious. "I do."

Lacey swallowed and nodded, ran a lone index finger along the other woman's cheek. Then she smiled and moved her hands lower to push up Rachel's shirt, exposing a pale stomach. She stopped, tilted her dark head silently as blue eyes studied the scars she found there.

A small sound escaped Rachel's lips and her verdant eyes reflected shame and panic. She tried to scoot away but Lacey moved tan hands to hold her around the waist, thumbs nearly meeting in the middle of the small woman's abdomen.

There was a large incision mark just above Rachel's navel, several inches long and jagged. Surrounding it were several small scars in a scattering formation that ended just below the young woman's breasts. She struggled again and Lacey glanced up to meet those eyes.

"What are you afraid of?" the husky voice asked gently.

Rachel dropped her eyes, moved her hands to cover her companion's. All sense of arousal had left her body. "Bad memories ... they're ugly."

"You're beautiful, sweetheart," Lacey murmured, leaning forward to kiss the scars, noticing the abdominal muscles tighten under her ministrations.

Rachel shook her head, tried to shrink away but was unsuccessful as the tall woman practically covered her entire body. There were tears in her emerald depths.

"Raich?" Lacey whispered, laying her body along her friend's, gathering the small woman in her arms and holding her gently. "Honey, you are beautiful. All of you. Your heart, your mind, your body. And some day we'll wake up naked in each other's arms ... after making love all night long." She grinned. "Of course we'll have to shut Karma out of the bedroom." She felt her companion relax against her.

"Oz made fun of my scars," she whispered after long moments of being lost in the embrace.

"You don't have to worry about him anymore," Lacey growled.

Rachel pushed away, blinked at her companion with an open mouth. "Did you kill him, Lacey?"

The dark woman loosened her embrace and evaded those searching jade orbs. "I didn't," she choked out at last. "But he's dead."

The blonde absorbed this information with a sickening turn of her stomach. The worst part was, deep down, she was grateful for it. She was relieved that she would never see his weaselly face again or feel his brutal hands. Suddenly, she realized what her stillness must be implying to her partner and she shook herself back. Rachel framed the dark woman's face in her hands, small fingers tangling with raven locks.

"I accept you for what you are, and what you've done ... but I don't want you to do those ... those things for me."

Lacey's expression reflected mild hurt as she gazed at her companion but then she nodded, she knew the young blonde was right. Until now she hadn't really thought about the life she lived, but suddenly she despised it. "It wasn't for you," she murmured softly. "It was for Vinnie. For the horses. We questioned him and killed him. Couldn't really turn him loose again." The words were cold and distant. Lacey wondered how true they were. She wondered if she did have him killed because of Rachel. "I'm sorry," she whispered.

She got a slight smile in response as Rachel leaned forward and hugged her tightly, choosing to dismiss the topic and change the subject. "How 'bout some breakfast, Crony Number Two? Cuz I sure am hungry."

It was almost noon when they pulled up to the barn and Lacey parked her small red sports car next to Rachel's Jeep. She got out with the younger woman and watched her as she pulled a harness from the floorboard of the passenger side of her own vehicle and secured it around Karma. Then she put the dog up in the seat and ran the seatbelt through the harness with nimble fingers.

When she turned back around, Lacey was giving her a slight smirk.

"Don't make fun of me," the young blonde warned.

Her companion shook her head, met her eyes with gentle blue. "Never. I like it. You're so ... tender."

They watched each other for a moment as a slight blush climbed up Rachel's face to settle in her features. The cold air whipped both of their hair and each tilted her head into the wind so it would blow the stray strands out of her face.

"So," Rachel said softly.

Two raised eyebrows, a gentle grin. "So ... you headed home?"

"Nah. I may stay for a bit, see if they're going to exercise the afternoon string. Sometimes I get to ride ... I could use it."

"What about her?" The dark woman sent a thumb the dog's direction.

"If they are, I'll come back and move her to the office. No time to take her home."

"I'll take her back to your apartment. It's on my way."

Rachel was silent for a moment, rocked back on her heels. "No it's not."

Lacey shrugged, smiled. "Not really. But I'd like to help you out. I can take her home and then you won't have to worry about her."

The young blonde felt warm inside at these simple words, blushed again, but she was grinning. "Okay. It's a deal ... but I only have the one key."

Her dark companion graced the young woman with even white teeth formed into a grin.

Rachel laughed. "You don't need keys?"

Lacey shook her head.

"Promise not to break down my door?"

The dark woman nodded. "Promise."

Rachel handed over the dog's leash and unhooked Karma from her seat and harness. "Go, ya ungrateful mutt."

Now they were back to standing awkwardly. Until Lacey leaned forward and kissed Rachel tentatively, then tilted back and met her eyes with a questioning gaze.

Luckily, the young blonde was smiling. "Are you going

out of town?"

"Shouldn't be."

"When will I see you again?"

Lacey looked away, ice eyes traveling across the pastures and paddocks surrounding them. "Soon."

"Be careful?" Rachel whispered and the tone in her voice brought back the dark woman's attention.

She got a half-grin in response as her companion battled with the inanely warming feeling inside of her. She couldn't remember ever hearing a request for her own safety, though she'd received plenty for the successful completion of a job. "Thanks."

Rachel smiled back, reached a hand out to smooth it down the forearm of the black leather coat in front of her. Then, after leaning forward to quickly press lips against ice cold cheek, she turned and trotted into the barn complex.

****

"Rico," Lacey sighed, running long nimble fingers through her tangled black hair. "Sit your god damned ass down. Bernard, what did Tony find at the deli?"

"Nothing," the burly man said succinctly as he watched the young teen stop pacing and throw himself on a plastic chair. Lacey, however, continued to pace.

Until she stopped to glare icy daggers in Bernard's direction.

"Oh. No sign of forced entry, just like we thought. No prints, no weapons, no money or drugs. Nothing."

"Except bodies," George, the lanky black man, helpfully supplied.

She started walking again, long legs eating up the space in the small office at one of the Russo restaurants on the edge of Brooklyn. The others could see the fury emanate from her and were frankly quite confused by it. Sure, it was dangerous that a drug runner for their main source had missed a meet, and that he'd been found dead with his family. They hadn't gotten their drugs but it's not like they'd never had a problem like this before. The dark woman had never before been like this.

Finally, Bernard decided to jump in feet first. "What's wrong, Lace?" He blinked at her with dark brown eyes framed in a slightly beefy face and brown curly hair. Rico could barely conceal a gasp at such forwardness.

Lacey stopped pacing again to look at him with bright sapphire eyes, which started hard but slowly softened. She sighed, looked to Rico and George, before returning her eyes to Bernard. "I'm sorry." There was still a tinge of edginess in her voice. "I really didn't want to be doing this tonight."

"You thrive at this, sugar," Bernard said gently.

The lovely mouth quirked into half a grin. "Not anymore." *And that's not all I don't like about this job anymore. Oh, Raich. What do I do?*

****

Rachel came into her apartment after her mid-afternoon ride and tossed her keys onto the phone table. No messages.

Her lock and door had seemed untouched, for which she was grateful. Though she had to admit it made her just a touch nervous to know these were barriers that meant nothing to her new friend. Karma met her happily at the door and, after a quick walk, Rachel started making dinner. The omelets they'd shared this morning, sitting at the snug table in Lacey's kitchen, had long since left her system and the young woman's stomach felt hollow with that absence.

After finishing her meal and cleaning her meager dishes, Rachel finally made her way to the bedroom to lay down for an hour or so. There she found on her pillow a single red rose resting on a white note card.

> "Miss you already. See you soon.
> Hope Karma didn't eat this ...
> L."

She held tightly to the card for several long moments,

studying the strong dark scrawl of the words, before going back to the kitchen to find a bud vase for her rose.

****

Lacey sat in a fine French restaurant on the south side of New York City. She'd brought Rico with her but left Bernard and George at the other restaurant they'd been prowling earlier. Their host was a jovial Cuban man with hair and eyes equally dark.

"You like the duck?" He motioned a wiry hand to Lacey's plate. The tall dark-haired woman nodded, raised a thin eyebrow at him.

"Great food, Raoul. What say you tell me what happened to our shipment."

The man's beady eyes sank away and then back, slightly intimidated by the ice blue before him. The young kid with this woman, however, practically shook in his shoes.

"We're still looking into that," he admitted, not wanting to reveal too much to this raven-haired woman.

She grinned, though it wasn't pleasant. "We're not gonna take the fall for your shitty security, Raoul. We need a new shipment. Kalzar was your man, not ours."

"We're working it. I assure you, Senorita. Please, enjoy the meal." The hand swept to indicate the veritable feast before them.

Lacey glanced to thin-faced Rico, regretting a young kid being in this business, but knew he must have impressed Vinnie to be her latest tag-along. Hold on, kid. Gonna be a bumpy ride. She jumped up from her chair and lunged across the table to grab Raoul's tie. Somehow, surprising the man's bodyguards, a thin knife had appeared in her hand.

Raoul's men pulled their weapons and aside from the noise from the main part of the restaurant, this group was bathed in silence. Lacey glanced at Raoul, pressing the sharp blade into giving skin. He got the hint and held up a hand to the men around him.

"Don't fuck with me, Raoul. Your losses are not my

problem, but you damn well better fix em. Cuz we've got bills to fill and you're making us late. I don't want your fucking food or your lame ass excuses. I want results." She drew the knife slowly down the side of his neck, allowing a bead of blood to follow her path.

"Lacey, look," he gasped, trying in vain to pull away from the iron grip and maniacal eyes.

"No you look, shit head. One day. One day or I'm gonna come back and rip this place up. And you and your fuckin' worthless cronies. Ya got me?" She yanked him again to make her point clear.

He nodded, swallowed loud enough for the whole room to hear.

The dark-haired woman shoved him back in his chair and mysteriously returned the knife to wherever it had been. The power exuding from her was absolutely unmistakable as she turned delicately in her black strapless dress and let her eyes rest on Rico. She held out her arm. "Shall we, Rico?"

The kid about wet himself as he gained his feet and offered his elbow. One of the bodyguards lunged at Lacey then, completely missing the look of terror from his boss at such a move. She stopped him with an open palm to his nose, sending blood spurting down the front of his tailored shirt. His partner, however, managed to get a solid punch into Lacey's stomach and a follow-up gun whip to her face before she disabled him and had him lying on the floor in agony. The glare she tossed to Raoul was easily interpreted and the whole room seemed to take two large steps back from her.

Rico then escorted Lacey out of the private room, through the dining room, and into the chilly New York night.

Chapter 7

Rachel and Karma came into the apartment just after dawn and Rachel tossed her keys on the phone table, disappointed that there wasn't a message. Karma bounced down the hall and into the bedroom, already anticipating the forthcoming nap.

Rachel stopped in the bathroom to brush her teeth, wash her face, and pull on T-shirt and shorts. Then she stepped into her bedroom to find her mattress already occupied. Sapphire eyes gazed at her quietly as the dark-haired woman held Karma in a loose hug.

"Hi," was all the blonde could think to say but the shy smile she was wearing lit up her face.

"Hi, yourself," Lacey whispered back, her voice husky and dark. Her hair was unkempt and she had pillow lines on one cheek. Those blue eyes looked barely awake.

"How long have you been here?"

"Hmm." Sleepy eyes glanced around for a clock, found it, and she tilted her head in concentration. "Coupla hours. Is this okay? I wanted to see you." She actually looked a little worried when she turned back to meet a light green gaze. She'd come here somewhat on a whim, realizing what a big step it was. But she also realized how much she'd wanted to see this young woman.

"Of course it's okay," the blonde breathed. *Better than okay. God, it's great to see you in my bed.*

"Are you gonna stand there or are you gonna get in here and keep me warm?" Lacey released her hold on the dog and pulled back the covers invitingly.

The bed bounced as Rachel leapt on it eagerly, sliding fair legs beneath the blankets to mingle with dark ones.

Lacey wrapped the young woman in her arms immediately and she swore she felt her heartbeat slow and the weight on her shoulders lessen. Rachel sank into the embrace naturally and pressed her face into long dark hair. "I missed you," the young blonde whispered.

Lacey's only response was a sullen nod. Rachel pushed away slightly to better look at her companion and found that her cheek was bruised and her lip was freshly split. She tilted her head and met blue eyes that were now slightly watery.

"What happened, Lace?" the light voice probed. Rachel moved her hands to touch the bruise with gentle fingertips. "Are you okay, honey?"

Lacey gave her companion a half-smirk. "I am," a deep breath, a shrug. "We ran into a little trouble. Not much."

"Did anyone get hurt? Besides you?" The green eyes implored gently.

Blue eyes slanted away. "None of us. For them, a broken nose, a few ribs. Nothing big."

"Does it hurt?"

Lacey shook her head, reaching up to grab her companion's arm and pull it back over her shoulder to hold the woman close again.

"I'm so glad you're okay," Rachel whispered, tickling the dark woman's ear with warm breath.

"C'mere." Lacey rolled slightly onto her back to drape the smaller woman over her. Then she reached down and pulled up the blankets to tuck them around their connected bodies. "Let's get some sleep. And then we'll go do something fun today."

"Mmmm," the young blonde agreed. "Sounds great."

Sleep was easy to claim for both of them.

****

The late morning sun cut through sheer drapes to form patterns across the floor and walls. Lacey blinked at them with lazy blue eyes and held the woman in her arms even tighter.

"Ugh," a sleepy voice responded. "I'm not gonna go anywhere."

"Sorry," Lacey whispered, loosening her hold.

"S'okay. What time is it?"

"Not yet noon. Are you ready to get up?"

"Oh, sure. Four hours of sleep, I'm such a lazy bum." Her voice was muffled where her face rested against the dark woman's neck. "I'm s'posed to ride this afternoon."

"What time?" the dark-haired woman asked gently, running slender hands along Rachel's head and back.

"Three prob'ly."

"So if we get up now, we can go have lunch and spend some time together figuring out the horse mess. Right?"

"Yeah, I guess so." The blonde's voice was still garbled. Then she seemed to remember something and her body shifted so her face was revealed. "The filly that fell down on the training track last week, after being brought back from Aqueduct?"

"Yeah?" Lacey acknowledged.

"She died yesterday morning some time."

"How?! Why didn't you tell me?"

Rachel managed an impish grin. "Ya see, there was this beautiful woman in my bed when I got home and I kinda forgot the rest of my day. They said she went down in her stall, had muscle tremors but didn't appear to be seizing or anything like that. They couldn't get her back up and she died. I guess it was dreadful. The body was already gone by the time I got there."

"They send her for a necropsy?"

"Yeah." Rachel nodded, snuggling herself back into the covers and the long body at her side.

Lacey was silent for a moment as she reviewed this new information. "You working tonight?"

"Yeah. Just one mare left. Had a baby last night. Filly."

"That's great, Raich," Lacey said softly, planting a kiss in the blonde hair at her lips. "Good for you."

"Was easy." The young woman tried to shrug though it didn't go too well in her current position of being wrapped around her companion's torso.

"Do you like your job?" the husky voice asked and Rachel realized with some resentment that she really was awake for the day now.

"Yeah. It's all right."

"What would you do if you could do anything?"

"Anything?" Rachel queried and the dark head nodded, though her companion couldn't see it. The young blonde pushed away to roll onto her back and stare silently at the white ceiling for several long minutes. "Hmmm. That's a tough one."

"You want to do this for the rest of your life?" Lacey moved now so she rested her head in the palm of one hand and looked down at her young friend.

"No." Bright emerald eyes met a dark sleepy indigo. "I wanted to be a vet for awhile. And then a teacher, I like kids a lot."

"What about now?"

"I'd love to be an author or write articles for an Equine magazine," the young woman admitted sheepishly, letting her gaze slide from the intent eyes above her.

Lacey moved one hand to rub it along her young friend's stomach. Her touch was sure and soothing. "Like an equine journalist?" she inquired and the blonde nodded. "So why don't you?"

Rachel shrugged. "I don't even have a high school diploma," she whispered. "I barely make enough money to feed Karma and me and pay for this crappy place. And the Jeep. Let alone my daughter." She shook her head hopelessly.

"Get your GED, Raich. Take college classes and then do some freelance writing. You can do it," Lacey urged gently, slowly pushing under the young woman's shirt to trail fingers along the scars she felt there. Neither flinched at this new move.

"Why do you care?" Rachel snorted softly.

"I want you to be happy, Raich. If you don't want to work for Briargate, then do something you want. I know you can do it. You're intelligent and motivated."

Green eyes met blue again to stare for a very long time. Then they started to water slightly.

"What'd I say?" Lacey asked, regretting any pain she may have caused. She leaned down to press a gentle kiss to her companion's forehead. She was shocked when arms wrapped around her neck and pulled her close, holding her in a tight embrace and forcing her to remove her hand from the other woman's abdomen.

"No one has had faith in me since Leslie died," Rachel whispered, choking on tears.

Lacey held the small woman fiercely. "I tell ya what, sweetheart. I'll make you a deal. You work on getting your GED and taking some classes and maybe writing a few articles. And I'll work on getting away from Vinnie."

Silence. Then Rachel pushed away to blink at the dark face before her. "You're serious?"

"Yeah, Raich. I am. Is it a deal?"

"You want to stop working for Vinnie?"

Lacey swallowed, framed the small face before her. Then she voiced the one thing she'd been thinking since the day she met this young woman. "I want out. I swear to God, I do. I can't do it anymore."

They stared at each other for very long minutes.

"Then do it," Rachel whispered at last. "We can do this."

"So, is it a deal, Raich?" the dark woman asked again,

her hands still firm on pale cheeks, her eyes still searching for something: acceptance, agreement, understanding.

"Yeah," was the quiet response. "It's a deal, Lacey. You and I ... we'll change our lives."

She got a slight smirk and watery eyes for her comments and was pulled back into an embrace. "Let's get outta here," the dark woman growled.

They had lunch at a nearby deli, where Rachel updated Lacey on the tests that had been run. She'd received a call the day before from the vet tech saying that the bloodwork had been inconclusive, only indicating raised white counts which was to be expected. The mineral blocks themselves had disappeared prior to testing, which actually surprised neither woman.

"I kept one block, though. It's at my apartment," Rachel cheerfully told her dining companion with a gentle shrug of her shoulders.

Lacey responded with a wry smirk and raised eyebrow. "Good thinking, Raich. I have a guy who I think can do something with it."

"The vet suggested biopsies from the horses. They were supposed to do that this morning and send the results to the lab," the blonde said, finishing her potato chips.

"Same lab?"

"Yeah, I guess."

Lacey scoffed. "That'll work." She shook her dark head. "Should we go visit the vet and see what we can find out? And then we'll go do something a little more exciting," she promised lightly.

The receptionist at the vet's office was evasive at best. The biopsies had already been sent to the lab. The horses appeared to be healthy.

"They're not, though," Rachel said softly as her tall friend escorted her from the treatment facility. In fact, they appeared to be getting worse and the filly's death the day before was a poor omen for the other horses' fates.

Lacey nodded her agreement, silently pondering the next step. "Who is Wheatridge's vet? Do you know?"

Rachel tilted her head in thought and then narrowed wide green eyes to slits. "These guys."

The tall dark woman stopped mid-stride to turn and look at her companion. "You're kidding?"

The blonde shook her head.

"Shit, Rachel. You coulda said something before. They're probably being bought as well." Lacey had already turned around and was storming back into the vet's office.

"Sorry," Rachel murmured to her retreating back before deciding to follow her companion.

Within minutes, Lacey and Rachel were headed across town to the lab where the samples had been sent. And mere minutes after that they were headed out of the lab with a cooler full of samples. Rachel had been impressed with Lacey's professional manner and her ability to refrain from knocking a few heads around, though she had used her intimidating ice blue stare to the best of its advantage. They also swung back by her apartment to get the final mineral block, which Lacey broke into two pieces first, leaving one and taking the other.

Minutes later, Lacey left Rachel in the car outside a Planned Parenthood clinic while she jogged in with the samples.

"Planned Parenthood?" Rachel questioned when her friend had returned and eased the small car into traffic.

"Friend works there. He can run the standard drug tests."

"For horses?"

"He'll find out. He's good. Now let's get on with the fun part of our day." She flashed a bright smile and sparkling sapphire eyes at her passenger.

They found an arcade that wasn't too overrun by teenagers playing hooky. There they spent nearly an hour playing air hockey and pinball before Rachel glanced at her watch reluctantly.

"Time to go?" her dark-haired companion asked gently.

Rachel nodded. "I have to go walk Karma and then get to the barn and tack up. Will ..." She paused, suddenly feeling awkward as they walked out of the arcade together and to Lacey's waiting sports car. "Will you watch me ride? And then we could get some dinner before I have to work tonight?" Silence. "Would that be okay?"

Lacey smiled, opened the door for her friend and let her hand trail along the young woman's thigh before responding. "I'd like that a lot."

"You have to work today?"

"Tonight. But it'll wait 'til after dinner." She closed the door and made her way around the vehicle.

****

Lacey stood quietly on the side of the track, warmly wrapped in her black leather trench coat. Her arms were crossed casually across her chest and she leaned against a light post, dark hair billowing around her face and shoulders. Ice blue eyes watched the young blonde intently.

The object of her gaze was nimbly perched atop a bright bay filly. The stirrups were dropped a little farther than normal jockey mount in order to give her more balance during this precarious part of the training. They were breaking from starting gates.

According to Rachel's earlier explanation, the filly had been walked through them on previous days. She'd heard the bells ringing, had been inside her own gate and closed in while other horses danced around her. But now she was being led forward for her first release.

There was a grey colt, as well as another bay filly. Both had already been trained to the gate and were there for moral support, more or less. The filly bounced on the way in, rearing slightly on back legs before planting front feet to the ground again. Rachel rode the rear easily and used hands and voice to bring the horse down. The two young men on the ground pushed rider and horse into the gate and closed the back doors. From Lacey's vantage point of about 100 feet away, she could hear the chatter of the riders, though she couldn't make it all out. But she could hear the trainer's voice over the speaker on the five stall starting gate.

"Rachel? Talk to me," he called.

"We're good. We're good." Lacey heard her friend's clear response above the horses' snorting and shuffling feet. Then there was a loud commotion and yelling. Again Rachel's voice rang out. "No go!"

Lacey squinted ice blue eyes to see the young blonde hanging from the side of the gate and not on the filly. The horse reared and slammed into the walls a few times until the two helpers had her calmed down and standing. It made the dark woman nervous to watch this. Rachel could be killed in an instant with one wrong move.

Back in the saddle, Rachel found her stirrups and raised herself again to balance over the young bay's neck. She was still dancing nervously and sweating but at least was staying mostly parallel to the ground.

"Ready?" the loudspeaker questioned again.

"We're good!" Rachel called back, leaning close for balance and safety, using her knees and hands to keep the filly's nose straight in front of her. Then the bell clanged and the doors flew open. The filly hesitated just a moment, on the verge of panicking, until she saw her companions already several lengths down the track. And then she was off.

They ran not even a furlong before pulling the horses up and circling them back to the gate. The other riders were cheering at Rachel and the young woman was laughing back.

"Do it again!" the loudspeaker roared.

Four more times they pushed the filly in and broke her from the gate. Only once more was there a hassle forcing Rachel to abandon her mount and hang from the metal walls. Then the trainer was sending them all back to the barn.

Lacey walked next to the bay filly's shoulder, wanting to reach up and touch her young friend but refraining from doing so in front of her peers. Instead, she merely offered her a slight smile and twinkling blue eyes.

The young blonde returned the smile as best she could but her hands were full with the dancing mount. It wasn't until then that Lacey noticed the other two horses had people at their heads as well as on their backs and the trainer followed several yards behind Lacey as if he wanted to replace her next to the horse.

"Grab her bridle," Rachel said softly, green eyes meeting blue for just an instant before the filly reared and came down.

"You're kidding," Lacey responded, instinctively stepping away when the filly's front feet left the ground.

"No, I'm not. Please grab her bridle. She'll calm down." The smaller woman's green eyes were slightly teasing this time as she sought out her companion's gaze. "Or aren't you up to the challenge?"

Lacey laughed in spite of herself and reached out to take the filly's bridle just above the large snaffle bit. She applied a little pressure to the filly's nose through her grip on the leather and, true to Rachel's words, the young horse stopped dancing and began walking more calmly.

"Works," the dark-haired woman murmured.

"It's what they're used to," Rachel responded with a shrug. "Thank you, she was wearing me out."

Lacey noticed that the trainer had stopped shadowing her and instead jogged ahead to speak with one of the other riders. "Is that all it takes to wear you out, Raich?" She grinned mischievously and was rewarded with a gentle laugh and a blush.

"Wouldn't you like to know," the blonde teased right back.

Lacey decided that pointing out how much she did want to know might be inappropriate right now and a tad forceful. So she chose to not respond at all. If you can't say something nice ...

She watched the young woman strip the filly down and sponge her off. Then Lacey fell into step beside her friend while they paced long lazy circles outside to cool the young horse. It reminded Lacey of her first meeting with the blonde over a week ago.

How long does it take to fall in love? she found herself wondering, slanting blue eyes to her companion who was peaceful and smiling.

"What's up with you?" the dark woman asked softly.

Rachel turned to her and grinned sheepishly, playing with the lead rope in both hands now. "Just ... just you and me, I guess."

Lacey nodded her agreement. "Yeah, me too," she responded tenderly, reaching out tentative fingers to run along Rachel's arm gently then stuffed the hand back in her pocket.

"Why me?" the blonde blurted, looking away at the increasing greyness of dusk.

"Pardon?" The husky voice sounded confused.

Slender shoulders shrugged silently. "Why me? I'm a nobody. You're ... so amazing. Surely you've had better offers."

"I've never in my life had a better offer, Raich," the dark-haired woman said seriously, reaching that hand out again to capture her friend's arm. "You are a wonderful woman: compassionate, funny, sweet, beautiful. You're not a nobody. Don't think that about yourself."

Green eyes glanced at her and then away, but Lacey easily read in them the uncertainty and self-doubt.

"I think we need to work a little on your self-esteem, hon," the dark woman said softly. "I'm having a lot of fun these last few days, getting to know you."

Rachel smiled softly. "I think you maybe need some self-esteem work yourself, Crony Number Two," the young blonde bantered recalling the timid look she'd received when discovering a dark-haired beauty in her bed. "I've had fun, too, Lace. I really have. I just ... is it only fun?"

Lacey tried to seek out her friend's gaze but she refused to meet the ice blue eyes and instead concentrated on fidgeting with the bay filly's mane. "Hey," she said softly, trying to get her companion's attention, wanting very much to see her expression. "Raich, honey," the dark voice soothed until Rachel did turn and meet her eyes. "No. It's not just fun. I want more. I've never wanted out from under Vinnie before. Kinda figured it was my lot in life. But suddenly, since knowing you, I want more from this life. You know? I want happiness and normalcy."

Rachel's look was carefully guarded and not easily interpreted. She tilted her head slowly. "I know that you're not one to give your heart easily. I see that in everything about you. But, maybe, you don't know that I feel the same. I've had ... a lot of disappointments in life. And I'd kind of assumed that I would just grow old alone and live in an apartment and work on a horse farm. That everything I could be is right here, right now. But, with you, I ..." She paused, looking sheepish, but the sapphire eyes that met her urged her to continue. "I want a future that's better. That's full of love and family and happiness; one that includes you and Molly. I didn't think it was something I could have."

They stood for several long moments just staring at each other. The filly waited patiently, eyes blinking into the early evening dusk. Then Lacey glanced around them, found that they were alone and the other walkers had gone elsewhere. So she stepped forward and wrapped the small woman in her arms, held her snugly, buried her face in fragrant blonde hair.

"God knows I don't deserve to be happy. But I do want it. And I want it with you," the dark woman said slowly, her voice catching slightly.

"What are you gonna do after Vinnie?" Rachel asked softly after returning the embrace for several quiet moments.

"Don't know." Lacey pushed away, wiped at her wet cheeks. "You want to help me find out?" An inviting grin accompanied the words.

Rachel smiled. "I'd like that."

"You ride tomorrow?"

"Probably, then mare watch again."

"One mare left?" They resumed walking now that the conversation was more casual.

"Yeah."

"What happens when she goes?"

"Then I go back to working days and I get to sleep at night."

"Show me this mare. I need to give her a stern talking to." Lacey grinned at her young companion, tossing an arm casually over her shoulders.

Chapter 8

It was several more days before they got the chance to see each other again. Rachel paged Lacey with a succinct message that scrolled across the dark woman's alphanumeric pager: colt born this morning. Free tonight, can we see each other?

A grin passed easily along the tanned face, though she smothered it fairly quickly and returned her attention to Vinnie and the present discussion of a drug bust. Though it wasn't on one of their routes, it was still something that concerned everyone in the business. As soon as she was able to bid her good-byes, she did and drove her RX-7 home to get things ready.

****

Rachel came into her apartment after her afternoon ride and tossed the Jeep keys casually on the counter. As she was putting a leash on Karma, she rewound the answering machine message.

"Pick you up at 6:30 sharp. Make sure you're hungry and pack to stay."

The blonde grinned. It was Friday, so did she pack for the weekend since she didn't work tomorrow or pack just for tonight? Best to play it safe, she decided.

She was sitting on the steps to her apartment watching the parking lot when she saw the Grand Cherokee pull into the lot. Rising to her feet and swinging her bag over one shoulder, she gave Karma a gentle tug to urge her forward.

Lacey jumped out of the driver's side dressed casually in jeans and the ever-present black leather trench coat. Her dark hair was pulled back into a ponytail, leaving just her bangs to tangle haphazardly over her eyebrows.

"Hey, gorgeous," she said by way of greeting and watched the young blonde blush furiously. Lacey opened the back to let Karma leap inside and then settled Rachel's bag as well. She turned and hugged the smaller woman quickly, placing a kiss just in front of her ear. "Has it only been three days? Seems like longer."

"It does," Rachel agreed, feeling a little awkward in these first moments together again. She knew it would go away soon.

"C'mon," Lacey said as she tugged her smaller friend to the passenger side and opened the door for her. Her excitement was poorly veiled and it made her blonde companion laugh softly.

"What do you have up your sleeve, Lace?" her lilting voice teased gently.

"Surprise. You're gonna love it." Then she walked around and was in the driver's seat in moments. "I can hardly wait."

"Then tell me," Rachel begged, grinning. "I'm so bad at surprises."

"My lips are sealed, hon. You'll just have to wait."

"Tell me about the biopsies, then." Rachel conceded, though she was still curious.

"Just heard from him today. He said there's nothing in the samples. He'd like to come out and draw some blood himself from one of the horses and maybe do another biopsy to make sure those samples weren't tainted at the other lab.

Think we can get in tomorrow and do that?"

"Covert or not covert?"

"Probably covert so no one's suspicious and speeds things up."

"I think we can handle that. Probably best to do it about midmorning and avoid the feeding and exercise rushes. I can get Sunny out pretty easily."

"Good. It's a plan, then."

"What about the mineral blocks?"

Lacey sighed and knitted dark eyebrows. "He said there's sugar in it? Is that right?"

"Should be salt and some basic minerals. No sugar, though that would explain why the horses were eating it so readily. What else?" Rachel tilted her head in concentration.

"He said there appeared to be some foreign substances. He's trying to isolate the minerals so he can figure out what's different. He had to send some samples to different labs for that work. He also needs the manufacturer so he can get exact ingredients."

"Well," Rachel said thoughtfully. "I can give him the manufacturer we normally use but my guess is that those were made by someone else."

Lacey nodded. "Yeah, but it may give him a baseline to work off of. We'll talk to him tomorrow about it."

They settled into a companionable silence while considering this new information.

When they entered the house, Karma went bounding ahead as she had on her previous visit but made her reconnaissance mission in much less time. Old hat now. Then the light-framed dog made for the screened-in porch where Lacey was standing by the door. The dark woman casually opened the door and Karma slipped through the opening into the dark night beyond.

"No!" Rachel yelled, confused at her friend's actions, and was running immediately. Visions of chasing her beloved pet caused her to panic. Lacey flipped on some external floodlights and grabbed the young blonde's arm so they stepped into the night together.

Rachel located Karma immediately and tried to shrug off her companion's grip but Lacey held tight. Finally, the young woman glanced around the yard and saw that it was now completely fenced in with six foot tall privacy fence. Nearly an acre of the land was fenced and Karma ran through the night with abandon.

Rachel glanced up at her friend, absolutely speechless.

"It's safe, I promise. I talked to a couple Siberian Husky breeders and trainers and they gave me some advice. There's cement under the gates so she can't dig out. And electric wire running along the bottom of the fence."

Rachel merely blinked at the dark-haired woman, unable to find a response. She hadn't realized how much this woman understood her until this moment.

"Is this my surprise?" she asked softly.

"Yeah." Sapphire eyes sparkled with the knowledge she'd hit the nail on the head.

"How did you? In February ... can they dig post holes?"

"They can if you're persuasive enough ... and the equipment's big enough." Lacey grinned. "C'mon, walk with me."

They walked the perimeter side by side, watching the stars. Karma raced around them and ran full tilt through the enclosure. She got hit by the electric wire once, yelped and ran, then gave the fence the respect it deserved.

About halfway through their stroll, Lacey felt the warm softness of a smaller hand curl into hers and their fingers entwined gently. The dark woman glanced to her companion, confident blue meeting shy green and she grinned, bringing their hands up to press against warm lips.

"I'm glad you came tonight, Raich," Lacey whispered against the knuckles still at her mouth. "I've been thinking about you since the other night."

The blonde head nodded in agreement and she turned a more confident smile to her companion. "This was ... really thoughtful, Lace. But so expensive, you really didn't have—"

"I wanted to," the dark-haired woman, interrupted.

"Doesn't hurt the value of the house, either. So it's okay. And there's a doggie door, so once she figures that out we won't have to get up with her." Her eyes sparkled. "See, some of the motivation was selfish."

"Hmmm," Rachel agreed, though she was skeptical about the woman's easy dismissal of a kind deed.

"There's more." They were at the door now and Lacey pushed it open, holding it for her smaller friend to walk through.

"More, hmm?" Rachel looked over her shoulder to glance at Karma one more time before going into the kitchen.

"Have a seat."

She took the offered chair and watched her friend with bright eyes.

"Okay." Lacey took a deep breath, slightly worried about Rachel's reaction to this next part of the plan. "Dinner's on its way, I ordered pizza." The blonde responded with a grin. "And ... yesterday I stopped at one of the New York Education Offices." The dark-haired woman pulled some papers from a drawer and slid them across the small table to lay in front of her companion.

"What are these?" Rachel raised a thin eyebrow before turning green eyes to the stack in front of her. She realized within moments that it was an application to take the GED. She glanced up at the tall woman who stood awkwardly across from the table. "What do I do?"

"You fill out the application and submit it back to the office, select a couple dates from the schedule and they'll let you know which one's available. The schedule's in there, too. There's one in a few weeks." She grew silent and watched the blonde intently. *Am I meddling too much? Did I go too far?*

But she was rewarded with a small smile. "Thank you, Lace. I'll fill it out tonight, after dinner. And we can put it into the mail tomorrow."

"So, it's okay?"

"Yeah," Rachel agreed softly. "It's great. Thank you for

thinking about me."

"A deal's a deal, right?" Lacey raised a dark, questioning eyebrow and smiled when Rachel nodded her agreement. "We'll apply for your test, then get a course catalog for the Community College."

"And what about you?"

The dark woman took a deep breath and let her blue gaze sweep away. "I have a couple big things coming up for Vinnie and I'm gonna do them. But when you go take your test, I'm gonna tell him."

"Why do them?"

"I have to, Raich. Regardless of what Vinnie is or what he's done, his family has saved me. I probably wouldn't be alive today if they hadn't taken me in."

"Hey," Rachel said softly, still sitting and still playing with the papers in front of her. She tried to meet sapphire eyes but was denied them. "Are you sure you want out? Cuz you don't need to do this for me. I already know who you are and what you do."

"Yes." Blue eyes flashed up to meet green. "Yes. There is no doubt in my mind."

"Will he let you go?"

She was silent for awhile, came around the table to kneel next to the young blonde. "I don't know. But I think so."

"What if he doesn't?"

That really was the question of the hour but Lacey didn't want to dwell on it. So, instead, she raised two dark eyebrows and grinned at her young companion. "You ever wanted to live in Tanzania?"

Rachel let her get away with the evasion and returned the smile. "Might be nice."

Later that night they gave up all pretenses of sleeping in separate rooms. Lacey pulled up the covers and tucked them gently around the smaller woman, pulling her tightly against her own body. "All right?" she whispered.

"Mmmm," Rachel affirmed, snuggling closer still to the long dark body. "I like this."

"Me, too," the dark woman whispered back and planted a warm kiss to Rachel's temple.

Rachel responded by sliding her body up slightly, placing a light kiss on a well-tanned neck, moving up the jaw line to Lacey's ear.

Gentle touches and kisses grew more heated as they progressed with their exploration. Soon Rachel was sprawled across her companion's body and they were lost in deep kisses of discovering tongues and lips.

Rachel moaned, pressing herself into the muscular body beneath her. Then she spread her legs to capture strong hips between her thighs.

"Raich, Raich," Lacey breathed heavily, her own hands reaching down to slide under the fair woman's shirt so she could trace shoulders well-defined from hours of riding. "Are you sure?"

She didn't get an answer as the young blonde found her way beneath Lacey's shirt and pulled it over her head, tossing it casually across the room. Her lips trailed to the now bare skin to lay burning kisses on exposed breasts. Then those busy hands traveled back down to tug at shorts until Lacey complied and sat up to pull them off. The dark woman now lay completely naked to her young companion.

"C'mon, gorgeous," Lacey growled. "Turnabout's fair play." She freed Rachel of her shorts first, then reached up to slide off her shirt.

The young blonde froze and grabbed her companion's wrists. She shook her head, her eyes slightly fearful. "Please?" Embarrassed by her scars, she wanted to leave her shirt in place.

"They don't bother me, Raich," her companion promised as they studied each other's features merely inches away in the darkness.

"They bother me," she whispered back.

"Okay, love," Lacey agreed huskily and smoothed the shirt back down. Then she leaned forward again to catch elusive lips with her own and restarted her exploration.

After many long minutes of touching and caressing,

kissing and holding, Rachel relaxed again. Swept away with the intensity of sensations, she forgot her fears and ran warm hands down the long body under her, stopping to stroke a firm breast and feel the hardened nipple push into her palm. She growled and replaced her hand with mouth, sucking and licking eagerly.

Lacey arched her back into the sensations, feeling the wetness grow between her legs and on her lower thighs where Rachel rested. She fought briefly with herself to take control of this situation, never one to be acted on and preferring, always, to be the aggressor. She started to shift her weight, preparing to flip them both over.

The young blonde sat up, placing both hands on the dark aching breasts beneath her. She met smoldering sapphire with dilated jade. "Let me," she commanded huskily. She read the trepidation in those blue depths, she understood this woman's need for power and control but she asked for it anyway. After a moment's consideration, Lacey nodded just once and arched back into the hands on her.

Given this permission, Rachel lowered herself again, reinitiating her attack on those firm breasts. She moved down slowly to her lover's apex where she found moist dark curls and musky heat. With nimble fingers and probing tongue she brought the dark woman to the edge and held her there, whispering words of affirmation and humming softly into moistness.

Teetered on the edge, Lacey gripped the sheets, Rachel's shoulders, Rachel's hair. Soft whimpered moans escaped those lips, her head thrown back, her eyes closed in passion. "Raich," she whispered hoarsely and it was a plea the young woman was ready to answer.

With a final twitch of fingers and a lingering suck of coral lips and tongue, Rachel let her go. She moved one arm to hold onto the rocking hips, leaving the other fingers embedded in silky heat to feel the internal pulsing and pull every last sensation out of the long body. The blonde rested her cheek on Lacey's sweaty abdomen and reeled in the satisfaction of pleasing this woman.

She was so lost in this concentration of emotions and movement that she was surprised when Lacey growled and flipped her over, separating their connection between probing fingers and pulsing canal. Green eyes blinked in surprise at the dark woman but there was nothing more there: no fear or apprehension.

Eager to return the pleasure, Lacey slid her long body down her partner's. She stopped to suck on aching nipples through the thin cotton material, leaving wet marks in her wake that chilled in the night air and caused the woman to squirm. The dark woman nipped her way slowly down the T-shirted abdomen until Rachel was writhing in anticipation, rocking her hips forward, pleading for contact.

Small hands captured raven locks and tugged plaintively and Lacey grinned at the gentle urging. As if she didn't know what the younger woman wanted. She rested her cheek on crisp honey blonde curls just to further the torment, blowing enticingly at the warmth below, holding on for the ride as hips rocked more.

"Please?" Rachel whispered softly, resorting to words since body language was getting her nowhere.

"Please what?" Lacey asked, smirking, her hot breath that formed the question nearly the young woman's undoing.

"Aagh!" Rachel moaned, trying to prepare some kind of response but didn't need to. Without moving her head, Lacey inserted long fingers inside the blonde, seeking, probing.

Lacey set up a gentle rhythm that was readily answered by yearning hips, then slid her mouth down to join in the pleasuring. The minutes stretched out endlessly as Rachel writhed beneath the dark woman's control, breathing heavily, whimpering softly, murmuring her lover's name over and over.

The stream of sounds heightened Lacey's senses again and she felt her hips rocking against the sheets between her lover's legs in reaction. She moaned into Rachel's center, the vibration causing another shot of pleasure to rattle the lithe body. Feeling the reaction, she did it again, accenting the vocal with tongue and teeth and pushed the young blonde into oblivion. Leaving one hand in place inside her lover, she lowered the other to her own dark curls, rocking against that friction, and finding another release as well. It hadn't been that far off with her lover's sounds of pleasure, the pulsing on her digits, and the musky scent she breathed.

Slowly, carefully, Lacey withdrew from the young woman and slid up her body to wrap the smaller woman in long strong arms. She turned them gently so that she was on the bottom and Rachel's limp sweat-slicked body shrouded her. The young blonde breathed heavily into the bare shoulder beneath her head, trying to regain some equilibrium. Lacey's breathing was equally labored and stirred the fair hair just beneath her chin.

"Okay?" Lacey whispered at last, long silent moments having passed as they each soaked in warmth.

"Great." Rachel leaned up and kissed the dark woman, sharing their flavor for a lingering moment before moving up to wrap strong arms around the other woman's neck. "Great. Thank you." She was quiet for a beat. "I love you, Lace."

The dark-haired woman closed her eyes for a long moment. A gentle tear escaped her eyelashes and fell quietly down her cheek. "Say it again, hon," she whispered softly. Not realizing until this very moment the healing power of those simple words. How her whole world suddenly seemed right and a void was filled that she hadn't even realized was wanting.

"I love you."

Lacey pushed away slightly to rain the face above her with tender kisses. "I love you, too, Raich."

****

Lacey crawled out from under her bed partner just after dawn, smoothing away her mumbled complaints with a kiss. She dressed in workout clothes and went to find Karma. Then they sneaked out the front and took a long run through the nearby woods.

"She loves me, Karma," she whispered conspiratorially to her four-footed jogging partner. She felt the giddiness rising through her body as she heard the soft words echo through her again.

Karma apparently didn't care one way or the other and merely continued her stretched out, tongue-lolling lope.

****

Rachel blinked open lazy emerald eyes and examined her surroundings with slight interest. Rather, she was recalling the evening she and Lacey had just spent together, remembering the dark woman's smooth skin and whispered words.

When she finally brought herself to consider the room and the surroundings, she realized that both her lover and her dog were missing. Deciding they must be together, she rolled to her side and studied the growing sunlight as it poured through a large double-paned window. She was watching the dust mites float in the sunshine when she heard a sound behind her. Then Karma hopped nonchalantly on the bed.

Rachel rolled over slowly, taking in the dark woman before her as she snuggled her mostly naked form deeper into the warm comforter. "'Morning." She smiled at the other woman, hungrily noticing her sweat-slicked body.

Lacey quickly shucked her clothes, leaving them in a haphazard pile on the bedroom carpet. "'Morning yourself, sleepy head."

The young blonde flashed her companion a gentle smile though she found herself a bit shy in the morning light. "Hey. Have a good run?"

"Yeah." The dark head bobbed agreement even as she made her way to the bathroom. She turned back slowly, tilting her head in contemplation. "Want to join me in the shower?"

Rachel smiled and put surprisingly little thought into her response. "Yeah."

She hopped out of bed and was halfway to pulling off her shirt, revealing the rest of her body to the naked woman in front of her before remembering the scars and her shame.

Lacey smiled, her ice blue eyes dancing with fondness, and it caused the young blonde to reconsider her hesitation. Then, slowly, she pulled the shirt over her head, slightly surprised when she tossed it aside and found herself immediately in strong tan arms. "Love you," the dark husky voice assured and Rachel easily slipped into the conviction of that familiar timbre.

"Too," was all that Rachel said but Lacey grinned at her. This dark woman easily understood word economy. It was something she lived by.

The shower head spewed hot water over the both of them and they showed remarkable restraint and actually managed to keep their hands to themselves until legs and underarms were shaved and hair was shampooed. Then they soaped each other with lingering fingers.

The young blonde winced visibly when her partner's hands ran across her scarred abdomen.

"Why does that bother you so much, Rachel?" Lacey murmured while studying her companion with hooded eyes.

The smaller woman shrugged slightly. "It's a reminder of that time. I'm not proud of it. Or myself. Or the fact that I managed to get my sister killed." The last words were barely audible as they were whispered through imperceptibly open lips.

"Not true, Raich." Lacey shook her partner slightly, not paying attention to the spraying water in her eyes and mouth. "You would never have done anything to harm her."

Silence.

"Would you have?"

The blonde gave a reluctant nod of agreement. What she wouldn't give to change that night.

"I love you," Lacey said again and somehow the tone of her voice made the young blonde realize what an admission that was.

She smiled, teeth gleaming in the bathroom's overhead

lights. "I love you too, Lacey. I never thought I could feel that again ... but I do."

Chapter 9

Rachel led Sunny through the training barn into the stocks near the wash stall where she settled him with expert hands and waited. The farm was busy this morning, being a Saturday in the breeding season. Owners were delivering or picking up mares, checking out stallions, and inspecting progeny. She hoped they could do this quickly and avoid questions.

It was only a few minutes before she heard footsteps coming up the concrete aisle and then saw Lacey and a tall bearded man rounding the corner.

"David, meet Rachel ... and Sunny," Lacey introduced as they came closer. The bearded man shook Rachel's hand and then eyed the young colt skeptically.

"Did you bring a sedative?"

"No." David shook his head. "I was hoping you had something more ... horse-like."

The blonde grinned. "Yeah, hold on. I'll get something out of the office. Watch him." She passed the lead line to her tall, dark partner.

"Raich, I don't think—" Blue eyes observed her warily before flashing to the bay.

"He'll be fine. Gentle as a lamb," Rachel called over her shoulder even as she was jogging back down the barn aisle.

They drew blood before administering the sedative and then gave it several minutes to sink in before inserting the large hollow needles for biopsies. David needed a lot of assistance from Rachel on where to insert and what to take samples of.

"I've never worked on a horse before," he explained meekly, meeting green eyes with gentle brown.

Rachel smiled. "I've never worked on a human. Cool, huh? Wanna let me try?"

Lacey laughed at David's worried expression before he realized the young blonde was kidding.

"This is the name and number of the mineral block manufacturer." Rachel handed the bearded man a piece of paper after he'd finished his work.

David nodded and pocketed it. "How's he doing otherwise?"

Rachel shrugged and pointed to him. "He's still doing that awkward standing thing. And now I sometimes see him shiver all over. Still stumbles a lot."

The man watched Sunny carefully, noting slight occasional tremors. The stance looked uncomfortable at best, splayed legs and slightly hunched back. He shook his head slowly before promising to run the samples as quickly as possible and walking away from the women and the colt, deep in thought.

Rachel and Lacey left soon afterwards and headed back to the house to enjoy the rest of their weekend.

****

Lacey knocked gently at the doorjamb to her own office, peering in the opening to the young blonde at her desk. She appeared lost in thought, fingers occasionally dancing across the keyboard, head tilted in concentration as the monitor's glow bounced off achingly familiar features. She hadn't heard the knock.

"Hey," the dark woman called gently, causing Rachel to look up.

A grin spread across her face as she leaned back and massaged her neck. Then she glanced over her lover's shoulder to the large window beyond. "It's dark. I didn't know I was at it so long."

"Yeah, you hungry?" Lacey asked gently, stepping into the room and laying her hands on the desktop and leaning her weight on them.

"I am. I didn't realize it." Rachel grinned fondly, reaching a hand across the desk to cover Lacey's.

"I have dinner ready if you want to come down and take a break."

"Yeah." The blonde glanced back to the screen. "I found some stuff. Can I print it out and bring it downstairs?"

"Sure." Lacey moved easily across the plush carpet and turned on the laser printer in the corner. "Give it just a minute. I'll be downstairs."

Several minutes later, Rachel was slicing into a grilled steak. Lacey was doing the same across from her at the smaller kitchen table.

"What did you find?" Lacey asked.

"I did a search on horses and poison and then I narrowed the list by symptoms. There are a couple of plants that may be culprits." The blonde pushed the papers she'd printed out across to her lover.

Lacey read them silently as she continued to eat. She finished off her baked potato in relative silence before she glanced up to see seeking emerald eyes. "Good job, Raich," the husky voice praised. "I think you're onto something." The pages outlined three potential poisonous plants with make-up and symptoms of each: ragwort, bracken fern, and astragalus.

Rachel beamed with pride at the gentle words. She'd been combing the Internet most of the afternoon, unable to relax when Sunny's life seemed in danger. "Can we get that information to David?" the young blonde asked, resuming the consumption of her meal.

"Yeah, I'll fax it to him right now." Lacey rose from her seat and leaned over to kiss her lover's cheek gently before leaving the room.

****

By late Sunday afternoon, Rachel and Lacey were standing back in the broodmare barn with David and Sunny.

"I think it's the bracken fern," David was explaining as he drew an amber liquid into a syringe. "The toxin in the fern is thiaminase, an enzyme that destroys thiamine which is vitamin B1," he explained softly while inserting the needle gently into Sunny's muscular neck. "The horse suffers from a vitamin deficiency of thiamine, which causes a loss of the fatty insulation layer to nerves that primarily control muscles. Symptoms are weight loss, weakness, gait abnormalities, abnormal heart rate and/or rhythm, inability to rise, sometimes death."

Rachel remembered all of this from her reading the day before but she listened intently just the same, needing the information to be confirmed by a professional.

"He was probably being poisoned for a couple of months before the onset of symptoms. It can be deadly if left untreated."

"What are you giving him?" Lacey asked, peering over the blonde's shoulder to watch the needle withdraw.

"Thiamine ... vitamin B1," he clarified in case the dark woman didn't remember what the word was. "He needs a daily injection for two weeks."

"And he'll be better?" Rachel asked softly.

"Well," David smiled gently, "according to my research, yes. And I called around and asked some vets. But this is all new to me. Let's go give some injections to the other horses."

****

Wednesday evening Rachel pulled up to the curb outside

of Lacey's grand home, realizing how stupid this move was. It's not like the self-appointed crony wouldn't notice a white Jeep parked in front of her own house. The closest neighbor was maybe a half mile away.

The young woman had come here on impulse after her work at Briargate was done for the day. She and Lacey had spent a wonderful weekend together and had spoken on the phone once since then to discuss the health of the horses as well as the vet's apparent involvement.

David didn't think that such a prognosis could have been overlooked by knowledgeable large animal veterinarians. Lacey passed this on to Vinnie, so the barn vet had been immediately changed and the prior vet questioned for involvement. But still the trail ended there and they couldn't tie anyone else at Briargate or a name at Wheatridge to the poisoning of the horses. Meanwhile, all of the remaining six horses were receiving their daily vitamin shots and appeared to be improving.

For now it looked as if Lacey's job at Briargate was done. Rachel had feared her association with the dark woman ended with the job but Lacey reassured her that it wasn't the case and they'd see each other soon.

So now, Rachel was outside the mafia crony's home. This was her first uninvited trip here. Her first time actually driving herself, in fact, and that newness had been illustrated in her inability to find the place on the first try.

She sat silently with the Jeep turned off and her wrists resting lightly at the top of the steering wheel. Karma whined plaintively in the passenger seat, pulling slightly against her restraints.

"Hush, would you?" her owner reprimanded softly. "I'm gaining courage." She watched the house curiously, noting that the porch light was on, freeing the front walk from early evening darkness. There were also a few lights on behind closed curtains: in the living room, front hallway, probably kitchen.

She was still considering all this when her door was yanked open and she was pulled bodily from the vehicle, immediately grateful that she'd taken off her seatbelt already and spared herself a strangling. The hand that held her was large and beefy and wrapped in her jacket and sweater. Her back was pressed firmly against the Jeep's canvas top and Karma screamed like a banshee from her side of the vehicle.

He was a large man, well over six feet tall, with a solid if not pudgy build. His almost black hair was cut short and his brown eyes were nearly as dark as his hair. He eyed her suspiciously, the cold look on his face chilling the young woman more than the night air. Slowly, his eyes left her to track to the squirming and yelping dog. He raised a silenced gun in the hand he wasn't using to hold Rachel against the vehicle and pointed it at Karma.

"No!" Rachel screamed and bucked hard against the Jeep, forcing her knee solidly into the large man's groin. He dropped his grip on her but managed to backhand her with the weapon before doubling over in agony. The young blonde slid to the ground, pain shooting through her face like hot fire. She tasted the metallic tang of blood. She jumped to her feet as quickly as she could and tried to duck around the Jeep, hoping to free Karma and make a run for it. But her assailant grabbed her hair and growled at her.

"You fucking bitch." He pulled her hard back towards him and she used that momentum to spin around and hit him in the face with her elbow.

God, his face is hard as rock. She winced at the jolt of pain through her arm.

But when he pressed the silencer solidly to her temple, she knew the fight was over and stopped struggling.

"Not so dumb after all, eh bitch?" the dark voice grumbled. Karma, thankfully, had quieted down during the struggle and now just watched them with blinking blue eyes.

"Don't hurt her," Rachel mumbled through painfully split lips, her head spinning, her stomach churning. *Damn me and my weak stomach.*

Silently, the man tugged on her hair and dragged her to Lacey's house.

****

Lacey stood in the kitchen watching George and Rico at the small table. They both were reading separate parts of the paper: George had the sports section and Rico read the comics. How fitting, the dark woman snorted and turned back to the soup she was heating.

"Where'd Bernard go?" Lacey asked, glancing back at her companions. George merely shrugged his shoulders but Rico looked up from his reading.

"Dunno. The john?"

"He touches one thing in my house and I'm gonna rip his fucking tongue out," she spoke loudly. "Ya hear that, Bernard?"

As if on cue, Bernard entered the kitchen from the front hallway and stood on the ceramic tiled floor. Only he wasn't alone and he watched in shock as his boss's look turned from good-natured teasing to one of passionate anger. "Found her sneakin' around—"

"For Christ's sake, Bernard! What the fuck did you do to her?" Lacey dropped her spoon and took a step towards the two, examining the bruises that marked the young blonde's features and the split lip. She had blood smeared across her face and her green eyes were frantic and darting. She didn't notice that Bernard's face sported its own set of bruises though she did see that he jammed the gun he held harder into the young woman's temple.

"What did I do to her?!" His eyes widened incredulously. "She's spying on your house. She's got some stupid ass dog out there screaming its fuckin' head off and when I went to shut it up ... this bitch lost her fuckin' mind!"

Lacey reached a hand out to her young friend, telling her as best she could with eyes alone that everything was all right. "You shot the dog?!"

"No, no." Bernard was beyond confused. George and Rico stood now as well, weapons drawn though there was no clear enemy. Bernard still held his own gun firmly to his young captive's head, trying to sort out why Lacey was angry at him and not the little peeping Tom.

"Let her go, Bernard," Lacey said softly, raising her other hand out to her side, indicating that George and Rico better hold their ground.

"Lace! She's watching your house. She could be with the assholes that killed Al!" The beefy man was nearly whining. "George, get me your cuffs. We'll question her."

"Let her go," Lacey repeated in a menacing growl, quickly losing her patience for this ludicrous game where the only loser was the young blonde before her.

The gun wavered and dark brown eyes met ice blue.

"Put down the fucking gun, Bernard, and LET HER GO!" Lacey shouted.

He dropped it as if it had bitten him and released his hold on long blonde hair.

The two woman took a step each and it was enough to find them in each other's arms. Lacey wrapped herself around the blonde, rocking her slightly, burying her face in soft hair.

"I'm so sorry, so sorry," Rachel was whispering over and over. "I shouldn't have come. I wanted to see you."

"Shhh, shhh," Lacey responded, rubbing the other woman's back. "It's okay." She cast a dark look to Bernard who simply stood still and looked dumb, having no other recourse at this moment in time.

Then the dark-haired woman pushed her companion away gently and cradled her face. "Let's get some ice on that jaw, huh sweetheart?" She wiped at errant tears on the pale face before her, smiled gently. "It's okay, love. C'mere, sit down."

George and Bernard exchanged bewildered looks.

"Sweetheart?" mouthed Bernard soundlessly.

George shrugged. "Love?" he returned in the same silent manner.

But Rico had the foresight to push his recently vacated chair towards the two women. Lacey couldn't suppress a grin: the kid was catching on pretty fast.

Rachel eyed everyone silently while Lacey pulled out a

dishtowel and filled it with crushed ice from the freezer door dispenser. The only sound in the room was the gentle mechanical churning of the ice machine at work.

Finally, the young blond kid ventured forward, sincerity in his blue eyes. He thrust out a hand awkwardly. "Hi, I'm Rico."

Rachel glanced at him, guessed him to be in his late teens at the oldest, and slowly returned his handshake. "Rachel." He beamed, looked to George and Bernard before casting a worried gaze to Lacey.

The dark woman smiled at him as she came back and knelt before Rachel, tenderly pressing the ice pack to her face. The young blonde flinched away and Lacey steadied her by cupping her free hand behind fair hair. She pursed her lips, met emerald eyes. "I know, it's gonna hurt like a bitch."

"Already does," her young companion affirmed.

"Uh ... Lace?" Bernard spoke at last, figured he was already in trouble for hurting this young woman so he may as well take the hit for all of them by asking the stupid question. "Who is she?"

Sapphire eyes twinkled for Rachel alone before she turned her attention to the beefy man still standing near the main entrance to the room. "This is my lover, Rachel. Rachel, this is Bernard, George ... and you met Rico."

Bernard's chin hit the floor and George let out a huge whoop.

"Oh, buddy!" the black man crooned. "You're gonna get promoted right into the graveyard! Holy shit! You tried to take out her lover?! You are so fucking dead!" But George really seemed delighted at the other man's misfortune.

"Oh my God," were the first words Bernard was able to mutter. He glanced angrily at George. "Shut up!" he growled, then looked back to Lacey with a mixture of guilt and downright fear. "Lace, I ... I didn't know. I was walking through the front room and I saw her pull up ... I didn't think ..." But his explanation faded out when the dark face watching him creased into a toothy grin.

"You're lucky she didn't kill you, Bernie." Lacey smiled at him, winking at Rachel. George was still chortling. "Give us some space, guys. Rico, there's a dog in her car. Go get her, don't hurt her."

The kid almost snapped a salute before flying out of the kitchen and down the front hall. The two large men followed him but detoured into the living room.

"Hey, honey," Lacey whispered, dropping her grin and turning a concerned gaze towards her young companion. "I'm sorry. I'm sorry he did that. We're all kinda on edge right now." She smoothed one hand over blonde hair, still holding the ice pack with the other.

"It's my fault," Rachel responded, pushing the cold sensation gently away. "I shouldn't have come. I thought, you know, that since this weekend and I missed you ... I thought ... it was stupid." She dropped her eyes.

"No, no it's not, Rachel. You're welcome to come here any time you want. I just wasn't expecting you. I'd have warned the guys. I'm glad you came.'" And she really was. It meant a lot to her that her young companion sought her out. Now she was sure Rachel felt the same connection as she did. "Always welcome here."

Their eyes met again for a very long moment and Rachel saw the conviction in blue depths. She ventured a small grin even though it tugged painfully at her lips.

"C'mere." Lacey gently pulled her friend to her feet and guided her over to the counter. She was helping the blonde sit on top of the Formica when the sound of nails came clattering down the hall and into the kitchen. Karma was absolutely frantic as she tried unsuccessfully to jump up to see her owner. So Lacey picked her up and held her as she reached out an exploring tongue to Rachel's face.

"Hey, easy, Karma," her owner whispered quietly, stroking soft fur. "I'm okay, see?"

When the dog seemed suitably subdued, Lacey placed her back on the floor and watched her shoot off into the front of the house. "Will she hurt Bernard?" the dark woman asked, not sure whether to encourage or discourage such action.

"I don't think so."

Lacey shrugged and turned her attention back to Rachel's face, which was now at eye level. She winced. "That's gonna be painful for awhile." She pressed the ice back. "Hold that there, it'll help." Then she examined the cut on the other woman's left cheek, also produced by the weapon's impact.

"This one needs stitches," Lacey murmured, using a moistened paper towel to dab at the blood.

"Your soup's boiling over."

"Hmm?" The dark-haired woman raised her eyes slowly to meet her companion's. Then caught what she was saying. "Ah." She turned around and clicked off the burner.

"Stitches?" A slight look of fear flickered across her friend's features when Lacey faced her again.

"Or it'll scar pretty badly."

"Can you take me?" she whispered.

Blue eyes ducked away for a minute, then back. Her lips were almost smirking. "I could do them."

"You can give me stitches?"

Her companion nodded, shrugged one broad shoulder. "You kinda learn how to do some of these things when you're avoiding police reports."

"I see." The young blonde grinned slightly at her companion's self-deprecating manner.

"She's good," a voice came from the hall entrance and both faces turned toward George. The man offered a gentle grin. "She's stitched me up a couple of times. No pain, no scars."

Lacey offered George a grateful smile before turning back to her patient. "Whaddya think? Trust me?"

"Yeah." Rachel nodded without hesitation.

"Let's go upstairs." She tugged on her friend's arm and led her towards the other opening in the kitchen that led through the dining room to the spiral staircase. "George," she turned back. "Send Bernard out for Chinese."

She was answered with a toothy grin. "Can do, Boss."

****

Rachel sat silently on the toilet lid, holding the ice to her face even though the towel was getting soggy. She watched Lacey work with slight trepidation. The darker woman rummaged through drawers and laid out needles, gauze, surgical thread, small scissors, and forceps. Then she went into the bedroom closet and came back with a small syringe.

Green eyes widened.

"Local, that's all," Lacey assured her gently.

"I'm bad at this," Rachel whispered nervously.

Her companion smiled reassuringly. "I'm good at this. Don't worry. Just a little prick ..." Rachel felt the poke but had the good sense to sit still. "And another one. Good, now we wait for a minute."

Lacey took the opportunity to examine her partner's face more closely. She pulled away the ice pack and set it in the sink, then held Rachel's chin and tilted her head gently. "He got you pretty good."

"I got him, too." The blonde grinned slightly, causing the other woman to laugh.

"Yeah, you did."

But then Rachel grimaced a little. "I kneed him in the groin. I hope he's okay."

"He deserved it."

"He was trying to protect you, Lace," Rachel said softly, defending the large man's loyalty.

"Yeah, well, Bernard's been with me long enough to know I can protect myself." The dark woman shook her head. "Ready?"

"I guess."

Long tan fingers tapped the skin surrounding the wound. "Feel that?" The blonde shook her head. "Here we go."

Rachel sat tall and still under the ministrations of large gentle hands, her own hands clutching nervously to her partner's shirt front. Lacey whispered to her occasionally, smiling with encouragement, her eyes flashing from worried green to the cut she stitched. Rachel could feel the tug of needle and sutures but not any pain so she was able to relax after several long minutes.

Finally, Lacey snipped the thread with small scissors and patted her friend on the knee. "All done."

"How many?"

"Four. But they're teeny. I don't think it'll scar."

"You're amazing." The blonde grinned.

Lacey returned it. "Spread that rumor. Let's get you some more ice. I'll put it in a bag this time."

Rachel followed the tall woman through the bedroom but tugged at the tail of her button shirt before they entered the hallway. "Lace?"

"Yeah?" She turned around, raven hair flying briefly before settling on shoulders again.

"Why are they here? Should I go?"

Lacey wrinkled her brow in thought, pursed her lips and evaded her partner's gaze for a few moments. "We're waiting for a call. S'posed to work tonight. Sometimes it's easier if we're all in one place, sometimes we stay here instead of Vinnie's."

"What are you supposed to do tonight?"

A slightly amused look was her only response.

"Can't say?"

"No."

"I should go, then. If you're going to get called away," Rachel decided reluctantly, wanting to stay right where she was.

Lacey shook her head slowly. "How 'bout we have some dinner and if the boys and I get called away, you wait here for me?"

The young blonde switched her weight nervously from foot to foot, studying the features in front of her. She found that she was slowly learning to read the stoic face and guarded eyes. Lacey wanted her here as much as she wanted to be here. The dark woman was disappointed that she had to work. "What if you don't come back tonight? What if you have to leave again?" Rachel whispered at last.

Lacey considered the questions, knew them to be realistic. She hoped tonight's meeting would go well, had no reason to think it wouldn't. "I'll do my best to come home. If I can't, I'll call here and you can pick it up if you hear me on the answering machine. Okay?"

Rachel nodded, gave her companion a small smile.

"Good. Settled. C'mon." The dark woman wrapped her large hand around a small one and led the blonde back downstairs to the kitchen.

****

Much later in the evening, Rachel was slightly tipsy from the wine Lacey had been handing her. The dark-haired woman had reasoned that the alcohol would help numb the pain in her face, which it did. So the young woman didn't complain.

She played cards with Rico and Bernard, grinning from ear to ear and taking them for all they were worth. Lacey peeked over her shoulder chewing on an egg roll and occasionally reaching out to run tender fingers through blonde tresses. The touches were warm and comforting and it pleased the young woman to no end that Lacey was confident enough to show affection in front of her companions.

"Unh unh," Lacey warned softly, tugging at a blonde lock when Rachel went to discard something.

"No?" She turned questioning green eyes to her friend.

"This one ... and this one." The dark-haired woman leaned forward to tap two cards, kissing Rachel on the temple before sitting back up.

"No fair," Bernard joked, feeling more at ease as the evening wore on. "You can't help her."

"George is helping you," Rachel bantered back.

"George is worthless. Lacey is the card shark."

"Hey," George lightly backhanded his friend, "a little respect."

"Not likely," Rico snorted.

Rachel laughed.

Lacey's cell phone rang and the two women's eyes met before Rachel glanced to the kitchen clock. It was nearly midnight.

"Yeah. Great." The dark woman turned her attention to her team. "Let's go."

Rachel stood with them and began cleaning up their glasses and plates. She rinsed them in the sink, her back to the group as they prepared. She heard muttered comments about ammunition and pieces. The men had the good grace to leave first.

She felt warm hands on her shoulders, gentle lips at the top of her head. "C'mere." Lacey turned the small woman around, hugged her close. "Be safe. Stay inside, Karma can use the doggy door. I'll set the alarm on the way out, if you have to leave I reset the code to your birthday for tonight ... day then month."

Rachel nodded against the familiar leather trench coat.

"I'll be back as soon as I can."

"Be careful," the blonde whispered. "I want to be with you for a long time to come."

Lacey chuckled, Rachel felt it bubble through the tall woman's body. "Me, too. I love you." She bent forward to capture the blonde's lips, careful to not hurt her further. But she wasn't satisfied with one kiss so she did it again.

"Love you, too."

They didn't say good-bye as they disentangled and stepped away.

Rachel decided it was going to be a long night as she heard the telltale beeping of the alarm being set and then the front door closing.

Chapter 10

Lacey stepped quietly into the front hall and disengaged the alarm quickly. Karma trotted through the darkness to greet her.

"No," Lacey whispered, waving the dog away. But Karma had already stopped several yards away, smelling the unfamiliar scent of blood and tissue. She sneezed, backed a few steps. "I know, girl," Lacey agreed wearily. She'd been gone almost six hours and had returned covered in blood.

She walked quietly to the downstairs bathroom, disappointed to find that there wasn't a bath towel there. She kicked off her shoes on the hard wood floor and shrugged off her coat before crossing to the stairs and going upstairs to the linen closet. Every muscle in her body ached.

Rachel heard her. "Lace?" she called quietly from the bedroom.

"Yeah, honey. It's okay. I need to take a shower." Please stay where you are, please. I don't want you to see this.

Of course, her silent pleas fell on deaf ears and she immediately saw the young blonde silhouetted by moonlight in the doorway.

"I'll shower downstairs, Raich. Go back to bed." Lacey was already retreating with a towel, hoping to make it to the stairway before her partner's eyes adjusted to the darkened hallway.

"Don't be silly," Rachel yawned and stepped into the corridor, extending a hand. "I'm awake, haven't slept yet."

"Don't touch me," Lacey barked, jumping away from the fingers reaching for her.

They were close enough now that Lacey could see the doubt and confusion on her young friend's face.

Fuck. "I don't want you to get dirty. Go ahead, I'll shower up here."

Rachel turned on the bedroom light on the way back in and turned around while speaking. "Are you hurt?" But her voice died in her throat when she fully faced the tall woman.

Lacey stood before her covered in blood. She was somewhat clean where she'd worn the trench coat but apparently hadn't buttoned it because her front was red. Her hair was sticky with blood and tissue fragments. Her ice blue eyes watched Rachel intently, preparing herself for hatred or rejection. Rachel saw the walls building up again.

The young blonde pressed the back of her hand to her mouth, trying to fight off nausea. She swallowed a few times, took a deep breath. "It's okay, Lace. Is any of it yours? Are you okay?"

"None of it's mine," the dark woman confirmed softly. "Are you going to be sick?"

"I hope not." Her partner grinned shyly but still looked a bit green around the edges.

"If you want to go ... I'd understand," Lacey whispered.

"Enough of that, love," Rachel assured her gently. "I knew. Remember?" Though she had to admit that the knowing and the seeing were two very different things. "Shower."

Rachel sat silently on the closed toilet lid while her partner showered, relieved that the initial nausea had passed without incident. Then she stood to help Lacey dry off once she stepped out onto the tile. She was glad to find that that there weren't any marks on the smooth, dark body.

"Let me see your face," Lacey whispered, tilting the blonde's chin upward. "How does it feel?"

"Bad."

"Looks better. Did you keep ice on it?"

The blonde head bobbed in agreement.

Lacey pulled on a sleeping shirt and went into the other room to crawl into bed. Rachel was right behind her. They snuggled silently for several long minutes and Rachel could feel the tension coiled in the strong body beside her.

"Can I ask what happened, Lacey? Did something happen to the guys?"

The dark-haired woman was quiet for so long that Rachel decided her question was going to go unanswered.

Finally, she cleared her throat and the husky voice rumbled forward. "Things are going down with the business. Some of our contacts have been picked up ... some of the traffickers have disappeared altogether or have been killed. Everyone's on edge. The other team was no exception. They were high-strung and young, made Rico high-strung. We were there for hours, arguing things that shouldn't have needed arguing. Everything was settled before hand, they were getting jumpy. One of them pulled a gun on us ... he was just stupid, I don't think he would have done anything. We were still talking cost and quality." She took a deep breath, Rachel feared for the outcome. "Rico pulled his gun, too, and I told him to put it away." I yelled at him, actually. "Took a step forward to stop him. The other kid was no more than a yard or two away, tracked me with his gun. I heard it cock and I went to put myself between him and Rico. I was a foot from the other kid when Rico pulled the trigger. One shot to the head, the kid was dead."

Silence. Then, hesitantly, "That was his ... uh ... on you?"

"Yeah. Rico panicked. It was all we could do to keep the other guys from opening fire," she sighed deeply, held her lover closer. "Finish the deal. Calm Rico down. His first kill."

"He thought the other kid was going to kill you."

"He may have."

"Rico's a good kid."

"I need out," she whispered hoarsely, tears on her cheeks. The suddenness of the statement surprised her as much as the blonde nestled against her.

"You will be," the blonde reassured her, scooting up her partner's body to wrap arms around dark head and shoulders. She rocked her and comforted her, could find no words to express her depth of feeling.

It could have been hours or minutes that they lay together like that, Rachel's small body curled around the other woman. She was surprised at her own strength. She really was sickened by what she'd seen and heard but was able to push it aside in Lacey's moment of need.

Their long moments of silence were interrupted when the alarm clock on the nightstand nearby started beeping. Rachel groaned, reached over to slap it off.

"What for?" Lacey asked huskily, her throat raw from crying.

"I have to go to work." And I haven't slept a wink. And she needs me to stay.

"Can you call in sick?" the quiet voice requested.

"Lace, I can't, love," she responded with regret. I need the money ... I can't miss a day this paycheck and still pay bills.

"Please?"

Her heart broke. A woman who could very likely conquer the world if she set her mind to it, was asking for her. Nothing more, just her presence and her companionship. "Okay."

The large frame relaxed visibly in response.

Rachel disentangled herself long enough to get a glass of water for her friend and call the stable. Lacey listened quietly to this end of the conversation while she sipped cool water into a parched throat.

"I know I did. I know ... can't be helped ... no shape to do any good for the horses. Bye."

She snuggled back under the comforter.

"What is it?" Lacey asked softly, leaning over her companion, brushing blonde bangs back.

"Nothing. I just asked for extra work this paycheck and he reminded me that I'd asked."

"Why?"

Rachel shrugged, met sapphire eyes in the growing dawn. "Bills. My daughter's coming to stay with me for her Spring break next week. Ya know ... things."

"Can I help?"

"Nah." Rachel brushed it off, even though her mind was already spinning with which bill could be put off or which meals she could go without. "It'll be okay. I'd rather be here with you."

White teeth flashed in a grin. "Thank you."

The grin was contagious. "No problem. Let's get some sleep."

****

Lacey had to shout to be heard over the road noise as the Jeep Wrangler flew down the highway.

"How much longer?"

"You're worse than a kid." Rachel smiled her response. "Maybe another twenty minutes is all."

It was closer to thirty, though, when they pulled to a stop in front of a suburban Rochester home and Rachel killed the ignition. She glanced back at Karma who stood expectantly on the rear seat, full tail waving gently back and forth.

"Are you nervous?" Lacey asked when she noticed her partner's hesitation.

"A little, yeah," the young blonde admitted, studying the manicured lawn and the well-kept home.

"Does she know ... about you and me?"

Rachel nodded. "I told her on the phone. She really is looking forward to meeting you. She and I talked about my lifestyle and preferences awhile ago."

Well that's good, anyway, the dark woman thought. "Why are you nervous?"

Rachel flashed white teeth in a gentle grin, shrugged one shoulder. "She's my family. I want her to like you. I haven't seen her in almost two months, too, because of extra duty at the barn."

"Well, let's go," Lacey said, reaching back to grab Karma's leash and then opening her door and hopping out. Within moments, Rachel was at her side and they were making their way up the sidewalk to the front step.

The door opened before they'd come within fifteen feet of it and a small blonde-haired, blue-eyed missile flew out the opening and into Rachel's arms.

"Mama!"

"Hey, baby," Rachel murmured, wrapping the girl in an embrace. "I missed you!"

Lacey was better able to observe the youngster when she stepped away from her mother. She came up to Rachel's elbows and wore a black T-shirt which, in X Files eerie green, encouraged people to trust no one. Her cotton pants were the same eerie color of green and her tennis shoes were black and ratty. Her hair was thin and about shoulder length, held away from her face by a braided leather headband. And her blue eyes absolutely sparkled with her glee.

The girl launched into animated banter, backing away to hold her mother's hand in both of hers while bouncing up and down. "Missed you too! Can we go to the zoo? Are there babies at the farm I can see? What happened to your cheek?"

"Just a cut ... an accident," Rachel said about the stitches, meeting Lacey's blue gaze. "We can talk about what you want to do when we're on the road. I want you to meet someone, Molly." Rachel turned her attention to her partner and extended her free hand to draw the dark woman closer. "This is Lacey. Lacey, this is Molly."

The girl offered her hand in a grown up shake while she beamed from ear to ear. "You sure are pretty," then aside to Rachel, "You were right, Mama. Her eyes are just like the sky."

Rachel blushed, Lacey offered a slight smirk. Then

Molly turned her attention to Karma who was dancing on the end of her leash, waiting for her turn at greetings.

"Can I hold her?" Molly asked, reaching to take the leash from Lacey's hand. It was relinquished readily.

"Molly, let me go say hello to Aunt Helen and then we'll go. Are you all packed? It's not even March, where's your jacket, young lady?"

"Yeah, it's by the door with my stuff." She rolled expressive eyes, looking to the dark-haired woman for support. "Lacey and I can put it in the Jeep? Is that okay?"

"Sounds great," Lacey agreed, nodding encouragingly to her partner who went ahead into the house.

"Can I call you Lacey? Or should I call you something else?" Molly asked awkwardly, shifting her slight weight from foot to foot.

"Lacey's fine, kiddo. Let's get your stuff loaded up, huh? And what say you put on your jacket?"

The child offered the older woman a full-toothed grin as she jogged with Karma into the house.

In the end, Rachel shouldn't have been worried. Her tall, dark partner lightened visibly in the presence of the child and they got along famously from the very first moment. In fact, Rachel experienced mild pangs of jealousy throughout the day, as she'd never had to share Lacey or Molly before. But they passed with some gentle reminders to herself and she found herself enjoying the day immensely.

The three snuggled down together in Lacey's bed late that night after a full day of going to the zoo, seeing the new foals at Briargate, and dinner at a loud Peter Piper Pizza. Now they watched a movie and tried to wind down the young girl who was still chattering aimlessly.

She held the dark woman's hand between her own, tracing the lines and fingers absently while she mused about school and Aunt Helen and the other two children who lived with her.

"Aren't you going to watch the movie at all?" Lacey asked in her husky voice. "You picked it out." *Lord knows George of the Jungle was not my first choice.*

"I've seen it before," she piped up.

Lacey glanced to Rachel who sat quietly on the other side of Molly and cast her a funny look as if to say 'why are we watching this crap then?'

Rachel laughed. "C'mon, honey. Let me take you to your bed and settle you in. It's late."

The child groaned her protests but followed her mother to the door willingly enough before stopping in the threshold of the room. Then she turned around abruptly to look at Lacey again. The dark woman rested comfortably on top of the covers, dressed in sweats and a T-shirt. Molly glanced briefly to her mother. "Can I say goodnight to Lacey, Mama?"

Rachel grinned, smoothed her daughter's mussed up blonde hair. "Of course, Molly. Go ahead."

For the first time that day, the young girl was shy as she moved back across the room to crawl on top of her mother's lover. She hugged her tightly around the neck and Lacey returned the embrace easily.

"Sleep well, squirt," Lacey whispered. "I'll see you in the morning."

"G'night, Lacey. I love you."

"Love you, too." Lacey grinned, looking over the small shoulder to meet her partner's emerald eyes. "Go on to bed." With a final squeeze, she disentangled and sent the young girl on her way.

Chapter 11

Lacey had dozed off when she felt the covers tugged from beneath her. She blinked sleepily and met shining green eyes.

"Hey, sleepy. Move over and let me in," Rachel's soft voice teased.

The dark woman lifted her hips then rolled onto her side to let her partner pull the covers down. Then she tucked her feet under them.

"Unh unh, crony. A little less clothes, please. At least ditch the sweats, you'll get hot," the blonde admonished as she stripped to t-shirt and underwear herself, expertly unhooking her bra and sliding it out one sleeve. All went unnoticed by her bleary-eyed partner who pulled off the sweats and then settled back into the pillows, opening her arms to invite her lover.

Rachel silently took the invitation and pulled the covers up over them both.

"I'm tired," Lacey murmured, placing a gentle kiss to the other woman's temple. "Little tike wore me out."

The young blonde laughed. "You didn't have to keep picking her up to show her things. It was a ploy."

"I know," Lacey agreed, snuggling closer to her partner. "She's wonderful, Raich." She could feel the excitement thrumming through the young woman she held. "You're not gonna let me sleep, are you?" She opened one wary blue eye to peer out.

"You can sleep, I'm sorry. I'm so excited, Lace." She clutched the arm holding her. "I've never been happier in my whole life. The two of you with me ..."

"Pretty spectacular, huh?"

She nodded eager agreement.

Lacey grinned at her young friend's happiness. "We have a week with her, Raich. You better get some sleep sometime."

"Yeah, I know. I love you. So much." She emphasized the statement with gentle kisses to the other woman's neck. Kisses which slowly became more arousing as they traveled across the dark woman's collarbone, then up to her earlobe.

"Rachel," her dark-haired lover growled softly, even as she found herself responding. Suddenly she wasn't as sleepy as she thought when the arousal traveled from the flesh the young woman touched, straight to her groin.

"Hmm?" the blonde responded innocently, trailing her fingertips under the other woman's t-shirt and up well-defined abs.

Lacey gave up and flipped her lover over, straddling her hips, meeting her emerald eyes with icy blue desire. "You win," she whispered huskily, taking the lips below her and dueling with an eager tongue.

The younger woman responded with a throaty chuckle. "You have no willpower, crony."

"Not when it comes to you, gorgeous," Lacey agreed readily, peeling the remainder of both of their clothes away to allow skin to entice skin. The friction was deliciously erotic and both women were lost in the sensations of touches, kisses, and whispered words.

****

It was a good thing they'd had the foresight to pull clothing back on after their lovemaking, because bright and early, Molly came bouncing into the room and did a cannonball rendition in the middle of the large bed. Karma wasn't far behind.

Lacey found herself reaching for her nightstand drawer at the rude awakening but her fingers were gently caught in her young lover's grasp. Their eyes met briefly and Rachel easily read the dark woman's self-disgust. The action had been pure instinct, since Lacey had removed any weapons from easy grasp and locked them away before the young girl came into the house.

"S'okay, love," Rachel whispered sleepily. "Old habits are hard to break." She kissed Lacey's cheek gently while squeezing the hand she still held.

"Yuck!" Molly announced loudly upon seeing the display of affection. "Do that on your own time." She stuck her tongue out and shook her head as if having a chill.

Lacey laughed. "You'll understand some day. You'll meet some cute boy—"

"Boys are not cute," the child said with obvious disdain.

"Girls then?" her mother teased.

"Kissing is gross!" Molly argued. "I don't care who it is."

"Oh yeah?" Lacey growled, crawling out from under the covers to sneak up on the little girl. "So then we shouldn't kiss you?" With that she tackled the squealing child and proceeded to rain kisses all over her face.

"Aaagh! Mama! Help me!!"

Rachel grinned and made as if to come to her daughter's rescue but only ended up tickling her ribs while her dark companion held the girl still.

"No fair! No fair, Mama," Molly screamed, though the words were barely intelligible through her gurgling laughter and Karma's excited howling.

After another minute of torture, both women backed away and watched the girl as she moaned and giggled and tried to catch her breath.

"'Morning, kiddo," Lacey smirked.

"'Mornin'," Molly responded weakly.

When everything had calmed down, Karma gave up on the excitement and made a bee-line to the door and down the stairs. The rest of the house's occupants followed shortly afterwards.

After realizing how long it might take, Lacey left her lover and Molly to make decisions on breakfast while she went into the office and checked up on business. She had an appointment this afternoon and a meeting in the evening with her team but otherwise, everything seemed under control. When she came back downstairs after nearly an hour of phone calls and email, she found Rachel and Molly working easily together, chatting softly.

"So," Lacey announced her presence from the doorway. "What are we having?"

"Waffles," Molly said proudly, seated on the counter in her long nightgown, stirring a huge bowl in her lap.

"Great. What can I do?"

"Do you have any juice or anything?" Rachel asked from the center island where she was slicing sausage patties off of a large roll.

"Hmmm," Lacey pondered a moment, raising slim dark eyebrows to mingle with her bangs. "Maybe. I'll go check the garage freezer."

Later, they all sat around the kitchen table. "These are good, Molly," Lacey complimented. "You did an excellent job, squirt."

"Mama helped," the child admitted but blushed from the kind words.

Lacey reached out a gentle hand and rubbed her partner's arm. "Your mom's a good cook."

Molly nodded. "What are we going to do today?"

"Well," Rachel said, wiping her mouth of syrupy remnants with her paper napkin. "I thought maybe the museum this morning while we're all together. And then just you and I get to spend some time together this afternoon. Maybe a movie?"

"Where's Lacey going?" the youngster asked, reluctant to give up the camaraderie of this instant family.

"I have to work this afternoon," Lacey said softly.

"Really? Do you ride horses like my mom?"

"No, honey," Rachel intercepted, not sure what the dark woman would say. "Lacey is kind of a business consultant. She handles merchandise purchasing for her boss." She got a raised eyebrow and a barely perceptible nod for her explanation.

"Sounds boring," Molly grumbled as she took her dishes to the sink and ran water over them.

"Oh yeah?" Lacey challenged, following the child. "What do you want to do when you grow up?"

"Well," the little girl began as scrubbed her dish absently. "When I was younger, I wanted to be a cat when I grew up."

Lacey turned around to cast her lover a raised eyebrow and a smirk. Rachel merely shrugged her shoulders.

"But I think maybe I want to be a teacher. Or a doctor. Or a veterinarian."

"Those are good goals, squirt," Lacey said softly, rubbing the child's shoulders with a gentle hand. "You've got a good heart."

She turned her head to the side to grin at the woman and it made Lacey's heart catch in her throat. She truly was beautiful. She was young and innocent, pure. She had her mother's features and ideals and the dark woman found herself, much to her own amazement, loving this little girl. She placed a kiss on the small forehead before moving to the sink and rinsing her own dishes, turning her back on the other occupants.

Rachel noticed the change in her partner's demeanor. "Hey, Molly, baby. Can you go upstairs and pick out some clothes for today? Once we finish cleaning up in here, we'll change and head out. All right?"

"Okay, Mama," the girl agreed readily, giving the dark woman next to her a quick hug before skipping to her mother for a hug as well. Then she spun around and ran out the doorway and into the dining room towards the spiral stairs beyond.

"Hey, love," Rachel whispered as she moved up with the rest of the dishes. "You okay, hon?"

She nodded and turned deep blue eyes to her young friend. She knew they were slightly moist. "I'm okay." She quirked a smile.

"You sure? If this is too much for you, we can go back to my apartment. I know it must be hard with all of us here."

"No." Lacey placed sudsy hands on either side of the young blonde's face. "It's hard in a good way. There's so much ..." she paused, searching for a word, " ... hope in this house now. So much life. It's hard for me to know that I do what I do and look in her face."

Rachel nodded her understanding.

"I love her. Isn't that funny? Two months ago I didn't love anyone. I did my job and that was it. And then you wheedled your way into my heart." The dark woman grinned gently to take away any sting that may have accompanied her words. "And now your little girl. My heart is so full ... I'm afraid it might burst. I'm not used to this feeling."

"I'll hold it together," her lover promised solemnly. "And don't be afraid to tell me you need space, Lace. I know how overbearing I can be. And I just kinda moved in here for the weekend with my dog and my kid."

"I wouldn't have it any other way, love."

"But still. You tell me, okay?"

Lacey nodded her agreement before leaning forward to place a kiss on the slim coral lips in front of her. "You, too."

Rachel grinned. 'Deal. Go on and get ready, I'll finish up here."

The dark woman agreed and turned over the task, wiping her hands quickly on a dishtowel. She stopped in the doorway to turn and watch her young partner's back. She observed her silently for several long moments. "I love you, Rachel."

Rachel glanced over her shoulder, obviously surprised at the dark woman's displayed emotions in both her words and her looks this morning. "I love you, too, Lace. Go on." She tilted her head towards the door. Lacey turned and disappeared.

****

By the middle of the week, an easy arrangement had been made. Rachel and Molly would go to Briargate in the morning where Molly amused herself for an hour or two until Lacey came by. The dark woman would take the little girl for some entertainment and lunch then come back in the middle of the afternoon to watch Rachel ride. Usually, they stayed until Rachel was finished for the day and they'd all go have dinner together.

Lacey and Molly were making their way through the training barn to the track beyond where they knew they'd find the young blonde rider when Molly suddenly grabbed the dark woman's hand. "Oh yeah! Mama told me this morning to tell you something and I forgot."

"What was that, squirt?" Lacey inquired, squeezing the little hand she now held in hers.

"She said something like she saw some guy named Benny ... said he was watching us ... something like that."

The dark woman stopped cold in her tracks. "Are you sure that's what she said? That Benny was watching you two?" She'd considered and dismissed the burly kid as a player but if he was still around, and watching Rachel, maybe he was.

"Yeah. I didn't understand it. I didn't see him." She shrugged her slim shoulders absently and began to swing their grasped hands, tugging the woman forward.

"Did she seem worried or afraid?"

The small blonde head cocked slightly, so much like her mother. "Maybe a little. But not a lot. Kinda surprised when she saw him. Told me not to go near him. She said he's not a very nice man."

"No, he's not, Molly. Stay away from him."

"Gosh." She rolled pale eyes. "I will. Having two

mothers is a lot of work."

Lacey grinned slightly at her murmured words, even though her insides were in turmoil.

When they approached the track railing, the dark woman took more care to look around at everyone. She didn't see the stumpy Benny anywhere.

Rachel was on a grey filly, milling around with a group of riders, when she saw her partner and daughter. She excused herself and trotted over.

"You saw him, Raich?" were the first words out of the tall woman's mouth.

"Yeah. Hey, Molly. How was your day?" the blonde said, trying to keep the mood light.

"Good, Mama. We went to the mall and walked around for awhile."

"Lacey? At a mall?" Rachel teased, meeting her partner's worried blue gaze. "Woulda liked to have seen that!"

"What's he doing watching you?"

"Lace, I don't know. As far as I know, he still works here. He just gave me the creeps, that's all. Can we talk about this later?" Rachel pointedly glanced at her daughter.

"We need to find out what he's up to," the dark woman responded immediately. She couldn't believe she'd left Rachel alone all day when there was potential danger.

"I know, love. We will." She glanced over her shoulder. "I gotta get back. See you two in a bit."

A few minutes later the barn trainer walked up to them, nodding to the dark woman who was becoming familiar and grinning to Molly. "Spectators!" he said cheerfully.

"Hi, Ray." Molly's response was equally cheerful.

"You wanna come in here and watch? We can walk over to the infield, the view's better," he offered, extending his hand to the young girl.

She glanced to the woman at her side first, then accepted the hand when the dark head nodded approval. They walked in front of the small starting gate while the horses were still dancing behind it and loading into stalls and ducked under the white pipe rail on the far side.

"Your mom's gonna come out of gate three. See her there now, that little grey filly?"

"Yeah." The child nodded eagerly. "Is that Smoke?"

"Good eye," he said approvingly. "Yes it is."

The little blonde beamed with pride and Lacey cast her a fond smirk.

"She's gonna bring her on the rail. Smoke's a front runner but shies from the rail. So the other horses are gonna push her that direction while your mom holds her at their pace. Teach her to run straight between a horse and the rail. She likes to bump the horse on her side."

Molly sucked up the information, nodding.

With a loud clang the horses surged from the gate not twenty feet in front of the small group watching. Lacey saw her partner gently guide her filly from the outside to the rail and then steady her surging with expert hands. Another horse slid next to her and they rode side by side. As they pulled away and the spectators leaned over the rail for a better view, Lacey saw what Ray had meant. The filly pulled to the right, bumping her running partner on nearly every stride.

"She's a stubborn little filly," the trainer muttered, realizing he'd have to use more drastic measures if she wasn't going to respond to a firm hand. "She'll get disqualified before the first turn in any race."

They were still watching the horses as they came around the bend and were completely unprepared for the mishap. Something popped, a loud cap gun sound, and white billows blew up right at the turn. Smoke freaked out, her partial blinders not protecting her from the commotion, and slammed hard into the horse at her side. He broke stride, got angry, and half-kicked the young filly.

Smoke turned sharply in response, finding herself right in front of the rail she so hated and in poor position for evasion. Too close to jump but not able to turn, she raised herself up on two legs, hitting her lower chest into the pipe and having enough forward motion to flip herself over the rail, throwing Rachel hard to the ground. Then the filly was on the ground, too, rolling to gain her feet, squealing in fear and dismay. Amazingly, Smoke was able to avoid her rider in her struggles and was back on her feet galloping across the turf.

The whole mess had taken less than three seconds.

"Mama!"

Lacey heard the blood-curdling scream at her side even as she was stretching long legs and running to her partner. She slowed down long enough to scoop up the girl and hold her. As she was situating the child so her blue eyes peered over the dark woman's shoulder, away from her prone mother, Lacey caught motion out of the corner of her eye.

It was Benny, his lumbering form running towards the barn. She was torn for only a second before she resumed her path to the fallen rider.

Rachel wasn't moving when they got there. One of the other riders had already run to call an ambulance and Ray knelt over the prone woman's body.

"Rachel?" he said loudly. "Rachel? Wake up!" He glanced worried caramel eyes to the tall woman at his side.

"Here," she said abruptly, handing him the screaming child in her arms. He took her willingly and pressed her head against his shoulder, whispering into her ear. The freedom enabled Lacey to kneel down beside her lover.

Rachel looked like she was just sleeping peacefully. Her arms and legs were arranged neatly at her side, indicating that she hadn't broken or twisted a limb. But when Lacey put a hand on the blonde woman's chest, she wasn't breathing.

"Oh, God," she murmured. "Raich, honey?"

Green eyes blinked open suddenly and Lacey saw in them panic and fear. The blonde started gasping for air.

"Easy, easy," the dark woman soothed. "Wind knocked outta you, baby."

Finally, she took a deep painful breath, then coughed it back out before breathing shallowly. Groaning, she tried to move.

"Don't move, Raich," Lacey whispered as she began to

run warm hands up and down the blonde woman's extremities. "Does anything hurt?" She unclasped the riding helmet and tugged it gently away, tossing it aside.

"Chest," she muttered.

"Anything else? Back, neck?"

"No ... don't think so. Head ... yeah, head." She began testing movements slowly, pleased to find that nothing appeared broken. "Just sore. Holy shit," she groaned. "D'ya get the license plate? Jesus Christ."

"Mama?"

It wasn't until that moment that both women realized they'd been hearing quiet crying and sniffling all along. Lacey looked up and nodded to Ray who let the girl go. She ran over to them but the dark woman grabbed her before she was able to throw herself on her mother.

"Easy, Molly," Lacey soothed, sitting down and pulling the girl into her lap.

"Give me a minute, baby," the blonde woman whispered, still coughing. "I'll be okay."

"Smoke tried to jump ... thought she landed on you ... oh, Mama," the girl whimpered incoherently.

"S'okay, squirt," Lacey murmured, holding the small girl tightly and rocking her back and forth. "Your mama's gonna be okay. We just need to let the doctors look at her."

Rachel glanced to her partner, ready to argue that she really just needed a minute to catch her breath, when she noticed the steely gaze. Maybe a doctor wasn't such a bad idea. "What happened? I didn't see."

Lacey glanced down the rail to where several riders were milling about an awkward contraption. "Don't touch it!" she warned. "I want to look at that." They all backed away. "Something on the rail spooked her," the dark woman said when she turned back to her partner.

"You know what?" Emerald eyes met her blue one questioningly.

The dark-haired woman nodded, but her expression begged her companion to drop the subject. She agreed easily enough, since she was pretty miserable and wasn't sure she wanted a lengthy conversation anyway.

When the girl had been reasonably calmed, Lacey was able to scoot closer and smooth her lover's bangs back. Molly held her mother's hand. Before too long, they heard the wail of a siren and then watched the van's progress through the large gates at the end of the track and across the well-turned dirt.

The paramedics hopped out and ducked under the rail, elbowing away the dark woman and her cargo. Soon they had the blonde rider loaded up on a stretcher and were moving her towards the van. "Lacey?" she called weakly.

Lacey moved to her side, glaring at the paramedic who tried to discourage her. "I'll bring Molly," Lacey said, wanting to get a look at the contraption on the rail and also thinking the ambulance ride may be too much for the young girl. "I'll call Bernie and George and have them go to the hospital. All right?"

Rachel nodded mutely.

"What hospital?" The dark woman directed her question to the nearest orange-suited person.

"Memorial."

"Okay." She looked back to Rachel. "It's okay. We'll be right there." She kissed her gently on the forehead. Molly did the same. "I love you."

"You too," she whispered. "Stay with Lacey, baby." She focused on the young girl who nodded meekly.

Then she was loaded up and rolling away.

It seemed as if the little girl's legs couldn't hold her as she stumbled behind the tall woman. Lacey noticed and picked her up, feeling scrawny legs wrap around her midsection and arms tighten about her neck.

With her awkward bundle, she examined the odd contraption attached to the rail. It wasn't any bigger than a soda can and looked like a modified firecracker with wiring for remote detonation. She tilted her head in silent scrutiny, before juggling the child in her arms and withdrawing the cell phone from her pocket.

"Bernie," she said without introduction. "Get to Memorial. An ambulance just took Rachel there. I need you and George to keep an eye on her. And send Rico out to Briargate with someone on the tech side ... Tony maybe. Get him here fast so I can go see Rachel."

"Sure thing, Boss." He hung up without saying goodbye.

"Now we wait a little bit, squirt," Lacey murmured as she sat in the grass near the incendiary, not wanting to give Benny a chance to come back and clean up his mess.

Chapter 12

The hospital corridors were starkly white and silent as the woman and child made their way through them hand in hand. They'd apparently entered from the wrong door and had been forced through a maze of hallways before reaching the Emergency Room and the receptionist there.

"Rachel Wilson was brought in by ambulance probably an hour or so ago?" Her words were casual enough but her look was intense. The receptionist's hazel eyes studied the dark-haired woman for just a moment before looking to her records.

"Are you family?"

"This is her daughter," Lacey responded, indicating the child next to her.

"And you're her—" Molly looked up quizzically when Lacey squeezed her shoulder and interrupted her.

"Friend. We'd like to see her."

"She's been checked in for observation on the third floor. Just go down that hall there and take the elevators up."

"Thank you." Lacey gave the effort of a smile before

taking Molly's hand and steering her away.

"Why didn't you tell her what you really are?" Molly asked softly. "Mama told me to be honest."

Lacey took a deep breath, curious as to how much water her explanation would really hold. "Sometimes people aren't very understanding of people like your mother and me. Women who love each other like we do. And sometimes it's easier to just ... kinda gloss over our relationship rather than get in an awkward situation or deal with people's criticism."

She wrinkled her small brow. "But Mama and Aunt Helen said it was okay to love someone ... anyone. That it's your heart that decides. Not other people."

The dark woman grinned, ushering the small girl in as the elevator doors slid open and emptied its cargo. "Well, your mom's pretty smart. It is okay. It's just a lot of people are ignorant or prejudiced. Do you know how sometimes people don't like other people whose skin is a different color?"

She nodded, her finger hovering over the three, pushing it when Lacey nodded.

"Well, it's kinda like that. Some people don't look beyond the color of someone's skin to see the human inside. And some people won't look past how your mother and I love each other to see the people we are." She silently cursed the slow-moving elevator. She'd never explained her sexuality to anyone, especially not a child.

"But people can't hide the color of their skin. They have to live with it and how people look at them. You and Mama shouldn't hide how you really feel."

"You, squirt, are too smart for your own good," Lacey teased gently.

The child grinned, but then turned thoughtful. "Does it bother you that people know you love my mama?"

"No, baby," Lacey said solemnly, kneeling in front of the girl even as the doors slid open. "Your mama is the best thing that's ever happened to me. I love her with all of my heart. I'll work harder at making sure people know that, okay?"

The small girl nodded and threw her arms around Lacey's neck. So the dark woman stood, holding her in a tight embrace and carrying her out of the elevator.

A huge bulky form was beside her in seconds. "Lace!"

"Hey, Bernard. George." She nodded to the tall black man who moved up as well. They'd apparently been in a nearby waiting area. "Molly, honey, I want you to meet some other guys Rico and I work with. This is Bernard and George. Guys, this is Molly. She's Rachel's daughter."

They hid their surprise well as Lacey shifted the girl so she could see the two men. The young child extended a tentative hand, which each man shook readily.

"Molly, why don't you come with me and help me pick out a candy bar? I just can't decide," George said gently, wanting to give his boss and Bernard some privacy.

"Can I?" She turned questioning blue eyes to the dark woman.

"Sure, squirt." Lacey set the girl on her feet and then fished in her pocket until she presented a dollar bill to the child. "Go ahead. I'll be right here."

Then, when man and child ambled away, the dark woman turned her attention to her companion. "Spill it."

Bernard could read the worry in his boss's eyes. "S'okay, Lace. She's okay. She has a concussion and will probably be really sore and stiff. They just wanted to keep her overnight to watch her head injury. No broken bones, nothing permanent."

The dark woman's sigh of relief was audible. "Can we see her? Are they allowing visitors?"

"I think we need to talk to the head nurse about the tike. I didn't know or I woulda buttered her up."

"You can't butter toast, Bernie," the tall woman scoffed. "But thanks for the offer."

"Yeah, like you're Miss Land O Lakes yourself, Boss." But he grinned at the return of her gentle banter. "So what happened, Lace?"

"That little shit Oz had a partner after all, I guess. Kid named Benny tried to take her out. I thought it was over.

Stupid."

"Oz? That guy we killed? He wasn't working alone?"

"Evidently not," she growled softly. "I shoulda been paying more attention."

"We'll find him, Lace."

She nodded her dark head, brushing black tendrils back with long fingers. "You bet your ass we will, Bernard. No one touches Rachel or the girl. Got me?"

"My life, Lace," the bulky man swore and Lacey met his dark eyes briefly. She wondered how such a cold-hearted bitch had inspired this kind of loyalty. "Go see her. George and I will work the nurse."

She pushed the door open slowly, trying to make no sound but not succeeding as the door hinges were apparently older than Hippocrates himself and squealed in protest. The blonde in the bed tilted her head slowly in the direction of the noise. A full-fledged grin lit up her weary features.

"Hey, you." Her voice was slightly hoarse from lack of use.

"Hey yourself, gorgeous," Lacey whispered, her own words thick with emotion. "Ya scared me out there."

"M'sorry."

"Nah." She pulled up a chair, the metal legs grating along linoleum. "Don't apologize. Just get better." But she grinned with the gentle order. "How do you feel?"

"I really am okay. I think I could use a good massage come tomorrow, though."

"I think I can manage that." The dark woman raised her eyebrows suggestively, but her blue eyes shined with only concern and love. "They took out your stitches," she observed after a quiet moment.

"Yeah." The blonde grinned gently. "Said it was the best job they'd seen."

"You lie," Lacey growled playfully. "Looks okay, though. Shouldn't scar."

"That's what the doc said, too," her young companion agreed. "I told them I walked into a stall door at the barn."

The dark woman shrugged her shoulders and nodded. It

was as good an explanation as any. Plus, it was much better than the truth.

"How's Molly?" Rachel yawned then reached out a hand towards her companion who took it readily and scooted closer.

"She's okay. A bit spooked. Wasn't a pretty sight, love," Lacey whispered gently, smoothing fine blonde hair with her free hand. "She did find time in her busy schedule to lecture me, though."

"Hmm? About what?"

The dark woman grinned and told her about the receptionist downstairs and the ensuing elevator conversation.

"I tried to hammer tolerance into her. Helen helped," the blonde explained, smiling.

"Yeah, I guess so. I just ... do you understand?" the tall woman faltered, surprising her partner.

"I do, Lace. I really do. There's a time and place for every battle. I'll work on Molly's subtlety." She grinned tenderly.

"I meant what I told her, Raich. I love you with all my heart. You're the best thing that's ever happened to me." Lacey's ice blue eyes had deepened in color with her gravity.

"I feel the same, Lacey. I knew how you felt that night in your house when you introduced me to the guys as your lover. I've never felt so honored before. I've done some pretty dumb things and made some pretty big mistakes ... but somewhere down the line the fates must have smiled at me because they led you to the track that morning."

"That was Vinnie. A little known Fate." The dark woman grinned impishly, the feelings overwhelming her. "I'll be sure to thank him."

There was a quiet knock on the door before it squeaked open. Rachel groaned in protest at the offending sound.

"Don't they have any WD40 around here?" she muttered.

Bernard poked his head in. "You up for another guest, Rachel honey?"

Lacey raised her eyebrows to the young blonde at the gentle term of endearment, but she simply shrugged. "I've charmed them."

Dark eyebrows quirked even higher as the tall woman smirked.

"Send 'em in, Bernie," Rachel requested, ignoring her partner's teasing look.

Molly tiptoed in slowly, her movements hindered by nerves. Lacey pulled the youngster into her lap. "Hey, squirt. C'mere. See, Mom's okay."

"Oh, Mama." The little girl's words were watery.

"Shh, baby," Rachel whispered, reaching a hand out to smooth her daughter's fears by tenderly stroking her hair and face. "Everything's okay."

The girl held her arms out towards her mother, needing so badly to be comforted. Lacey glanced to her partner who nodded.

"Okay, here we go." The dark woman lifted the child up and settled her on the hospital bed at Rachel's side. Then the little girl wrapped her arms around her mother and snuggled into her neck, crying large messy tears.

Rachel let her cry, murmuring words of love and stroking her back with strong fingers. There was a lot of healing in tears and the blonde woman knew her daughter needed this. It took several minutes before the sobs quieted into gentle hiccups.

"Let me see your face, sweetie," Rachel crooned softly, placing hands on the girl's cheeks. Immediately she found tissues held in her direction and she took them gratefully, cleaning up her daughter's face. "Feel better?"

The girl nodded mutely.

"It was pretty scary, I know, baby. But Smoke didn't land on me at all. I just fell off of her and knocked the wind out of me. And I kinda hurt my head so they want me to stay here tonight. Everything's okay."

"Where will I stay?" she questioned plaintively.

"With me, silly," Lacey interrupted, running a strong hand up and down the little girl's back. "You know that. We can keep each other company."

"Can I sleep with you?" The little girl turned waterlogged blue eyes to this mafia big wig and left her weak in the knees.

"Yeah," Lacey agreed easily. "I think that would be good."

"So it's settled then," Rachel whispered, placing a kiss on the girl's forehead. "You go on with Lacey, now, baby. I think they're about ready to kick the two of you out."

Molly leaned forward to hug her mother fiercely once more before she allowed herself to be lifted down. Lacey showed her to the door and opened it, pointing down the hall. "Go sit with Bernie just a minute, okay? I need to tell your mom one more thing." The child left willingly enough with one last glance at her mother.

"What's up?" Rachel asked when the door was closed.

Lacey resumed her seat. "It wasn't an accident," she said bluntly. "It was Benny, you were right. I saw him running from the track. He knew Smoke was shy on the rail so he set up something to spook her. I think he was hoping for more than a concussion."

"Why?" Rachel had trouble believing she'd be significant enough to him for this kind of action.

"I don't know. Maybe cuz he lost money from Wheatridge? Or maybe to get back at me for Oz. We'll find out, but Bernard and George are staying here tonight to watch you. Rico's going to come back to the house and be with Molly and me. I just want you to know what's going on."

The blonde head nodded solemnly.

"You look sleepy, love. I'm going to go." She leaned forward for a lingering kiss on responsive lips. "I promise you Molly will be fine."

"I know," her lover assured her. "Sleep well."

"You too, Raich." With a few lingering touches and words, the dark woman was on her way.

****

"My mama was in jail for awhile." The child's soft voice, though it was quiet and plaintive, pierced the room's darkness. Her little blonde head was snuggled up against Lacey's shoulder in much the same way her mother slept.

"I know," she told the little girl, glancing first to the bedside clock, which showed a ridiculous hour, and then to the moonlit window. Karma shifted in her position at the end of the bed, stretching against Lacey's long legs.

"She's not a bad person, though. Aunt Helen said she helped the police and saved some people's lives."

"That's true," the dark woman agreed, realizing the cathartic nature of this discussion for the little girl. "She made some mistakes, some bad decisions. But in the end, she did what was right."

"She got shot in the belly. She can't have any more babies."

That was something Lacey hadn't known. It somewhat explained her closeness to Molly and her aching desire to take her child back and live as mother and daughter. After all, she had been in prison nearly four years, separated from her daughter another two years in addition to that. She hadn't been a hands-on mother to Molly for more than half of the young girl's life. "Your mama loves you very much," Lacey whispered softly.

The girl nodded, shifted her weight slightly. "I want to come stay with her for good. Would that be fun? Would you visit us?"

"All the time, squirt," the dark-haired woman promised softly. "What about Aunt Helen?"

"I love her, but she's not my mom, you know? I want my for-real-mom who helps me with homework and talks to me about school."

"Have you told your mom what you want?" Lacey asked, wondering if Rachel knew they all yearned for the same thing.

"Yeah and Aunt Helen. Mama said that they still need to work out some issues with her history. Said she'd made a promise to Aunt Helen and she had to keep it first, then we would be together."

The dark woman would have to remember to ask Rachel

about this later. "That'll be a good day."

"Yeah," the child agreed wistfully, finally seeming to be relaxed enough for sleep. Moments later her breathing evened in slumber.

Lacey watched the moonlight through the window and thought of Rico who was sleeping downstairs on the sofa. He'd been parked outside when they got home. He'd had the foresight to stop at Rachel's apartment to get items for Molly, as well as retrieving Karma and bringing her to the house. Lacey was quietly impressed with how quickly the gawky kid was catching on to things even as she cursed herself for turning him into a criminal.

The prints on the incendiary had matched Benny's, but that wasn't much help unless they chose to pursue this legally, which wasn't an option at this point. Lacey and Rico had easily convinced the barn manager to not take this to the police by reminding him who owned the barn. There were too many more difficult questions to answer about poisoned horses and beaten-out confessions.

The smoking contraption itself was a clever little device that was apparently homemade. This worried the dark woman to no end because while she hadn't been worried about Oz, who beat just a hair above stupid, Benny may prove to be more clever. She didn't like having to deal with the unknown.

It was barely an hour before dawn when ice blue eyes finally fluttered closed and fell into sleep.

Chapter 13

Lacey had been up long enough to have a cup of coffee and shove Molly towards the shower when the phone rang. The caller ID showed it to be Briargate. She answered the phone and the barn manager announced himself.

"What is it?"

"Something happened last night. Coupla horses were killed."

"What?!" the dark woman shouted. Rico was next to her in seconds, but she shook her head and pushed him away gently.

"Shot. Night watch didn't hear anything, but I guess they could have used silencers."

"Yeah," Lacey agreed. "Which horses?" She already knew the answer.

"The poisoned ones. All of 'em."

"Sunny?"

"Yeah."

Lacey groaned. This would be hard on Rachel. "Are they still there?"

"Yeah. Just found 'em about an hour ago. There's a

bunch of stuff we have to do about the vet and insurance paperwork before the bodies can be removed."

"Thanks for telling me. Keep in touch about the vet."

"Will do. And Benny's gone."

"No shock there," Lacey muttered, disappointing the other man by her lack of surprise. "He was the one who set up the little device, I'm pretty sure. Keep an eye out for him."

"Yeah," he agreed.

She sighed in thought. "Okay. Let me know about the horses and Benny. We'll come by later today."

Lacey hung up without saying goodbye, concentrating for several long moments before feeling Rico's inquisitive stare. "Horses at Briargate were killed last night."

"Should we send someone out there?"

"Yeah. Do that, Rico. And we have a wild card. Benny Brown. Check out his personnel records in my office. We need to find him. I'm gonna go get ready and then we'll head for the hospital."

****

Rachel was awake and arguing to be released by the time the trio got off the elevator and walked down the hall. They could hear her soft convincing voice easily. Bernard and George hovered outside the open door, looking as tired as she felt.

"Trying your charm again?" Lacey announced her entrance into the room with a gentle tease. Molly bounced in and up onto the hospital bed.

"Hush, crony, you're not helping," the bed ridden woman teased back. "Hi, sweetie." She hugged and kissed Molly.

"As soon as Dr. Evans can come up and check on you, we'll be ready to sign release papers. Nothing overnight suggested we need to keep you longer," the nurse promised. "I'll let you visit and I'll bring the doctor in as soon as he's here."

"Thank you." Rachel smiled sweetly and the nurse retreated from the room as Bernard and George came in. Rachel turned to Lacey, held out a hand. "C'mere tall, dark, and trouble."

The dark woman grinned and took the offered hand, then leaned over and kissed her soundly. They both ignored the "yuck" coming from the foot of the bed.

"You look good," Lacey said softly, smoothing back blonde hair.

"Feel better. Let's get out of here."

"We will." She pulled the chair up and took a seat. "Molly, can you go outside with the guys for a little bit?"

She hopped down from the bed willingly and took the hand Bernard held out to her. "Are you gonna smooch some more?"

"Maybe." Rachel grinned. "Skedaddle, kiddo."

Lacey met her partner's moss green eyes with her own blue ones for several long seconds, formulating the words in her mind.

"Bad news," Rachel guessed easily.

"The horses that were poisoned ... were killed last night." Subtlety had never been the dark woman's strong suit.

The young blonde's eyes grew wide. "All of them?" she whispered.

"Yeah. Sunny, too," Lacey said gently, trying to soften the blow with eyes and voice.

"How?" she choked, tears in her eyes.

"Gunshot. I want the guys to take Molly home and you and I go to the barn. Can you handle that?"

"Are the bodies still there?"

"Yeah."

Rachel considered for only a moment before she nodded. "I can do it. I want to see him."

"I thought you might. As soon as we spring you, we'll go."

****

To say Rachel was a little stiff would have been the understatement of the century. She moved very slowly at Lacey's side once the taller woman had helped her down from the Grand Cherokee.

"Didja take that muscle relaxer?" the dark-haired woman questioned as they made their way tediously from the parking area towards the main training barn.

"Not yet," the young rider muttered, ready for her partner's quick response.

"What? Why not? You can barely move!"

"It'll make me sleepy. I want to be a little closer to a bed first," Rachel replied, reaching a hand out to catch Lacey's and twine their fingers together.

Lacey nodded, squeezing the fingers wrapped in her own. She knew that Rachel was really struggling to stay calm between what happened yesterday and the overnight deaths. "All right, you win."

"And where's my damn tape recorder when I need it?" the younger woman joked gently. They stood now at the entrance to the large barn. Looking down the cement aisle they could see many people milling around towards the middle of the structure.

"Ready?" Lacey's husky voice whispered.

"I guess," she murmured.

"Rachel!" A stocky man in his mid fifties turned and started jogging towards the two women.

"Hey, Frank," she greeted the barn manager with a stiff smile and an extended hand, releasing Lacey's fingers.

"Didn't expect to see you today. How do you feel?" He fell into step beside them, slowing his gait to match the young rider's. He'd known that Lacey would come in, but hadn't counted on his young employee.

"Sore. But okay. I wanted to see the horses. They still here?"

"Yeah, we're finishing up with the vet. They all need to be autopsied for insurance claims. They're sending some trucks to take them to the lab."

"What lab?" Lacey spoke up and Frank flinched at the

dark woman's voice. He'd spent many years fearing this woman's wrath.

"Whichever lab the vet uses. I don't know the name."

"Which vet?" This question was asked with the young blonde's soft voice.

"New barn vet, Rachel. Michaels," the manager answered impatiently.

Rachel glanced quickly to her dark companion and shrugged her shoulders.

"Frank, those horses aren't going anywhere yet. I'm gonna make some phone calls and we'll send the bodies to a different lab." She wasn't taking any chances this time. Let the new vet prove himself on something a little less important.

"But, Lacey," the short man started to complain but stopped mid-sentence. "Sounds good. I'll go call 'em off." He trotted away, leaving Lacey and Rachel by themselves as they neared Sunny's stall.

The entire front panel had been removed to allow access to the stiff body when it was time. The surrounding stalls had been emptied of their occupants.

Rachel stepped forward slowly, kneeling in the thick bedding of wood shavings. Taking a deep breath, she pulled the blanket away and looked at the large still form beneath. She watched him quietly for several long moments with watery eyes before suddenly tilting her head. Then she started moving frantically, pushing the rest of the blanket off and crawling around the huge form.

"What is it, Raich?" Lacey asked softly, kneeling down as well.

"Not him," she murmured, moving stiffly to the horse's withers and running her index finger up under the mane resting there. "It isn't him." Mist green eyes looked up quickly to meet ice blue.

"You're sure?"

"Yeah. Sunny has a scar here, at the top of his withers. When he was a yearling he tried to run under the top half of a stall door. He was following me out."

"How could that be? Otherwise does it look like him?"

She nodded quickly. "But it would be easy to duplicate him. He's got no real distinguishing white marks. Solid bay, tall for his age, but not outrageously so. The teeth would check with a horse the right age."

"Tattoo?" Lacey asked.

Rachel moved over next to her partner to peel back cold stiff lips. "It's right. But so what? That wouldn't be hard either."

"But why?" the dark-haired woman murmured, rocking back on her heels.

"They stole him. Wheatridge?"

"Maybe. Let's go check out the others." Lacey got to her feet and helped her partner up, steadying her on painful muscles.

"I don't know the others as well."

"Well then, let's find someone who does," the taller woman insisted as Rachel pulled the blanket back over the unfortunate beast's body.

It was several hours later before the other six horses had been checked out with the help of a couple other barn hands and groomers. Lacey had also called around until she found an appropriate vet and lab to take over the autopsies and the two women waited silently in the main office with the rest of the barn staff until the trucks arrived and the bodies were removed.

By the time Lacey loaded her young lover back into the Grand Cherokee, the blonde could barely move and the pain was evident in her eyes and face.

"Take that pill now, love," Lacey whispered as she started up the vehicle. "We'll be home soon."

"We need to go to Wheatridge," Rachel protested.

"Honey, there's no way we're going there now. You can barely move. First thing in the morning, okay?"

The blonde shook her head slowly. "If he's there, we don't have much time."

"That's not true," Lacey argued. "They took him for a reason. We didn't tell anyone that wasn't Sunny, so there's no way that information could leak back to Wheatridge. Whatever their original plan was, they're still following it."

"I hate logic," her blonde companion muttered, opening the glove compartment to extract the prescription bottle she'd shoved there earlier.

****

Lacey had to gently wake the young woman and help her walk into the house. Rico and George sat at the kitchen table and watched the two women as they entered.

"Hey," Rachel muttered and half-waved.

"Hey, darlin'," George said softly. "Ya look like hell."

"So do you, George, only you don't have an excuse," the young blonde responded sleepily.

Rico laughed.

"How's Molly?" Lacey asked quietly.

George turned his attention to the tall, dark woman. "Fine. Bernard's upstairs with her. They're watching a movie."

"In my room?"

"Yeah."

"Thanks. C'mon, love." She tugged the young blonde's hand gently.

Bernard stood up from the large bed when he saw the two women entering the room. He helped Molly pull the covers back and watched as his boss settled her lover's light frame into the sheets. Rachel grinned and waved her thanks at Bernie who nodded his head and backed out of the room.

The young blonde was asleep before Bernard was even out of the room. Molly stayed and sat cross-legged on the bed while Lacey gently undressed the small woman and put a T-shirt and loose flannel pants on her.

"She okay?" Molly raised questioning blue eyes to her mother's caretaker.

"Yeah. Just tired. The doctors gave her some medicine to take to help her not be so sore and it makes her sleepy. That's all."

"I can hear her belly rumble," the small girl mused and Lacey stopped her ministrations to tilt her head and listen. Sure enough, she could hear the gentle rolling sounds.

"Should we wake her up and feed her?" the dark woman asked Molly.

The young girl nodded.

"Well, go have the guys make some soup and maybe a grilled cheese sandwich? Sound good?"

Molly nodded again and hopped off the bed to run downstairs and deliver the order.

Lacey settled next to her young lover and pulled the woman comfortably against her. She tugged up the covers and tucked them in gently. She glanced up and saw what the two previous residents had been watching: George of the Jungle ... again. She groaned.

George was just making himself unwanted at a large dinner party when Molly came back upstairs with Rico in tow. Rico held a lap tray with a mug of soup, a sandwich, and a glass of milk.

"Hey, love," Lacey whispered softly, jostling the young woman resting against her.

"No," Rachel moaned softly.

"C'mon. Wake up, sleepy. Let's put something in that pit you call a belly."

Weary green eyes blinked open and the young woman righted herself, leaning back against the headboard. She drank her soup wordlessly and ate about half the sandwich before pushing it away. Lacey finished it while the blonde drank her milk.

"Done?" Lacey asked around a mouthful of crust and was answered by a mute nod. "My thanks to the chefs." Lacey grinned at Molly and Rico as she settled Rachel back into the bed. Then she turned her attention to Molly. "Honey, can you turn off the TV? I'm gonna lay with your mom for a bit."

The little girl did as requested and watched the two women silently for a moment, wanting to crawl into bed with them as well. Rico realized his boss needed some private time and reached out for the child's hand. "Why don't you show me how to play that card game, Molly? The one we picked up at the apartment?"

"Uno," Molly supplied easily, waving slightly to Lacey as she turned and followed Rico out.

When the door had closed and left the two women alone, Lacey let out a huge sigh of relief. Then she wrapped her long body around her partner's smaller one and held her fiercely. "I've wanted to do this since I saw you hit the ground yesterday," she whispered. "You scared the shit out of me. I won't lose you now that I've just found you."

"Love you, Lace," the sleepy woman murmured, snuggling into the warm embrace.

"You, too," Lacey responded and just absorbed her companion's presence while looking out the window into the late afternoon sunshine.

****

Lacey sat at her dining room table and observed the occupants with quiet interest. They'd been forced to abandon the smaller kitchen table, as they needed six place settings.

George and Bernard shoveled the omelets into their mouths without a word or glance to anyone else. Rico spoke gently to young Molly, teasing her and poking at her as an older doting brother would. She giggled in response, her fair hair pulled back into a ponytail and her blue eyes dancing with amusement. She showed no after effects from the last two days of adventure.

The sixth place setting was empty, waiting for Rachel to come downstairs. She had been awake and in the shower when Lacey had last visited the bedroom.

"Lacey?" Molly's soft voice brought the dark woman out of her thoughts.

"Hmm, baby?"

"Are we gonna go see the baby horses today?"

The dark-haired woman cast her eyes slowly to the men,

realizing no one had told the small girl of the deaths at the farm the previous day. She wasn't sure there was much of a point in sharing that news now. "I don't think so," she said instead. "I think maybe we just need to take it easy today. What do you think we should do?"

"We could go to Central Park and feed the ducks," Rico piped up.

"In March? Are there ducks?" George asked skeptically.

"They stay year round cuz people feed them," the blond man responded easily. "I go there all the time."

Bernard was busy choking on his omelet and the dark woman could tell that he was itching to come back with a biting retort. She pointed at the heavy-set man. "You, hush." Then she turned to Rico. "You are so not cut out for this business."

He grinned sheepishly, shrugged his shoulders, and was thankfully saved from any further ribbing by a gentle voice calling from upstairs.

"Lace?"

The dark-haired woman pushed back her chair and stood, still shaking her head and grinning as she bounded up the spiral staircase and down the hall into her bedroom.

Rachel stood there, still mostly wet, wrapped in a towel.

"What can I do for you, gorgeous?" Lacey smiled, embracing the other woman warmly.

"I need a little help," she said quietly. The young blonde motioned to her hair. She'd been trying to dry it but was too sore and weary to hold her arms up and complete the task.

"C'mere." Lacey led the other woman to the bed and pushed her down gently before returning to the bathroom to retrieve a dry towel. She rubbed the towel over blonde tresses for several minutes before satisfied that they were about as dry as she could get them without a hair dryer. Then she ran a comb through the tangles and plaited the resulting smooth hair into a braid.

"Better?" she asked softly, observing her handiwork.

"Yes, thank you." The blonde smiled.

"Good. Now let's get you dressed."

When the two women walked down the stairs, the group at the table was discussing the conspiracy on the X Files. It was evident that Molly was the driving force behind the conversation.

"You guys don't have anything better to talk about?" Lacey jibed as she pulled out a chair for the blonde woman.

"This is important," Molly argued before continuing the discussion. The precocious little girl sure didn't sound eight years old when she talked about aliens and FBI cover-ups.

After listening for a moment, Rachel jumped in. Lacey rolled her eyes but was smiling gently. She never thought, as Crony Number Two, she'd be sharing breakfast with friends and family and listening to debates about a television show. It was so ... domestic.

The dark woman went into the kitchen to retrieve Rachel's omelet from the warm oven, switching it off and grabbing a glass before making her way back.

"Here ya go, love." She set down the plate in front of the young woman. "Orange juice or apple juice?"

"Apple, please." The blonde grinned her thanks at her companion before turning back to her conversation about the cigarette smoking man.

"You all are hopeless," the dark woman muttered as she regained her seat. She caught George's eyes when he looked over to her and knew he saw through her posturing. He saw the peace in her.

He smiled, the expression meeting and encompassing his caramel eyes. And he winked at her.

She shook her head and went back to finishing breakfast. So much for her reputation, she mused.

In the end, George and Bernard went to see if they could track down Benny while Rico, the women, and Molly stayed at the house. They'd decided that Rachel wasn't quite up to going to Wheatridge and that they may have a better chance of finding the colt, anyway, if they let yesterday's tragedy blow over. The young blonde rider had eventually conceded to this argument.

Now, Lacey and Rachel sat quietly in the winterized screened-in porch, watching the little girl and the teenage boy romp around the backyard in the early afternoon chill. The dog ran with them and between the noise all three were making, it was a wonder they weren't waking the dead.

"Can I ask you some questions?" Lacey ventured after they watched the action outside for the better part of an hour. She sounded hesitant.

Rachel turned her eyes from the children at play to her lover. Lacey leaned back in her chair, the front two feet off the ground the back two teetering as she balanced with her fingertip on the glass patio table. She was dressed in faded blue jeans and a thick forest green sweater. Her hair was loose around her shoulders and her light blue eyes were nervously darting around.

"Of course," the blonde woman said softly, reaching a hand out to brush against dark locks. "What's bothering you?"

"Did you know that Molly wants to stay with you for good?"

She was a little surprised by the question, thinking the inquiries would have to do with the farm or the horses. "She tell you that?" she asked carefully.

"Yeah. When you were in the hospital. She was pretty worked up. She talked my ear off all night long." The dark woman chuckled softly at the memory.

"What else did she say?"

Lacey took a breath, released it. "Rachel, I'd assumed that Molly was with Helen on court order. That you'd lost custody. But that's not the case, is it?"

"No," the blonde sighed. "I granted guardianship while I was in prison. We were worried that if I left the decision up to social services, my aunt and uncle would step in and she'd have to go to them. We couldn't let that happen. Helen understood so once I gave up parental rights, Helen proved that Molly had a stable environment. The ... arrangements were made by us at that point. Helen would keep Molly while I got on my feet and I could visit her whenever I wanted to."

"Molly said that you made a promise to Helen that you have to keep before Molly can come back to you," the dark-haired woman continued the prompting.

Rachel laughed softly. "Well, it's not quite that simple. There's a lot involved. I have to be able to support myself and a child. Right now I'm not really there and as long as I stay at Briargate, I won't be. The criminal record isn't helping me out much, unfortunately. I have to get my GED." She turned gentle green eyes to her partner, gratitude showing in them. "Which you're helping me with. And Helen wants me to resolve the issues with my aunt and uncle. She's worried that if I take Molly in, they'll petition for custody and try to prove they have a more stable environment."

"You think they will?"

The blonde shrugged, turning weary eyes back to the games outside. Rico was spinning Molly in the air by an arm and a leg. "They might. I haven't spoken to them since I got out of prison. I think that's the real barrier. If I went and spoke with them, I could probably find out what's going on and maybe there really isn't even an issue. I just ... I don't want to go back there."

They sat in silence for a little while, interrupted only by the squeaking of Lacey's chair as she rocked it back and forth on two legs. "Not even for Molly?"

"Don't say that," Rachel whispered angrily, tears in her eyes. "You don't understand."

"I understand that you have a little girl who loves you very much and wants to be with you. I understand you have a crony who loves you just as much and would do anything for you, including but not limited to, facing past demons."

"Lacey," the blonde said gently, reaching a hand out to capture her lover's. "You have to know that this doesn't help, right? What court would ever grant me custody with a criminal record, working odd hours at a horse barn, having sexual relations with a woman who also happens to be Vinnie Russo's right hand?"

"It doesn't sound so good when you put it that way."

The dark woman grinned ruefully, squeezing the fingers in hers. "But you don't even know if your aunt and uncle will step in. You have no reason to believe they will. Do you? Did they even come looking for you and Leslie when you left?"

"They knew where we were. The police returned us once and we ran away again."

"If they didn't want you, why would they want your daughter?" the taller woman asked reasonably.

"I can't risk it, Lace," Rachel whispered. "I won't let them touch her. I won't let them near her."

"Okay, Raich, honey." Lacey slid from her chair to kneel next to Rachel's, clasping the young woman's smaller hands in her own large tanned ones. "Give up your apartment and the job. Move in with me and get your GED. I can support you and Molly while you do that and start some college classes. Even after I leave Vinnie, I have enough in savings to last us awhile. That takes care of the first two requirements."

"I can't ask you to do that, Lace." Rachel leaned forward and pressed her forehead into her partner's. "We aren't your responsibility."

Lacey met the other woman's liquid green eyes. "I ... love ... you. Okay? I want to be with you. You've changed the way I look at life and I don't want to go back to who I was. You are my responsibility because I choose for it to be that way. I want to help you."

She nodded her agreement, her pale eyes reflecting confusion but acceptance.

"As for your aunt and uncle, we'll go visit them when we take Molly back and see what their real story is. Then we'll know what to do next. I think we should wait for the school year to be over before we change Molly's life, anyway, right?"

"Yeah," Rachel agreed, still looking a little shell-shocked. "You promise not to pound on them?" she teased weakly.

The dark woman saw the nervous tension for what it was

so she couldn't possibly take offense at the statement. She grinned gently. "I'll only pound on them if they give me reason to."

"That's fair," Rachel acquiesced, leaning forward to kiss the other woman's nose. "Couldn't ask for more." She reached up her hands to frame the face before her and met the searching blue eyes with grateful emerald. "Thank you," she whispered.

The emotions were palpable between them as they clung to each other knowing, regardless, that they'd found a home. The moment was interrupted when Molly and Karma came flying into the small room, bringing the cold from outside in with them.

Even the child could feel the emotions in the air and slid to a silent halt to watch the two women before her. Karma bounded forward and kissed both women before flying into the main house. Molly stood awkwardly, watching them, feeling left out, until Lacey snaked out an arm and pulled her to them.

The girl squealed and hugged the dark-haired woman, laughing. Rachel embraced them both, pressing warm lips to the child's cool face. Then the moment was over and Molly bounced away, following Karma into the house just as Rico came in from the outside. He glanced to the two women and grinned before moving along.

"You okay?" Lacey whispered, helping the younger woman to stand, smoothing back the errant hair that had fallen loose from the braid.

"I'm great. I love you."

"You better." The dark woman grinned, tugging Rachel's hand and leading her back into the house where they were cajoled into playing Uno.

Chapter 14

Taking Molly home was a sad affair all the way around. The little girl cried most of the drive and both women had to assure her that everything would be all right. They'd decided not to tell her any of their plans until things were more certain, not wanting to give her false hopes.

The three had been inseparable the last few days, temporarily putting the farm and horses on hold until Molly left. The most work Lacey had done was a late night meeting for Vinnie and some phone calls the previous morning in reference to the horse autopsies. Only one had been completed and the bracken fern poisoning had been confirmed by the evidence of myelin degeneration.

George, Bernard, and Rico had been in and about the house consistently, but no further attempts on Rachel had been made and their searches for Benny had come up empty.

Now Rachel, Lacey, and Molly stood on the front step to the suburban home where Molly lived. Rachel held her daughter closely, whispering words of assurance and love.

"Mama," she whimpered. "I want to stay with you."

"I know, baby," the young blonde responded, tears on

her cheeks. "I love you, you know that. And some day we'll work everything out."

Lacey swung the child up in her arms and hugged her fiercely. "You be good, kiddo. Okay? We'll come get you for the weekend before you know it."

She nodded, small arms wrapped around the tall woman's neck, hands tangled in her long hair.

"Here." The dark woman set the little girl back on the step and pulled out a business card. "This is my home number, pager number, and cell phone number. If you ever need anything at all, you call okay? Any time."

Molly nodded, hugged the dark woman again. "I love you."

"You too, Molly."

"Take care of my mama." She grinned, blue eyes watery.

"I promise." She parted from the child gently and Helen took Molly's hand, pulling her slightly toward the house.

The retired teacher nodded to the two women and smiled at them. They knew the little girl would be okay. They waved one last time before turning and going back to Lacey's Grand Cherokee.

"Let's go grab a bite to eat first," Lacey said softly once they were pulling out of the subdivision. She knew the young blonde had to regroup before they could go meet with the aunt and uncle she'd been dreading seeing.

Rachel nodded her agreement.

They shared a medium supreme pizza, talking casually over the meal. The two women made plans for moving Rachel into the house during the upcoming week and her ensuing GED exam on the weekend.

Lacey watched her young lover push around a pizza crust for the better part of ten minutes before she pointed out the obvious. "It's time to go, Raich."

The young blonde sighed deeply and met her partner's blue gaze. "Do you think Molly's in any danger from Benny?" she asked, trying to put off the inevitable, even though they'd already discussed this very topic.

"Nah. I think he's more focused on the barn and on me. I think Molly will be fine. 'Sides, I have someone watching her."

"Really?" Rachel raised her eyebrows. That was something that hadn't come up before.

"Mmm," the dark woman nodded slowly, "it's time."

Rachel just watched her quietly.

Lacey read apprehension in those green eyes she'd grown to know so well. "I won't let them hurt you, love. I promise you that," she said softly, reaching across the table to hold a small trembling hand.

Rachel smiled weakly. "I know. Just so many memories. I never wanted to see them again. What if they don't live in the same house?"

"They do," Lacey assured her. "I checked it out. C'mon." She tugged on the hand until her partner was standing and then guided her to the cashier to pay before leaving.

Minutes later they were on the doorstep Rachel had hoped never to stand on again. She was fidgeting nervously, fighting butterflies. "I'm gonna be sick," she moaned.

"No, you're not," Lacey chided gently. "C'mon. Confidence, stand tall. Remember the first day you met me? Remember how forward and brash you were?"

Rachel grinned at the memory, knowing that even then there had been something between the two of them.

"That's the Rachel we need right now." She rang the doorbell before her young companion could say anything else.

It seemed like forever before the front door was pulled open, revealing a slight woman in her fifties. Her grey eyes blinked for several moments before recognition hit.

"Rachel?" she whispered softly.

Rachel simply nodded and made no attempt to offer any kind of familial greeting.

The older woman leaned back into the house. "Harold, come out here and look who's ringing our doorbell." There was no tenderness in the wrinkled features when she turned back to the two women.

They stared at each other silently until Harold came up and stood next to his wife. He looked at the two women and practically sneered. "What do you want?"

Well, that was the question. She didn't want to tip her hand, didn't want them to know that it would kill her if they pursued custody of her daughter. So she stuck to the plan that Lacey had outlined. "I ... I was in town and I thought, maybe, I could stop by and say hello."

The two people blinked at her.

"This is my friend, Lacey," Rachel trudged on. "Lace, this is my Aunt Jean and Uncle Harold. They kinda raised me."

"We don't take credit for you, child," Harold said slowly. "You spent two miserable years here and it was two years too many. Ungrateful for our love and care. You drove your mother, my only sister, to her death—"

"I didn't," Rachel argued shakily. "You know I didn't. She wanted to be with Dad. She loved him so much."

"Shut up, child," the greying man snapped. "Some things never change."

"I'm trying to change things," Rachel said softly, drawing strength from the dark woman who stepped nearer. Easily able to feel the anger and hatred rolling off of her lover, she forged ahead to their reason for being here. "I was in town to visit my daughter."

"That bastard child? If you think we're cleaning up any more of your mistakes, you're wrong. We don't want anything to do with you or that child. You're not welcome here and you're no relative of ours. Murderer," he spat angrily, his face turning red with his fury. "Your mother would be ashamed, thank God she's not here to see what you've become!" He pulled his wife away from the door and slammed it on the two women.

Lacey stood stunned, her hands clenching and unclenching as she'd had to fight to control herself. Finally, she shook her head in amazement and heard the sniffling beside her.

"Okay, baby," the dark woman whispered. "Okay.

Come on, let's get out of here," she encouraged gently, taking the elbow nearest her and ushering the young woman back down the sidewalk and into her vehicle. She belted Rachel in and wiped at her tears. "Shh, honey. I know it hurts."

Lacey jumped in the driver's side and left the neighborhood quickly. She pulled over as soon as she could and unbuckled her silent passenger's seatbelt. Then she crawled into the back seat and tugged Rachel with her, pulling her onto her lap.

"Okay, it's okay," she crooned and, finally, Rachel let it go. She clung to the dark woman and cried heavily into her shoulder. "That's it, Raich," Lacey encouraged, rocking the small body. "It's over. You never have to see them again and Molly can come home. They won't bother you again," she assured the young woman, though she did wonder, on the edge of her mind, if the couple was malicious enough to come after Molly despite their hateful words.

"My mom wouldn't be ashamed of me," the young woman whispered hoarsely, choking on her own sobs.

"No, she wouldn't, love. She'd be proud of what you've become."

"They were so mean to us. They said Mama killed herself because Leslie and I were so bad. We were just kids, that wasn't fair."

"No, it wasn't," Lacey agreed, rubbing the smaller woman's back firmly. "They were wrong, you know that."

"But it still hurts," she cried.

"I know it does, baby."

"He used to beat us and she'd just stand by and let him do it." The young blonde was on a roll now and it all came pouring out, accompanied by hiccups and whimpers. "He was so hateful. He loved Mama so much and he was so mad that she was gone. He never liked Dad ..." The rest of Rachel's words were mumbled and incoherent, but it didn't matter. Lacey knew she was lightening her load and simply soothed her young lover with hands and voice.

It was much later that she was finally silent, breathing

raggedly into the dark woman's neck. The Grand Cherokee had become humid and stuffy with her tears and the windows steamed faintly.

"Let's get home," Lacey said at last, holding the smaller woman away from her and wiping her face clean. "It's all over, Raich. You don't need them."

"But I never wanted them to hate me," she whispered.

"I know."

"They were all I had left of my mama ... and of Leslie."

"No, honey. They're nothing. Leslie and your mom are in your heart. They really loved you. Not those old fogies. They never cared, okay? They're not worth it." She nodded encouragingly, pulling the smaller woman to her for another fierce hug. Then she pushed her forward gently. "Climb up there. We need to go."

The young woman fell asleep on the drive home, clutching desperately to her lover's hand.

Chapter 15

"I feel like an idiot," the dark-haired woman muttered under her breath as she and her partner crossed Wheatridge's visitor parking lot. She glanced at Rachel, who was dressed in baggy clothes with her hair tucked under a baseball cap. Her dark sunglasses completed the outfit. Lacey's own outfit was incredibly out of character with white linen pants, a yellow sweater, and black hair braided into two thick ropes that fell across her shoulders.

"Hush, crony," Rachel whispered back, admitting to herself that the Mary Sunshine approach just didn't work for her tall lover.

"You shoulda stayed with Bernie and George." Lacey evidently wasn't listening to the young blonde at her side. She ran nimble fingers through raven bangs, then flipped one braid back over the saffron knit.

"And you can identify Sunny?"

Whatever response may have come from Lacey's lips was so unintelligible that Rachel didn't understand it. She just shrugged slim shoulders and pushed her hands back into the pockets of her barn coat, deciding she probably hadn't wanted to hear the biting words anyway.

The weather had turned icy overnight and the early morning fog had yet to dissipate. The young blonde watched her breath frost in the air with interest, then caught her partner's blue eyes watching her.

"Hmm?"

Lacey replied with a gentle shake of her head, unable to voice the emotions she felt for this slight woman at her side. The night had been silent and solemn, spent holding and talking. But, upon waking, Rachel had apparently decided to let bygones be bygones and not mentioned the previous day's encounter with her hateful aunt and uncle.

Instead she'd formulated a plan to come to Wheatridge and act as mare owners in search of a suitable stud. Lacey had argued, of course, that it was too dangerous but the deciding factor had been that the tall dark woman couldn't tell bay from chestnut from buckskin. George had worried that the stable employees might recognize Lacey since she wasn't exactly low profile in their dark world. But Lacey refused to let Rachel go with anyone but her. So this ridiculous outfit had been developed. They'd also tried to hide Rachel's features as some of the barn hands might recognize her from her work at Aqueduct.

So here they were, on enemy territory, rounding the corner towards the stallion barn. They'd called ahead so had been able to get through the farm's large front gate though now they were prepared to be accosted at any time.

Rachel was peering into the last stallion stall when they were discovered.

"Can I help you?" The dark voice was borderline curious and hostile.

The two women turned simultaneously to take in the man at the end of the aisle. He was about Rachel's size with light brown hair pulled away from his face in a tight ponytail. His searching eyes were grey.

"Yes." Lacey stepped forward first, placing herself between this man and her lover. She extended her hand. "I'm Laura Cranberry. We called about looking at your stallions for our mare?"

"Ah." He nodded his head slowly. "That's right. You spoke with me. I'm Wheatridge's barn manager. Name's Chris. And who is this?" He tilted his head towards the woman leaning against the stall door.

"That's my trainer, Rita." Lacey grinned, her white teeth contrasting with tan skin and accenting blue eyes. Chris was immediately disarmed and barely noticed the young blonde standing several yards away.

Rachel had to smother a laugh at the look on his face. "Ms. Cranberry wants a bay stud for her Abigail."

"Surely, Ms. Cranberry, you understand that color is not really a serious consideration when looking for good matches. We need to consider stamina, spirit, build. Color is merely the wrapping."

"I want bay," Lacey said slowly and dangerously. It caught Chris slightly off guard. "Little or no white. White markings are so unseemly, don't you think?"

Chris knit his brows in confusion and finally chanced a look at the smaller woman whose expression was nearly impossible to read under those large sunglasses. "Uhh ... well. Only one of our studs is bay. And he has four high whites." He thought he heard the tall woman gag. "That's all we have. I can show you his pedigree and his race records. He's an outstanding stallion and his offspring have already started proving themselves on the track."

"But he has four white socks?"

Chris ran his tongue over his teeth, glanced from one woman to the next. "Yeah. But—"

Rachel stepped forward and took the man's elbow, pulling him a few steps away. "Ah, Chris? Right, Chris?"

"Yeah?"

She glanced over her shoulder, met amused blue eyes. "I've worked for Ms. Cranberry for several years now and, well, let's just say she's a touch eccentric. I brought her here because I heard you had a no markings bay ... a colt who maybe wasn't in the breeding program this year. If we could see him, maybe get on his bookings for next season or the following ... I could probably talk her into Music Man." She referred by name to a stunning chestnut stallion at the end of the aisle. "He's my first choice for Abigail, he accents her well."

"We don't have such a horse as this bay you're talking about," Chris insisted. Rachel watched his features and body language. He appeared nervous, but whether it was because he thought they might be onto something or because he was surrounded by insane women was unclear.

"You're sure? One of Abigail's exercise boys said he saw such a colt on the track. He was under your colors."

"No." He shook his head, ran a large hand over his face to rest on his chin. "No solid bay colt. I wish I could help you."

Rachel considered this, pursing her lips thoughtfully. "Okay." She nodded. "Do you mind if I walk her through your training barn, show her some of your offspring to let her see what kind of talent your stallions throw?"

"No, not at all," he said almost cheerfully, seemingly glad to have an excuse to abandon these two women. "You two go ahead. I have some other things to get back to. If you need anything else, let me know." With one final awkward wave to Lacey, he quickly turned and walked back down the aisle.

"Well?" the dark woman questioned as she came up beside Rachel.

"He said he doesn't have a horse like that here."

"Could they have put white markings on Sunny?" Lacey questioned under her breath, her face close to her young lover's.

"No. It's hard to put markings on a horse, easy to cover them up."

"Did he seem nervous?"

"He thought you were insane." Rachel grinned with twinkling eyes. "But I couldn't tell if he was worried we might discover something or that we might sprout horns and start spewing things from our mouths."

"Nice picture, Raich. Thanks," the dark-haired woman muttered sarcastically. "I'm thinking he wouldn't have abandoned us to check out the training barn if he were hiding something there."

"I agree." Rachel nodded, removing her sunglasses and chewing on the stem absently. "But I gotta look." Mist green eyes looked up expectantly and Lacey sighed.

"I know, love. Let's go." She placed her hand at the small of the other woman's back and escorted her gently from the barn.

As suspected, the training barn had shown nothing out of the ordinary. There was no trace of a solid bay gangly colt. With obvious disappointment, Rachel climbed into Lacey's third car: a seven series BMW. She sank into the soft leather seats with a deep sigh.

"Let's get back to the house and see what the boys found," Lacey said gently as she drove down the long, treed driveway towards the front gate. Once she turned on the highway several minutes later, she started steering with her knee and undoing the tight braids in her hair.

Rachel grinned and reached over to hold the wheel.

"I feel like I belong on a commercial, waving around dish washing fluid," the dark woman grumbled, indicating her bright clothing before taking back control of the sleek grey car.

"Or floor cleaning supplies," Rachel supplied helpfully.

"You be quiet," Lacey growled but she was grinning.

"I like the dark look better, Lace," the young blonde conceded. "But you look beautiful in anything."

The dark-haired woman glanced to her partner and smiled tenderly. "You sucking up, love?" She reached out to capture a blonde lock.

"Nah. Only the truth."

Lacey turned her attention back to the road and pulled out her cell phone, hitting a memory button to speed dial Bernard.

"Hey, Boss." The voice on the other end sounded cheerful.

"What's up?"

"Well, we got those overview maps you wanted. I think

you'll like what we found. Rico went to the track and wandered through Wheatridge's barn there, but he didn't see anything that could remotely match Sunny's description."

"Aah, it was a long shot anyway." Lacey shrugged. "Chances are, they wouldn't steal him and then put him in broad daylight. What do the maps show?"

"There are a couple decent places on the Wheatridge property that are away from the main barns. We can check them out tonight."

"Great." Lacey nodded her approval, winked to her passenger. "We'll be to the house within an hour and we can talk about our next step." After hanging up, she reached over to hold Rachel's hand and squeeze it tenderly. "We'll get to the bottom of this."

****

Their evening plans set and still most of the afternoon to kill, Lacey had talked her team into moving stuff out of Rachel's apartment. She'd had to pay a penalty to the leasing office for breaking Rachel's contract, but she wasn't really worried about it.

George and Rico did most of the work loading the bright yellow Ryder truck in the lot. Bernard was a decent foreman but his bulk made it difficult for him to move boxes and furniture down the narrow outdoor stairs. Rachel and Lacey tossed things into boxes.

"Ya know, you really don't have much," Lacey observed, looking at the few boxes they'd packed and glancing around at the mostly bare walls.

The young blonde shrugged. "Don't need much." Plus she couldn't really afford much, so she wasn't into gadgets or miscellaneous. Most of what they'd packed was shelves of books and a few memorable trinkets. The rest were clothes and kitchen items.

"Thank goodness you're not a packrat," Lacey teased gently, sensing the mood change and wanting to lighten it. "Cuz you and your stuff would be out on your ear."

Rachel snorted her amusement and went back to wrapping dishes in newspaper. "What are we gonna do with the kitchen stuff? You don't need it."

"I dunno." Lacey paused in thought and then yelled to the group that had just come in the kitchen. "Hey, Rico. You need some dishes and things?"

The teen stopped and tilted his head. "I guess I could."

"Where do you live, anyway?" Rachel asked, watching this young man she'd come to like a lot in the last few days.

"Closer to Vinnie's."

"Roommate?" the blonde woman kept pushing. Rico blushed. "Ah ha! Do tell, Rico!"

George laughed. "Rachel, honey, you're embarrassing the kid."

"You don't belong here, Rico," Rachel said more solemnly, inclining her head slightly to observe the lanky form in front of her.

"Where would you rather I be?" He grinned playfully, trying to divert the conversation.

"No. I mean it, Rico. Or George, you have a family. And Bernard, you're just a big teddy bear."

"Not so, hon," Bernie said gently.

"Rachel," Lacey warned softly but her young lover was on a roll.

"Maybe you should all leave when Lacey does. Maybe that would work. Do you think so, Lace?" Rachel turned to regard her partner and saw a distant look in her eyes. She realized, suddenly, that Lacey hadn't revealed her plans to her team.

"What? Leave?" Bernard was the first to speak.

"Aw, shit, Lace," Rachel whispered. "I'm so sorry."

The dark woman smiled tightly. "S'okay, love." The three men looked at her with bewildered expressions and she heaved her shoulders in a sigh. "Close the door. Let's all sit down."

The only place to sit was the floor in the living room. They pushed away newspaper and flat boxes to clear room. Rachel sat close to her lover, crossing her legs and resting her hands on her knees. She felt like an idiot for spilling the beans.

"So," Lacey began slowly, looking to the small group around her. She'd known Bernard for nearly a decade and George just under that. She'd watched George's kids grow up, she'd been to Bernard's wedding. Despite their violent jobs, she knew the hearts in these men and she knew this would be the hardest part of leaving Vinnie. Because, as much as she liked to portray her hard-hearted exterior, these men were the only family she'd known in a very long time.

"Does Vinnie know?" George asked softly.

Lacey shook her head, gave him half a grin for trying to make things easier for her. "I haven't talked to him yet. I promised myself I'd finish out this mess with Kalzar and Raoul before I left. I don't even know if he'll let me go."

"You're the best, Lace," Bernard said gently. "There's been no one to replace you for years. Operations have never run smoother."

Lacey grinned at the compliment and let a little of her feralness show in her eyes. "They're afraid of me."

"But it works." George grinned back, then he turned serious. "Vinnie will be reluctant."

"I know."

"Umm." Rachel spoke for the first time since letting the cat out of the bag. "Are you in danger? Will he hurt you?"

Lacey looked to her lover before glancing at her team members. "Maybe."

The young blonde tried to jump to her feet but her wrist was caught in a cast iron grip. She was pulled back to the floor with an audible thump.

"Maybe he will. But I don't think so. I've been loyal to him for a long time. He knows he can trust me not to change sides or to go after him."

The men in the room nodded their agreement.

"I want to finish this up for him, then I'm going to ask to be let go. Free and clear."

"What about us?" Rico asked slowly. He hadn't been in the business long but he readily recognized how lucky he was to have been assigned to Lacey's team.

"I can't make those decisions for you, Rico. But if you want to go when I do, I'll do everything in my power to keep you safe," the dark woman swore. "All of you."

"What are you gonna do?" George asked.

Lacey shrugged, moved her grip from Rachel's wrist to slide down and tangle their fingers. "You have any ideas?" she grinned slowly.

Bernard smiled. "Let's see ... professional hit man?"

Lacey cleared her throat and glanced to her young lover.

"Okay, maybe not ... How about ... Private Investigator?" George had to add his input.

"No, no, no," Rico spoke up, getting entirely too excited with the direction of the conversation. "How about a security consultant ... kinda like that movie Sneakers!"

"Great." Lacey rolled ice blue eyes. "Look. The point of all this was to tell you that yes, I am planning to leave the business. I've had enough. I want a more sane life with less drugs and death and more Rachel and Molly." She looked down at their entwined hands. "It's time."

They were silent for a moment, realizing their boss was embarrassed by the confession. "Well, for what it's worth, Lace," Bernard spoke up at last, meeting her eyes earnestly. "I've never seen you happier. And I've known you a very long time. You're not the woman I worked for last year."

George nodded his agreement.

"I will do my best to keep you guys safe, if you leave or stay. You've ... stuck with me through a lot. And though maybe I never showed my appreciation for you, it's there."

"We knew." George smiled gently. "You've always had a good heart."

The dark woman snorted, growing entirely too uncomfortable with the emotional conversation, and jumped to her feet. She pulled Rachel up next to her. "Let's get back to work. We need to have Rachel packed before dark so we can go do a little prowling at Wheatridge."

Chapter 16

The darkness was all-encompassing, even the stars seemed to be hiding from sight tonight. Rachel tilted back on her heels, stretched her neck back to stare at the sky above.

"Stop fidgeting," Lacey whispered in front of her and tugged at the young blonde's jacket yet again to bring her attention back.

"Sorry," the rider responded, rocking forward again to stand flat-footed. She tilted her head down to watch what her lover was doing.

"Raich, honey. I can't see," the dark woman whispered, trying her best not to sound impatient or frustrated. She turned blue eyes to Bernard who stood silently at her side. He winked.

"Sorry," Rachel said again softly. She stopped watching the nimble hands at her jacket and instead redirected her attention to the dark head in front of her.

"Thanks," Lacey said softly.

"What are you doing?"

"I'm putting a tracker on you in case we get separated." With those words, Rachel felt the long fingers slide up under her shirt into her bra. They were cold as ice and caused her to jump. "Chilly?"

"Mmm," Rachel agreed softly.

"Okay." She made a few more adjustments, then pulled her hands out. "Go ahead and tuck your shirt in."

Rachel obliged.

"Now," the dark woman said as she was pulling items out of a bag. "Carrots into your inside pocket." Lacey described her actions as she tucked the vegetables neatly inside the leather jacket Rachel wore. "This," she held up a gun for Rachel, "is a small frame nine millimeter. It'll fit your hand better."

"Lace, I don't think—"

"Hush," the dark woman said quickly. "Listen," she murmured, ejecting the cartridge. "It's loaded." She slammed the clip back in after showing Rachel the bullets. "The safety's on. Right here. When you hold it in your hand, you can flip the safety off with your thumb. See?" She demonstrated and waited for Rachel's reluctant nod. "Flip the safety, aim, fire. You don't have to cock the gun. The first trigger pull will be hardest because it also chambers a round. You may have to give it a good tug. After that, each round will chamber so the pulls will be easier. It's a nine round clip."

Rachel met her lover's eyes with hesitant green. "I don't want to fire that," she whispered.

"And I don't want you to unless you're in danger, okay? It's just a precaution. Leave the safety on." She flipped it back in place and put the gun into Rachel's other inside pocket.

"I don't like it." Rachel felt herself getting nauseous.

"Are you going to be sick?" Lacey asked warily, watching her friend's face change to different shades of green. She'd become pretty used to Rachel's sensitive stomach over the last weeks. The young blonde had spent most of the night hanging over the toilet after her confrontation with her aunt and uncle.

"Maybe."

"It's making you nervous?"

"Yeah," the blonde said softly.

Lacey pursed her lips in thought, glanced from the young woman's face to her team. George shook his head, Bernard shrugged, Rico was busy scratching some of his dinner off his coat. "All right," she said at last, pulling it out and handing it over to George.

Rachel heaved a sigh of relief and her color slowly came back.

George slapped something else in his boss's extended hand and she glanced at it briefly and then grinned to the dark man.

"Good idea. Here, this is better." Lacey held up a canister for Rachel to see, illuminated by the Maglite Bernard held. "Pepper spray."

"Why do you have pepper spray, crony?" Some of Rachel's confidence was returning.

"Dogs, mostly. But you use it for anything, okay? Aim for the eyes."

The blonde nodded as Lacey shoved the spray into her pocket. Then Lacey zipped up her lover's jacket and kissed her on the nose.

"Stay with me," the dark woman repeated for the umpteenth time. "Or with the guys. Once we find the horse, you know what to do?"

Rachel nodded and patted the backpack she held in one hand.

"Good, let's go."

George acted on the order and moved forward with bolt cutters. He easily snipped through the chain on the gate in front of him, using Bernie's light for guidance. The chain fell to the ground and George pulled the gate open.

Then the whole group jumped into Lacey's black Grand Cherokee. George drove while the other men filled in the seats. Lacey and Rachel sat in the back compartment with the doors open and their feet dangling towards the darkened ground.

"Are you okay?" Rachel whispered after a moment, noting her friend's increasing distance. She reached over and latched onto Lacey's forearm.

"Yeah," she confirmed quietly, even though it was a lie.

Rachel recognized it easily and reached her other hand over to tug at a long black braid. "Talk to me. Is it just a work mode thing or is it something else?"

Lacey sighed, turning ice blue eyes quickly to her young lover before looking away again. "Just memories. Another job."

"Tell me," the blonde urged softly.

"It's about a past lover," Lacey whispered, warning her friend.

Rachel shrugged. "I can take it."

Lacey sighed again and looked thoughtfully at her long fingers before continuing. The rocking of the four wheel drive along the barely traveled dirt road was almost soothing.

Rachel considered further prompting, but decided instead to wait the dark woman out. Her patience was rewarded before too long.

"It was a gun deal. George, Bernard, Susan, and I. She was more of a sidekick than anything. Shouldn't have been on our team, shoulda been in a less active group. She didn't have natural instincts like Rico does. She wasn't a quick learner. She was only there because we were sleeping together and I let her talk me into bringing her along. She thought it was her opportunity to prove herself. She was Vinnie's niece, new in the business, wanted to be like me. So I let myself be convinced." The husky voice stopped as Lacey looked up to the sky, seeing just a few stars peeking from behind the clouds. She felt increased warmth on her hands as Rachel reached over and covered them with her own.

With this support, she continued. "So, we met ahead of time only Susan wasn't there. We waited, I paged her, tried her cell phone, her house. No good. So we gave up on her and decided to go just the three of us. We entered the warehouse." She sighed, easily recalling what she'd seen.

"There should have been a small group of Miami gun runners with a shipment. But instead there was ... I saw Susan. She was hanging by her neck, head tilted at a grotesque angle, and eyes open and staring. Obviously dead. There was a note pinned to her shirt explaining she'd tried to make the buy on her own and failed. Her body was marked up enough to indicate that she'd been beaten, her death had been slow. I don't know how early she got there."

Lacey felt a gentle squeeze from her lover. Then Rachel leaned into her shoulder in a show of comfort. She wasn't sure she really wanted to subject her young companion to the rest.

"Go ahead," the blonde whispered softly. "I'm listening."

The dark woman quirked a grin at the softly spoken words. "There was movement from behind some abandoned cargo crates across the main floor so we were all drawn and ready. On edge. Angry. The gun runners swaggered out, their own weapons drawn casually, looking smug. The first guy ... he said ..." She took a breath, closing her eyes and hearing the voice in her memory. "He said 'Your little friend screamed like a baby before she died'." The words echoed in Lacey's dark head today as they had echoed in the warehouse so many years ago.

"I lost it. I wanted to finish the deal, kill them all, take her body and get out of there. But I knew I couldn't do all of those things and still complete the job. So I stepped forward and grabbed the nearest guy's shirt front, pushed him to his knees, and placed my Glock right on his forehead." Lacey tapped her own forehead in the exact spot with a long index finger. "I looked right in his eyes when I pulled the trigger. I saw him know he was going to die. I saw his fear and his panic and I reveled in it because I knew he'd seen the same in Susan's eyes. Then I shoved the lifeless body to the floor and walked back to George and Bernard. The other guys were stunned. My own had expected it from me. But no one retaliated because they knew they were wrong. We finished the deal and we walked away."

"Did you take her with you?" Rachel asked softly, fighting nausea for the second time in less than an hour.

Lacey must have sensed this in her companion because she reached over and gently rubbed Rachel's stomach through her layers of clothing.

"Yeah. I did. We sent her home to be buried. Vinnie chewed us up one side and down the other. But he believed us ... believed that she had done it herself." They were both silent for a very long time, listening to the rumble of the vehicle and the quiet mutters of the men closer to the front.

"Thank you for telling me," Rachel whispered at last. "I know it was hard for you."

"I didn't love her," Lacey said softly in response, surprised at the blonde's chuckle.

"You don't have to say that for me, Lace. I know we each have pasts."

"I'm not." The ice blue eyes that met mist green were honest. "I didn't love her. It was more physical. I ... I didn't really love anyone. Not even myself. She was attracted to me and I needed a release. I guess I led her on. That was four years ago ... I didn't get attached to anyone else until you."

"Really?" Rachel asked, interested.

"I ... I didn't want just release anymore. I didn't want anything because it didn't get me anywhere and just got someone else hurt."

"So you had no one?"

"No."

"How did you survive?" The blonde tilted her head gently. "You need someone to love you. You crave it."

Lacey surprised her partner with a soft chortle. Rachel had eased that deep aching part of herself that needed love and commitment. "Yeah. But I just closed off from it. Until you."

"What was so different about me?"

"I love you," the dark-haired woman said simply, shrugging leather-clad shoulders.

"From that first moment?" Rachel asked skeptically.

"I think so. But it wasn't until later that I realized it. Must be fate." She flashed teeth to her partner in a grin, their white almost blinding in the darkness.

"Must be." Rachel returned the smile with a beam of her own and then leaned forward to claim wind-chilled lips. "I love you," she muttered, barely pulling away so their lips touched with the movement.

"I sure hope so," Lacey responded easily, "cuz this would be too much trouble for someone who hated me."

"Hey, ladies," George called back, completely clueless to the thick emotions in the end of the Grand Cherokee. "We're almost to the first place."

They'd outlined four different areas to look for the colt. One was a network of caves, one was a run down shed, and the other two were heavily forested sections that would be hidden from the road and the air.

It was well past midnight and they were in the second section of woods when Lacey called to her group. "It looks like traffic has been going through here." She indicated a narrow path between trees, looking down to see a tire track.

"Wheelbarrow, probably," Rachel said as she came up to her partner's elbow.

"Yeah." The dark head nodded agreement, guiding the beam of her flashlight up the narrow trail and into the trees. "Let's go."

They'd only traveled twenty yards into the dense underbrush when they heard frantic nickering and stomping of feet. Lacey didn't need her flashlight with the light from Rachel's ear to ear grin.

The young woman ran the rest of the distance, tripping a few times on exposed roots, then climbed a green paneled steel fence and threw herself at the waiting colt.

Sunny stood for the overflow of emotions, pushing affectionately on Rachel's shoulder and back. He whuffled her hair and nickered over and over.

"Am I intruding on a moment?" Lacey asked wryly and got a smile for her question.

"God, he's beautiful," Rachel whispered, running her

hands under his blanket and over his body. Then she did the same with his legs. She pushed gently on his shoulder until he shifted his weight and she picked up the hoof to examine it. "They kept his shoes on." She quickly checked his other feet in the same manner, nodding her approval. "Good, that'll be better. I wonder if they kept up with the vitamin shots." She stepped back to watch him stand and he did look better, the hunched back, leg-splayed stance gone.

Meanwhile, her dark lover leaned casually against the gate Rachel had scampered over and watched the surrounding forest. After a moment she raised her weapon and pointed it at the small trail they followed in until she recognized Rico's blond head.

"Good." She dropped her gun back to her side. "Call the guys back in. I'll meet you at the truck in a minute."

He nodded curtly and turned around to trot away.

"I need a hand," Rachel called from inside the enclosure so Lacey obliged and tucked her gun in her waistband before climbing the gate. "Hold his head." Rachel had already pulled a snaffle bridle out of her backpack and slipped it over the colt's ears.

Now she adjusted the bit and fastened the cheek strap. "When I was a kid ... twelve, I think," Rachel began speaking softly and Lacey listened intently. Rachel didn't talk about her past much outside her daughter and her crime. Plus the whimpered words the night after facing her aunt and uncle. "I had a horse show at the barn where I took lessons. I was riding a little Arabian gelding named Tyler. After our first class I put him back in his stall to rest and my dad wanted to help me. He didn't know a thing about horses but he was eager to be with Leslie and me. So I asked him to take off Tyler's bridle for me."

The young blonde finished with the bit and settled the brow band. "When I went to get Tyler to warm up for my next class, I found the bridle sitting on a chair outside his stall. Every single buckle and strap had been unfastened. It was a pile of leather and a loose bit." She laughed softly at the memory. "I thanked him for his help and took the jumble into the stall to sort it all out. I was almost late to my class." Rachel finished her story with a wistful smile and pushed the reins into Lacey's hands.

"How did you do in the class?" Lacey asked tenderly, reaching out her free hand to run it down her companion's arm as she turned to the backpack.

The colt danced excitedly when Rachel pulled out a tiny racing saddle she'd borrowed from Briargate. She cocked her head slightly in thought. "Second, I think. I don't remember." The young rider pulled off Sunny's blanket, letting it drop to the leaf littered ground, then tossed the saddle over tall withers.

"Did you show a lot?"

"Almost every weekend during the show season. But always on borrowed horses or lesson horses. I've never had a horse of my own," Rachel responded, cinching up the saddle with expert hands.

"Never?" Lacey asked, surprised.

"Nope." The blonde was busy adjusting the stirrups from racing height to a more comfortable riding seat.

"We may need to do something about that," Lacey said softly, giving her companion a warm smile, which was returned readily.

"I just might hold you to that."

"I hope you do," the tall woman responded sincerely.

"We're set," Rachel told her dark-haired companion, who gladly handed over the reins and opened the gate. Rachel led Sunny through the opening while he snorted and spun. "Shit, buddy. They had you in there since last week?" she chided the excited colt gently. "Spit and fire," Rachel muttered, secretly happy that he appeared to be doing so well despite his ordeal with the bracken fern.

"Pardon?" Lacey asked, falling into step behind the colt and woman as they headed back down the trail. She did her best to shine her flashlight in front of Rachel.

"He's gonna be a handful, I'm afraid."

"Can you ride him?" Lacey asked, suddenly concerned. She hadn't been worried about this part of the plan, but her lover was a little sore still and hadn't been on a horse since her bad fall. She cursed herself for not considering Rachel's part in the horsenapping.

The young blonde snorted as if she'd never heard anything so silly. "Can I ride him?" she repeated cockily.

Lacey laughed softly, dismissing her worries.

They emerged from the trees and the underbrush to stand about fifty yards from where the Grand Cherokee was parked. Lacey glanced over and could see the men milling around the area of the vehicle and nodded her approval.

"I need a leg," Rachel called, pulling Lacey's attention back to the horse and woman.

"You have two," Lacey responded teasingly, not understanding the request and misinterpreting it on purpose.

"A leg up, crony," Rachel growled.

"Show me how." The dark woman stepped forward and looked to Rachel's hands. The young rider had intertwined her fingers and held her two hands cupped together.

"I put my knee in there and you give me a little toss up into the saddle. Little. Don't you dare throw me over him to the ground on the other side," Rachel warned.

Lacey nodded and put her flashlight on the grass, holding her hands as she'd been instructed. Rachel gathered the reins and a handful of hair at Sunny's withers and then placed her knee into her partner's grip. She was impressed when Lacey executed the move perfectly and Rachel was able to toss her leg over and land neatly in the saddle. She found her stirrups quickly and stood in them for a moment to test their length.

"Okay?" the dark-haired woman asked, picking her flashlight back up.

"One more thing," Rachel murmured and she leaned over to run the fingers of one hand under the girth to test its tightness again. In order to loosen the restricting girth, some horses let out deep breaths once they have a rider up. Sunny was no exception so Rachel had to control the colt with one hand while dropping her stirrup and placing that foot up on the saddle's pommel. This contortion allowed her to reach under the saddle flap and pull up a billet, tightening the girth another notch or two.

Lacey observed these acrobatics warily. "Is that safe."

"You handle the guns and attire, hon. Leave the horse stuff up to me." She grinned at her dark lover as she settled her foot back into its proper place.

"Deal," Lacey responded, returning the look with a smirk of her own.

Suddenly, some shouting from the direction of the Grand Cherokee caught her attention and both women glanced over at the vehicle to see the men jumping in. Then Lacey tracked her eyes further across the field to see headlights bouncing their way from the barns.

"Shit," Lacey groaned. "Go, Raich. Meet us at the trailer."

The colt spun with excitement but his rider glanced from the woman at their side, to the waiting Grand Cherokee, to the headlights. "You won't make it, Lace," she said frantically.

"Go," the woman shouted, shoving at the broad shoulder next to her. Sunny was more than ready to listen to her pleas.

"Lace! They're pulling away." Sure enough, George had waited as long as he felt comfortable but had begun to move the vehicle. She had always taught them how to split up and regroup and he easily followed those ingrained instructions.

"I'll be fine," Lacey argued, her voice raised angrily, eyes flashing back to the headlights, which were gaining quickly. They must have seen their vehicle. "I'll go into the woods. You get out of here."

Rachel reached down and gripped her lover's shoulder with an iron hand, strengthened from years of handling reins. "Come with me." Her emerald eyes sought Lacey's blue and found them. Their gazes locked for a long moment.

Slowly, reluctantly, Lacey nodded. Because she wouldn't have survived if she had to ride out and leave

Rachel here. How could she expect anything less of her lover?

Rachel was greatly relieved as she maneuvered the colt back into the edge of the woods until she found a downed tree. "Hop up here."

"Oh, Raich," Lacey groaned, doing as she was bade. "I've only ever ridden once and it was a pony on one of those little go around things."

"S'okay, hon," Rachel reassured her. "Get on behind me." Rachel was going to tell her to hold on once she did but Sunny lurched forward as soon as he felt the unfamiliar extra weight and the dark woman reached out reflexively, wrapping long fingers into the leather coat in front of her.

"Raich?" The husky voice sounded a little worried and Rachel took just a moment to reflect in the irony that this woman could face down gun fights but was afraid of this act.

"Put your arms around me," Rachel commanded, looking at the headlights that lit the path they'd left and caught them in the peripheral. "Hold onto his mane instead of me, more secure," the blonde grasped her partner's hands and shoved them into the colt's wiry black mane, nodding approval as long tan fingers wound into the coarse hair.

"Will it hurt him?"

"No. Horses don't have nerve endings in their hair like we do. Hold on as tight as you can. And grip with your legs."

Rachel glanced over her shoulder to check out the dark woman and saw that Lacey looked more secure. Now or never, she mused. "Here we go!" she yelled and it took very little encouragement for Sunny to go from a dancing stand to a dead run. Rachel leaned over his neck; Lacey leaned over Rachel.

"Smooth," Lacey commented after her initial yelp of surprise.

"Yeah, well hold on anyway," Rachel called back, the mane whipping her face, the wind catching her words and dulling them before they reached her partner's ears.

Rachel turned the colt with expert hands until he was

flying down the rutted dirt road. She prayed he wouldn't take a hard stumble as she wasn't sure Lacey could stay on with that kind of jolt at this speed. With that thought in mind, she guided him away from the road and onto the less traveled grass at its side.

Lacey was warm against her back and she felt the tautness of the dark woman's muscles as she held on for everything she was worth.

"What do you see?" Rachel asked after a moment of running full tilt towards the fence line near the gate they'd broken.

She felt Lacey move as she glanced over her shoulder and around to each side. "George is almost to the gate. The truck is right on his heels."

"Do they see us?"

"I don't think so. But we won't make the gate."

Rachel calculated quickly, remembering where they'd parked the rented truck and trailer. She hoped George would go out the gate and turn right, leading their pursuers the opposite direction.

"George'll remember," Lacey reassured the blonde as if reading her mind. "Shit, there's another truck, Raich. He must have called for backup."

Suddenly their whole world lit up as the second truck swung around and shone bright headlights directly onto them.

"Fuck," Rachel growled. Sunny flicked back black-tipped ears at her exclamation. Without a moment's hesitation, Rachel swung the colt to the left and headed at an angle towards the fence line to where she guessed the trailer to be.

"What are you doing?" Lacey asked, releasing her death grip on the black mane to reach for her weapon as the truck gained on them.

"We're gonna go over."

"What?!"

"Don't get your gun. I need you to hold on."

Lacey was a moment away from arguing until she realized how correct her young lover was. She snaked her hand back around and gripped the mane again. The fence loomed before them, the moon had finally broken the clouds and silver shards of light reflected off the white in front of them.

"They'll drive through it," Lacey argued.

"No. It's metal poles, look at it. They'll crash right into it." Rachel tilted her head back so Lacey could hear her.

The dark woman peered over the blonde's shoulder to examine the fence more closely as they approached. She was right. It was five horizontal poles, connected every ten feet to a sunken metal pole. "If he hits his feet on that, we'll all die."

Rachel nodded her agreement, the adrenaline pumping through her and refusing to let her feel that fear. "He better not then, huh?" she murmured, knowing her lover couldn't hear her.

Thirty feet. Pounding hoofs. They could hear his labored breaths, smell the sweat that poured off of him. Twenty feet and they felt him tense as he watched the moonlit fence before him.

"Oh God, Sun," Rachel yelled. "Please don't balk. You can do this, buddy." She knew if he refused the fence at this speed, she and Lacey would fly right into it. It was more than likely the colt would slide into it as well and tangle his long limbs with metal.

"Trust in me, Sun," she called to those hesitant flicking ears. She gave him every cue she could think of to take the jump. She leaned forward, taking Lacey with her. She raised in her stirrups so her weight was on his shoulders and she slid her hands up his neck to give him a half release. This would allow him his head for the jump but gave her contact to keep him straight. She pressed her legs harder into his sweating sides.

Fifteen feet. Rachel tensed. One more stride and he should be leaving the ground. She held her breath, felt Lacey do the same.

Then he did it. He shifted his tall frame to his haunches, had faith in the small woman on his back who had welcomed him into the world and raised him and trained him. He made adjustments for the extra weight of the dark woman who smelled funny to him but had enough of his rider's scent on her to make him feel it was okay. Pushing off with powerful hind legs, he stretched his neck, tucked his knees tight against his body so that his shoes actually touched his elbows. His alert ears flew forward, already paying attention to the ground on the other side. And then his front feet were connecting with the earth, denied any longer flight without the wings of Pegasus.

The first jolt tossed the women forward and Rachel steadied them both, dropping one hand from the reins to reach back and hold her lover's thigh. The second jolt as back feet hit balanced them and gave Rachel a chance to grab the reins with both hands. Rachel heard the joyous whoop of her partner even as she herself remembered to finally breathe.

She let him run full out until they hit the tree line and then she pulled him down into a controlled canter. Just as they passed into the first trees, they heard the horrifying crash behind them. The sound of metal wrenching into metal nearly caused Sunny to jump out from under them in his panic. Rachel used calm hands to steady him even as she heard the steam rising and popping sounds of a mutilated engine. She trembled at the thought of the dreadful scene behind them.

"It's okay, Raich," Lacey murmured, squeezing her partner. She was much more comfortable now as Rachel pulled the panting colt down to a hurried walk and broke from the trees out onto the road.

"Trailer?" Rachel asked, breathing hard herself.

"Up there." Lacey pointed, her eyes focusing on the truck and trailer about a quarter mile up the road.

"Hold on." Rachel nudged the tired colt back into a canter and ran along the berm of the road until they were across from the rig. Then she pulled him to a stop. "Train stops here, love," she said softly.

Lacey slid off to rubbery legs and caught her partner as the young woman did the same. Together they led the colt across the black-top road. Rachel gave the reins over to the dark-haired woman and jogged ahead to unhook the large back door and swing it open. It was a standard stock trailer without any barriers.

Sunny stepped in easily behind Lacey.

"Go out and push the door mostly closed. I'm gonna untack him really quick so he doesn't hurt himself."

Lacey nodded at the instructions and stepped back into the cold night. Moments later, Rachel was elbowing her way through the small opening. She watched Lacey close and latch the door before they jogged to the truck and each hopped in. Rachel tossed the tack to the floor at her feet while her dark companion started the truck and eased it back onto the road.

They rode in silence for a few moments before Lacey heaved a huge sigh of relief.

Rachel laughed out loud.

"That was something." Lacey shook her head in amazement. "Kinda fun." She threw a slightly feral grin to her passenger. "When can we ride like that again?"

"Okay, we are never ever ... ever riding like that again," Rachel chuckled. "Holy shit. We really got him."

"We sure did. There's a phone in the glove compartment, love. Get it out so I can call George."

Moments later, Lacey was holding the phone up to her ear. It was actually Bernard who answered the ringing. "Bernie!" she shouted.

"Oh my God, Boss. Where the fuck are you?"

"We're all right," Lacey said instead, not willing to give out such information over the cell line. "How are you guys?"

"All in one piece. We're following the plan, still. Is Rachel okay?"

"Yeah," Lacey chuckled. "She's right here. We'll see you soon." She handed the phone over to her passenger who hit the end button and stowed it back in the glove compartment.

****

Bernard and George sat in the cold night, watching their breath frost into the air in front of them. They exchanged few words in these hours just before dawn and instead focused on the horse and women across the yard.

Rachel was walking out Sunny carefully. She'd sponged him off, put liniment on his legs and wrapped them. Then she'd covered his body with a warm wool liner and an outer shell. She fully expected him to be lame in the morning. His lithe legs weren't meant for that kind of weight and that kind of full-fledged run across open land.

Lacey walked beside her, entwining their fingers, whispering words every now and then.

Rico was in the house with Karma, going from room to room and ensuring the security systems were all functioning properly.

By the time the early morning sun was forcing crimson rays through foggy mist, Rachel had at last turned the colt loose. Now the two women stood in the enclosed porch and watched him eagerly graze on the sparse grass in the huge backyard.

"Get some sleep," George suggested quietly from the doorway. "We have everything covered."

It didn't take too much convincing for the dark woman to drag her lover up the stairs where they took a quick, hot shower together before piling into the king sized bed. The morning sun cast orange streaks across the floor and the bedding as they each found sleep.

Chapter 17

Rachel nearly skipped out of the building and into the parking lot. Her jade eyes scanned the vehicles until she found a familiar one. It was the black Grand Cherokee from their illicit horsenapping nearly a week a before.

She jogged over and jumped into the front seat, casting a quick hello to the three men crammed into the backseat before leaning over to kiss Lacey's cheek. The dark woman grinned easily as she put the vehicle into drive.

"How'd it go?" Lacey asked gently, as if she couldn't tell from the sheer joy pouring off the woman next to her.

"Great. Thank you for your help."

"Any time." The dark-haired woman smiled.

"Are you ready?"

"Ready as I'll ever be."

"Am I staying in the car?" The blonde grinned mischievously. "I promise not to play with the windshield wipers. The radio I can't guarantee, though."

Lacey grinned as well. "Actually, you even get to come in. It's a security risk to have people sitting in the car. Kind of a get away set-up." She regretted the words as soon as they left her mouth and she must have winced visibly because the young blonde's haunted look faded slightly.

"S'okay," she assured her friend, laying a warm hand on a sweater-ensconced arm.

Everyone in the vehicle remained silent for the rest of the trip to Vinnie's sprawling mansion.

Rachel waited silently in the passenger seat of the Grand Cherokee while her dark companion made her way around the vehicle. Then she opened the door and hopped out to stand next to the woman. The men piled out beside them and the five stood there looking at the front double doors for long moments before Lacey took a step forward. Everyone else followed.

They walked in quietly, the two women not touching, but no more than an inch or two apart.

"Lace." A tall, olive-skinned man opened the door for them, glancing easily over Lacey's lithe form to take in the small beauty beside her. He moved his gaze along the others with familiarity.

"'Berto," Lacey mumbled by way of greeting as they stepped into the foyer. "This is Rachel."

He nodded his greeting and Rachel glanced at him briefly and smiled before moving her attention to take in the room. It was huge and well-lit. A large open entryway went farther into the house and a grand winding staircase found its way upstairs. The floors were a light oak, as were the banisters to the stairway and the trim on all the doorways. Light poured in from the solitary skylight and bathed the floor with glistening highlights.

They were led down the hallway into a large anteroom with sofas and an assortment of coffee and end tables. There was a silver tray set out with coffee and tea for guests.

Much to Rachel's surprise, 'Berto moved up behind her and lifted her arms to start frisking her. She yelped and squirmed away.

Lacey cast the offender a dark glare and stepped closer to her young friend.

"Policy, Lace. You know that."

"Yeah, but don't sneak up on her for Christ's sake," the

dark-haired woman growled. She turned to Rachel, offered her half a shrug. "It's okay."

The young blonde nodded, raised her arms again to allow 'Berto access. He frisked her quickly and a touch too intimately for Rachel's tastes but Lacey was watching closely and made no comment so it must not have been out of the ordinary.

Apparently, Crony Number Two had reached the status of not being frisked because 'Berto simply nodded to her before frisking her team with quick expert hands. He walked across the lush burgundy carpet to the only door in the room.

Vinnie himself emerged after a brief knock, though Rachel wouldn't have known it except he introduced himself.

"Rachel Wilson," she responded quietly, shaking his hand and meeting his dark eyes. She found them warm and friendly and this confused her. She glanced to Lacey who offered no smile in the presence of this man but her sapphire gaze told the blonde that everything was okay.

Vinnie's brow wrinkled slightly as he tried to recall the name and its connection to him.

"Briargate," Lacey supplied when it was obvious her superior wasn't going to come up with it quickly.

"Ah," he nodded, remembering now, "If you'll please excuse us, Ms. Wilson." He inclined his head slightly in her direction and then stepped back towards the room from which he'd emerged, knowing that Lacey and the others would be right behind him.

When the dark woman looked to her companion, she saw the beginning of worry in the emerald depths. Rachel glanced from her friend to the tall dark man still standing in the anteroom, waiting. The rest of the team had already gone inside.

Lacey stepped forward and touched the young woman's arm gently. "Just wait here for me, you're safe. I'll be right back." Her eyes turned from ice blue to gentle violet and Rachel nodded dumbly.

It seemed like hours she waited there, sipping coffee, flipping through inane magazines and watching 'Berto watch her. Finally, her tall dark companion emerged from the office with Vinnie on her heels. The rest of the men were right behind and though none of them were outright smiling, neither did they look like they feared for their lives.

****

They were silent until all five of them piled back into the Grand Cherokee and Lacey maneuvered the vehicle away.

"Well?" Rachel asked at last, unable to hold her questions any longer.

"Our threats to Wheatridge apparently worked and they have no interest in pursuing Sunny further," Lacey began, referring to the conflicts that had happened since the horsenapping. Wheatridge had known the culprits but since their ventures had been less than legal as well, they had little to stand on. Lacey responded with some harsh words and well placed threats. "And Vinnie's agreed that we can keep Sunny on our property as long as we don't geld him and Briargate maintains breeding rights," she continued, knowing, though welcome information, this wasn't the question her young lover wanted answered.

Rachel grinned at this news, even though the dark woman had counted on it and a barn was already being built behind the backyard's fence. Luckily, Lacey's property was zoned for horses.

"They found Benny," Lacey continued, noticing Rachel's grin fade.

"And?"

The backseat seemed to grumble as the men muttered to each other. Lacey hesitated. "You don't really want to know, love."

"Who did it? Your side or theirs?"

"Ours," Lacey answered honestly. The husky man had been found hiding just outside of Chicago and had been disposed of after questioning. What Lacey didn't admit was that she somewhat regretted it hadn't been at her hands.

Benny had revealed Oz as his accomplice in poisoning the Briargate horses for profit. He'd even described how he'd pureed the bracken fern and made the mineral blocks with sugar so the horses would eat more of it.

"What about the rest, Lacey?" Rachel glanced into the backseat to see three wide grins and she knew it was good news.

"We're all free to walk. He asked that we wait until Kalzar is finished and that we stagger our departures so we can train incoming before we go. I'll be the last. Rico's the first."

Rachel nearly screeched her joy and the whole vehicle cringed with the ear-shattering sound. The young blonde lunged across the front and hugged her partner awkwardly.

Lacey laughed. "You're gonna make me have an accident, Raich. We can do this in a minute."

Rachel disengaged her hold and reached back to squeeze each of the men's hands in turn. Then she settled back in her seat and belted herself in. "How about lunch?" she asked excitedly.

Lacey nodded her agreement as she cast her glance sideways to the other woman's fair profile. Her green eyes blazed with pleasure. God willing, they'd live long happy lives raising Rachel's daughter.

Making Strides

Prologue

The early December wind was frigid and biting as it cut across the small crowd, lifting long coats and dancing with the snow around and between the mourners' feet. The casket was settled sturdily on a stand next to where the grave would be dug when the ground had thawed enough.

The small group bent their heads in prayer as the graveside service continued. Muffled sobs could be heard throughout the mourners, but one woman stood silently still, right hand stuffed in the pocket of her leather overcoat, the other holding the small hand of the child at her side. The child was crying, using their joined hands to wipe at the mucous and tears on her face, her other hand also being held firmly by the blonde woman on her left side.

Lacey dropped ice blue eyes to regard her wet-cheeked partner and the sniffling child. She felt again the odd mixture of affection for these two important people in her life and the caged feeling of entrapment.

Molly looked up at her as the service ended, her eyes worried.

"What is it?" Lacey asked, gentling her voice for the young girl and kneeling beside her.

The blonde child glanced from the dark woman's face to the large casket a scant few yards in front of her. "They can't leave him like that," she whispered. "He can't stay there. He needs to go in the ground." She was starting to tremble, her small frame wracked with sorrow.

Lacey looked over the girl's shoulder to Rachel, who had knelt down as well, meeting the smaller woman's misty green eyes wet with tears. She looked back to Molly. "Honey." Lacey wiped at her cheeks, framed the small face in her large tanned hands. "Remember we talked about this. The ground is frozen so they need to put him over in that building," Lacey removed a hand to point across the graveyard to the small stone mausoleum, "until they can dig the grave here."

Molly's lower lip trembled and she tried to catch it between even white teeth before continuing. "When we visit him, will it be here?"

"Yes, baby," the dark woman assured her, smoothing back fine blonde bangs. "This is where we'll bring him flowers and tell him how we're doing."

"Will he hear us?"

"I think so," Lacey said softly, pulling the small girl into a warm embrace. She again met her partner's eyes before closing her own and placing her lips on the child's head. "Come on, let's go say our goodbyes."

Lacey picked up the girl and held her in her arms, even though she really was too big to be carried in this manner. Together, the three of them walked silently to the grieving widow and two young children. The families had grown close since the team had left Vinnie and Molly had come to live with the two women permanently. Lacey, Rachel, and Molly offered hugs and kind words and assistance if needed. Then they went to the raised casket and told Bernard goodbye before turning and making their way to the parked Grand Cherokee behind the small crowd.

Chapter 1

Lacey stepped out onto the balcony through the sliding glass door in the master bedroom. During the summer she'd spent many long hours here, reading, thinking, watching her young lover ride. The balcony provided an excellent vantage point for observation across the backyard and over the privacy fence into the small arena beyond.

Today the wind was icy cold as it reached through her sweatshirt and jeans. The yard beneath her held remnants of last week's snow, well tracked by dog and child prints. There was a melting snowman in the far corner of the yard. His listing head wore one of Lacey's baseball caps. She grinned.

The tall woman wrapped her arms around her torso, breathing in the cold air and pulsing out breaths of vapor. Even from here she could see that Rachel and the horse did the same with their breaths.

There was a portable CD player set up near the barn and Lacey could hear the deep bass of Eurythmic's Sweet Dreams echoing across the arena and into the yard. Rachel always worked to music, and it was almost always a heavy loud beat. She'd said it helped her concentrate, that if she could match Sunny's strides to the beats in the songs then she'd accomplished something. George had burned a CD that played her favorite riding songs for her on his computer. She treasured the gift and used it often.

Though Lacey didn't understand the finer points of what her lover was doing, she admired the artistry of it. Horse and rider moved smoothly about the ring and the dark woman knew if she were closer she would hear Rachel intermittently making kissing or clicking sounds, often whispering praise, always singing to the music in between. Her fair face lit up in a grin when the stallion behaved properly, though Lacey's untrained eye rarely noticed any difference in his stride or his appearance.

Lost in thought, she watched them. Her vision tunneling to the woman and the horse. She recalled easily the many months of love and commitment between them, the raising of Rachel's daughter, the life now in this large house that had once been so empty. But still, she felt herself backing away from it all. It was so much: this instant family and its demanding needs. Her young beautiful lover offered her heart so easily but unintentionally managed to take as much as she gave, leaving Lacey bewildered and disconcerted. She was in uncharted territory.

She had never in her life lived for anyone but herself, until she met Rachel: emerald eyes and reeling spirit bundled into a small package of open affection. Her life had changed with the first touch, the first smile, and had led her to this place of uncertainty. She balanced precariously on a plank between a life she'd hated but grown accustomed to and a life she loved but feared because of its lack of familiarity. Had she gone down the wrong path? Should she have let Rachel be?

Because now they were in danger and she had only herself to blame.

The dark woman ran a trembling hand through her hair and scratched the back of her neck. *I will not go to your funeral, too, Rachel. I won't do it.*

Her watch alarm went off, the beeping reminding her it was time to pick Molly up from school.

Lacey sighed and stepped back inside, sliding the heavy door closed behind her. Though the barrier sealed the wind outside, it couldn't protect Lacey from the coldness she felt growing inside.

As much as the dark woman tried to deny it, having this child and her mother in her life had definitely been worth the trouble. She was a better person for it.

Now if she could only keep them alive.

****

Rachel nudged her heels into Sunny's sides, jiggling the reins gently and relaxing her tailbone back until it looked like she was almost slouching. This dramatic shift of weight caused Sunny to drop onto his haunches and come off the bit even as he moved forward in a trot and held steady contact with his rider's hands.

"Good boy," she murmured, releasing the reins slightly as his reward. She trotted him in a large figure eight, sitting the rough beat with practiced skill. "Sweet dreams are made of this ... who am I to disagree," she sang under her breath, oblivious to the cold or the blue eyes watching her from the bedroom balcony.

"Gimme," she whispered, jiggling the inside rein and rattling the snaffle gently until Sunny acquiesced and curved his neck inside. The motion caused his whole body to bend into a supple turn and Rachel grinned. "Good for you."

She was proud of him. The young stallion had shown an aptitude that far surpassed the racetrack he'd grown up on.

He was proving to be a calm hunter mount with ground eating strides and silk smooth gaits. Though still green, he responded well to gentle persuasion and rarely blew up out of frustration.

She halted him squarely in the middle of the arena, applying calf pressure and bit pressure to keep him contained and equally balanced on all four legs. They stood silently this way for several long seconds before Rachel released him. The young stallion heaved a sigh of relief and relaxed.

"Everybody's lookin' for somethin'," Rachel murmured, patting the broad bay shoulder firmly. "Some of them want to use you." She dropped her stirrups and slid down from his back, flipping the reins over his ears. "Some of them want to get used by you," she continued to sing as she led him back to the barn. "Some of them want to abuse you, some of them want to be abused."

Sunny pushed into her small body, dropping his head to wipe his sweaty poll on her shoulder.

"Unh unh, ya big lug," she corrected him gently. "Back off, bucko." The blonde shoved at the large head and Sunny resigned himself to plodding calmly beside his rider.

Having untacked horses countless times, and this one more than any other, it was a rote task and her mind wandered while accomplishing it. Rachel thought of the funeral and Bernard. She considered her lover's attitude of late, which was even more stoic than her normal somber persona. She didn't understand the change in demeanor, but also didn't want to dwell on it, so her mind quickly traveled on to the upcoming holidays.

****

Rachel pushed a blonde tendril behind her ear with the thick glove she wore before hefting the rake again and starting back in on the stall. Sunny stomped at the closed door from the outside where she'd put him after brushing him down and she yelled at him to be patient.

"Good advice." She heard the dark voice behind her and nearly jumped out of her skin before turning to look at her partner leaning over the inside half door.

"What's up?" Rachel asked, setting the rake against the wall and stepping closer to the dark woman.

"Just got Molly from school. We're going to do some Christmas shopping. You need anything?"

"Today right now? Or for Christmas?" Rachel grinned easily, loving the holiday and the spirit surrounding it.

Lacey returned the smile, an expression that had become incredibly rare in these last few weeks, especially since Bernard's accident. "Let's stick to today for now. You have class tonight?"

"Yeah, I need to start getting ready for it." The blonde nodded, pushing another troublesome tendril back. "Prep for next week's final. I'm not sure how late we'll be."

Lacey nodded, watching her partner with those unsettling ice blue eyes.

"Molly have homework?" Rachel asked.

"She has a spelling test tomorrow and some reading vocabulary."

"That's right. I forgot about the test. I promised her I'd help her study." The small rider cringed, knowing she couldn't miss her own class tonight.

"I can do that." The dark woman nodded again. She'd taken her role in Molly's life quite seriously and easily picked up the slack when Rachel was in class or unable to help with homework. "Anything from the store?"

"Nah. I'll pick up some milk on the way home from class."

"Great. See you tonight." Lacey turned and started to walk down the wide aisle and out of the barn.

"Lace?" Rachel called after quite a bit of hesitation.

The dark woman turned back, raised an eyebrow.

"Are you okay? Really?"

Lacey wrinkled her brow in thought, as if considering a more complex answer, before she simply nodded. "Yeah. Great."

Something was very wrong with the ex-mafia crony. Things had been going extremely well since they'd moved in together, bringing Molly home permanently towards the end of the summer and enrolling her in the fourth grade. Rachel had started taking college courses towards her bachelor's degree. Lacey had opened up a network security contracting firm with Rico, George, and Bernard. Although George had ventured out on his own a month or more previous, it had been a mutual parting to the best of Rachel's knowledge. Then Bernard had died a week ago in a car accident. Since that final incident, the dark woman had been withdrawn and angry. Her moods were unpredictable and she usually worked late and left early, seemingly avoiding the rest of the household.

"Are you sure?" Rachel asked, pushing more than she should, but uncertain where she stood right now with her tall partner. They'd not been very close since the accident.

"Yeah." She flashed a smile, shrugged her shoulders. She knew she was pushing them away. She also knew she had been very difficult to live with these past few days.

"I love you," Rachel said softly, reaching out to pick her rake up again and get back to work.

The smile on Lacey's face seemed to fade before being replaced by a more plastic one. "Love you, too, Raich." Then she disappeared, leaving Rachel to fight off her tears as she finished mucking the stall.

****

Lacey was in the office, typing away on the computer when Rachel got home. She said hello to Karma and peeked in on her sleeping daughter before venturing into the large office.

"Hey," she said softly, smiling into the blue eyes that greeted her.

"Hey yourself."

"How was shopping?"

The dark woman shrugged, leaned back in her swivel chair to stretch out long arms above her head. "S'okay. Not too crowded yet. I think we're done with yours." She grinned.

"Did you tell my little snitch what you want for when I take her shopping?" Rachel teased gently.

Lacey laughed out loud. "She was working me pretty good. I gave her some ideas."

They watched each other silently for several long moments and then each spoke at the same time.

"How was class?"

"Is she ready for her spelling test?"

Rachel smiled, the awkwardness almost painful. "Class was fine. I feel ready for next week."

"Good. Spelling went well. She's a smart little girl."

Rachel nodded agreement. "She feed the horses?"

"Yeah. And Karma."

"Okay." More silence. "I'm gonna head to bed and do some reading. You coming soon?"

Lacey gestured to the computer. "I have a while yet. Don't wait up for me."

Rachel nodded and silently made her retreat. She'd been asleep for hours when Lacey finally crawled under the covers next to her.

Chapter 2

The blowup was inevitable, so Rachel shouldn't have been as surprised as she was when it actually happened. It was two weeks after Bernard's funeral and a week and a half before Christmas when she was standing in the kitchen preparing dinner.

The latest phase in Lacey's distance had been running herself ragged at night. After one such expedition, she entered the kitchen preceded by Karma, who trotted right by Rachel, tongue dragging on the ground, to go find her water bowl. Lacey liberated a bottled water from the refrigerator.

"Dinner will be ready in about an hour," Rachel said without turning around.

"Not hungry," Lacey responded. Another new habit had been skipping meals with Molly and Rachel and working in the office instead.

"Sit with us? Have something to drink anyway?" Rachel prompted, too afraid to look at her partner's face so concentrating instead on chopping the vegetables and not her fingers.

"Busy."

If Rachel had learned anything from nearly a year with the tall dark woman, it was to face things head on and not skirt the issues. Why her partner was doing it now was beyond her, so she took it upon herself to force the confrontation and she turned around, facing the sweat-covered woman. "What's wrong lately? And don't you dare say nothing."

Blue eyes widened in mild shock as she took another swig of water, seemingly savoring the cool liquid. She shrugged broad shoulders. "Don't know. Out of sorts."

"Is it Bernie?"

"Nah."

Silence as they watched each other. "Is it me or Molly?"

Lacey shook her head wordlessly, looking very much like a trapped animal hoping for an escape route to open up.

"Is it the funeral? Did that worry you? Maybe if you just talked about it, worked it out with us..." Rachel ventured slowly and knew immediately by the fire in her lover's eyes that she'd gone too far.

"Dammit, Rachel," she growled. "Everything is not solved by a good cry and a carton of chocolate ice cream."

"I know that, Lace," Rachel said softly. "I just want to help you. I don't like how we've been lately."

"Sorry. Didn't want to mess up your perfect little world by being a bitch," Lacey barked, slamming the water bottle on the counter. She realized her anger was completely disproportionate to the discussion at hand, but she found herself unable to control it.

"Lace, c'mon," Rachel cajoled gently, putting down the vegetables and knife, taking a step closer.

"Fuck you!" the ex-mafia crony growled, appearing every bit the frightening woman of years past.

Rachel blinked at her in momentary shock. Though she'd seen Lacey's anger on many occasions, she'd never had the privilege of being the target of it.

"Maybe I just need to be alone. Didja think of that? Maybe I don't need you pestering me or a little girl following me around. Maybe I need—"

"Do you want us to go?" Rachel interrupted, her own anger rising even as some part of her mind wandered back to what kind of jobs she could apply for to support her and her daughter. One thing was certain, she wasn't giving up Molly again. Another part of her was breaking at the thought that Lacey didn't want her anymore.

"Something needs to change. I'm not a damn babysitter. That wasn't part of the deal—" Her tirade stopped mid-sentence and the sapphire eyes that had been blazing with fury a moment before dulled to ashamed guilt.

Rachel's own eyes widened with realization as she spun around to look behind her at the doorway leading into the dining room. Molly stood uncertainly with one hand on the doorjamb and her weight shifting from foot to foot.

Rachel stepped back so she might better be able to look at both of them. She knew it was up to her to diffuse this situation. Her dark lover was on the brink of something that Rachel couldn't understand or fathom and her own daughter was very close to tears, if her trembling lower lip was any indication.

She extended a hand to each of them. "Okay, we need to talk."

But Molly turned and ran through the dining room and up the spiral stairs, her sobs audible as she fled.

"Shit," muttered Rachel as she turned back to her lover who, for the first time in months, looked like she was going to cry. "I gotta go to her."

Lacey nodded dumbly. "Raich, I didn't ... I said ... I love her so much. And you."

"Oh, baby," Rachel murmured. "I know. It's okay." She really did understand that Lacey was on a short fuse and, though she'd said some pretty hurtful things, there was a good chance she hadn't meant them. It was, after all, Rachel who had pushed even after seeing the dark woman's anger.

She didn't have a lot of time to consider all these thoughts as she left the kitchen to follow her daughter up the stairs and to her room.

Rachel entered slowly, surrounded, by moonlit darkness, but so used to the bright cheery bedroom that she could picture it even now in its shadows and shrouds. On the walls there were horse and dog posters. There was even a picture of Rachel and Molly in the winner's circle with one of Vinnie's colts. That photograph was the child's pride and joy and Lacey'd had it mounted and framed beautifully. Shelves lined the walls about a foot down from the ceiling and held prancing model horses, each one with a specific place and name. Lacey had helped her build stables and pens for them that were stored under the bed. Rachel had stayed up late sewing blankets, halters, coolers, and leg wraps. It was a room that shouted little girl all the way from the horse bedside lamp to the dolls on the frilly pink pillow sham.

But now the dolls were strewn on the floor and Molly had wrapped herself around her favorite teddy bear where she cried into his worn brown fur with heaving sobs. Rachel crawled onto the soft queen bed beside her and covered the shuddering body with her own.

"Easy," she murmured. "Slow down or you're going to be sick, baby."

"Sorry," she heaved, nearly hyperventilating. "Lace ... I ... must be bad for her not to love me." Each syllable was strangled out between sobs and Rachel felt her heart tear at the words. "I ruined it Mama. Without me she would love you."

"Oh, baby," Rachel whispered, rocking the slight form and stroking the little girl's trembling back. "Lacey loves us just like she always has. You're just like her own daughter.

If anything happened to Lacey and me, you would still get to visit her."

"She said ... babysitting. Said I followed her ..." The heaves were getting worse and Rachel knew she'd have to take the girl to the toilet pretty soon if she didn't calm down.

"Molly, honey, Lacey is really hurting inside. Bernard was one of her best friends. She doesn't know how to say goodbye to him. Sometimes when you hurt so much inside, you say things you don't mean just to try and get rid of the pain. You say hurtful things because you want someone else to feel as bad as you do. Lacey was trying to hurt me, not you. She wanted me to share her sadness but she didn't know how to do that."

"But—"

"No buts, baby. She loves you very much. I know you heard her say some bad things, but she didn't mean them, believe me. Lacey loves you."

The words seemed to work eventually and the sobs calmed but remained. Then Molly turned over and captured her mother in a fierce hug, holding her tightly, burying her wet face in Rachel's neck.

"I love her, too, Mama. I never want to say goodbye to her like we had to to Bernard."

Rachel stroked her child's back and smiled that they should share that same emotion. "Not for a long time, Molly."

They stayed that way in silence for several more beats. "What say we lay here and calm down for awhile, then we get cleaned up and go downstairs and have dinner with Lacey. Are you up to that?"

"I think so. Hold me awhile longer, Mama?"

"I'll hold you forever, sweetheart."

****

Lacey stood stunned for several long moments after her lover's departure. *Oh my God, what have I done?* She'd been battling with herself for weeks because half of her wanted to push Rachel and Molly away to safety while the other half wanted to hold them near and protect them. She'd been hiding the threats from her younger partner for the better part of a month, but she had to admit she'd all but lost it when Bernard had been killed. She'd known from the moment she'd found out that it was no accident. And George hadn't left to start his own company, he'd run away to protect himself and his family.

The team should have known it wouldn't be so easy to walk away from organized crime. Maybe they had suspected it, but had decided it was worth the risk. Lacey'd dragged the fair-haired woman and her beautiful daughter along with her on her journey of leaving behind the only life she'd known. Now the people Lacey loved most in the world were in danger as well.

Gathering her senses and trying hard not to wallow in guilt, the dark woman fought both the urge to run out the door and disappear and the urge to climb the steps to hold the little girl. She knew Rachel was better at these kinds of things and would smooth it over as best she could. It was in Lacey's best interest not to go up there and insert her foot into her mouth ... again.

So she finished chopping the vegetables Rachel had left and bagged and refrigerated them all, plus the other fixings that had been on the counter. Then she cleaned up the remaining dishes and called for a pizza before finally going upstairs to take a long-awaited shower.

Lacey was barely under the hot stream long enough to soap up and rinse off the dried sticky sweat before she was winding long dark hair into a wet braid and pulling on flannel pants and a T-shirt. Then she was walking down the plush carpet of the hallway to Molly's room.

She stood just inside the door, watching the profile of her lover and the little girl, wrapped tightly around each other. At first she thought they'd fallen asleep until she caught a glint of green eyes reflecting the gentle moonlight coming through the window.

"Molly," Rachel whispered, nudging at her daughter's still form. She'd known the little girl was still awake but in that hazy exhausted state that always follows a hard cry. "Lacey's here."

Molly moved from her mother and turned to look at the dark woman standing in the doorway. She wiped at her tears with the back of her hand before crawling across the bed and landing lightly on the floor. Then she took a few tentative steps towards the woman.

Unable to handle the little girl's uncertainty, Lacey stepped forward and swooped her into the air, crushing her in an embrace. She felt the thin bare legs wrap around her midriff and the little girl's hot breath on the side of her neck.

"I love you, Molly. I said horrible, horrible things and I didn't mean them. I was scared and sad and worried."

Molly clung to this woman as if a remora feeding on the skin of a shark. Her whole being was concentrating on the effort it took to absorb the warm body she'd latched on to. She couldn't speak in response, but Lacey knew from the deathgrip that she was being forgiven. It was something she hadn't deserved and certainly wouldn't have expected. She'd said plenty of hateful things in her life, meant less than half of them probably. Had Rachel been the only one to hear the words they would have sparred for a few more minutes and then backed to neutral corners with minor wounds.

The walls had ears. They were raising a small child together and it had been completely irresponsible of her to revert to the darkness she'd hidden so well.

The upstairs speakers announced the chiming of the doorbell and Rachel rose from her position on the bed to glance quizzically at her lover.

"Pizza," Lacey explained concisely and Rachel nodded, moving past the two-headed, four-legged creature in the doorway.

She stopped before leaving to place a kiss on each head. "We're okay," she promised them. "We just need to talk through some things and understand each other."

The other two nodded mutely and Rachel left them to their few moments of silence as she went downstairs to find the checkbook and relieve the delivery guy of their dinner.

Rachel could tell that Lacey wasn't going to reveal anything over dinner. The dark woman's mood was somber and resolute, her sapphire eyes reflected guilt when she glanced at either of them.

Molly, showing the natural mood swings she'd always been prone to, bounced back rather quickly. She chatted animatedly about a kid at school and how he'd talked back to the teacher. She was prompted through the story by Rachel's inquiries while Lacey watched the two silently.

It was hours later before Rachel had a chance to get Lacey alone. They'd put Molly to bed with Karma tucked neatly over her feet and said their goodnights.

"Come to the barn with me?" Rachel asked her lover gently, casting eyes in her direction and trying to gauge the dark woman's present mood.

"Sounds good," Lacey gave in easily. She knew they needed to discuss things and the barn was a good place to do it, in case the conversation became heated again.

The night air was brisk and cold as they walked through the backyard and opened the gate out the back, allowing them access to the barn beyond. The horses whinnied when they heard the yard gate open and close.

"You already ate," Rachel called back to them, stepping into the structure behind her partner. The barn had four box stalls on one side, the other being taken up by a tack room and hay storage. Though not heated, the several tons of hay and three warm horse bodies lent to keeping the building bearable. Rachel shrugged out of her winter jacket and took a seat on a convenient hay bale. Lacey did the same.

Both women silently watched the horses watching them. There were three right now. Sunny had moved in to stay, but occasionally had visiting mares from the main barn at Briargate as was the case now. The third horse was Molly's Morgan gelding, bought several months ago from a training barn near Rochester. Molly had wanted a mare but Rachel decided the logistics of keeping a stallion and a mare in the same barn year round just weren't worth the trouble. The little girl had been happy regardless and Jester had come home to stay as an early Christmas present of sorts.

Rachel smiled at the Morgan's inquisitive gaze and bright eyes. He was typical to the breed in his continuous desire for handouts.

"So," Lacey said at last, heaving a sigh and smiling slightly. Sensitive chats had never been her strong suit though she was getting better since Rachel had become such an important part of her life.

"Yup," Rachel responded. She watched her partner quietly for several more moments, noticing her lips were drawn thin and her jaw clenched and unclenched rhythmically. "If I asked you some questions, would you answer them?"

"Calmly?" Lacey inserted wryly, turning to the younger woman and raising a dark eyebrow clear into her bangs.

Rachel smiled gently, shrugged one shoulder. "Or not, I can take it." She left the rest unspoken, knowing it wasn't necessary to discuss the argument that had happened earlier and the danger of saying hurtful things when a third party might be around.

Lacey nodded slowly, grateful for what had gone unsaid. She was still kicking herself for losing control of her emotions. "Shoot."

"Is Bernard's death bothering you?"

"Yes." Lacey nodded honestly, turning her attention away from seeking green eyes towards the towering hay behind them. She remembered the hot day in August when they'd filled this barn. George, Bernard, two workers from the farm where they'd bought it, Rachel, and Lacey had slaved the afternoon away taking the tons of hay from the flatbed and stacking it in here. The horses had drooled with hope and Molly had hopped from bale to bale and climbed the mountain with abandon until they yelled at her to get down and clean the stalls. Lacey smiled fondly at the memory.

"Are you feeling mortal at having lost such a close friend or is there more to it?"

"More." Lacey met the woman's eyes.

A year ago the monosyllabic answers would have bothered the younger woman, but she took it in stride now. She nodded, pursing her lips in thought as she considered her next questions. "Do you feel trapped here with us? With a regular job?"

Lacey rubbed the back of her neck and stood up to begin pacing. "No. Well ... that's not it, though."

"Go on."

"I do feel a little trapped, you know? I'm not used to being responsible for a family and worrying about things like who'll be home when and dinner and homework. Grocery shopping."

Rachel swallowed back her fear. She needed to know these answers, even though she didn't want to hear them. "You've been alone a long time," she allowed softly. "It's a big adjustment."

Lacey shrugged, stopped to play with a bridle hanging on the tack room door. "You were alone, too."

Rachel smiled. "Yeah, but I didn't want to be. You were by choice."

"This is everything you've always wanted?" Lacey moved one hand to take in their surroundings.

The blonde considered the question for several long moments. She knew what the answer was: she'd never been happier until Bernie's death. It was the family she'd always wanted, horses in her backyard, classes that challenged yet rewarded her, a lover who was attentive and brilliant and warm, and her little girl living with them full time. But Lacey had to make decisions based on her own wants and needs, not those of the people around her.

"I'm really happy, Lace," she answered at last, realizing it didn't answer the question directly, but hoping it was enough at the moment.

Lacey nodded, took up pacing again.

Rachel watched for several more silent moments before she took a deep breath and cleared her throat. "Lace, I know you love Molly as if she were your own." She waited just the split second it took for the dark-haired woman to nod her agreement. "I want you to know that ... regardless of what may happen to us ... you're a big part of Molly's life. And I'd want you to be able to still see her, if you wanted. I'd like you to, in fact. You two are good for each other."

The other woman turned and gaped with wide eyes and dropped chin. It suddenly dawned on her where this conversation was headed and she didn't like the route or the destination much at all. She recalled quickly her words in the kitchen: Rachel's questions and her own heated responses. "I didn't—"

The blonde interrupted her with a raised hand. "If you want us to leave for awhile, if you need some space, I can do that. Molly and I can find some place to live ... I think the horses would have to stay or go back to Briargate. But I think—"

"Stop." Lacey finally shook herself out of her stupor and interrupted the younger woman. Jade eyes looked up at her from the hands they'd been studying. "That's not what I want." Then fear gripped her. "Is that what you want?"

"No." Rachel shook her head adamantly. "But I want you to be happy, Lace. I know you never thought in a million years you'd have a family and a dog and be worried about spelling tests or math homework. You never thought you'd be taking a nine-year-old to dental appointments or arranging your schedule around her needs. It was too much to ask of you. And I can tell that you're not happy."

Lacey wrinkled her brow, confused again. "I want this, Raich. I love you and that little girl. Sometimes it's overwhelming and sometimes I get pretty scared or I worry too much. I'm so busy trying to figure out how to protect both of you and I think that if it weren't for me, you wouldn't need protection."

"Protection? From what, Lace?" Rachel had the eerie feeling they were finally getting close to the heart of the matter.

Lacey took a deep breath, met her lover's gentle gaze, and exhaled slowly. "Bernard wasn't an accident."

Rachel chuckled with relief. She was thinking Lacey was going to drop a bomb on her. "Of course it was, sweetheart. Freak accident. Hit and run outside of the hardware store. Police thought the driver may have been drunk. Is that what you're worried about?"

The dark woman moved like lightening across the hay-littered floor to kneel in front of her smaller companion and grasp her hands in an almost painful grip. "No, Raich. No. They killed him."

Her reassuring smile faded. This wasn't Lacey being paranoid. There was more going on here. "Who," she choked slightly, had to clear her throat. "Who killed him?"

"The same person who was sending threats to George. Who forced him to leave."

"George? Threats?"

"Yeah." The dark head bobbed in a solemn nod.

"Now's not a good time to ask why you were keeping secrets, huh?" the blonde asked slowly, knowing she should be angry that she was hearing this belatedly. But she was really too confused to pursue the other emotions right now.

"No. But I'm sure it'll come up later," Lacey said softly, finding she still had her dry sense of humor.

Rachel considered this new information very sluggishly, running it through the cogwheels of her mind until the obvious clicked into place. "You've had threats, too." It wasn't a question but Lacey nodded anyway. "What?!" Rachel leapt to her feet, pulling her hands away from Lacey's and taking several steps away. "Who? What kind of threats?"

"I don't know who. It's an enemy of Vinnie's, I think. We've been going through old records trying to narrow it down. But there are so many. Maybe it's someone who is feuding with Vinnie now and they're just cleaning up loose ends."

"Have you talked to Vinnie?" Rachel calmed slightly and stepped back to Lacey to capture her large hands again.

"Not yet." Still holding hands, Lacey smoothed the back of her fingers along the fair woman's cheek. "I didn't want to. I didn't want to have to go back there."

"But?" Rachel prompted, feeling the other woman was leaving some words unsaid.

"It's time to do that."

"They killed him?"

She nodded slowly, watching the green eyes fill with tears.

"What did the threats say, Lace?"

The dark woman quirked her lips into a fair representation of a smirk. "You don't want to know, really."

"About me and Molly?"

"Yeah."

Thank goodness realization doesn't carry a lot of physical weight behind it, because it would have knocked Rachel over when it hit her. "You wanted us to be with you, but were afraid that being with you was endangering our lives. You were trying to push us away..." She trailed off, watching the confirmation of her words in the sapphire eyes opposite her.

"But I couldn't in the end. Even if it was better for you. I didn't want to be alone again ... I didn't want to be without you." The words were nearly forced from the dark woman's mouth. Admitting needs had never been a strong point for her, but she knew, without a doubt, all of that had changed when this young woman had bounced into her life. They'd shared such intense emotions that first month, shared thoughts and feelings Lacey had never let herself voice before. In the months since then, the darker woman had been more verbally withdrawn but every kind action and every smoldering look let Rachel know that she was wanted.

It was nice to hear it sometimes, too. The young blonde stepped forward to wrap her companion in strong arms. "We're right here."

"I thought maybe I could do it. After Bernie's funeral, when I knew they were serious." The words were in monotone as they tumbled forth, the dam having shattered beneath the force of her need to finally get it out.

"I'm glad you didn't," Rachel whispered, knowing her words weren't nearly as important as her touch and her love.

"And tonight I thought ... I was so scared and worried. It's been building up. I just snapped. I lost control and yelled at you."

"It doesn't matter."

"I thought that if I hurt you enough you would leave. And it would be easier for you to hate me. For you to leave me."

Though stunned by the admissions flowing into her ear,

Rachel continued her gentle murmuring. "I could never hate you."

"I shouldn't have said those things. As hard as the instant family has been at times, I don't regret it. The rewards outweigh any trouble."

"I know you didn't mean them."

"Does Molly know?" Silent tears tracked their way down Lacey's olive-toned skin as she asked the question.

"She does. It hurt her a lot, but I think she understands. Just make an extra effort to tell her how much she means to you. She's pretty forgiving."

Lacey nodded, crushing the smaller body to her. "If you weren't in my heart, it would collapse from being empty."

Rachel smiled, squeezed her lover back. "We won't let that happen. You ready to go inside?"

"Yeah." She wiped at her tears and moved out of the embrace where she'd regained some strength. "I love you," she whispered sincerely, her ice blue eyes reflecting some of her shock at being so easily forgiven.

"I love you, too, Lace. C'mon." They shrugged their jackets back on and walked to the house hand in hand.

Chapter 3

It was the Thursday before Molly's Christmas break and it had taken nearly all of Lacey's patience and control to get the small girl ready for school and into the Grand Cherokee. Lacey had been taking Molly to school and picking her up since well before Bernie's death. And though her lover had noticed and questioned her, she'd just shrugged and said she didn't like the idea of Molly standing at a cold bus stop. Rachel had accepted the answer readily enough and thought it touching that her partner and daughter spent that time together. This morning, Molly's reluctance was borne of her readiness for the two weeks without homework or tests. She'd dragged her feet until Lacey'd nearly picked her up and tossed her in the running vehicle, driving the few short blocks to the private school she and Rachel had picked out.

That had been another debate between the two women in the summer. Lacey'd wanted Molly to have the best opportunities and when she'd researched the public school district their zoning fell into, she'd been disappointed with the results. That was when she'd started looking into private schools. The one she'd liked best was close and academically sound. Rachel, though very much interested in the idea of a school that would better attend to her daughter's needs, had been loathe to spend the kind of money the private tuition demanded. It had taken a lot of fast talking on Lacey's part to get Rachel to submit the application and then attend the ensuing interviews until the girl was accepted. After that, Lacey had been sure to intercept and pay the bills before Rachel had a chance to look at them.

Now, nearing lunchtime, Lacey was cooking something for Rachel. Her own business had been slow during this holiday month and she'd had time to be home a lot, though she'd not taken advantage of it up until these last few days, after their talk in the barn. She enjoyed getting Molly ready for school, most mornings having been easier than this one, and letting her lover study. Rachel had been upstairs preparing for a final since late last night.

"Raich, honey?" Lacey called up the spiral stairs. "Lunch is almost ready. Come down and eat something before you go."

When Rachel entered the kitchen several minutes later, she looked weary and exhausted.

"You should have slept some," Lacey reprimanded gently, steering the blonde to a chair at the kitchen table then presenting her with soup and a sandwich.

"Too much to study."

"You'll be tired for your exam," Lacey said reasonably, filling a large mug with coffee and fixing it to her lover's preference of sugar and cream. When she sat the mug down, it barely hit the wood of the table before it was in Rachel's hands. The smaller woman chugged the coffee like it was necessary to sustain life. Lacey smirked. "Would you like your caffeine intravenously, love?"

"Smart ass," Rachel murmured before beginning her meal.

Lacey sat opposite her, taking a bite out of her own sandwich. "You'll be fine. You know this stuff a lot better than you give yourself credit for."

"I wish I didn't have to take the sciences, too, to get a literature degree," the blonde mumbled around a mouthful of ham and cheese.

"They want you to be well-rounded. You'll be fine."

"The professor is letting us use an index card with formulas on it. I didn't think I could write so small."

The dark-haired woman grinned. "But will you be able to read it as bleary eyed as you are?"

Rachel nodded, sparing her partner a smile. "Yeah. How was Molly this morning? Sounded like she was giving you a hard time."

Lacey shrugged, sipping at her coffee with much less gusto than her blonde companion. "She was okay. I had to light a fire under her though, to get her going. She's all starry eyed for the holidays, doesn't want to be in school."

"I still need to get that game for her we'd talked about. Maybe I can find it today after the exam."

Lacey nodded. "Raich, do you think she's happy at school?"

The blonde stopped with the spoon halfway to her mouth and cocked her head, wondering what may have brought on such a question. "I think so, why?"

"Does she ever talk to you about friends or doing things after school? She never has anyone over."

Rachel thought about that for a moment before shaking her head. She hadn't really realized that a child her age should be doing those things. This was her first stab at full time parenting, after all. "Her grades are good."

The darker woman shrugged broad shoulders. "So. That's not everything and you know it. She should have friends."

"Maybe she does and just doesn't talk about them."

Lacey snorted her laughter. "Are you kidding, Raich? That little girl doesn't shut up. Why would we not hear about friends?"

Rachel conceded the point with a grin. "Well, what about that boy she was talking about the other night? The one who talked back to the teacher and got in trouble?"

"I think that was a factual reporting, love."

"Okay. Then how do we help her?" Rachel scraped the rest of the soup off the bottom of her bowl before returning to her coffee mug and emptying the contents.

"I don't know. Is there a pony club or something she could join? Youth riding groups? She's really good at that and she has her own horse, maybe that would help?"

Rachel nodded in thought, searching her mind for anything she'd heard along those lines. "I'll work on that." She got up and rinsed out her bowl in the sink before placing it in the dishwasher. Her plate followed and then she retrieved Lacey's dishes to do the same. "After this test."

"Deal."

"Thanks for lunch, I feel better now."

"Good." Lacey came up to the smaller woman and wrapped her in long arms. "You'll do fine. Go kick some butt."

The blonde grinned and squeezed the hard body tightly against her. "Thanks. See you guys just before dinner, probably. I'll call otherwise."

Rachel's departure left Lacey to wander around the house listlessly. She didn't like having so much time on her hands, never having to deal with that in her previous job. She decided to surprise her lover and cleaned the horse stalls, dumping the manure in the pit well away from the house and laying fresh shavings. She was filling the water buckets when the phone rang on the barn wall. She turned off the water and jogged over before the answering machine in the house picked up.

"Yeah?"

"Hello, is Mrs. Wilson there?" the tinny voice asked.

Lacey decided not to correct her on the title she'd bestowed upon Rachel and instead answered negatively. "No, she's not. Is there something I could help you with?"

"Umm ... this is Creekside Elementary calling—"

"Is Molly okay?" Lacey interrupted, fear gripping at her. She'd been worried enough about the threats to be delivering Molly to and from school, and having someone follow Rachel while she was on campus, but maybe these actions hadn't been enough. Her heart leapt into her throat.

"No, no, no," the woman said hastily. "I'm sorry, I didn't mean to worry you. Molly's fine. We've had a little disciplinary incident and, well, we need someone to come pick her up. She's been suspended."

"Suspended?" Lacey repeated, shocked.

"Yes. Could you get a hold of her mother?"

Lacey considered paging Rachel and pulling her away from the exam, but realized immediately that this was part of taking responsibility for her lover and the child. "I'm a legal guardian," Lacey responded. "I'll come get her."

"Uhh..." The woman seemed at a loss. "We'll need the paperwork to prove that to release her to you. And a picture identification."

"No problem," the dark woman responded. "I'm on my way, we live about ten minutes out."

"Great. Thank you."

She made sure the stall doors were secured into the barn and open into the paddocks beyond before going to the house and washing up quickly. "What did you do, Molly-girl?" she muttered to herself while searching for her keys.

Surely her own elementary school hadn't been this small, thought the dark-haired woman as she parked the Grand Cherokee and made her way past the flagpole and to the sign for the main office. Though she'd been to the school countless times to pick Molly up and drop her off, she'd never been inside the small building. It had been Rachel who'd attended back-to-school nights and parent-teacher conferences.

She'd barely opened the door to let herself inside the large glass room, when Molly propelled her little body across the carpeted floor and into the tall woman's body.

"Hey, hey," she soothed gently, picking the girl up and holding her close. Pretty soon, Molly would be way too big to hold like this and Lacey found herself dreading that day. "What happened?"

Apparently Molly was beyond tears, whether she'd already shed them or didn't have them to spare, Lacey didn't know. Regardless, the little girl just held her silently, resting her head on a strong shoulder.

"Do you think you could tell me what's going on, baby?"

The secretary watched the two silently. Lacey guessed this was the woman who had made the call and nodded to her, taking a step closer. She extended a hand. "Lacey Montgomery."

"Abby Pritchard, Administrative Assistant. Principal Walters has a few moments if you'd like to discuss the issue."

"Sure. In fact, I'd love to know what the issue is," Lacey responded, retrieving her hand to better distribute the child's weight.

"Called Mama and you dykes," Molly murmured.

Lacey's blue eyes widened in surprise. "Ah. Who did, baby?"

"Stupid sixth graders. Onna playground."

Lacey nodded, pursing her lips in thought. She met Abby's curious gaze with a smirk and a shrug. "Can I get the whole story or am I gonna have to pry it out of you?"

Molly sighed heavily, never moving from her position.

"Talking about Christmas and what we got our parents. I told them what I got Mama and what I got you. They asked who you were. And I told them."

"What did you say?"

"That you and Mama were my parents. That you were like my dad but not my dad, more like another mom. Then they asked me some questions about if you guys did things like hold hands and kiss like their parents did and I said yes. Was that wrong?" The little girl finally pushed away to meet Lacey's blue eyes, so much like her own.

"No, honey. But I have the feeling we're coming up to the wrong part. Keep going."

"He said you were dykes."

"We covered that. And?"

She sighed, laid her head back on the woman's shoulder. "And I punched him in the nose as hard as I could."

Ah ha. Lacey nodded, trying not to smirk, knowing this was serious. She set Molly on the counter that divided them from the attentive administrative assistant and cupped her cheeks. "Molly-girl, we are dykes, honey. Not a great word choice for grade schoolers, but true. You hitting him for saying that was like if he were to hit you for telling him that we're your parents."

"But he was mean." Now the tears did come. "He was mean about it. He said it like a curse word."

"Sweetie, I'm sorry it hurts so bad, but you're going to have to learn that you'll face this over and over again. We talked about this a little before school started."

She nodded numbly, pale eyelashes wet and clinging together, making them seem darker than their normal light blonde. "But they don't know you, how could they hate you?"

"*Because* they don't know us. Because it's different and people are afraid of different things. You have to make decisions on how you're going to handle it, baby. If you want to just not talk about it or tell the truth. But either way, hitting someone is wrong. You shouldn't have punched him."

"I know," she murmured eyes studying the floor between her swinging feet.

"What should you have done?" Lacey pressed the issue, her face inches from the child's, the weight of her upper body resting on hands planted on the counter at either side of the girl's slim hips.

"Shoulda walked away. Doesn't matter what he thinks of you, cuz I love you."

Lacey smiled and tugged the girl into an embrace. "Good. Remember that next time. No matter what they say or do, you come home to us and we love you."

Principal Walters stepped out of his office to see the two women and the child. He looked to his assistant who smiled warmly at him, touched by the affection displayed between Lacey and Molly.

"Uh, Ms. Montgomery, Principal Walters is available now."

Lacey looked up at Abby's voice and met the man's eyes. He was younger than she expected, though she suspected her preconceived idea was because her own principal had looked so old when she was nine. She set Molly on the floor and squatted in front of her. "You stay with Mrs. Pritchard, I'll just be a few minutes, okay?"

The child nodded glumly.

"Then we'll go home. Maybe we need to talk about some things you can say or do to help people understand?"

She nodded again.

"I love you, baby. Go siddown."

Principal Walters was struck immediately by the beauty of this woman. She was easily six feet tall with long raven black hair pulled into a thick braid. Her eyes were the iciest blue he'd ever seen and she carried herself with a quiet confidence he envied. She was tender with the child, her love obvious to anyone who cared to see it, but turned into a businesswoman when she faced him. She was obviously a woman of great bearing, maybe having schooled her expressions for boardrooms, though this day's outfit of jeans and button flannel shirt over a turtleneck spoke of a softer soul who'd never been on the inside track of the corporate world.

"Please, sit down." He motioned to a chair by his desk before moving to claim his own seat. "Do you know why we're here?"

"Yes," she responded politely. "Molly explained the situation to me. Do you understand it fully?"

He was surprised by her question and tilted his head, clearing his throat awkwardly. "Umm ... Gary Nelson called her mother a ... uh ... dyke. She punched him."

"Well, that would be the short version, yes." Lacey smiled softly. "But the longer version would be that we are, indeed, same-sex partners and Molly's learning to deal with the prejudices behind that."

He was startled by her honesty and nodded. "She punched him."

"Yes, she did. And I'm glad you called me and I'm glad she's being reprimanded for it. I just want you to understand her a little bit. Maybe schools need to work on some tolerance issues as part of the educational curriculum."

He nodded. "Ms. Montgomery—"

"Lacey, please." No one had ever called her by her last name. Her previous position as Vinnie's right hand had warranted her first name notoriety.

He smiled politely, inclined his head. "Lacey, we do have programs that deal with tolerance of sexual preferences and racial differences. Try as we might, however, we can't always convince everyone, especially if their home teachings are different."

She nodded at the validity of the statement.

"Molly is a very special little girl. She's smart as a

whip, does all her work, works hard to please everyone. The other kids don't know how to deal with her anyway and she doesn't appear to be interested in any of them. She keeps to herself. Frankly, I'm surprised this situation even arose because I've never seen her speak with other children on the playground. Usually, she sits under a tree and reads a book all recess."

The dark woman knew Molly was a voracious reader, but it hadn't dawned on her to question how the little girl finished her books so quickly. "Do you think they came to her to provoke her?"

"No, I don't think so. Unfortunately, I think she's pretty excited about the holiday and actually ventured out on her own to be a part of the conversation. The sixth graders were sitting at a table not far from her tree."

Lacey sighed, rubbed her temples. Poor Molly. "So she finally decides to get herself involved and this is what happens. They ridicule the people she loves most in the world."

He nodded. "I understand why she did what she did, Lacey, but I am forced to respond appropriately. I'm sorry." His dark eyes appeared to show genuine compassion for Molly and her plight.

The tall woman shrugged, blinked impossibly blue eyes at him. "How long is she suspended?"

"Today and tomorrow. Hopefully after the long holiday break, things will have simmered down. Gary's parents were in earlier and picked him up. He's bruised and a little bloody, but nothing serious. They, however, weren't as understanding as I would have liked."

Lacey sat up straight, suddenly concerned. "Did they speak with her? The parents?" Molly had a lot of respect for adults and they could have wounded her badly with harmful words.

"No," he assured her immediately, raising placating hands to the woman before him. "Molly was with the nurse's assistant in the first aid office when they came. We didn't want them to meet her, didn't think it was in her best interests."

Lacey relaxed back into the chair, shifted her weight and crossed her legs. "Why did you wait to call us?"

He smiled gently. "We weren't sure it was in the parents' best interests to meet at this stage either. Gary needed to be attended to first since he was bleeding."

She nodded silently, accepting that reasoning. "Were you ever worried about her not being involved with her peers?" Lacey realized it was ironic that she and Rachel had discussed this exact thing over lunch.

"Not really. We worry if they seem withdrawn or anti-social. But she's a well-adjusted little girl. She's remarkably well behaved and appears quite normal in the way she deals with children and adults. She just prefers to be alone." He shrugged. "We can't begrudge her that."

"Do you think she's lonely?" Lacey asked softly, hesitantly. She'd always been a loner as a child and often wished for more friends to confide in, other girls to laugh with. She remembered many lonely days on the playground. She imagined that Molly's own mother had been a social butterfly. Rachel was gregarious and outgoing, quick-witted and charming.

The man raised dark bushy eyebrows in thought. "I don't get that impression, no. We do try to keep up with the children and give them the best environment we can."

Lacey nodded, believing his words and appreciating his understanding attitude. "Did anyone know before today about her mother and me?"

"Before today? I doubt it. We didn't know, her teacher didn't know. But I really think it's because she's never said, not because she's hiding it. She just didn't think it was an important detail. Usually we learn about families in kindergarten and first grade when they're drawing and coloring pictures. We know what to expect and maybe can help head off problems. We never had reason to know with Molly, her age group doesn't draw family portraits."

"Am I on her paperwork as a contact?"

"I don't know, let's go see."

Molly still sat in the outer office, seemingly swallowed by the large chair she'd chosen. Her thin jean clad legs swung back and forth, unable to reach the ground. The small girl had inherited Rachel's height and was shorter than most of her age group. Lacey only remembered that when seeing her around other children, or when she seemed to disappear in furniture. Molly looked up hopefully and the dark woman recognized the pained expression she wore. She was so nervous, she was borderline being sick. Like mother like daughter.

"One more minute, baby," Lacey assured her from across the room. "If you need to go to the bathroom, you can and I'll meet you there." She glanced to the other adults quickly, pleading with her eyes that they allow the child this small dignity. Throwing up in the main office in front of the principal with the glass walls displaying her crime would be hard on her.

They nodded their approval, though they appeared confused. Molly was on her feet and flying down the hallway before anything else was said.

"Uhh..." Principal Walters started stupidly.

Lacey half smiled at him. "She throws up when she's nervous or worked up. Her mother's the same way."

"That's another good thing to know," Abby murmured, pulling out the small girl's file and annotating it.

Principal Walters took it from her when she was finished and flipped through the paperwork in it. "We do have you here as a legal guardian."

Lacey nodded. It had been a big step but a necessary one. Rachel'd wanted Lacey to have some control in case something happened to her. Being a legal guardian made adoption procedures easier. Neither had doubted that if Rachel were to die, Lacey would raise Molly on her own.

"We still do require a picture ID, though," he stated softly. "For the safety of the children. I don't mean to offend you."

She shrugged; she wasn't offended. It was a relief really that anyone couldn't walk in and claim her child. She stopped mid-thought. She'd never actually allowed herself to call Molly hers. A few more words were exchanged as she showed her driver's license and then repocketed it. Principal Walter suggested that both Rachel and Lacey meet with Molly's teacher after the holidays, to which Lacey easily agreed.

Then she got directions to the restroom and went to retrieve the little girl.

"Molly-girl," she called gently into the echoing tiled room.

"I'm here." She emerged from the handicapped stall, her eyes red rimmed, both from the exertion of being sick and from crying.

"C'mere, let's get you cleaned up and then we'll go home." The tall woman moistened a paper towel and wiped at the little girl's face. She was ready to leave when a bell rang and they heard voices in the hall.

Molly looked up at her. "Afternoon recess."

"Do you want to stay here until they're gone?" Lacey offered gently.

Molly shook her head, smiled shyly. "Will you hold my hand?"

They walked down the hallway through the swarm of children, Molly's small hand securely gripped in Lacey's larger one. Children stopped to stare as any strange adult in the halls was new and different, especially since they recognized Molly as the girl who'd bloodied a sixth grader's nose.

Most of them also knew why.

One little girl stepped up beside them and stopped. "Hi, Molly," she said softly. She had carrot orange hair and bright blue eyes. Her fair skin was freckled.

"Hi, Lauren," Molly responded, gripping tightly to Lacey's hand. They stopped their progression as well and Lacey knelt down on one knee to be on the same level as the girls.

The two children stared awkwardly at each other and Lacey wondered what she should say to ease the obvious tension when Lauren spoke first.

"Is this your other Mom?"

Molly merely nodded, looking to Lacey to find strength and acceptance of that title in her sapphire gaze. It was there and she drew on it.

"I'm Lacey." The dark woman offered her hand, after prying it from Molly's grip. Lauren shook it in a grown up way.

Then she leaned forward and touched a small hand to Molly's arm. "No one knows," she whispered. "But I had two dads. My other dad got really sick and died last year. We miss him."

Lacey's heart reached out to this little girl, laying it all on the line to offer Molly some support. She'd kept her secret pretty well, apparently. Either that, or Molly wasn't the prying conspirator her mother was.

"The other kids might make fun of you, but I never will."

Molly met her classmate's eyes. "I'm sorry about your other dad."

"Me too." She nodded. "Thank you."

"Can we ... maybe play after Christmas?"

Lauren smiled. "I'd like that."

A slow grin crossed Molly's face. "Have a Merry Christmas, Lauren."

The halls had all but emptied and Lauren backed away towards the door leading to the playground. "You, too. Bye, Molly, bye, Miss Lacey."

When Lacey looked to the little girl's face, she thought Molly's smile might take sail and lift her away it was so huge. She grinned back. "Let's go, Squirt."

****

It was just after six when Karma heard the Wrangler before the garage door opener even sounded. Though Rachel didn't park in the garage, she always came through that way. The little Siberian Husky stood at the kitchen door, wagging her bushy tail and whining her greeting, warming up for the chorus of woos and howls that was sure to follow. Molly was sitting at the table reading a book while Lacey was working on dinner.

Rachel burst in and dropped her book bag to hug the overzealous dog, who vocalized her satisfaction with life. Then she looked up to the rest of the kitchen's inhabitants as she closed the door behind her.

"Hey! How are you guys? You look great, Lacey." She kissed her lover on the cheek, not wanting to interrupt her food preparations. "Molly, honey, how was school?"

The whole room seemed to get silent and Karma slinked away. Molly looked at Lacey with slightly liquid eyes.

"I missed something?" Rachel guessed, not having to use any intuitive skills to reach that conclusion.

Lacey smiled. "Yeah, we'll fill you in. Tell us about the test."

Rachel looked from her daughter to her companion and knew something had happened. But her partner's raised eyebrow asked her to step away from it for now, so she gave in. "It went great. I stayed a little later so I could wait for the results. End of the alphabet ... you know. Anyway, I got an

A." She tried to say it offhandedly, but her big grin and sparkling eyes gave her away.

Lacey put down the wooden spatula she'd been using to sauté and captured the smaller woman in a hug. "Good for you, love. I knew you could do it."

Molly skipped over to get a hug as well. Her head reached just below Rachel's breasts as she embraced her fiercely, nearly crushing her mother's ribs. The little girl preferred the whole-body-elevated hugs that Lacey gave, but Rachel couldn't carry the growing girl around like the taller woman could.

"You did good, Mama," she said softly, her warm breath seeping through Rachel's sweatshirt.

"Thank you, baby." She kissed her head. "One more paper to turn in and I've finished my first semester."

"We're proud of you, Raich." Lacey smiled, rubbing her partner's back affectionately before turning to stir the sautéing vegetables again.

"It takes a good support team, huh?" The blonde tousled her child's hair and led her to the kitchen table where she claimed a chair and pulled Molly into her lap to hug her closer. "I missed you today."

Molly nodded, wrapped small arms around her mother's neck. "Missed you, too, Mama."

Rachel was dying to know what was going on. She glanced back to her partner who shook her head and offered a grin. *It's not so bad*, her expression seemed to say. "During dinner," she mouthed silently. Rachel nodded.

Molly was grateful that it was Lacey who told of the crime that had been committed. She was nearly in tears already just from the guilt at disappointing them both. When the story was finished, Rachel looked quietly at her daughter, who refused to meet her gaze.

"Molly, honey?"

"I'll be good next time, Mama," she whispered.

"Oh, sweetie," Rachel said softly, reaching over the table to draw the little girl's chin up. "It's not a question of being good. I know you're good. You couldn't be better. Lacey and I are blessed by having such a wonderful child with us."

Teary blue eyes looked from her mother to Lacey, finding conviction in both gazes.

"It's a matter of learning to control your temper. And knowing how to handle things peacefully even when it really hurts inside. You get that from me, baby. I have trouble controlling my anger, too."

Lacey snorted, remembering for the first time in months when she'd had to pry a flailing Rachel off of Oz nearly a year ago. The little blonde had had the scrawny man down and was beating him senseless.

"Hush, crony." Rachel glanced sideways at her smirking partner. "I'm sorry that it came to that and I'm sorry the boy hurt your feelings. But I'm not disappointed in you."

"You're not?" Molly asked, almost hopeful. That had been her biggest fear. At nine, she did her best to be mature and grown up, to not give Lacey a reason to dislike her or her mother a reason to send her away again. And then she goes and bloodies up a little boy. No matter how much he may have deserved it, she would have taken it back in a heartbeat to not have that blemish on her desperately good record.

"No, honey. How can Lacey and I help you?"

They talked over stir-fry beef and rice about the possibility of a pony club or youth group. Lacey told Rachel about Lauren and the prospect of the new friend seemed to cheer Molly up greatly. Then they discussed the more intimate issues of how Molly chose to deal with their sexuality.

"Lauren said no one knew," Molly said softly as they were clearing away the dishes and storing leftovers.

"Well, that was Lauren's choice to make. You don't

have to tell everyone you meet about us, honey. Maybe just tell close friends or don't tell anyone. We'll respect whatever you decide."

"You said when I was living with Aunt Helen that it was something to accept, not to shy away from. Remember?" The little girl looked from her mother to Lacey. "Remember in the hospital, Lacey?"

"I remember, kiddo. Do you remember what I told you then?"

"That it didn't matter what they thought you were, as long as we know how much you love each other."

"That's right," Lacey praised the youngster's good memory as she rinsed off their dinner dishes and placed them in the dishwasher. Rachel stood at her side, putting leftovers in small Tupperware containers.

"You said that sometimes it's easier not to say anything. But they asked me. And I couldn't lie. I'm not supposed to lie."

"Ooo boy," Lacey muttered, elbowing Rachel. "Ball's in your court." The dark-haired woman took the Tupperware containers and placed them in the fridge.

"Chicken," the smaller woman murmured back. "Molly, it wouldn't be lying to say that Lacey was a friend that you cared about very much. Or to say that she's someone we lived with. They probably would have let that slide. You know the truth in your heart."

The child seemed to consider this for a very long time, running a damp rag over the kitchen table. "But I want everyone to know that I have someone who loves me as much as my mama does. That's pretty cool, isn't it?" She raised an eyebrow in question and could have been Lacey's daughter by blood with that expression.

"It's really cool, honey. But if that's what you're going to say to people then you just need to have tougher skin. Because I think you'll find that most of your classmates aren't going to be thrilled for you."

The child hummed softly in response, then went to the sink to rinse out her rag and drape it over the faucet. "I'm going to go up to my room and read."

"Horses cleaned yet?" Rachel called to her daughter as the little girl trotted out of the room.

"Yup. Barn fairy did 'em." Then she was gone.

"Barn fairy?" Rachel quizzed her companion, who shrugged a shoulder.

"Had some time to kill today ... *before* I got called to the principal's office. Not my first time in a principal's office, mind you." She grinned rakishly, tugging fondly on Rachel's hair on the way by.

"You know," Rachel said softly, taking a deep breath. "You could have called me out of class. I would have come, you didn't need to deal with it." She flashed back to their conversation a couple of nights ago and Lacey's resentment on some levels of the family role she'd been forced to play.

Lacey knew what she was getting at. "I didn't mind, gorgeous. Not at all. Please believe me when I tell you that the love you guys give me far outweighs the hassles. I was just frustrated before. I feel better now."

"Did you talk to Vinnie?" Though not completely convinced, the pleading in her lover's eyes persuaded Rachel to start a subject change.

"No," she chuckled dryly, holding out a hand to her partner and then leading her into the living room where they snuggled on the white leather sofa. "Would you believe his right hand is giving me the runaround?"

Rachel laughed, tucking herself securely into the large woman's arms. These were the best moments of the day. "His job, right?"

"Yeah ... but this is me. Robbie knows me. I'm not sure what's up. I didn't really get around to pursuing it today."

"Any more threats?"

"No," Lacey murmured, brushing aside her lover's golden mane to nuzzle at her neck. "Not since before the funeral."

"Any word from George?" Rachel asked softly though her attention was being divided rather quickly. With her back against Lacey's chest she could feel the dark woman's nipples tighten. She recalled easily the taste and texture of them beneath her exploring tongue and lips.

"Unh unh." Lacey's hands wandered under the blonde's sweatshirt, journeying upwards to rub large palms against bra-encased breasts. She bit an earlobe, causing her lover to gasp and arch her back.

"No more talk," Rachel growled, flipping around to straddle the older woman and capture her mouth with seeking lips.

Lacey chuckled. "S'okay. I wasn't all that interested in talking anyway," she muttered between kisses.

More minutes of heated kissing and fondling followed until Rachel was panting, rubbing her body against Lacey's, wanting to be rid of the clothes and feel that silky skin she knew so well. "Upstairs. Room. Locked door," she breathed out, nibbling on Lacey's neck.

"Great idea," her dark lover responded. Her heavy breathing indicated she was in the same state of no-return arousal. She stood up, taking the smaller woman with her, and they retreated to the bedroom where they could lock the door and continue their exploration in private.

Chapter 4

The next morning caused some logistics problems only because they hadn't planned on having Molly home from school.

Rachel needed a few uninterrupted hours to put the finishing touches on a paper that was due by four o'clock. She had yet to edit it and print it out, though at least it was completely written.

Rachel muttered to herself as she chewed on a pen cap and watched the screen intently, trying to formulate her next thought. She should have finished this last night but after a long bout of lovemaking and no sleep the night before, she'd curled up in Lacey's arms and hadn't even ventured off the mattress until this morning.

Lacey was downstairs with Molly and had finally gotten through to Vinnie. She was going to pick up Rico and have the long-awaited discussion with their former boss. The dark woman hoped it would be revealing, but didn't hold her breath that Vinnie would have the answers to all her problems.

The young blonde woman's deep thoughts and sporadic typing were interrupted by a gentle knock on the door. She looked up. "Hey, Lace." She grinned.

"Hey. I'm headed out."

"Where's Molly?"

"Playing Nintendo."

"Wait a sec. She gets suspended from school and as punishment she gets to play Nintendo all morning?"

"You have a better idea, Raich?" Lacey asked pointedly. "Because I'm open for suggestions, but she can't come with me and you need to finish your paper."

Rachel sighed, Lacey was right. Molly couldn't go to Vinnie's and Rachel really couldn't entertain her and get this paper in on time. "No, you're right. Do me a favor, though. Tell her one hour on Nintendo and then she has to go to her room and do one of her workbooks. I'll check up on her."

"Deal." Lacey nodded and padded across the plush carpet to kiss her partner goodbye.

"Be careful," Rachel whispered, not liking that Lacey was walking back into the family she'd left last February.

"No sweat, baby," Lacey promised, smoothing golden hair with a large hand before heading out of the room. Rachel heard Lacey's hollered instructions to the child downstairs in the television room before the sound of the garage door opening indicated her lover was on her way.

"Please be okay," she murmured, trying to concentrate on her paper once more.

****

Lacey had chosen the little Mazda RX-7, knowing that Rico liked to drive the sports car. It had been nearly a week since she'd seen the young man and he'd still been pretty torn up over Bernard's death. The two had been close.

Though Rico had received threats as well, they were

more vague than the rest and the group used to joke that they were sympathy threats. Whoever was writing them didn't want Rico to feel left out. They didn't joke about them anymore.

Rico was a brilliant kid. He'd been assigned to Lacey's team just a few short months before she left the organization but had proven in that time to be loyal. Now that he worked for Lacey in the computer security firm, his skills really shined. He was a computer geek at heart and was responsible for most of the research and development team. Lacey ran the business side of bidding for contracts and shmoozing prospective buyers, though she did dabble in the programming end from time to time. She was no slouch herself in the computer environment, she just didn't enjoy the tedium of it.

Rico was standing outside his apartment complex in the parking lot. His toothy grin widened at the sight of the little red car. Lacey put the car in neutral, set the emergency brake, and hopped out. "Hey, Rico."

"Hi, Lace." His blue eyes danced in merriment as he ran his hand through too-long shaggy blonde hair.

"All yours." The dark woman gestured to the driver's seat as she stepped around to let herself into the passenger side. She adjusted the seat to her longer legs and looked over as Rico did the reverse, accommodating his smaller stature. "Just leave more rubber on the tires than the road, bucko."

"No problem." He grinned as he squealed out of the parking lot.

Berto let them into Vinnie's mansion when they arrived. He didn't spare them so much as a lingering glance, even though it wasn't common practice for mafia personnel to be released and then waltz back in nearly a year later. He frisked them both and Lacey put on her best glower for him, never caring much for the pompous ass anyway.

The house was just as she remembered as she walked down the hallway into the plushly carpeted anteroom. Rico was hot on her heels. "Stop steamin' up my tail," Lacey teased.

Rico looked at her stupidly for a moment before grinning. "Heh. Bugs Bunny. That's pretty cute, Lace. How about 'Spear and Magic Helmet'."

"Magic Helmet?" Lacey bantered back.

They were in full swing by the time Berto showed them into Vinnie's office. The room itself was stifling enough that it demanded their silence long before Vinnie could.

He stood quietly behind the desk regarding them both. Lacey had been his best associate for many long years. His family had pulled her away from her abusive mother and nickel and dime dealing to raise her here with his family. He remembered her fondly as an angry young woman with a chip on her shoulder who'd matured into the best business mind he knew. She'd been loyal and ruthless, earned the family only slightly more than she'd saved. If his family hadn't been so indebted to her, hadn't loved her so, she never would have left alive.

He didn't know Rico well at all. They'd just gotten him out of a homeless shelter where Rico'd been holding up a volunteer for drug money, when one of the family members had spotted him. He'd immediately liked the kid's bravado and recruited him. Rico had shown promise since day one, but showed more loyalty to Lacey than the family. It had been a hard fight, but Vinnie had given in when Lacey asked for his freedom as well. If he didn't know she was shacking up with the young rider from Briargate, he would have assumed there was more to the relationship before him.

No one spoke for a very long time, each lost in separate memories. It was finally Vinnie who broke the silence.

"You look good, Lace. Better than you've looked in a long time." It was a completely true statement. Though she still wore the black leather trench coat he'd grown to know so well over black slacks and a white silk shirt, there was something different about her expression. It was something softer and it suited her well. He noted immediately, however, that her ice blue eyes were just as keen, sweeping the room, sizing him up.

"Ya look good, too, Vinnie. A little more grey, maybe."

He smiled. He'd always been fond of her. She'd never once backed away from him merely because of the power he wielded. She was not a yes-man and he'd never had a better right hand. Robbie was no comparison.

"You get bored without me?"

"Robbie, that slime, gave me the runaround. He thinks he runs the world now?" Lacey avoided the question. She was a little bored, in reality, but not bored enough to become the cold killing machine she'd once been. There was no going back there. She'd been ready to leave that life for a long time before Rachel showed up. Rachel had just given her a solid reason to walk away. The decision had been easy after that. No looking back.

"Please, sit." Vinnie motioned to the deep leather chairs framing his large oak desk. "You did when you had that position."

"Ah." Lacey nodded with a knowing smirk, taking the seat he'd indicated. Rico followed her lead. "But I did run the world. He has delusions of grandeur."

Vinnie laughed. "Fair enough. He's no Lacey Montgomery, that's for sure."

"Don't hurt his feelings, Vinnie. I'm sure he's doing his best."

"Hah," the tall, dark-skinned man snorted, straightening his silk blazer. "Everyone's been comparing him to you since he stepped into those shoes. He's pretty pissed off at you right now. That's why he was giving you the runaround. Why did you ask to see me? He said you wouldn't tell him."

"I wouldn't tell the little fucker who won the Super Bowl, Vinnie." Lacey grinned evilly. "He doesn't deserve to know. I'm here because I need your help on something."

"If I can do it, I will," he promised generously.

She outlined as much of the problem she was willing to share, starting with the mild threats and ending with Bernard's death.

"I'd heard about that, I'm sorry," Vinnie offered. Bernard had been a hard worker and a good guy. "The threats are getting worse, now?"

Lacey nodded and extracted an envelope from the inside of her trench coat. She unfolded the letter and handed it over.

Vinnie's eyes skimmed the note twice before raising salt and pepper eyebrows. "How recent is this?"

"Couple weeks. Before Bernard's death."

"Lacey." Vinnie met her blue eyes with his own dark brown ones. Hers showed absolutely no emotion. "It's not normal protocol to threaten families like this."

"I know." The letter outlined in disgusting detail how Rachel and Molly were going to die. Organized Crime members usually attacked head on, no forewarning letters, always in person. And almost never was the family directly targeted. Wives and children were killed as a matter of course, but not as primary targets. "The letters threatened Bernard's family as well but in the end, he was killed, not his wife and children."

"You think it's a scare tactic? That you're actually in danger and not them?"

"Yes. And let's hope I'm right because aside from having a tail on Rachel, I've not had them protected as if they're targets."

"Rico, you have letters like this, too?"

The young man nodded, reaching into his pocket and extending his own version of the same letter. The target was his girlfriend Mary.

"Lacey, I can't think of anyone right away. That's why you came here, right? To see if it was an enemy you gained while here."

She nodded.

"You're free to go through my records, you built most of them anyway. If I can offer you people or a place to stay—"

"No," Lacey interrupted, shaking her head. "I was reluctant to come here. I'm not interested in being in the business again or owing you that much. I just want our families to be safe."

"You would owe me nothing, Lacey. My family is indebted to you beyond our means."

She remained silent, indicating she was still declining his offer of protection.

"The files and copy machine are at your disposal. Just use discretion, as I know you will."

Lacey nodded and left Vinnie's office through a back door, which led to a large library. She'd been here countless times before. She knew that Vinnie trusted her not to expose anything she shouldn't or show records to anyone who could harm him. She valued that trust, had spent over half her life building it, so she wouldn't do anything to destroy it now.

****

Rachel was driving to the college campus to drop off her paper, Molly in tow, when she received a page from Lacey. It said simply "Meet me at office ASAP."

She hoped it was good news.

"Lacey?" Molly inquired, looking from the vinyl window of the Jeep to her mother.

"Yeah. As soon as we get rid of this paper, we're going to the office."

Her eyes lit up. "Is Rico there?"

"Maybe," Rachel laughed. Molly loved Lacey's young partner like an older brother. They bantered and fought like siblings as well. "He was at her morning meeting, but I'm not sure if he was planning on hanging around."

They parked behind the small building and let themselves in the back door. It was a little office attached to a much larger complex and held spaces for Rico and Lacey with a large suite for developers. Everyone had been given the weeks before Christmas off, as business had been slow and most of their developers were contracted out anyway.

Rico and Lacey were sprawled on the floor in the front office, files and papers scattered on the carpeting.

"Hurricane strike?" Rachel asked by way of introduction and got a good-natured grin in response. Molly bounced across the room to give Rico a huge hug.

"Hey there, Molly." He smiled. "How's life treating you?"

"Good. No complaints." She grinned. "I was hoping you were here. I have to talk to you."

The adults all exchanged curious looks, wondering what this was all about. They didn't have to wait long.

"Have you gotten past the Deku tree in Zelda? And gone to the castle?"

Lacey and Rachel laughed, the darker woman gaining her feet and ushering her lover across the room where they could speak in relative private.

"How did it go?"

"Vinnie couldn't think of anyone but he let us copy his business folders, prior transactions and such. We're going through them now but haven't really come up with anything. It'll take days just to sift through all this shit."

Rachel nodded, looking at the files laying around.

"Figured you two could join us for dinner and then we'll take all this back to the house to work on."

"Sounds like a plan," the young blonde agreed.

"Get your paper in okay?"

"Yup." Rachel grinned. "No more pencils, no more books, no more teacher's dirty looks."

"Until after Christmas, anyway." Lacey returned the grin. "Don't go writing your valedictorian speech yet, Raich."

"You really know how to bring a girl down," Rachel frowned, but couldn't keep from laughing when Lacey leaned forward and nipped at her neck.

"But I can cheer you up later, can't I?" She growled playfully.

"Roger that," Rachel whispered, wrapping her lover in a strong embrace and guiding the dark woman's lips to her own. They shared a lingering kiss that spoke more of belonging than of passion. When they broke, they headed back across the room to Rico and Molly.

"No," Molly was insisting, seated cross-legged by Rico's side. "You have to get the chickens. There are six of them, I think. You put them in the pen."

"I can't find the last one," Rico said, shaking his head. "Do I need to save the chickens? Can't I just go up Death Mountain?"

She shook her head. "You get the flask from the chicken lady. You need to have that."

"So where's the last chicken?"

"There's a crate by one of the buildings. Link can roll into it and break it. Did you find that one?" Molly asked helpfully, rising to her feet when she saw her mother and her partner approach.

"No, I think I missed that one. I'll have to go back and look." Rico stood as well.

"I hate to interrupt Nintendo's Greatest Secrets Revealed, but I'm hungry," Rachel announced. The others agreed. "You can work out the finer points of chicken collecting over dinner."

They all joined in to gather the files and carry them out to Lacey's car. They settled them in the hatchback.

"I thought Jose's?" Lacey suggested.

"Sounds great," Rachel agreed and Rico nodded.

"Follow me, then."

The little caravan started up and was on its way.

****

Lacey and Rachel sat next to each other in the booth they'd acquired while Rico and Molly shared the other side.

"Mary couldn't join us?" Rachel asked, munching on the tortilla chips in the middle of the table. One taste of the salsa was enough for her to claim it too hot. Her partner, on the other hand, scooped the tangy mix into her mouth with abandon.

"She's with her mom tonight. They're doing some shopping together or something."

"You two doing okay?" Rachel probed gently and got a poke in the ribs for her question. "What? We're like his family. It's our job to be nosy."

Lacey smirked at her indignant partner. "For you, it's a way of life, hon. Maybe equine journalism isn't what you should do. You should look into the gossip rags."

Rachel glared at her, but there was no heat behind it. She turned her attention back to Rico and her expression immediately sweetened. "Anyway ..." she drawled.

"We're doing great," Rico said, watching their suspicious gazes. "Really. It's almost sick, actually. We don't argue over anything, we like to do the same things. We're having a lot of fun."

"That is sick," Lacey mutteringly concurred. "What's the fun in a relationship without a few good fights?"

Molly blanched slightly at the joking words and Lacey felt guilty immediately. She reached across the table and captured the young girl's hand. "I'm teasing, sweetie. Your mom and I don't fight much at all. Just that one time you saw. We're all going to be together for a long time to come, I promise."

Rachel knew there was more unsaid behind the words. Lacey was also vowing to protect them from this unknown enemy. She reached under the table to pat her lover's thigh. "So," she decided it was time to lighten the mood, "does Mary play this Zelda game, too?"

"Oh yeah." Rico grinned. "But she's not as good at it as Molly and me." With this he turned his attention back to the child at his side. "It took me forever to get into the castle because of those guards. I couldn't tell which way they were facing to sneak behind them."

Molly nodded. "I had the same problem on the television upstairs, so Lacey moved it to the big screen. Then I could see what they were doing. But Lacey thinks it has more to do with how far you are from them and not which way they're looking."

"Yeah," Lacey agreed. "You need a big screen, Rico. And run it through stereo. Makes all the difference. I was getting tired of talking to all the people in the market place so Molly showed me where to go so I only had to talk to the people that trigger game changes."

Rachel stared open-mouthed at her partner, who turned and grinned at her.

"Close your mouth, Raich."

"You play the game, too? I thought you were working on your laptop when you were both in that room."

"Heh." Lacey grinned. "It started out that way ... but that game is addictive. You should try it."

"Yeah, Mama," Molly piped up, eager to get her mother involved in their little Nintendo circle. "There's space for one more player on the game."

"Yeah, Mama," Lacey teased. "I think it's a great idea."

"Kids today," Rachel murmured, leaning back so the waitress could set down her plate of chicken enchiladas cautioning, as always, that it was hot.

****

Rico and Lacey followed the familiar white Wrangler in the dark woman's little Mazda. Rico was, happily, behind the wheel. It was about a twenty-minute drive back to the house and they passed the first part in comfortable silence.

Their peacefulness was disturbed when they watched Rachel go through a green light ahead of them and a car come barreling at the Wrangler's side.

"Lace!" Rico yelled, leaning forward, urging the little car to somehow catch up and prevent the horror in front of them.

"Fuck!" Lacey growled, also leaning her tall frame forward. She was in a front row seat to watch a horrible collision involving her family. The car entering the intersection was a sleek dark sedan, details undetectable in the night.

Rachel saw the headlights out of the corner of her eyes, engrossed as she was in Molly's summarizing of a recent story she'd read. The headlights, she realized after a moment's consideration, were not stopping at the oncoming traffic's red light.

"Shit!" she cried out and slammed on the accelerator, knowing she was going to get clipped in the tail end and knowing that the speed of the oncoming vehicle as well as the Wrangler's could result in an ugly collision that would send the Jeep into an uncontrollable pirouette. So she decided to control the spin instead, applying the brakes and taking a hard right which twisted the backside of the Jeep around, bouncing the tires along the pavement and colliding with the curb on the far side. When the wheels rolled to a dead stop, she was facing oncoming traffic and aside from being jostled, everything was okay. She stalled the Wrangler out when she lifted her feet off the pedals, giving it one last lurch into silence. She stepped down on the parking brake.

"Molly?" Rachel asked immediately, reaching across the narrow interior to lay her hands on her daughter.

"M'okay, Mama," she muttered, eyes wide, hands shaking.

Both the passenger and driver's side doors were yanked open and concerned faces peered in. Rachel undid her seatbelt and collapsed into Lacey's arms.

"Thank God," the dark woman murmured, clutching the trembling woman to her, feeling their racing heartbeats compete for tempo. "You were brilliant, baby," she whispered, smoothing her hair. "C'mon out of there."

Rachel accepted her partner's help to climb down from the Jeep and stand on rubbery legs. She leaned into the taller woman's arms and found strength and safety in the embrace. She could feel Lacey trembling as well.

"It's okay, Lace," Rachel assured her. "We're okay, just shaken up."

Lacey nodded numbly, pressing her lips into Rachel's soft hair. "You were great, the way you avoided him."

"Couldn't think of anything else to do," the blonde murmured, feeling her heartbeat slow and her legs become steadier.

"Did just the right thing," the dark-haired woman assured her. "I love you."

"You, too."

Rico was pulling Molly out of the Jeep on the other side and leading the equally shaken girl around to be with the women. Lacey disentangled from Rachel and picked the child up to hold her close.

"We need to get out of the middle of the road," Rachel observed quietly, turning to see that Rico had parked the sports car nose to nose with the Wrangler. She stood close to her lover and her daughter, one hand on each of them, needing that solidarity. A few other people had stopped and were cautiously making their way to the small group.

"Fuck them," Lacey growled. "They can wait a minute."

"They have other lanes to use," Rico supplied a little more helpfully. It was true. Their vehicles were parked in the far right lane, leaving two open for westbound traffic.

"Hey." The first man approached a little timidly, taking in the tall dark woman fiercely holding a child and the other smaller woman standing unsteadily at her side. Rico leaned quietly against the Jeep, always right on the outskirts, ready to provide support whenever the two women needed it. Rachel looked pale and shaken still. "I saw everything. I don't know, but I think that guy was aiming for you, even when you spun out."

Rachel looked over to meet her lover's eyes. Lacey nodded solemnly.

"Are you okay?" the man continued. "I can call the police ... or the paramedics. Did anyone hit their head?"

"No," Rachel sighed. "We're okay. Just really shaken up. Did you hit anything, Molly?" Her tone softened when addressing her child. She couldn't hear the muffled response.

"She said no," Lacey replied. "She's just scared."

Rico turned to the man offering help, taking in him and the quiet woman at his side in one gaze. "Did you get the license plate number or anything?"

"No." He looked away with evident shame. "I'm sorry. It all happened so fast. I've never seen anything like it. If he'd hit you going that speed ..." He let his voice trail off when he caught the taller woman's warning gaze.

"I got it," said the smaller woman beside him and he turned to her in surprise. She shrugged. "I looked. I thought he was going to clip her and just keep going." She held out a piece of paper. "Our name and number are on there, too, if you need witnesses for anything. He wanted to hit you."

Rachel nodded glumly as Rico took the offered paper with much gratitude.

The other cars that had stopped were beginning to merge back into traffic again, as it looked like everything was under control. The man and woman retreated to their own vehicle after accepting a lot of heartfelt thanks from the small entourage.

Lacey set the little girl down, steadying her. "Go see your mama for a minute, Molly-girl." She stepped over to Rico to claim the paper, already dialing her cell phone. Molly obligingly went into her mother's welcoming embrace and wrapped small arms around the woman's waist.

"Robbie, put me through to Vinnie right now. I don't care ... right now or I'll come over there myself and shove the telephone down your fucking throat." Silence as she looked to Rico and shrugged, offering him a smirk.

"Some people never lose that charming touch," he murmured teasingly.

"Vinnie ... sorry about interrupting dinner. I need your current DMV contact ... someone just tried to run into Rachel, I have the plate. Sure ... thanks ..." She read the plate number into the phone. Evidently, Vinnie had agreed to handle it himself. "Call me on my cell when you find something. Same number." She tucked the phone away and nodded her head towards the little red car. "Follow us. I'm gonna drive them."

Rico nodded and returned to the driver's seat to watch Lacey pile her family back into the Jeep and slide behind the wheel. She backed it up and then waited for traffic to clear before performing a tight U-turn and starting on their way again.

The ride was pretty silent, there really not being much to say. When Lacey wasn't shifting, she rested her right hand on Rachel's thigh where the younger woman clutched the long strong fingers.

They were already settled in the house, files tossed across the living room floor where Lacey and Rachel had camped out, when the cell phone rang.

"Great. Yeah, thanks." The dark woman was scribbling on a piece of paper in her hands. Rachel listened halfheartedly to her while the rest of her attention was centered on the voices coming from the television room where Rico and Molly were playing Mario Kart. "They're okay. No injuries. Okay ... bye."

Rachel turned to her partner, waiting for her to volunteer information. Sometimes that could amount to a pretty long wait, but tonight was not such a case.

"Stolen plates. They belong to a red Ford Expedition."

"Ah." Rachel nodded, knowing the vehicle that had been aimed at her didn't come close to fitting that description.

"He gave me the information on the Expedition, but I think it's a dead end."

The young blonde nodded again, watching her partner with misty green eyes.

Lacey couldn't take it anymore, she set aside paper and phone and crawled across the littering of files to gather the smaller woman in her arms. Rachel went gratefully into the embrace.

"You're not leaving my sight until we figure this out."

"I was in your sight," Rachel pointed out softly, snuggling deeper into the protective arms. She could hear her partner swallow.

"I wouldn't have survived watching that," Lacey admitted hoarsely, rocking the small body slightly. "I don't think... I've done a lot of things in my life, seen a lot of horrible stuff ... but that would have killed me."

Rachel remained silent, knowing there were no words to express what she was feeling: a mixture of relief, fear, gratitude, and love. Lacey's emotions ran the same gambit and left the normally stoic woman choked up.

"I knew it was going to be dangerous for us to try to lead a normal life. I just didn't expect this. It's been almost a year since I left that scene. Why now?"

"Do they think your guard is down?"

"Maybe it is," the dark woman responded softly. "Two years ago, I never would have let someone get that close. I'm getting soft."

"Love," Rachel said gently. "Two years ago you never would have let *me* get this close. Things change. You've changed. There's nothing wrong with that."

"Yes, there is," Lacey growled. "I could have lost you both tonight."

"I think, Lace, that if you hadn't changed enough to let us into your life, we wouldn't have been here to lose."

The taller woman considered those words for a very long time. Rachel was right, of course. She had chosen Rachel and Molly over the darkness of her previous life and it had been, in all reality, a startlingly easy choice to make. She'd never once regretted it. "It's better to have loved and lost than to have never loved at all," Lacey whispered huskily, her breath tickling the small woman's neck as she held her tightly. She knew the statement was true for her. She knew that this time with Rachel and her daughter had enriched her life beyond understanding, but was the improved quality of her life worth risking theirs? "Do you think that's true? That even though your lives are risked by being with me, it's worth it?" Lacey asked her lover softly.

"Worth every minute, Lace," Rachel assured her, smoothing taut back muscles with small warm hands. "I never thought I deserved the happiness you've shown me. If I died tomorrow, I would die happy."

"Don't say that," Lacey growled softly. "Not tomorrow or the next day. Or next month. I want you forever." It was a startling admission not because it was unbelievable but because it had always gone unspoken. Everything they had said and done implied a commitment together. Every moment since they'd first met had seemed to lead into a shared life, whether it be destiny or good fortune that brought them together that icy morning in January nearly a year ago.

"Forever's a long time," Rachel teased gently. "Can you stand me that long?" She felt the body against hers move with a soundless chuckle.

"That long and more. You can't shake me that easily."

Rachel absorbed the warmth of the body and the words. Lacey was a complex character. Her emotions swung strongly one direction to another with very little warning. Not even a week ago, she'd been sullen and withdrawn, pushing Rachel away with angry voice and hurtful words. Now, she was declaring a lasting love and a lifelong commitment. Rachel knew the first had been a defense mechanism. Lacey had been confused and shaken, she'd wanted to protect her lover and the small girl and thought removing them from her presence would do that. Her lashing out had been a combination of emotional overload, something the dark woman rarely dealt with, and downright fear, an even more alien feeling.

The words she spoke now were honest, blatant truth. She realized the danger, realized the pressure she now carried to protect them both, but gladly paid the price to continue the lives they'd begun sharing. No more pushing away.

"I wouldn't want to," Rachel said at last, the words seeming a non sequitor after so much silence. Lacey understood, kissed Rachel's fair head.

"I'm not sure I can do this work tonight. I can't stop holding you," she murmured.

"Then let's not. The alarm is on, we're all safe. Let's go watch them play."

Making Strides

Lacey agreed readily, standing and bringing the smaller woman up with her. They straightened the mess of folders and set them up on an end table to prevent Karma from flying through them at top speed and scattering them worse. Then they went into the television room to claim the couch behind the two players and snuggle into each other's warmth.

Rachel absently stroked Molly's hair where it fanned out on the couch cushion, the small girl's back leaning against the leather furniture while sitting on the floor. Molly glanced up at them and offered them a smile. She still appeared a little shaken, but the women presumed she didn't understand the danger enough to be as frightened as she should be.

Lacey sighed, buried her face in fragrant blonde hair. How was she going to get them out of this one?

****

"Lace," Rachel whispered hoarsely, arching into the other woman while also pushing away.

Lacey grinned at the mixed signals, wiggling long fingers where they rested deep inside of her lover. "Hmm?"

"I can't."

Lacey's sexual appetite was directly proportional to her need to feel emotions. Where words failed her, she showed with her actions, ravishing the small woman's body over and over again. She was insatiable in her cravings to feel her partner, taste her, smell her. She wanted to hear the moans that let her know the young woman was alive and well, that they'd survived another day.

She'd denied her younger lover's roving fingers and seeking lips, finding pleasure only in bringing release to Rachel.

"No more," Rachel whispered wearily, burning from repeated internal friction, bruised on the tender skin over her pelvic bone.

"More," Lacey growled, withdrawing her fingers but settling her long frame over her lover and separating her legs with a still-slick thigh. She pressed it solidly against the smaller woman's center. Rachel groaned with pleasure.

"Lace," she complained softly, running her fingers through the tangled dark hair.

"I can't get enough of you," Lacey admitted softly, licking and nibbling her way along the blonde's jawline. One hand caressed a tender nipple, the other stroked Rachel's cheek, bringing with it the scent of her own arousal.

"Sore," the blonde woman gasped out, even as her hips tilted into the warm iron muscle of her lover's thigh. She was reduced to single word sentences in the heated passion.

"I'll be gentle," Lacey promised, knowing she'd been pretty rough earlier in her need to satisfy the smaller woman. She slid down her lover's body to replace thigh with mouth and delicately licked at the swollen lips. Rachel moaned, clutched at the sheets. Any protests died with the building of another orgasm. Using only lips and tongue on the burning flesh, Lacey pushed her over the edge again.

Rachel lay panting, tired.

"Again," the dark woman whispered.

Rachel only whimpered.

"One more," Lacey vowed, all of her previous fervor replaced with complete tenderness. She savored this one, tasting the sweet saltiness on her tongue, smelling the familiar tang of her lover's pleasure. She let this one last, being ever so gentle on the already sore flesh. It took only moments for Rachel to respond, raising her hips slightly to the invading tongue, dropping her knees wider.

"I love you," Lacey hummed on the bundle of nerves beneath her lips. "I will always love you."

Beyond words, Rachel simply reached down to stroke the dark wet hair, smoothing it with trembling fingers.

Lacey continued her gentle assault and whispered endearments. She had to consciously keep herself from using fingers and teeth on this last sweet climb, knowing it would be painful for her lover at this point.

Slowly, Rachel's hips gained more momentum, rising off the bed to meet the dark woman's seeking tongue, feeling only twinges of pain behind the much larger mountain of pleasure. Her eyes were closed to the silver moonlight, leaving her features trusting and vulnerable to Lacey's searching gaze.

The darker woman watched her lover's brow wrinkle in concentration, knew she was on the edge, her breathing irregular, her hips more frantic. She very willingly pushed her over with one final, gentle suck. Rachel groaned her release, her hips jerking in the aftermath, her face relaxing finally into peace.

"No more," she murmured, reaching for Lacey's shoulders to tug her up. "Hold me."

Keeping her promise, the dark woman left her sweet haven and crawled up the smaller woman, past the familiar abdominal scars and pink swollen nipples. She took the slight frame into her arms and rolled both of them to their sides. "Always," she whispered, placing honey-scented kisses along cheeks and forehead.

Weary as she was, Rachel wasn't one to endorse single-sided lovemaking. With a slight smirk, pale eyelids still closed, she slid a slim thigh in between her lover's.

Lacey smiled. "You're too tired."

"Unh unh," she whispered back. "Give me this."

It was an easy request that she knew wouldn't be denied. The dark woman was nearly dripping with arousal, having orgasmed several times simply from riding out her lover's climaxes. It took no more than heated kisses, tender hands, and firm thrusts of hips and thigh to bring her to release again.

"I love you, too," Rachel murmured into the dark woman's sweaty neck. She licked the saltiness there, the contact sending another jolt through Lacey. The young blonde smiled, snuggling closer to her long lover's form and easing gently into much deserved sleep.

Lacey only made it halfway through the night before nightmare images of car crashes and bloody limp bodies awakened her. The rest of the night was spent in silent vigil, holding her partner's naked, well-loved body as tightly as she dared.

Chapter 5

Saturday morning always started early in this house. Even Rico, who'd slept on the sofabed in the television room, fell easily into the routine. The only difference this morning was the hawk-like blue eyes that kept track of every move the others made.

Rico and Molly watched morning cartoons in between completing the little girl's chores, which included vacuuming the downstairs and cleaning the guest bathroom. It went a lot quicker with Rico's assistance and each was quickly seated back in front of the television as Rachel tidied the kitchen and Lacey prepared Molly's favorite breakfast of blueberry crepes.

The two women had spent the better part of an hour cleaning themselves and the bedroom of the smells of their lovemaking. The chore had been interrupted by occasional breaks for lingering kisses. Lacey had to admit a small surge of guilt when she watched her young lover sit gingerly at the kitchen table to whip cream for the crepes, but it didn't diminish the peace she felt this morning compared to the frustration and helplessness of last night. Even after not sleeping half the night, their consummated love had settled her nerves.

After breakfast and clearing the table, Lacey even followed Rachel and Molly to the barn for their morning ride. Rico tagged behind Lacey, mostly because he had nothing better to do.

The two watched silently from the side of the small corral, leaning on plastic white rails. It was cold enough they could easily see their breaths, making it uncomfortable at best to stand still and watch the action inside the ring. Molly grew increasingly frustrated at the way the reins slid through her gloved hands.

"Molly," Rachel called, annoyance in her voice. "Those gloves have grips on them. Just hold the reins tighter. He's getting away with too much."

It was true. The gentle Morgan gelding had an inquisitive nature that far outweighed his years of schooling. He'd learned quickly that Molly wasn't keeping a good hand on the reins and he'd jerk his head up, freeing him of the annoying restriction and allowing him to trot over to Rico and Lacey.

Rico raised his hand when the gelding approached but Lacey stopped him. "Don't pet him. It's a reward for an improper response," she quoted, having obviously been told that before.

"Can we put the martingale on him? He's tossing his head," Molly requested, gathering her reins again and nudging him back along the rail.

"No martingale." Rachel shook her head, stomping her feet to keep warm. "He's tossing his head because you aren't holding him right. You can do this, no aids."

Molly grumbled something as she trotted back by Rico and Lacey, giving the gelding an extra prod to go by the people. Neither heard what she might have said.

Making Strides

It went from bad to worse. Jester was repeatedly taking advantage of the little girl, Molly was growing more and more frustrated, and within twenty minutes she was jerking on the Morgan's mouth and he was stomping and shaking his head angrily.

"Off," Rachel said at last, walking up to child and horse. She captured the reins.

Molly stared at her, making no move to dismount. "I'm sorry, I'll do better. I know I'm pulling on him too much."

Rachel hated to see a horse's mouth abused and her daughter was quickly approaching that. "You're doing fine, sweetie. Just go stand by Lacey and calm down a little. Jester and I are going to have a little chat."

Molly did as she was told and Lacey wrapped the little girl up in her leather trench coat, leaning over to blow hot breath on her cheeks. "Dumb horse," she said, poking Molly in the ribs.

The little girl laughed. "Dumb horse," she agreed, but she was smiling.

They watched Rachel adjust her stirrups and gather the reins to mount. She looked over to Lacey and grimaced at the pain she knew was coming and Lacey actually did a decent job of appearing apologetic.

The small woman gathered the four reins Jester wore, situating the snaffle's by her pinkies and the curb inside further. He danced the entire time, tossing his head and jingling the two bits in his mouth together.

"Doesn't that hurt, stupid?" Rachel muttered, ignoring the painful bouncing. She withdrew a riding crop from its place in her boot and popped him on the shoulder. "Stand still, butthead."

Jester stopped immediately, realizing the game was over. He planted his feet solidly and stretched out to stand in a Morgan park. "Thank you." Rachel grimaced, straightening her reins again before urging him into a walk.

"How many reins does she have?" Rico asked, tilting his head to watch Rachel, squinting to better see her. He'd seen Jester in the barn before but had never been here when he was ridden.

"Four," Molly said. "Two bits. He's a Park Morgan ... but I ride him Saddleseat. Mama said he should come down enough to go to some schooling shows in the spring."

It meant nothing to Rico and his expression said just that. Lacey tried to help since she'd been through the same crash course training.

"It's a style of English riding. The stirrups are longer, the front flaps of the saddle are straight." She gestured with one hand to illustrate her point. "The horses are flashier, higher stepping. The other English you're used to is hunt seat, that's what you see at the Olympics. Those horses are supposed to be quiet and calm, their style more appropriate for long rides after fox or something. This style is showier, these horses are supposed to appear barely contained."

"He looks barely controllable," Rico agreed.

"He's not," Molly assured him. "He gets a little full of himself, but he's easy to handle. It's mostly an act."

"Why two bits. Isn't that hard on him?"

Molly shrugged. "It's not hard on him if they're handled correctly. You're supposed to use the snaffle for most things and a curb as a back up. The snaffle's a pretty gentle bit."

"My little walking trivia book," Lacey cooed, bending down to kiss the little girl's head. Molly elbowed the tall woman's hip.

Rico laughed. "So you're going to show him in the spring?"

"Maybe. If I can handle him."

Meanwhile, Rachel had put Jester through his paces. It took only one more pop to the shoulder to convince the gelding that he wasn't getting away with his antics anymore.

Now he was all business, head high but nose tucked, knees reaching up in front of his chest. She stopped him in the middle of the arena, seemingly without moving body or hands and he parked out again, back feet stretched behind him. Rachel hopped off and signaled to her daughter.

"You're up again. No gloves this time." She took the hand warmers and stuffed them in her pockets before giving the girl a leg up.

"Can I have the crop?"

"See how he does first. I think he's done sight seeing."

He was. He responded more easily to her now and her hands quieted as the frustration left her. He had the same general look of contained spirit, but it was obvious that the little girl had no trouble controlling him.

Finally, after Lacey and Rico thought their arms may just freeze and drop off, Rachel called horse and rider into the center of the ring.

"Great job, Molly. You looked really good. We can get some rides in during the week now, too, since you're off for break."

She slid down, grinning at her mother's praise. "Do you think we'll be ready for any shows? Maybe Rico and Mary would come watch."

"I think you will be. He's a nice horse, Molly. You just need to learn how to react to him when he's doing poorly. Horses are just like people: they have good days and bad days."

Molly nodded, walking beside her mother towards the gate and then the barn. The three adults sat on hay bales there while the girl untacked her mount and brushed him down.

"You gonna ride Sunny?" Lacey inquired innocently and Rachel cast her a dirty look.

"You are such a smart ass."

Lacey laughed, Rico looked at them with confusion.

"I don't think I'll be riding anymore today, thank you. That was more than enough for me."

"I don't get you two half the time." Rico shook his head and went over to help Molly with the finishing touches.

Lacey watched his departure with a grin.

"You're too proud of yourself," Rachel pointed out.

The dark woman turned to meet her gaze, piercing her with suddenly serious blue eyes. "I do feel a teensy bit bad if that helps."

"A teensy bit?"

"Yeah. I feel too good to feel really bad."

Rachel smiled and leaned in to kiss her partner's cheek. "I guess I'll have to settle for teensy then. What are your plans for this afternoon?"

"We are all staying put while Rico and I look through all those files."

"Not much of a plan," Rachel observed.

"Not for you, anyway. Maybe you can learn how to play Zelda. I bet my Link will kick your Link's butt," Lacey teased as she got up to join Molly and Rico, who were now ready to leave the barn.

"You are so competitive, Lace." Rachel shook her head as she stepped into stride beside them.

"But you love me anyway?" The dark woman wrapped an arm around her partner's shoulders to hold her closer.

Rachel sighed as if she were greatly put out by such an admission. "But I love you anyway, ya old crony."

****

Lacey and Rico spent all afternoon flipping through the files they'd gotten from Vinnie. On the first time through, they ditched over half of them based on either personal knowledge of the subjects or on information within the file itself. On the second pass through they made a few phone calls, did a few Internet checks and were able to bring the possible list down to five.

It was nearly dinnertime when Rico retrieved Rachel from Molly's bedroom where they'd been working on some flashcards.

"Lacey has some stuff for you to look at," he said softly, not wanting to interrupt their work but knowing what Lacey needed was important as well.

"Thanks." She held the cards out to Rico. "Do you mind?"

"Nope."

"Did you get a hold of Mary?"

"Yeah. She's gonna come for dinner and then I'll leave with her."

Rachel nodded as she made her escape, traveling the hallway that wrapped around and looked down into the lower living room and heading towards the office at the far end. She knocked gently on the doorframe.

Lacey looked up, smiled warmly at seeing her. "C'mon in, Raich. I want you to look at these."

Rachel went around the desk to stand beside her lover, who pushed her chair out and stood, giving the seat to the young blonde. She took it, looking at the photographs in front of her. There were dozens of them.

"These five here," she tapped the ones on top of each pile, "are the most likely candidates, I think. Below them are pictures of their best known cronies." She grinned at using Rachel's word. "I want you to take a really close look and let me know if you've seen any of them, maybe in your classes or on campus."

"Vinnie let you take his pictures?" Rachel looked up and Lacey shook her head. Didn't she understand the severity of the situation? She was worried about pictures?

"Yeah. Please take a look. I'll give you some time ... I want you to really study them, gorgeous."

"Okay." She nodded, already starting to flip through the first stack.

"I'll be downstairs," Lacey said before slipping out of the room and going down the front stairwell into the living room. She decided she might as well make herself useful and start dinner.

****

Either Rachel had decided to take studying the pictures seriously or she'd fallen asleep, Lacey mused as she put dinner on the table with Molly's help. Rico and the girl had come downstairs when Mary showed up.

Mary was a petite woman, barely Rico's age, with long brown hair and brown eyes. She was painfully quiet and incredibly shy around Lacey. Though she'd not known of Rico's occupation until he was no longer family, she'd spent plenty of time with Rico, George, and Bernard afterwards to get a clear picture of what he had done.

No less than ninety percent of their tales involved a retelling of something amazing Lacey had done. They never shied away from her darkness in their stories, rather they seemed to embrace it as they did her, accepting it fully as part of the woman. They all held a sort of hero worship for the tall, dark beauty and spoke easily of her feral nature and trigger-quick thinking.

Mary had gone through the jealous girlfriend routine right at the beginning. Rico loved the woman, that much was clear, but it had taken her awhile to realize that he loved her like a big sister and a mentor. Besides, the first time she'd seen Lacey and Rachel in a room together, she had known jealousy was a stupid emotion. It was quite clear that the tall dark woman was completely and obliviously taken. The entire world could hit on her and she'd never notice them while she was watching the small blonde woman to whom she was committed.

Once Mary had moved past the jealousy issue, she'd simply been in awe over this woman. She had realized that the laurels the team placed on Lacey were well earned and easily deserved. She was a woman with confidence and tightly held emotions. She walked into a room and took it over on presence alone and was incredibly, undoubtedly, intimidating. So even though Rico bantered easily with the dark woman and she'd seen the others do the same, Mary was still too intimidated to do much more than sit silently in Lacey's presence. What surprised her the most, though, was Molly's abandon with the other woman. It was that open emotion which would some day lead Mary to be more comfortable with her boyfriend's mentor.

They were sitting down at the dining room table, the group being too big for the small kitchen table, when Rachel leaned over the balcony in the living room.

"Hey, Lace!" she called.

Her summons was delivered into the kitchen and the dark woman came out.

"Got somethin' to show you," Rachel said softly and Lacey set down the drink she'd been carrying before climbing the spiral staircase and following her lover back to the office.

There were two pictures sitting on the desk and Lacey picked up both of them.

"First I went through and looked at everyone in the pictures and I didn't see anything. So I went back through them and started looking at the whole picture," she said, hands on hips, obviously quite proud of herself.

Lacey looked at the pictures and then at the young blonde. The photos she held were of two different people from two different files. "Ya lost me."

Rachel sighed. "The whole picture, Lace."

The dark-haired woman looked back at the photographs

again. She noticed that each one had the same man in the background. She nodded. "Good job," she praised, leaning forward to hug the smaller woman. "Where do you know him from?"

"He ... uh ... hit on me on campus."

"He what?" Lacey narrowed her eyes and pursed her lips.

"I saw him a bunch of times at the cafeteria by the student union. He asked me out once or twice, I declined."

"Once or twice?"

"Maybe three times," Rachel admitted sheepishly. "Doesn't matter ... I declined."

Lacey was more caught up in feeling jealous than in the true implications. She hadn't really thought of losing Rachel to someone else before. She'd thought a dozen times at least about losing her young lover to her own dark past and violent streak, but never had it crossed her mind that she needed to worry about outside influences.

"Lace," Rachel prodded 'gently, rubbing the taller woman's stomach. "No big deal, right? He asked me out, I said no."

"Didja want to say yes?" she asked softly.

The young blonde's brow crinkled in confusion. "Hello? Crony? I love you, I live with you, you're the one who ravishes me at night." She grinned gently. "Why would I have wanted to say yes to someone else?" She'd never suspected this insecure part of her lover. "Always you."

"Not even for a sec—"

"Lacey!" Rachel growled her interruption, shaking the other woman by the shoulders. "Are you not listening to me?"

"Sorry ... sorry," Lacey sighed. "I just ... never really thought of you leaving me for someone else."

"That's because I wouldn't," Rachel pointed out helpfully.

"And the thought of someone else wanting to be with you and you maybe wanting to be with someone else ... just got my mind spinning."

"Okay, well kick it out of the rut it's in because I only want to be with you. All right?"

"Yeah."

Rachel was still confused. Gone was the brash confident woman who commanded every room. "Tell me who this guy is? If he works for these people, then he wasn't really interested in me anyway, right?"

"I don't know who he is. Obviously your tail didn't recognize him as a threat. We'll have to run some searches. I'm assuming he's a freelancer if he was seen with both groups. That makes this harder. Do you still see him?"

"Not that I remember. But I haven't been around the student union for a few days and now I won't be back until the new semester starts." Rachel still watched her partner carefully, even though she seemed to be sliding back into a comfortable rhythm. "I have a tail?" she asked, registering the comment belatedly.

Lacey grinned sheepishly and nodded. "Yeah. On campus. Some guy I hired to keep an eye on you once the threats started coming."

Rachel was on the verge of bristling, partially angry that she had a babysitter, partially touched that her lover had been so concerned. She let the latter part win out, knowing the argument about the former concern would have been far from productive. "Why am I always the last to know?" she murmured instead, letting her anger simmer down and keeping it from her voice.

The dark woman shrugged. "I didn't want to worry you. I thought I could handle everything without telling you the details. Plus, you would have found the guy and struck up a conversation with him," she teased gently.

Despite herself, the blonde woman grinned at the comment, knowing it was probably true. She did want to discuss the entire withholding secrets subject that recently appeared to be a recurring theme, but understood her partner's side of it too well to take a strong stand herself, so she let it slide. "Is that why you take Molly to school?"

"Yeah."

"That's thoughtful," Rachel observed.

Lacey raised a dark eyebrow, her ice blue eyes questioning. "I'm not going to be read the riot act for this?"

"Mmm." The smaller woman grinned. "I thought about it, but realized it wouldn't get us anywhere. I know that you did what you did because you love us. That's enough."

"Wow," Lacey mused. "That's a pretty mature approach, Raich."

"Yes, but I reserve the right to argue this point later when I need a good fight."

The dark-haired woman inclined her head, smiling. "You got it."

They continued to look into each other's eyes for another moment before Lacey dropped her gaze back to the pictures in her hand. "You're sure it's him?"

"Positive."

"Good." She tossed the photos back on the desk and slung her arm around Rachel's shoulders. "Let's go have some dinner before it's all gone."

Rachel wrapped one arm around her lover's waist and slapped the taut abdomen with her other hand. "You're not really worried about that guy talking to me, are you, Lacey? Surely you know that I plan to be here for a very long time."

"I know," the darker woman whispered, turning to place a kiss on Rachel's forehead. "I ... always thought that if we weren't together it would be because of something I did or said. Or because my past was too dark for you or you couldn't handle my anger. I never thought about having to worry about other people, too. Silly ... I mean, you're beautiful and smart and gentle. Of course other people are going to be attracted to you, too."

"Baby, please don't worry about things like that," Rachel requested sincerely. "The only way I'll leave here is kicking and screaming, being dragged out bodily."

"Promise?" Lacey managed a grin, knowing it was ridiculous to be concerned about such a thing. It was really the shock of realization that was slowing her down.

"Promise. Besides, how do you think I feel? Every time we walk into a room, the whole damn place drools when they see you. You're about as eligible as they come and I know there are much better catches out there than me."

"I'm incredibly ineligible, Raich, because I'm absolutely taken. And there is no better 'catch' as you say, than you. So enough of this bullshit insecurity. Let's eat."

"I'm starving," the blonde agreed.

"You always are," her lover teased gently, squeezing her shoulders one last time before releasing her and giving her room to head down the stairs.

Chapter 6

Rico and Mary left shortly after dinner. Lacey had shown him the pictures but the man Rachel had seen wasn't familiar to him either. Lacey hadn't expected Rico would know him since the shaggy blond hadn't been in the business nearly as long as she had, but it was worth a try. She went upstairs to the office for some more searching and phone calls while Rachel finished cleaning up the kitchen.

Once she was satisfied with the level of cleanliness, Rachel left the room and started looking for Molly. The little girl was sitting at the foot of the Christmas tree in the living room.

Molly had wanted a real tree but Lacey and Rachel both decided an artificial one would be better for cleanliness and because something about chopping down millions of trees each year just to sit in people's living rooms had always rubbed Rachel the wrong way. So they'd gone out and found a nice fake one and put it up the weekend after Thanksgiving. Lacey had never had any reason to care about the holidays and aside from some casual gift giving with her team, she'd really not participated in anything festive as far back as she could remember. She was incredibly unprepared for sharing the holidays with a nine-year-old.

They'd bought ornaments and light strands, a star for the top. They'd found a tree skirt and stockings. Molly had even goaded the dark woman into decorating the front of the house and the trees and bushes there. Nearly every room held something of holiday flavor from flower arrangements to stuffed reindeer and it all changed the atmosphere of the home dramatically. Lacey'd found rather quickly that Christmas could be a lot of fun if you spent it with the right people. She and Rachel had been forced to have long discussions about spending limits and what Molly did or did not need. They'd finally reached a mutual agreement, though Rachel still feared her daughter would be overwhelmed come Christmas morning. Molly had been raised to this point in a foster home with other children and a single adult. Though Rachel had done her best to provide gifts, money had always been tight and the gifts were never huge or expensive. Lacey didn't have those limitations and her extravagance showed.

Now Molly sat silently in front of the tree, the flashing lights reflecting on the golden hues of her hair. She was sorting presents.

"No fair shaking them," Rachel teased gently, sliding to the carpet next to her daughter.

Molly looked at her and Rachel immediately knew that there were other things churning behind those pale eyes.

"What's up, baby?" the blonde woman asked gently, reaching out a hand to rub her daughter's jean clad knee.

By way of response she held a present up to her mother. Rachel read the tag. "To: Bernard From: Molly."

"It's hard, isn't it?" Rachel asked sympathetically.

"He's never coming back, is he?"

"No, sweetie."

"I've never known anybody who died before," Molly said softly, crawling into her mother's lap to be held there by secure arms.

"Doesn't matter. Every time is hard, it always hurts."

"Are you and Lacey going to die?" Her voice was murmured into her mother's chest.

"Some day. Everyone has to die. But we plan on being with you for many, many years."

"But you can't promise that," she stated softly.

"No, baby. We can't promise that because we don't know."

"Would I go back to Aunt Helen?"

Rachel took a deep breath. She'd never really planned on having this conversation with Molly, but she needed to be honest with her. "Well, I hadn't thought about it. I figured if something happened to me, you'd stay with Lacey. Would you rather go back to Aunt Helen? She loves you very much, too."

"I'd like to live with Lacey. Would she keep me?"

Rachel almost laughed at the oddity of the question. The way she said it sounded like she was some stray Lacey might take in out of the goodness of her heart. Well, maybe that wasn't so far from the truth. "Of course she would. You'd have to help her out, though, because I think she would really miss me and be very sad."

"We could help each other."

"Yeah." She kissed her daughter's head.

"What if something happened to both of you?"

"Do you really want to talk about these things Molly? It's very sad to think about them."

"I do. It's not sad because you're right here," Molly said reasonably. Death and loneliness seemed very far away when she was tucked into her mother's lap like this.

"Probably Aunt Helen, then. We'd have to ask her permission to do that."

"Will you ask her when she comes for Christmas?"

"Sure. But, honey, if she doesn't want the responsibility it's not because she doesn't love you. She's older than we are and it's a lot of work raising a little girl. She may think you'd be better off with someone else."

Molly nodded, apparently not bothered by the thought. "Not gonna happen anyway," she decided stubbornly.

"No, not likely," Rachel agreed, rocking their bodies on the soft cream carpet.

They were silent for a long time. "Was it hard coming here, Molly? Moving into this house and leaving Aunt Helen and your friends?"

"I was a little scared at first. I didn't know if it would be for real. I'd had dreams about being with you and Lacey and having a family that was mine and not someone else's. Then I worried that I would mess it up. A lot of the kids who came to Aunt Helen's ended up there because other foster families didn't work out. I wondered what that meant. Do you know?" She twisted in her mother's lap to peer up at green eyes.

"Mmmm ... it can mean a lot of things I suppose. Maybe that the children needed more attention than the other family could give. Maybe the school they went to with the other family didn't meet the child's needs."

"Do you think it could be because the children were bad?"

"It could mean that. Were they bad when they came to live with you and Aunt Helen?"

"Sometimes," Molly said softly. "Sometimes they were loud and mean and yelled at Aunt Helen. But you know what she did?"

"What, honey?"

"She'd hold them like this," she indicated how she was sitting, "and let them scream all they wanted while she hugged them. They'd tell her they hated her and she just hugged them and said she loved them. Sometimes they even hit or bit her but she never got angry."

"Your Aunt Helen is a very amazing woman, Molly. That's why I left you with her. I knew she would take good care of you until I could again."

"I'm glad you came back."

"I always came back, baby." It was true. Once she'd been released from prison, Rachel had always visited regularly and brought Molly here for visits. She'd never once entertained the idea of leaving Molly for good.

There was lingering silence as they watched the Christmas lights chase each other around the tree.

"You know what's the very worst part?" Molly whispered softly, tears in her voice.

"What?"

"This is the happiest Christmas of my whole life ... and ... I shouldn't be happy because Bernard is gone. And Brian and Tracey are lonely."

Rachel hugged her daughter more tightly at the mention of Bernard's children. "Honey, you have every right to be happy. Bernard was thrilled for you, coming here and living with us. You know that. He would want this to be a very special Christmas for you."

"He'll never have Christmas again," she cried softly.

"I really think that he can see us and hear us. That Christmas morning he'll be watching Brian and Tracey and blowing them kisses."

"He was always very nice to me."

"He was a good man and we all miss him very much." Rachel listened to her child's gentle sobs for a few long moments. "Tell you what. Every time we miss him really badly like we do right now, let's stop and remember something really good he did." The blonde woman paused in thought.

"I remember when Lacey was away on business and you

had just started living here. You got really sick and I didn't know any doctors or who to call or what to do. Bernard came over and took us to Tracey's doctor, remember? And he stayed with us the whole time and calmed us both down. Do you remember?" It sounded so much simpler than it had been. At the end of the summer everything had been in such upheaval as Lacey was trying to get her business started and Rachel was trying to become a full time mother. It had only been the flu, really, but Molly had been throwing up all night long, leaving both exhausted and weary by morning. She'd been in tears when she'd called Bernard.

He'd come right over, no questions asked, and whisked them away, carrying a weak Molly and holding Rachel's hand in his big, meaty grip. He never once teased her about it being just the flu and her overreacting. He never once looked at her as if she had no right raising a child if she couldn't get through one sleepless night. The support he'd offered that day had given Rachel the strength she needed to keep trying. She would be eternally grateful for that.

"Your turn," Rachel whispered to Molly.

"Brian and I were playing in his backyard and we climbed way up high in that big tree. We got so high we were scared and we couldn't get down. We started crying. Tracey went to get him and he brought out a ladder and pulled us out of the tree. When we were on the ground he just hugged us. I thought he was going to yell at us for being so dumb." Her voice gained strength near the end of the story.

Rachel grinned into the fine blonde hair by her chin. She remembered Bernard's half of the story. He'd been laughing when he told it, said the kids were just like mewling kittens waiting for a fireman. He said he'd thought about lecturing them, but realized they'd scared themselves senseless enough and just needed a good hug. "That's a good memory, baby," Rachel said softly.

"I have lots of good memories."

"Good for you. Try to remember those when you're really sad, okay?"

"I can do that." She nodded, the advice taking a stronghold. She leaned back and smiled up at her mother, her eyes still moist but no longer shedding new tears. "He would like that."

"Yes, he would."

They sat in silence for what seemed like hours, wrapped in the comfort of each other and fond memories. The Christmas tree lights shined cheerfully on the inviting packages beneath it, promising of treasures to come. Karma sauntered in and curled up next to them, placing a soft, white muzzle in Molly's lap.

That was the picture that Lacey walked in on.

"A Norman Rockwell Christmas," the dark woman joked gently, kneeling beside them.

Rachel smiled at her and reached out a hand to stroke a high cheekbone. Her touch was tender and Lacey leaned into it.

"We were remembering happy things about Bernard," Molly piped up, never being one to let a quiet moment last.

"That's really nice, baby," Lacey said softly, leaning forward to cup the back of Molly's head and kiss her forehead.

Ice blue eyes met gentle green and Rachel read in them her lover's need to talk.

"Hop on up, Molly." She gave her a helpful shove and rose to her feet as well, stretching muscles stiff from sitting so long.

"Are we gonna go to the movies?" the little girl inquired, reminding them of their normal Saturday night activity. It had become a ritual of sorts.

Rachel glanced to her partner and realized that the dark woman had every intention of keeping them under lock and key at the house. "Not tonight. Maybe we'll check out the pay per view movies after a little while, okay?"

Only mildly disappointed, the little girl acquiesced. "Then can I play some Nintendo?" she asked instead, already moving towards the television room.

Rachel laughed. "Go ahead. We'll be upstairs in the office."

Lacey was a perfectionist if there ever was one. Everything from her car to her home to her refrigerator was always spotless and well organized. This personality attribute had made getting used to a dog and a child more than a little difficult. But, thankfully, the dark woman never expected that same trait in others. As long as no one else in the house was a blatant slob, she could live with straightening her own things and badgering the others until they did the same, which was why Rachel was shocked when she walked back into the upstairs office. She hadn't been out of it that long, a couple hours at the most, but the storm that had happened since her departure was startling.

She looked at her partner with wide-eyed wonder and was answered with a smirk and raised eyebrow, daring her to vocalize her comment.

The smaller woman was never one to back down from a challenge, so she smirked right back, letting her eyes wander over the strewn files and the open cabinets. "D'ja finally get that letter bomb I sent? Figured it was lost in the mail."

"Funny girl." Her partner grinned. "Come sit down."

"Is there a clean spot to sit, crony?"

"Sit." The dark woman hauled her companion over to the desk chair and applied pressure to her shoulders until she took the seat.

"Control freak," Rachel murmured, but she was grinning and Lacey chuckled dryly at the comment.

"I want you to look at the rest of these pictures I pulled out."

"Who are they?" Rachel asked, turning serious and beginning to examine the photographs laid out in front of her.

"That guy you recognized is named Peter Grazier. He's a freelance hit man, top caliber, discreet and very clean. He's pretty new to the block, apparently, but has left quite an impression. These are pictures of the people who usually work for him on a job."

Rachel felt her stomach flip at the description of hit man. "He's trying to kill us?" She looked up to her partner, the fear hitting her for the first time. Her green eyes were wide with it.

Lacey knelt down, her brow crinkled. "Baby, what did you think that car was trying to do?"

She shrugged, looked back at the pictures without seeing them. "I guess I knew that. But it seems surreal somehow that someone would want me dead enough to hire a killer."

The dark woman chewed on her lip for awhile, looking at the pictures her lover pushed around with a blunt-nailed finger. "They're after me, Raich. And they're trying to hurt me by getting you. They know I'll be less efficient without you."

The blonde still didn't raise her head. "You'd be more efficient without me, Lace. Because you'd be bent on killing whoever did it."

Silence prevailed for a very long time until Lacey nodded slowly. "Yes. You're right."

"Why can't they see that?"

"I don't think they care. They want to cut me to ribbons and that's the best way to do it."

"I'm pretty sure I don't want to die this way," Rachel said simply, finally raising her head to meet her companion's steady sapphire gaze.

Lacey gave her a lopsided smile, her heart hurting. "It's not too late to walk away. They might refocus their efforts on me."

Rachel smiled affectionately, shook her head. "Way too late, love. I can't walk away."

The dark-haired woman tried not to show her relief, but could tell by the warmth in the emerald eyes watching her that she'd been unsuccessful. "We need to get through this then."

The smaller woman nodded. "Do you know who this Grazier guy is working for?"

"No. That's what I'm trying to figure out. None of my sources have a clue, didn't even know he was on a job right now. But from what I hear, he's one of the best, Raich, so it'll be hard to figure out who's paying the bills. I'm hoping that if you've seen some of these other guys that I may be able to narrow it down by how big the job is."

"Whether the person behind it is small change or not."

"Exactly." The dark head nodded confirmation.

Rachel seemed to think for a long time, quiet and withdrawn. Then she started shuffling through the pictures. She took her time, studying each one carefully. She looked at the whole picture, and then covered hair and mouth to focus on the eyes, before deciding. Lacey paced the office, stepping around the scattered files and growing impatient.

"Do you think they were counting on you not recognizing him?" Rachel asked suddenly, interrupting Lacey's thoughts of a Grazier massacre. "Since you've been gone?"

"I doubt it. I don't think I was meant to see him at all, if he's been at school. I didn't recognize any of those guys and I've never seen a tail when we're out together, but maybe they're only interested in you right now."

Rachel was silent again as she studied the pictures. "Do you think this is the same guy that killed Bernard?"

"Or one of his cronies." Lacey shrugged. "It really is irrelevant who actually did it. I want the person behind it all."

Finally, Rachel set aside the pictures, withholding a few. These last ones she handed to Lacey, who'd stopped pacing in front of the desk.

The dark woman flipped through them. "Are you sure, Raich?"

"Not would-you-stake-your-life-on-it sure. But pretty sure."

There were five pictures total and Lacey studied each one. "All at school?"

The blonde shook her head and left her seat to stand at Lacey's elbow. "That guy was in my critical writing class. That guy in the grocery store last week. The woman was waiting with me in the doctor's office when I went for that sinus infection last month. And the other two are familiar but I don't know why."

"You have a good memory," Lacey praised gently.

Rachel smiled and shrugged. "Can't do names, but I'm pretty good at faces."

"I have a tough one for you, then. This guy in your class. What did he say his name was?"

"Lionel somebody or other." The blonde shook her head. "He's not registered. He asked to sit in and observe for no grade and the professor agreed."

Lacey grumbled slightly. "Figures. Can't track him that way."

Rachel stood quietly in the center of the room next to her lover, watching the dark woman's long fingers trace along the pictures. "Five people is a lot, isn't it Lacey?"

Her companion nodded slowly, pursing her lips. "There are more, too. Kinda like mice ... for every one you see, there are several you don't. Maybe this is bigger than I thought. But it's so personal, Raich. That's what gets me."

"Didn't they threaten Bernard or did they threaten just his family?"

"Family."

"But they killed Bernie."

Lacey nodded again, the frustration coming off of her in dark waves. Rachel could picture in her now a little of the woman she was when they'd first met. It had been so long since Rachel had seen the working crony that she'd forgotten the power her companion held.

"So why were they trying to kill me and not you."

"They want to hurt me. Not kill me. It's personal. Never in all the time that I worked for Vinnie did I do anything more than threaten family. Family is everything in that world, Raich, and you make a real statement by killing them."

"We're your family?"

Lacey looked up from the pictures in her hands to cast a glance sideways at her young lover, who had a mixture of emotions on her face. "Of course, doofus," she teased gently.

Rachel laughed. "What's Vinnie, then? He was family."

"Was. Not anymore. You walk away from the life, you leave the family as well." She paused in thought as realization dawned. "In fact, this isn't even about Vinnie, Raich. This is about me. They killed Bernard, chased away George. They're after you."

"Rico's in danger." Rachel was suddenly alarmed. "Real danger, Lace. They're going from the outside in."

She shook her head, the long dark braid smacking her shoulder blades. "No ... that doesn't explain the attack on you last night."

"You have to get him and bring him back here. He's safe here. Lacey—" The blonde woman was becoming frantic.

Lacey set the pictures down and captured Rachel's face between her palms. "Stop. Stop. Listen to me. I'll call Rico. We'll bring him and Mary here. But you need to understand something. If they wanted you dead, you would be dead already. I haven't been with you every second, Molly's been at school, so have you. You walk to the barn at least three times a day and only the house is alarmed. Bernard was a professional like me, but he still didn't see it coming. They wanted him dead, he is dead."

"You're not making me feel better," Rachel said softly, her eyes growing misty.

"I'm trying to be honest, love. The car meant something ... maybe it was just a scare or maybe it was an intent to kill ... but it was out of place. You're right about their approach: outside in. If they follow that pattern they'll go for Rico next. Maybe find George. Then you and Molly. But they're waiting to make their move, because otherwise we'd have attended a few more funerals."

Rachel stood silently for a very long time, staring into the depths of her lover's eyes, realizing for the first time since Lacey had come home after Rico's first kill what she'd walked into. There was no turning back now, that much she knew. Since she needed Lacey as surely as she needed air, leaving the dark woman wouldn't save her life.

The young blonde was frightened and it showed in her face and the way she held her slim body. Lacey waited for something, anything, to happen.

The taller woman realized now that the fear she'd felt last night hadn't been shared. They hadn't really talked about the car or its implications, though Lacey had dwelt on them all night long. It was just now, this moment, that her smaller lover was facing reality. Her haunted emerald eyes reflected the depths of her understanding.

"C'mere," Lacey said at last, being the one to break the silence for quite possibly the first time in their relationship. Rachel usually reserved that right. She tugged the small blonde into her arms and sank to the floor with her, settling her in her lap.

"Wow. You lived with this every day?" Rachel asked

finally, searching to understand this woman she'd committed to.

"No." Lacey shook her head. "Not this. I never cared before, I never had anything to live for so it didn't scare me. You changed all that. I knew before I met you that it was starting to drag on me, that I couldn't do it forever. But when I started to get to know you, I understood it was time to go. It was an easy decision really, I'd been headed that way for a long time. You can't do that job and have too strong of a desire to live to see tomorrow."

"What about Bernard and George? Rico?"

"I think Bernard and George would have left a long time ago if they thought they could. Bernard carried a picture of his kids in his pocket on every job. Every damn one. And he kissed that photo after he cocked his gun. Rico was just too young. He needed a job, he was a street rat. Easy pickings."

Rachel nodded; she understood that. She would have done anything to survive while she was living on the streets. Almost anything. She wouldn't have joined Vinnie's family ... unless of course she'd met Lacey as part of the interview process. She grinned at the thought and it seemed oddly out of place, but Lacey didn't comment.

"I don't like having to worry about seeing my daughter in the morning, or waking up next to you in a week. These were things I took for granted," Rachel said softly, her grin from moments before dissolving into nothing.

Lacey nodded her agreement, holding her lover close and kissing just behind her ear. "I'll fix it, I promise."

"You have to come out of it alive, too, Lace," Rachel pointed out. It was a gentle reminder that times were different, that the dark woman couldn't go into this situation full throttle with guns blazing.

She smiled. "Wouldn't want it any other way. I want to see Molly every morning and wake up beside you for a long time to come," she assured her lover warmly.

"Are you afraid?" Rachel asked softly.

"You know the answer to that, Raich," Lacey responded, avoiding saying it out loud.

"I knew you needed to be with me last night." The blonde nodded solemnly. "I understood that. It was part of being alive and you wanted to dwell in it."

"Very much so."

"I guess I didn't think a lot about what happened yesterday and what you would have seen ..." She let her voice trail off to silence.

"I couldn't think of anything else," Lacey whispered softly.

Rachel was quiet for a very long time, her cheek pressed into the silk of her lover's shirt, the denim of Lacey's jeans leaving imprints on her bare feet where she had them tucked beneath a well muscled thigh. "I understand you better at this moment than I ever have," the blonde said slowly into the silence that ensconced them.

"Yeah?" Lacey leaned back to see her partner's face, one dark eyebrow raised.

"Everything you do is so ... big. You were afraid to lose me last night so you couldn't get enough of me. You used to live your life not caring about each coming day, but now you need to see tomorrow so much that you'll do anything to get us there. You want to be a mother to Molly, but you feel you aren't enough. You push away when you can't hold us closer. Last night you were just as likely to turn your back and lick your wounds as hold me. You never knew fear until you knew love."

The dark woman swallowed, pressed her wet cheek against golden hair. "What, you writing a biography?"

"I want to know you."

"No one knows me better, love."

"Do you think?" Rachel grinned slowly, leaning back to

see her lover and wiping at her wet cheeks. "Do you think you could teach me the finer techniques of emotional release through lovemaking?"

Lacey smiled. "Sure. But it's not all it's cracked up to be. It's more of an in-the-moment kind of thing. You still spend the night thinking about it."

"Not if you're too tired to think." Green eyes twinkled mischievously and Lacey knew she was in for some revenge.

"You're too sore."

"Not talkin' about me, crony."

The dark woman laughed gently and held her lover close.

Chapter 7

Try as Rachel might, all the gentle kisses and sensual touches in the world couldn't keep the morning at bay. They were still awake, exhausted, weary and greatly sated, but awake nonetheless when the morning sun started trickling across the room. It sneaked silently between the white horizontal blinds and chased itself across the plushly carpeted floor, before tentatively reaching out and touching the edge of the bed.

Both women watched it as if it were alive. As if, at any moment, it could change its course and spring on them.

"Do you think hamsters are nocturnal because they have sex all night long?" Rachel murmured softly, tightening her grip on the solid frame beside her.

Lacey laughed out loud, bouncing both bodies and the bed. "Where do you come up with this shit, Raich?"

"I'm creative," the blonde said defensively.

"You're borderline psychotic, baby," Lacey corrected gently, brushing at the errant golden locks surrounding her lover's features. "Did it work?" she asked after a moment of silence, meaning the diversion technique.

"Mmm," Rachel sighed, snuggled deeper into the covers and the arms of her partner. "Not really. Don't get me wrong," she grinned, "I'm not complaining. But you were right ... I still can't shake being afraid."

"I have an idea, Rachel," Lacey said softly, the seriousness in her voice letting the small blonde know that this was something big.

"Do tell," she prodded gently.

"I think we should leave here."

"Here as in bed, here as in the house?"

"Here as in New York."

"Come again?" Rachel leaned back and halfway sat up to better see the dark woman's somber profile. "We're running?"

Lacey grimaced. "Don't say it like that," she chided. "Not running ... protecting."

"Please, I'm all ears." Rachel settled back into her comfortable position of moments before.

"We're at a disadvantage here. They know the area, they know our routine, we don't even know who they are. If we move the field to neutral turf, we're all on the same level. The only advantage would be skill and desire. And believe me love, they couldn't possibly want to hurt you and Molly more than I want to protect you."

"And you are one of the best cronies around," Rachel supplied helpfully, getting a poke in the ribs.

"*The* best, you mean."

"Oh yeah. No ego problem here. Do you walk through doors sideways?"

"It's a damn good thing I love you," the dark woman growled playfully, nipping at Rachel's ear.

"So where are we going?"

Lacey shrugged, stretched her long limbs and unsettled the woman draped over her. "Where do you want to go?

Where have you never been?"

"Uh ... anywhere but New York?" the young blonde teased, never having been out of the state except for short jaunts over to New Jersey or Connecticut.

"It's Christmas ... we should go to the Rockies."

"I think that's a song," Rachel murmured, already deep in thought.

"Whaddya think? Colorado?"

"I don't need to point out to you that we have a week until Christmas and unless we drive or hitchhike, there's not much chance of us getting there. And when we do get there, we'll have to sleep on the streets because nothing's reserved."

"Pessimist. Leave that to me."

"What about Mary and Rico?" The two had come back over the previous night and spent it on the sleeper sofa in the television room.

"The more the merrier," Lacey replied, completely undaunted by her lover's unusual cynicism. "You game?"

"You think it's necessary? Really?" Rachel asked seriously, not wanting to uproot everyone and drag them halfway across the country. But it was a small price to pay if it would keep them alive.

"I'm not saying we couldn't get through this without leaving. But I think it betters our odds. And I'd prefer to do it this way," the dark-haired woman said honestly.

Rachel began to softly warble John Denver's *Rocky Mountain High* slightly off key. Lacey knew the decision had been made.

****

It took hours and plenty of called-in favors to set everything up. Very little sleep for the two previous nights and all day on the phone left Lacey wearily lying on the bed while

Rachel packed for them.

"Mama?" Molly hollered, flying in from her room down the hallway. "Should I bring my winter hat? Do you think I'll need it?"

"Probably, squirt," Lacey murmured her response. "And mittens. But bring some cooler clothes too, T-shirts and such. Colorado has unpredictable weather this time of year."

"Weather channel says it's sixty degrees there now," Rico announced, as he walked in the room. He and Mary had gone home earlier to pack and now had their bags downstairs.

Lacey nodded. "And it could snow a foot tomorrow."

Molly heaved a huge sigh and turned around. "I'm gonna have to pack my whole room!" she yelled as she stomped out.

"Only the left half, baby," Lacey called after her, grinning. "Leave the nightstand and the hope chest. And break down the bed ... it's easier to pack that way."

Rachel smiled. "Stop teasing her," she scolded, but it wasn't a statement meant to be taken seriously. You had to learn to hold your own in this crowd.

"She seems excited," Lacey said hopefully, turning her attention to her young lover. Rachel read the comment for what it was.

"Don't feel guilty, Lace. This is fine. It'll be fun. You can catch the assholes that are hunting us down and we get to visit the mountains."

Lacey smiled at the gentle reassurance. "Aren't you done packing, yet?"

"Well, if you'd get off your ass—"

The dark woman started to do just that.

"No, no. I'm kidding. You look beat. Just stay still, I'm almost done." The blonde's teasing banter had dropped away to reveal quiet sincerity.

"Briargate's coming for the horses in two hours," Rico

said, still standing in the doorway. "They just called."

Rachel looked from Rico to her lover. "We'll be gone by then."

"Love, I'm sure they can handle our three horses. All of them trailer fine, right?" Lacey asked softly.

"Yeah," she agreed reluctantly. She hated leaving her horses in other people's care, especially when it came to things like transportation. But they'd decided during the course of making arrangements that it was better to remove the horses than put someone in danger by continuously coming to the house.

"How about Karma?" Rico asked.

"Lacey took her to the vet earlier for her health certificate and we have her kennel ready. Let's hope she likes to fly."

Rico grinned from ear to ear. "You're kidding. She's coming with us?"

Lacey snorted from her prone position across the room. "Are you serious? Do you think they'd let me leave her?"

"What's Christmas without family?" Rachel grinned. "Can't leave her behind."

"That is so cool," Rico laughed. "The whole damn family's going!"

"Mama?"

"What, honey?" Rachel called, zipping up the suitcase at last, feeling she hadn't packed nearly enough.

"What about the presents?" Molly stepped into the room. Karma bounced in behind her and leapt on the bed to circle once and then settle on Lacey's feet.

All three pairs of adult eyes widened. Oops. Hadn't thought of that.

It was then that Mary stepped into the room and cleared her throat gently. "Uh ... I thought, maybe, we could open some now, take some smaller ones with us, and leave the rest as welcome home presents."

Lacey beamed, giving the smaller woman a grateful smile. "I think that's a great idea. Molly, why don't you finish packing and then go pick two presents to open now and four to take with you. Okay?"

"Do you mean pick out presents I want to give or ones I want to open?"

"Both," Rachel answered. "Scoot or we're never going to get out of here."

When the child had left and only adults and a recumbent pooch remained, Rachel looked to her lover. "Exactly how much does it cost to buy five roundtrip tickets to Colorado with one day notice a week before Christmas?"

"Oh ... you really don't want to know, love," Lacey assured her. They'd been unable to secure all five seats on the same flight or the same airline. But she'd searched long and hard and pleaded and pulled strings to get three on one flight and two on another so Mary, Rachel, and Molly would be protected. They would arrive at Denver International within an hour of each other.

"I think you're right." Rachel nodded her agreement. "Forget I asked."

"All set?" Lacey asked as she sat up and swung her feet over the side of the bed. Karma jumped to her feet to lick the woman's face profusely. "Just you wait, fuzzball. I hope they don't pressurize baggage."

"That's not funny, Lace," Rachel said solemnly.

The dark-haired woman regretted the words as soon as they left her mouth. "You're right. I'm sorry. She'll be fine, Raich. I wouldn't be doing this if I didn't think everyone would be all right." She hugged the Siberian Husky to her as a show of good faith.

Rachel nodded, believing her partner and trusting in her implicitly. "Let's go see how Molly's doing."

Chapter 8

Denver International Airport was huge and artistic, filled with yuppy images to match the yuppy attitude of the young city's population. They arrived in terminal C, welcomed by a soothing recorded voice and pictures of the mountains on every available wall space. The tram to take them to baggage claim was sunken into an ornately carved marble pit, which also held a planter with water fountains and beautiful lush foliage. The floor was covered in marble tiling and every few blocks of the gray stone were embossed with brass fossil shapes.

Molly studied these intently as she held her mother's hand and bounced from tile to tile.

"When is their flight coming in?" Rachel asked for at least the tenth time. Lacey sighed, frustrated both with holiday traveling and the stress of their situation.

"Another forty minutes. Let's jump on the tram and go to terminal B ... that's where they're coming in."

"Have you been to this airport before?" the blonde woman asked, following her lover through the throng of people towards the escalators.

"Couple of times. Was at the old airport, too. This is a vast improvement."

"Isn't this the one that was so late in opening because of baggage problems?"

"Yeah," Lacey confirmed, turning to lean her back against the side of the escalator as it took them slowly downwards into the marble pit. She looked at Rachel, her position having them at eye level. "Something about the software used or the developers. I was kinda busy at the time, I don't remember."

Rachel grinned, enjoying seeing her lover in the eye without craning her neck. "Busy? Doing what?"

Lacey smirked and her ice blue eyes twinkled slightly, letting Rachel know that she didn't really want to say what she'd been doing in such a public place. Odds on it had been illegal and deadly.

"Mama, look at the water," Molly interrupted, tugging at Rachel's sleeve and pointing into the planter.

"That's pretty, sweetie," Rachel acknowledged then turned back to Lacey. "Don't you think they went a bit overboard? Does an airport need to look like a botanical garden?"

The dark-haired woman shrugged, turned her attention back in front of her. "I don't pay Colorado state tax."

The man in front of her glanced over and grinned. "I do. And they did go overboard." He looked to Rachel, smiling at her.

"How late was it in opening?" the blonde asked curiously and Lacey smiled. Rachel could start a conversation with a fire hydrant, if she were so inclined. It didn't surprise her at all that the young woman was being congenial to a total stranger in an airport while they were running from killers.

The man shrugged. "I don't remember exactly. They

kept pushing it back, but the worst part was all of the vendors and stores in the old airport lost money because they'd started their leases here, but it wasn't open yet."

Rachel grimaced.

"Yeah. It was a lot of bad press for transportation and commerce."

"But it's okay now?" Rachel suggested, gesturing around them at the swarms of people as they stepped off the escalator and lined up at the tram doors.

"Sure. An airport's an airport, right?" He offered them a last smile before stepping away towards a group of business types.

"Nice man," Rachel said softly and got a raised eyebrow for her comment. She laughed.

"Mama? Can I sit with Lacey on the way back?" Molly piped up, gripping Rachel's hand with both of hers while she swiveled around wide eyed and took in the scenery. This was her first trip anywhere and she'd been amazed from the first moment they'd stepped into the airport in New York.

Lacey hadn't been able to get three seats together so Rachel and Molly had sat in first class while the dark-haired woman made do with a middle seat in coach. The experience had left Lacey uncomfortable and cranky.

"I think that's a good idea. Maybe she'll have a better attitude, then," Rachel poked gently.

"I wanted you two to have the nice seats," Lacey grumbled, looking away and not finding any humor in her young lover's antagonizing.

"Yeah, but, baby, it doesn't do any good when you're so gracious as to offer us those seats and then you turn into a hag because you hated your seat. Next time, you get the good seats with Molly and I'll sit with my knees in my chin."

Lacey conceded the point with a bashful grin. She really was being difficult and it didn't make sense to offer up the first class position and then make the young woman feel guilty about taking it. "Sorry," she murmured, reaching out to squeeze Rachel's elbow. "I'll be good."

The young blonde was mildly surprised at how quickly her partner gave in, but did her best not to show it. Instead, she simply smiled warmly as they made their way into the tram where they were fortunate enough to be packed like sardines.

Rico and Mary were only twenty minutes late in arriving and appeared to have survived the trip with no difficulties. The group made their way to baggage claim, loading onto the tram once again.

The huge luggage area was completely open, without anyone checking tickets or stopping people from leaving with incorrect bags. That struck Rachel as unusual, given the higher security of most airports these days.

The next thing she noticed was the baggage carousel against the wall, which had tall slotted compartments that moved quietly through the room. She eyed it, tilting her head.

"Mama? What's that for?" Molly asked.

"I have no idea," Rachel said honestly.

Her lover chuckled. "It's for skis. A lot of people bring skis with them here."

"Enough that they have a special rack?"

"It's mostly full, isn't it?"

Rachel conceded, realizing that nearly every compartment was filled with a tall canvas bag. She turned away, the novelty having worn off. "Where will Karma come out?"

They put the dog on Rico's flight, deciding it would be easier to wait with her on that end than to have her arrive here and wait an hour for Rico and Mary's flight.

"Over here, I think." Rico tilted his head towards an enclosed office in the wall as the ski carousel. "There, look."

Sure enough, once they'd opened the door they saw the

familiar tan colored plastic crate with live animal stickers all over it.

"Pooch," Rachel said softly and Karma started emitting a series of howls and woos.

"Yours, I take it." The woman behind the counter smiled. "Do you have your claim tickets?"

Rico produced the requested documents while Rachel brought Karma out and checked her over.

"Was it okay, girl? Were you scared?"

"Oh yeah," Lacey scoffed, looking at her lover and the little girl as they fawned over Karma. "She looks petrified, Raich." The only thing the dog seemed concerned about was who to lick first and how much drool she should impose on them.

It seemed to take forever to collect the rest of their baggage and get the rental car settled. Finally, they were on their way out of the airport parking lot. Molly turned in her seat to watch the complex shrink behind them. "It looks funny. Like it could be in X Files," she commented.

She got no argument from anyone in the car. The structure looked like a series of glowing white tents mashed together on the plains, rising from darkness to glowing peaks.

"I think it's supposed to look like the mountains," Rico offered.

It was as good an explanation as any and they let it go at that.

Lacey had an old associate who owned a condo in Breckenridge. With a bit of nagging and a great sum of money, she'd managed to talk him into rescinding the reservations already holding the place and opened it for Lacey's use. The dark woman felt a little bad that she'd ruined someone else's Christmas, until her acquaintance assured her that it was a rich business man and his mistress who'd decided on France instead.

The Budget car rental people had been kind enough to give her a map and directions along with the keys to the minivan they now occupied, so Lacey was able to navigate onto I-70, which wrapped its way lazily around the northern borders of downtown Denver before heading straight into the mountains. Through the darkness they could only see silver moonlight bouncing off snow-capped peaks. Rachel observed them silently from her position in the front passenger seat. She wasn't sure she'd ever seen anything more beautiful.

The condo was freezing and dark when they pushed open the front door and stepped inside. Lacey went first, turning on lights and checking each room. She hadn't been subtle about their departure, using their own names for all of the reservations. She wanted to draw the enemy out more than she wanted to hide.

The place was empty and they all came in carrying bags and staking out rooms. There were three bedrooms and two pull-out couches. Rachel and Lacey settled downstairs where there were two bedrooms side by side so they could be by Molly. That left Rico and Mary in the bedroom upstairs close to the kitchen.

While her lover unpacked, Lacey turned up the heat and started a fire. Then she set a kettle to boiling for hot chocolate. Soon they were all seated in the living room, dressed warmly, watching a roaring fire in the fireplace.

"I think we should ski while we're here," Lacey announced. "What's the point of coming to Colorado and not skiing?"

"I'm sure it can be done, Lace," her partner said softly, snuggling deeper into the warm arms around her.

"Sure, but why would you want to?" The dark woman grinned, raising an eyebrow to Rico to encourage him into joining her side.

"I think I'd try snowboarding." The young man smiled,

jumping in and trying to bring Mary with him. "What about you? You up for it?"

"Sure." Mary shrugged, smiling at Lacey's eager look.

"Molly?" Lacey asked. She felt the body she held tense and her grin faded. She planted a kiss at Rachel's ear.

"I'd love to!" the little girl enthused. "I've seen it on television. It doesn't look so hard ... just go over the jumps and tuck up." She bounced to her feet to show by example what she had seen.

Rachel shook her head slowly, wanting to deny the activity, being afraid to death of it herself, but not wanting to influence her daughter. "Not me. You guys go ahead."

"C'mon, baby," Lacey said softly. "We'll all go tomorrow, it'll be fun. We can rent the equipment."

Rachel turned slightly in her lover's arms so they could see each other's eyes. "I can't," she whispered. "Please?"

The dark woman saw fear there and it surprised her. As well as she knew this young woman and as much as they'd been through, she'd only seen genuine fear a few times. One of them had been just last night when they'd talked about Bernie's murderers, one had been after the incident with the car a few days ago, and the other was right now. She hadn't ever wanted to ease someone's dread as much as she did at that moment. She hated most of all that she'd caused every one of her lover's fears. "Okay," Lacey soothed gently, rubbing her hand along the young blonde's back, feeling the muscles relax. "Okay, no skiing for Raich. Would you mind going with us? Staying in the lodge?"

"That would be okay," she agreed softly, kissing Lacey on the lips before leaning in to bury her face in the warmth of her neck. "Take care of our little girl," she whispered for only Lacey's ears.

It wasn't until later when they were all in bed that Lacey had a chance to quiz her smaller partner. Rachel was securely wrapped around her lover, face in neck, arm and leg across strong body. "Baby?" Lacey started softly.

"Hmm?" Rachel didn't move, but she was awake and not even really sleepy. She could hear Karma trotting up and down the hardwood floor hallways looking for trouble or mischief. The vet in New York had warned that Karma may need some extra water and food at this altitude and climate. Apparently altitude sickness was pretty common to both humans and animals.

"Why don't you want to ski?"

"Mmm." She rolled to her back, resting her head in the crook of Lacey's shoulder and entwining her fingers with the long ones that stroked her belly. "It's always frightened me. How they show all the horrible accidents and you hear about people being paralyzed or getting killed. I've never wanted to ski, going that fast downhill on a slick surface never appealed to me."

"But you'll ride a twelve hundred pound horse at thirty miles an hour surrounded by other horses. That's probably more dangerous," her lover pointed out quietly.

"Maybe. But I can control that horse and my riding controls the situation, whether I'm on the rail or off, in the pack or out. It doesn't worry me."

"Once you learn to ski, you can control your speed and direction. It's the same thing, you have to learn how to do it."

"I don't want to," Rachel said firmly, tilting her head to see Lacey's dark profile. "I know it's silly but I'm afraid. And over ninety percent of trying something new is confidence. I don't have the confidence to do it and my fear will just get me hurt. No thanks."

"You don't want Molly to, either?" Lacey asked carefully, knowing the answer to the question. As much as they shared in the raising of the little girl, when it came down to it, Rachel was her mother. And if Rachel made a decision about Molly or her future, Lacey felt she had no choice but to abide by it.

Rachel sighed, rolled onto her stomach so she could rest her chin on the hand she'd splayed above Lacey's breast. "I don't want her to, no, but it's not my choice to make. She's old enough to want to try things and learn things. I can't stand in her way. It just frightens me. I don't want her to live in fear of the things I do. She has more opportunities and more available to her than I ever did. I think you should take her skiing. Besides, she's really excited about it now, we can't say no after promising."

"Raich, honey ... I," Lacey was recalling her lover's tenseness when she'd asked Molly to go. "I had no right to ask her without talking to you first. I'm sorry. If I'd known and not asked, we wouldn't be in a corner."

Rachel's brow wrinkled, Lacey could just make it out by the moonlight coming in from the window across the room. "Of course you had a right. I'm not the veto committee. Questions and activities don't have to be run by me first."

"She's your daughter," Lacey said softly.

"Ah. Well, let me tell you something, crony. I think of her as our daughter. Hush—" She laid her fingers on the dark woman's lips when she felt her chest move with an intake of breath. "Before she came here, I raised her for two years and then went to prison. Right?" Lacey nodded mutely, her lips still covered by soft fingers. "And then I saw her once a month and a few weeks in the summer until you and I were together. You have had as much influence on raising her as I have. You're as much her mother, really, as I am. I gave birth to her, but she doesn't remember much of me before we were us. So you have every right to make decisions and plan events. Don't feel like you need my approval to do things with your little girl."

The room was achingly silent for many long moments. Rachel was afraid she'd gone too far, pushed too hard. Maybe telling a woman who was always on the verge of backing away that she was a mother figure wasn't a good idea. Perhaps someone who's already feeling trapped doesn't really need to hear the gate close with the clang of commitment.

The young blonde was ready to apologize and withdraw her words when the arms around her tightened and lifted, settling her small body squarely on top of the length of her lover.

"When I went to the school last week and talked to the principal ... I thought of her as mine. It was the first time I had, really. I liked it. And that other little girl asked Molly if I was her other mother." She laughed softly. "Molly looked to me to see if I'd accept her saying yes. I did. I hadn't wanted to, I thought it was reserved for you and the bond you share with her. But to hear her agree that I was her other mother ... it was a good feeling."

Lacey sighed, kissed Rachel gently on the nose. "I know I've been difficult lately, pushing you away then pulling you close. Telling you I can't live without you and then yelling at you that I need to be alone. I'm sorry."

"It's okay," the blonde whispered. "I understand it's hard. Believe it or not, it was kind of hard for me at first, too. I was used to having my own time and doing my own thing and then I suddenly had to plan my schedule around having Molly. I think I resented that at first because I wasn't used to it. But now ... I wouldn't change it for anything. It must have been worse for you because Molly wasn't even yours."

"It wasn't so hard, then. I was so head over heels, it didn't matter. I was glad to have you both there even though I was struggling to find my own place and change my world to fit yours. It wasn't until the threats and until Bernard's death that it started to overwhelm me. I don't think it struck me until then that I was responsible for your safety and that simply being with me jeopardized it."

Rachel nodded slowly. It had appeared that way. Everything had been going very well until the last month or so. It was then that Lacey had become incredibly moody and stand-offish. Before had been amazingly comfortable and happy. "I love you."

Lacey smiled, leaned her head forward to touch her lips to her lover's. She lingered there in a warm kiss that became more sensual with each passing moment. "I love you, too ... even when I'm being a bitch," she whispered, going back for more and nibbling gently and Rachel's chin.

The young blonde grinned and spread her legs so her knees fell on either side of her lover's thighs. She pressed her pelvis into Lacey's. It didn't take long for gentle exploration to turn into tender passion. In no time at all, Lacey had stripped her companion of her sleep clothes and was covering the smaller body with her own lankier form.

Rachel reached down, shifting closer to the foot of the bed so she could pull her lover's flannel pants off and toss them on the floor. From there she moved lower, Lacey watching her silently with a raised eyebrow as the dark woman supported her own weight on hands and knees.

Rachel grinned, running her hands up smooth thighs and settling her face between her partner's legs. She gently cupped Lacey's hipbones and pulled her down until she bumped her nose on crisp, dark curls. Then she snaked her tongue out to touch the moistness there.

Lacey groaned, relaxing into the gentle searching of tongue and lips. She shifted her weight back so her hands were now at her lover's knees and her face and breasts raised to the ceiling.

Rachel was a gentle lover. That was one of the first things Lacey had discovered about her young partner. She was tender with fingers and tongue, using teeth at just the right times, showing a great amount of skill and concentration. She seemed to study the woman before her and store knowledge away as if learning from a book and taking notes. She was able to discern the dark woman's moods and decide what she most wanted. Sometimes Lacey needed fast and aggressive, other times warm and sensuous. Tonight was one of the latter.

Lacey climbed slowly, watching the ceiling, rocking her hips into the mouth below her, relishing in the warmth from the body laid out beneath hers. Everything was about this. All the frustration and anger and rage boiled down to this small blonde woman and how she made her feel. It was about being wanted and needed. It was about being loved today as every other day, despite moods or problems or outside forces. It was about loving someone so much, you only wanted to please them and fill them and honor them with your body.

Lacey felt this reverence in each touch and kiss. She felt it in the way Rachel ran small warm hands over her thighs and up her abdomen to cup full breasts and achingly taut nipples. It was more than Lacey could stand to sit there, so she broke away to muted protests and groping hands only to turn around and lower herself again. Lacey spread her lover's legs and found her treasure there while Rachel's tongue resumed its duty.

They rose together, knowing each other's bodies well and bringing the other to the edge and beyond. They convulsed against each other, clenching muscles spasming around slick tongues, fingers coated in sweet-smelling nectar. Then Lacey relaxed her body, feeling Rachel turn her head and breathe warm air on the inside of her thigh. The small blonde wrapped her arms up and around the hips above her, making it quite clear she wanted Lacey to stay where she was for a moment.

"I don't deserve this," the blonde said at last, the air of her words brushing against Lacey's thigh and making the dark woman twitch. "I don't deserve you."

Lacey pulled away so she could turn and gather the woman in her arms. They exchanged warm, flavored kisses for several moments until Lacey pressed her face into Rachel's neck.

"You deserve more. I just can't give it to you," she assured her lover gently. "But I'll give you everything I can. All of me belongs to you."

"I like the way you see me." Rachel grinned softly. "No one has ever looked at me like you do. No one has ever loved me knowing what I've done and how I've screwed up." A hand floated to her scarred abdomen out of reflex.

Lacey slid her hand down as well to stroke the rough skin she found there. "I could say the same of you, love. No one else has ever tried to get past the walls to see the person behind them. You barged right through."

The blonde smiled, fingering the long, dark hair beneath her touch. "I always loved a challenge."

Lacey snorted her laugh, puffing air against Rachel's neck.

"Get some sleep. You have some skiing to do tomorrow," Rachel murmured, feeling herself grow sleepy now that she was sated and warm.

"Hold on." Lacey disentangled herself long enough to pull her flannel pants back on and to gently dress her lover as well. "Just in case we have middle-of-the-night visitors," she mumbled softly, crawling back into her warm position and wrapping the smaller woman in arms and blankets.

"Good idea," Rachel sighed. "Love you."

"You, too, baby."

Silence and darkness shrouded them as each woman's breath evened in sleep.

Chapter 9

The first day on the slopes was a success all the way around. Lacey set up morning lessons for Rico and Molly, while she and Mary did a little skiing together.

Mary was relieved to have something in common with the dark woman, as their skills were fairly evenly matched. They rode the chair up together over and over throughout the morning, always veering towards the lesson groups on the way down so they could pass Rico learning to snowboard and Molly learning to ski.

The young girl really was showing an aptitude for it and her face lit up in a grin every time she saw Lacey pass. She'd holler and wave a pink mittened hand. Lacey returned the wave.

"She really loves you," Mary observed quietly as they loaded onto the chair again and started the ride up. The child's blue eyes watched them ascend until the instructor called her attention back with patience borne of giving young children lessons day after day.

"What's not to love?" Lacey joked, resituating her poles

into her right hand so she could hold the lift with her left. She noticed her young companion wasn't smiling. "That was a joke, Mary."

Mary grinned sheepishly, glancing to the dark woman. "Not really. It's true. Everyone loves you."

The older woman chuckled dryly and shook her head. "Evidently not or I wouldn't have this problem, huh?" She paused, squinting into the bright sunlight. "No. I have some loyal friends, a wonderful lover, and a beautiful child. I'm lucky." She shrugged. "But I have my share of enemies and I can't ever forget that or someone's likely to get hurt."

Mary was silent for a really long time, watching the brightly colored hats of skiers below them. Finally, she cleared her throat. "I don't understand how Rico and you did ... what you did. I can't see it."

The dark woman's profile hardened as she thought about this. She looked up the mountain and back down before she responded. "Not much to understand. We each needed a family, didn't have one of our own, and that's what Vinnie offered us. It's hard to turn that down."

"Are you ... um ... sorry to have left it?" Mary ventured. She'd never said more than three sentences to this woman before today, yet here she was prying. She figured she deserved to be pushed off the lift at any moment so she better get her questions in while she could.

"No." Lacey didn't hesitate. She glanced to Mary and saw how tense she looked. "I won't bite," she grinned, flashing even white teeth which reflected the sun's midday rays.

Mary laughed nervously, glanced to her companion before looking away. "Actually I was envisioning a tumble off the lift."

The darker woman laughed and arched one eyebrow. "Now that's not a bad idea." Mary tensed. "I'm kidding," she said gently. "Kidding. I'm glad you're here with us. It'll be good to get to know you better."

Mary nodded quietly and turned to give the other woman a hesitant smile. It was getting easier to be with them and to understand this dark woman and her passions. Lacey Montgomery was not a woman who did things half-heartedly, she had a driving need to give two hundred percent of herself to family and friends. Her loyalty could never be questioned and it was that trait that had probably led her to the top of Vinnie's organization.

They slid off the chair together, coming down the small ramp and veering to the right where they settled sunglasses and poles before glancing at each other.

"Ready?" Mary asked. Her only response was a toothy grin and a flip of black hair before Lacey was on her way.

****

Rachel, for her part, entertained herself by sitting at an outside table and reading the Denver Post. From her position she could see both of the lessons and catch an occasional glimpse of Lacey and Mary as they made their way to the chair lift from the slopes. She sipped her coffee, barely feeling the heat of it through the Styrofoam cup and her insulated mittens, but it warmed her belly nicely enough. She was content to spend the day here, enjoying the blinding sunshine and the smell of snow and wool. Karma was tied to the table and curled happily around her owner's legs, occasionally rising to stretch and solicit praise from passers-by.

She'd never been at this altitude and though it was cold out, the sun was so bright it warmed her cheeks and the top of her head. Some of the skiers said it also made the slopes a little icy, but that the snow was pretty good anyway for the amount of traffic on it. Rachel took them at their words and simply flipped to the sports section where she read about how Broncos-crazed the entire state seemed to be. That infatuation was further evidenced by the many jackets, knit caps, and scarves that bore the emblem of a horse's head in a field of orange and blue. Personally, the young blonde thought orange and blue were pretty stupid colors for a professional football team but she wisely kept that observation to herself.

While she was deep into reading about the Broncos' mascot Thunder and the young Arabian stallion's unfortunate injury last season, Karma jumped to her feet and started wooing. Rachel looked up to see her dark-haired lover tromping over in heavy plastic boots. She pushed her sunglasses up to perch on her head and revealed ice blue eyes twinkling with good humor.

She sat down heavily on the bench next to Rachel. "Hey, gorgeous. A pretty lady like you shouldn't be here all alone. Interested in grabbin' a beer later?"

Rachel grinned and leaned in to press warm lips to Lacey's wind chilled cheek. "Mmmm ... thanks for the offer but I'm kinda involved with someone."

Lacey raised a dark eyebrow in humor. "Yeah? Well then you shouldn't go kissing strangers who sit down next to you."

"I'll take my chances."

Lacey chuckled. "You will, huh?"

"Mhmm." Rachel kissed her again, targeting her lips this time and lingering there.

"People are staring," Lacey murmured.

"Let 'em stare," Rachel replied, kissing her lover again.

"You'd think they'd never seen women kiss before."

Rachel laughed gently. "Most of them probably haven't, love."

"We could give them a real show, then," Lacey growled, scooting closer. Rachel put her hands up to stop her.

"Easy there, crony. Not interested in being a floor show, but thanks anyway."

"Hmph." Lacey pretended to be put off as she slid back

slightly on the bench and folded her arms on the table.

"Where's the rest of the crew?" Rachel asked, ignoring the dark woman's mock sulking.

Lacey grinned, her little acts never worked on Rachel. "The two lesson goers are finishing up by noon. Mary went over to watch their last trip down. Then we'll be ready for some food. How are you doing?"

"Great!" Rachel smiled, her eyes showing her enthusiasm. "It's beautiful here. I've never seen so much snow in my life. Amazing how many people participate in this sport."

Lacey nodded slowly. "Didja see anyone you recognize?"

The young blonde paused to think about that and shook her head. "No. Should I have?"

"I wouldn't expect them so soon, but they'll find us. Maybe tomorrow or the next day."

"Should I be worried?" Rachel asked softly, her previous good humor having all but disappeared.

"Not here, I wouldn't think. Too many people, way too public," Lacey assured her lover. "C'mon. There's everyone now ... let's go get some grub."

****

That night an exhausted and content Molly crawled into bed with the two women. Karma joined them, slinking to the end of the mattress where she curled into a ball and hoped no one would notice and kick her off.

Lacey rolled over to toss a long arm over her lover and the child between them. Molly yawned, snuggling deeper into the covers.

"Did you have fun today, baby?" Rachel asked sleepily.

The child nodded her response.

"I'm glad," Lacey whispered softly, leaning in to kiss

the child's temple. "I did, too. Thank you for going skiing with me."

Molly grinned and rolled to her left where she could snuggle closer to the dark woman. "Thank you," she murmured. "Love you."

"You, too." Lacey hugged the child to her, feeling her drift off immediately. Then she looked up and met twinkling green eyes.

Rachel had watched the four of them all afternoon take to the slopes again and again. Molly had caught on very quickly, as most kids do, enabling her to go on the same slopes as Lacey. She'd treasured the time spent with the tall, dark woman. It was a day well spent healing wounds and solidifying relationships.

Dinner had been a joyous affair at the condo where they'd barbecued out and had a good time telling of the day's adventures and planning more to come. Even Mary had participated, making a dessert of berries and crumb cake and telling some of the things she'd seen throughout the day.

Here, in the darkness of the night, Lacey and Rachel lay silently wrapped around the child.

"Thank you for letting her go," Lacey whispered at last. "It felt good. Like all that stuff I said last week never happened."

"You don't have to thank me, Lace," Rachel whispered, her breath blowing around the fine wisps of her daughter's hair. "It was the best thing for both of you. I doubt she even remembers what was said."

"I hope not," the dark woman agreed softly.

Chapter 10

They'd debated what to do for the day over breakfast. There were a lot of small shops bordering the main street in Breckenridge, barely even a block from the bottom of the slopes. Also, a shuttle would take them over to Keystone or Arapahoe Basin, if they were so inclined. In the end, they settled for Breckenridge again, deciding that the closeness to both the condo and the shops would enable Rachel to do some wandering around while the others skied.

Rachel watched her companions strap on skis and snowboard while she stood in her warm parka holding onto Karma's leash. The young dog bounced with excitement, the snow and climate suiting her heritage well.

"Okay," Lacey announced. "I think we're ready. You gonna hit the shops?"

Rachel nodded as the dark-haired woman skied closer. "That was my plan." She smiled gently, straightening her lover's bangs with fondness and flipping the long dark braid back over her shoulder to fall between her shoulder blades.

"Don't go hog wild on us." Lacey grinned. "We have to

fit everything on the plane."

"Ha ha," Rachel said softly.

"Be careful." The dark woman's icy gaze turned somber. "Look for any of those familiar faces. Stay in crowds. Okay?"

Lacey was more than a little worried about splitting up today, though she'd no reason to be. Everything had gone smoothly thus far and they had no indication that they were being followed here. But she believed in being careful, especially when it came to the lives of those she loved.

"I'll be fine. You guys are the ones who should be careful." Rachel shivered at the thought of flying down the icy slopes. "Go on. I'll meet you back here by lunch time."

Rachel wandered up and down the street slowly, visiting all kinds of stores that offered everything from sterling silver jewelry to cheap souvenir T-shirts. She tied Karma outside of the stores she ventured into and kept her eyes open and scanning for any sign of trouble. It wasn't until she was headed back towards the bottom of the runs with several small packages that she noticed a familiar face for a split second. Then he was gone. Her heart froze. Had she imagined he was there? Was she so keyed up that she was seeing danger where there wasn't any?

She hurried back to the slopes to see Lacey and the others already seated around a large table on the outdoor patio. The dark woman saw her lover approaching and patted the bench next to her.

"There you are," she said warmly. "I got you a bowl of chili and some bread. Is that okay?" The words nearly froze in her mouth as she saw the look on Rachel's face. She rose to her feet to greet the younger woman and guide her away from the others.

"What is it, baby?" she asked softly, stroking Rachel's coat ensconced arm with sure sweeps of her large hand.

"I think I recognized someone from the pictures."

Lacey's breath caught briefly before she released it. Well, this was why they were here. "You think?"

"I'm not sure. I just got a glimpse and when I looked back he was gone. It wasn't one of the ones I saw in New York, it was just one of the pictures."

"Okay, relax, gorgeous," Lacey soothed. "We'll be okay. We're all here together. Rico and I are ready for this. Come sit down and act like everything's okay."

"I'm worried."

"I know," Lacey assured her, taking the bags and Karma's leash from her hands and tugging her gently to the table. "It's okay," she whispered again before urging the blonde to sit.

Rachel ate her chili automatically, glancing around the room and barely listening to the conversation at the table. The only thing that kept her grounded was Lacey's large hand splayed on her thigh. Her dark lover would make sure everything worked out, of that she was certain. She choked down the meat and beans in relative silence.

Lacey toyed with the idea of calling it a day and packing everyone away, but then she decided that they weren't going to get much more public than the slopes in Breckenridge on Christmas week, so she devised a slightly different plan. Rico and Lacey would alternate sitting on the patio with Rachel. That way no one was on the slopes unaccompanied and no one was waiting unaccompanied. She felt reasonably certain that they would be safe and she and Molly set off for the first lift ride up of the afternoon, the small girl chatting away, oblivious to the tension in the air.

****

It was nearly time to wrap up for the day when Lacey and Molly got off the lift and slid to a stop at the bottom of the ramp. Lacey checked the girl over to make sure she was bundled up and her goggles and helmet were securely in place before she grinned at her.

"Ready? Last run of the day, then Rico and Mary get one more."

Molly nodded, patted her helmet and started shuffling her skis towards the downwards slope.

Lacey followed her as she zigzagged across the terrain, the child using her slight body weight to navigate her turns, having decided not to be encumbered by poles. They rounded a corner where a couple was in a heap in the snow and they both slid to a stop.

"Hey," Lacey said, sidestepping up to the jumble of limbs and skis. "Need a hand?"

"Ugh," a male's voice groaned out as he rolled over, catching his ski on that of his companion. She yelped in protest. "Sorry."

"Are you okay?" Lacey popped her bindings so she could step closer and kneel down beside them, attempting to untangle limbs.

"My leg is killing me," the woman whimpered.

Lacey probed the leg in question and grimaced, flashing the woman's companion a worried look. "You're gonna be okay. Gimme your poles. You get your skis off." This she said to the man who was still partially entangled with the woman.

He obliged and popped his bindings, this new freedom allowing him to completely stand and withdraw his skis and poles from the pile of his partner. Now she lay alone on the slope, her leg at an odd angle.

Lacey took the poles the man offered her and tenderly straightened the woman's leg, taking off her skis and tossing them aside.

Someone slid to a stop next to them. "Need the ski patrol?" a young man asked, hopping over on his snowboard.

"Yeah. Send 'em up with a snowmobile and a basket."

Lacey glanced over her shoulder gratefully. "And the faster the better, temperature's dropping."

It was true enough. As the sun lowered behind the mountain, it left the snow slopes shrouded in shadow. Without the bright rays to warm from above anymore, the cold wind whipped around them and whistled through the trees at their side.

"Gotcha!" the young man yelled before hopping around and continuing down the hill at break neck speed.

"You're gonna be all right," Lacey reassured the woman, turning back to her frightened brown eyes. "It looks like a clean break, we just need to get you off the mountain is all." She continued her work of lining the leg up between poles.

"Are you going to set it?" the man asked incredulously.

The dark woman shook her head. "I'll leave that to the experts. I'm just trying to make it immobile. No need to damage it any more, huh?" She looked back to the woman. "How ya doin'?"

"Cold," she mumbled.

"Warm her up. Don't let her go into shock," Lacey commanded the young man. He clasped the woman's hands in his and chafed them, breathing warm air onto them.

"L-lacey?" Molly whispered, sidestepping closer.

"I'm sorry, baby." Lacey looked over immediately, pulling the girl to her and embracing her. She'd completely forgotten the child was right there with her. "Are you okay?"

She nodded slowly, blue eyes round behind the protective goggles. She watched the woman quietly.

"Molly, honey, this is ..." she trailed off, hoping the other two would catch on.

"Ah. Bob." He offered his hand to Lacey, who shook it firmly. "And my wife, Janet."

"I'm Lacey. This is Molly," Lacey finished the introductions. "Honey, Janet's going to be fine. She took a bad fall and she broke her leg, that's all. The doctors will fix it up."

She had her arms wrapped around the little girl still and felt her tremors. "Are you cold?"

"Mmmhmm," she acknowledged.

"Tell you what. You remember this slope? Just goes around this bend and then one other before it heads straight to the bottom?"

Molly nodded. They'd spent most of their day on this run and she'd managed to navigate it incredibly well.

"Can you do it by yourself? Go straight down to your mom and Rico and wait for me there?" Lacey was anxious to get the child down to the bottom and warm. Molly was a little upset about seeing the injury and didn't need to be here when the ski patrol showed up.

Molly nodded again, hugging Lacey close and placing a sloppy kiss on her cheek.

"Good girl." The dark woman squeezed back before releasing her and checking helmet and goggles. "Go on now and be careful. I love you."

"Love you." Molly hugged her again. "Bye." She waved shyly to the couple on the snow before meeting Lacey's blue gaze with her own sapphire eyes. "I'll tell Mama you'll be right down."

"Careful," Lacey hollered after her, watching her turn and head down the slope and around the bend before she focused her attention back to the people in front of her. "They should be here soon," she assured them.

The man nodded, looking to his wife. He slid down in the snow next to her and wrapped her warmly in his arms.

"C-cold," she whispered.

The patrol arrived with a roar of the snowmobile engine. The rider hopped off and trotted over to check out the situation. Lacey updated him.

They tossed blankets over the prone woman as they examined the leg and completed the field splint for moving her.

"You're going to be fine, Janet," the red-coated man assured her. "We're going to put you in the basket and take you downhill. Sir, you can ride on the snowmobile."

The two patrolmen settled the young woman in the basket, tucking warm blankets around her. Lacey smiled and patted her shoulder, then shook the husband's hand before he mounted the snowmobile behind the driver. With a loud growl, the vehicle started slowly down the hill.

Lacey put her skis back on, clicking her boots into the bindings, then she and the second patrolman finished the run together.

Once at the bottom, she spotted Rachel and the others at the same table where they'd had lunch. She coasted over to them and then poked her binding release with her pole, stepping out of the skis.

"We stopped to help an injury. Sorry you missed your last run, guys."

Rico shrugged.

"Where's Molly?" Rachel asked, standing up and beginning to gather the bags around her. Karma also hopped to her feet, wagging her thick bushy tail.

Lacey stood frozen. She swore her heart stopped beating before starting again in overtime. She glanced around. "I sent her down to be with you guys."

"No, Lace," Rachel said slowly, the first itchings of worry eating at her mind. "She was with you."

"No, no, no." Lacey spun around, speaking quickly, feeling sick to her stomach. "She was afraid of the injury and we were over halfway down. I told her to go ahead and come down here to you. That I'd be along in a minute."

Rachel's eyes were suddenly wide and filled with tears. "She never came down, Lace," she whispered hoarsely. "We were watching for you two."

"No!" Lacey yelled angrily. "God dammit." She reached into one of their bags of belongings and pulled out her shoes. She quickly replaced her ski boots with the more comfortable footwear and then ran to the ski patrol. "Stay with Rachel!" she yelled to Rico before disappearing around the corner of the building.

Chapter 11

It was well past midnight when they called the search off for the night. The police had been brought in along with volunteers, dogs, and snowmobiles. They'd combed the mountainside, but found nothing. Finally, the sheriff announced it was too dark and cold to continue the search without risking the patrols and volunteers. They all stood solemnly in the bottom level of the main ski lodge.

"Ms. Wilson, we're at a loss tonight. We can start again at first light," the sheriff said softly, glancing from the distraught woman in front of him to young Rico at her side. "You go back to the condo and we'll get you in the morning."

"I can't leave here without her," Rachel mumbled, wiping at her continuously wet cheeks. "She's so cold up there."

Lacey came in from a side entrance, stomping her numb feet on the floor before stepping closer to her friends. "Honey, she's not up there," she whispered, touching a hand to Rachel's side. "I think you need to redirect your investigation." Lacey turned to the sheriff. "Molly was most likely kidnapped."

"Why do you think that?" he asked, startled.

Lacey glanced around at the many eyes watching her. She was faced with an odd mixture of people: seasoned officers, teenagers working the slopes, shop owners who'd heard the call for help. Every last one of them was cold and exhausted from the efforts on the mountainside. Lacey'd been up there for hours herself, trudging through the drifts and calling the little girl's name. "We ... uh ... we've gotten threats in the last couple of weeks. It wouldn't be ... surprising ... if someone had taken her," she stated awkwardly, knowing these people deserved some sort of explanation for all their time and effort but she was unwilling to tell the truth.

"Is there someone investigating the threats?" the sheriff asked slowly, the timbre of his voice slightly aggressive. This definitely put a new twist on things.

"No. We were ignoring them," Lacey said softly, unable to meet her lover's eyes, knowing that the younger woman would only see guilt there. She felt her partner close by, though, the heat of her body warming the dark woman's as well. It was that gentle support that kept her on her feet talking to these men instead of on her knees begging Rachel's forgiveness.

"Can you come to the station and fill me in?" the grizzly sheriff inquired, looking at the small group that stood before him, lost in their grief.

"Yeah," Lacey whispered, unable to make her voice sound any louder or more commanding. "Rico, can you take Mary and Rachel back to the condo? I'll be there as soon as I can."

The young man nodded, taking the blonde's elbow and guiding her gently from the room and down towards a patrol car that had been offered to drive them. Lacey watched them go, hating herself for letting her lover and the young girl down.

Rachel glanced over her shoulder, her brow wrinkled in confusion, wanting the tall woman to offer a hug or a warm touch. Something. Anything. She'd never felt more alone in her life as she focused in front of her again and followed Rico.

It was an exercise in futility, really, Lacey decided. Because of the sketchy information she was willing to provide, the sheriff couldn't help at all except to have his people keep an eye out for a girl matching Molly's description. It wasn't as if Lacey could go into the whole sordid history about her involvement in organized crime and Bernard's death. She gave him a brief description of the threatening notes and suspecting foul play from a business associate.

The sheriff, normally a gentle back woods kind of guy, grew angrier moment by moment. At one point he accused Lacey of not wanting to find the girl, that if she really wanted to locate Molly, she'd come clean with everything. The words stung the dark woman. She imagined their biting force had left a red mark on her face, but she took the blow because she'd deserved it. She deserved to rot in hell for this transgression. She simply nodded to the sheriff, thanking him for his help. She requested quietly that he allow some men to look for abduction evidence the following day and maybe ask some of the remote lift workers if they'd seen a girl fitting Molly's description appear unwilling to be with an adult.

Then the dark woman bade him goodnight and left the small office quietly. He couldn't possibly have known what she was or the darkness she was capable of as she fairly shuffled from the room, her bearing and confidence all but gone. Ice blue eyes no longer shined with challenge, but were dulled with the reality of ultimate defeat.

Whoever had done this was well above the means of this

ski town police station, anyway, and had executed their plan seamlessly. Chances were good that Molly wasn't even in Breckenridge anymore. Too bad Lacey had no clue where to start looking.

She let herself into the condo silently, turning to close the door with slumped shoulders. Karma trotted out to meet her, tags jingling merrily in the darkness. She whimpered.

"Hey girl," Lacey whispered, crumpling to her knees and gathering the beast into a hug. "It'll be okay. It has to be," she whispered, allowing herself for the first time to feel the tragedy that had been lurking in her heart.

"Lace?"

The whispered word caught the dark woman's attention and she lifted her face from Karma's soft fur to see her lover leaning quietly against the wall at the end of the hallway. Lacey stood immediately, wiping angrily at her tears. She had no right to cry, it was all her fault. She stepped forward, intent on being strong for her heartbroken partner.

"Hey, baby," the dark-haired woman breathed softly, moving towards the young blonde. She was met halfway down the hall and wrapped in a fierce hug. Lacey sighed, part of her had feared Rachel wouldn't even want to be around her.

"No news?"

"No," Lacey confirmed, kissing the top of the blonde head beneath her chin.

"You really think they have her?" Rachel asked, her voice raw from crying.

"I do."

"That's better than being out there alone, right. They won't hurt her, will they?" She leaned back, her liquid emerald eyes begging for Lacey to agree. So the dark woman did.

She shook her head. "I'm sure they won't hurt her. We'll hear from them."

"They killed Bernie," Rachel whispered.

Lacey swallowed hard, the sound clearly audible to the small woman in her arms. She bit back her tears. "If anyone lays one hand on her, I'll kill them," she swore softly.

They stood like that for what seemed like hours before Rico stepped into the hallway and guided them gently into the living room where Mary waited. Unable to sleep and unwilling to be alone, everyone spent the night in silence there, bathed in the flickering flames of the blazing fire on the west side of the room.

Finally, near dawn, Lacey untangled herself from Rachel's still form and leapt to her feet. "I'm gonna go for a run," she announced, unable to sit still a moment longer.

"No," Rachel blurted, rising as well. "Don't go. Please?" She had an inexplicable fear that if the tall woman started running, she may not be able to stop. And Rachel very much needed her right here.

"Raich, honey," Lacey said softly. "I have to go do something. I can't handle sitting here."

"You think I can?!" the blonde shouted, amazed. "Do you think any of us can? We all lost her, Lace."

"No." The dark woman spun, shaking her head. "No. *I* lost her. *I* sent her ahead without me. *I* risked her safety for some young couple I didn't even know."

"Lace," Rachel said softly, stepping closer. This all needed to be aired. The dark-haired woman had been harboring this guilt since that moment of realization, but hadn't voiced it. "It's not your fault. We don't blame you."

"*I* blame me!" Lacey shouted. "God dammit! Don't you patronize me. I know you're angry at me. You should hate me. Go ahead and yell."

"I don't want to yell at you, baby," Rachel whispered. "I could never hate you."

"It's my fault," Lacey growled, wanting so badly for someone else to share her hatred. Wanting one of them, any of them, to yell at her and condemn her. "I lost her, Raich. I couldn't protect her as I'd promised. I didn't love her enough to keep her safe."

"Lacey," Rachel said softly, her heart aching again at this display of anguish in front of her. "Baby, don't do this." She couldn't conjure up the blame Lacey wanted. As much as Rachel needed to point the finger at someone, it wasn't her dark-haired lover. It was the bastards who'd gotten away with her child. Lacey had done nothing wrong. Molly walked to and from the barn every single day at home, brushing the horses for hours. She walked Karma around the block without an escort and that was twice the distance she'd skied alone today. She'd only been out of sight for maybe a minute while she made the bend between the two women. It had been a minute too long. But there was no blame to lay with Rachel's dark lover. No matter how much the other woman wanted it.

"Yell at me," she whispered. "Please?" Her tirade was losing steam in the face of her lover's devotion. "Make me feel like shit."

"You already do," Rachel responded gently, approaching her lover as if she were a frightened animal. "I love you, Lace. I know you wouldn't have intentionally put her in danger. You've gone to such lengths to get us this far."

"Not enough," Lacey whimpered, dropping to her knees. "Never enough. I kept Vinnie alive for a decade or more and I can't keep the two of you safe for even a year."

Rico and Mary stared from the side of the room, not wanting to see the dark woman's fall, but unable to avert their gaze from the tragedy before them. Never had Lacey been so vulnerable. She knelt on the floor, inner arms and palms exposed to the ceiling, her head bent in shame. Jet black hair that was usually braided or pulled back into a ponytail had ended up loose after the night's adventures and fell in a long tangled mass about her head and shoulders, like the dark veil of a mourner, obscuring her expression from the probing eyes of her friends. It was a moment none of them would ever forget, though they desperately did not want to remember the noble woman this way.

Rachel knelt next to her, scooting closer, wanting so much just to grab her and hold on, but knowing Lacey was very close to running from it all. The pain was almost too much for her to handle. "Honey, I know it hurts. I know you feel guilty and I wish I could relieve you of that, but I can't."

"It would be easier if you were angry at me," Lacey whispered, her voice broken and torn.

"Sorry, love, I can't help you there," Rachel murmured. "But what I really need right now is for you to stick with us here. You're the only one who can figure this out. You know how these people work, you know what they'll do."

"Because I'm a monster, too." Lacey toppled to her rear and scooted back so she leaned against the breakfast bar across the room.

"C'mon, baby," Rachel soothed. "Self-pity doesn't become you."

Lacey looked up from her hands, which had moments before been interesting enough to garner her full attention. Now she met the seeking jade eyes across the room. She saw there, beneath the sorrow and guilt, undeniable love and dedication.

"You can do this because you're the best. Remember?" Rachel managed a weak grin filled with warm affection.

"Not the best. I didn't see it coming like this. I didn't think it would happen on the slopes. I was more worried about you sitting down there by yourself."

"So we adjust the plan. It's not over, Lace, and I won't let you give up." She paused for a moment, trying to read the stoic features across from her. "You feel so damn guilty about this, then you fix it," the blonde demanded, knowing sympathy wasn't the right direction to take with her dark lover.

Lacey's ice blue eyes blazed with cold heat. "What do you mean?"

"Bring our little girl back, Lacey. Quit worrying about what happened and how we could have avoided it and let's start looking to the future. You said they'll contact us? How will we be ready? What can we do then?"

The small room was filled with silence except the clicking of Karma's nails as she trotted across the room to curl up at Lacey's side. Her slight frame leaned heavily into the tall woman as she tried to lick her chin. Lacey pulled the animal into a hug, pressing her cheek along the top of Karma's head.

Rachel acknowledged the immediate threat was past and Lacey was starting to appear more her normal confident self. But they weren't over it, yet. Lacey would harbor that guilt until well after they had Molly home. She felt she'd failed as their self-appointed protector.

They must have all sat in silence for a full twenty minutes before Lacey looked up from where she'd been petting Karma's back. "They know we're here. We need to get a wire on these phones. We have to stay until they contact us. They probably took her to Denver, this place is too small to try to hide a kidnapped child."

Rachel breathed a sigh of relief as she crawled across the floor and into her lover's lap. Lacey wrapped the young woman in a tight hug.

"I'm sorry I lost her," Lacey murmured for Rachel's ears only.

"You didn't, baby. It'll be okay."

****

She'd never had a lot of friends. She was a child who enjoyed her solitude and got along better with adults than kids her own age. She was used to being alone. But this was different. Now her friends were the darkness and cold that surrounded her and set her teeth to chattering. She wasn't chilly, really, but she was scared and she didn't know what else to do so she let the sound of her clicking teeth echo around the room and fill her silence.

The stench of herself made her nose itch and she became more embarrassed with each passing moment. When the man had jumped out from the trees and lifted her off the snow, she'd been so frightened she'd wet herself. She recalled the moment with growing amounts of shame and almost hoped her mother and Lacey wouldn't find her this way: a shivering little girl with smelly pants.

The man had covered her mouth and whispered horrible, horrible things in her ear about what he'd do to Lacey if she screamed. She'd so wanted to scream. So wanted Lacey to come find her and take her home. But the sound wouldn't leave her throat, even as he dragged her, skis and all, up through the woods past where Lacey was with the others.

She'd seen the dark woman talking to a man in a red jacket and she cried silent tears into the darkness, willing her second mother to look up at that minute and see her through the camouflage of trees. She'd prayed that Lacey would sense her near. She prayed that her voice would be found and she could yell and alert her. But fear had made her mute and her silent prayers had gone unanswered.

The man had said rude things to her and described things her young mind couldn't even fathom except to know they were bad and involved her mother and Lacey. She thought he probably meant they would be dead, too, but she chose not to linger on those thoughts.

She'd done her best to be good, to not give him reason to hurt her family. She'd sat on the chair lift with him and went down the slope on the other side that she hadn't been on yet. It was harder than the other runs and she'd fallen a couple of times only to be dragged to her feet. The man had attached a rope to her for the trip down to the bottom of the slope, not giving her a chance to veer into the trees or try to avoid him. She wouldn't have tried anyway, she acknowledged, because she was too afraid of what he might do.

So now she sat in her pants which had long since dried, but still reeked of urine, having been relieved of her snowpants, jacket, and boots so she wore only jeans, a turtleneck, and socks. The cot was far from comfortable, the mattress lumpy and holey. She imagined it smelt nearly as bad as she did and that gave her some odd comfort. The mean man had put handcuffs on her and tightened them as far as they would go. It still gave her some play but that only chafed her worse as she spun her bony wrists in the constricting circles. The cuffs were chained to an eyebolt in the wall at the head of the bed but it had enough slack that she could sit as she was now: knees drawn to chest and arms hugging them. She rested her chin on her knees, wrinkling her nose again at the scent of herself, and surveyed her surroundings.

She was about cried out and for that she was grateful. She'd cried so hard in the back of the van that she'd thrown up all over her jacket several times until she was reduced to dry aching heaves. She'd regretted that. Her mother had helped her pick out the jacket; it was a soft shade of pink with purple piping. Lacey had teased her that pink and purple didn't go well together but once she'd tried it on for the tall woman, Lacey had beamed. She'd told her how beautiful she was and that she could even make purple and pink look good. The memory warmed her heart a little but also helped a lone tear find its way down her cheek.

The mean man had pulled her retching body from the van and dragged her through the darkness into a house. There he stripped her of her outer clothing, calling her a sniveling baby and teasing her for her soiled pants. Then he'd taken her down some stairs and into the room she now occupied.

It was smaller than her room at home, smaller even than Jester's stall, she thought. The only furniture was the cot she sat on and a small wooden cart of some sort across from the foot of the bed. Even if she laid on her back and stretched her body fully, she couldn't reach the cart with her toe. She knew because she'd spent a good part of the night trying to do just that for no better reason than it was an obstacle to overcome. Finally, when the first rays of dawn had crept by the sides of the cardboard taped into the window, she'd given up and moved to this new position. She liked how she sat now with her back to the wall and her body curled in on itself, it made her feel safer, even though she knew she wasn't. Even though the thought of the mean man coming back down here set her teeth to rattling again.

She didn't know why he wanted her and had no clue what she could give him. She hadn't heard anything aside from some occasional thumps upstairs since she'd been deposited here and no one had come to see her. She hoped that Lacey and her mom would find her soon. Even though they would be mad that she wet her jeans and threw up on her coat, they would still take her home. She hoped it was soon because she was hungry and frightened and she didn't think she'd ever be warm again.

Chapter 12

Rachel hated the skiers here for their holidays. She hated their smiling faces and trickling laughter and she wanted to scream at all of them. *My child is lost! How dare you have fun, how dare you plan a merry Christmas?* The anger nearly seethed from her pores as she cast green-eyed daggers to the oblivious crowds around her.

Lacey easily felt the anger rolling off her partner in dark, wicked waves. She stood beside her and touched her occasionally, trying to ground her, trying to offer all the support she could muster. She knew that her young lover was grateful for her presence, even if she was unable to show that at the moment.

They waited for the sheriff to come back from talking to the ski patrol. He was getting some of the snowmobiles to take them back up to the spot where the woman and child had encountered the accident yesterday. From there they would walk down the slope and look for any clues indicating what might have happened. Last night they'd been focused solely on finding her and not on scouring for prints of someone else.

Lacey kicked herself for that now. Had she not let her pride get in the way, had she not been denying that she'd failed them, she would have realized the truth sooner. Molly wasn't lost. She hadn't gotten injured or wandered off into the trees lining the runs. She'd been taken. By the time Lacey was ready to admit that to herself, and share that information with others, Molly had been off the mountain and halfway to Denver probably, and it had been too cold and dark to take the dogs back up and look for tracks.

The sun was just glittering orange and red across the snow-covered peaks. Early risers were seated on the patios enjoying hot chocolate and flavored yuppy coffees. The same image had been beautiful to Rachel the morning before, but she didn't even notice it now. The sunrise danced off her golden hair and reflected in her emerald eyes where it was appreciated for a moment by her tall lover. She studied her young partner resolutely.

"I love you," Lacey murmured, reaching an awkward, mittened hand up to brush at fine blonde tendrils.

Rachel glanced from the slope she'd been scrutinizing to meet her lover's blue eyes. They were nearly violet in the morning sun, laden as they were with layers of guilt, shame, and love. The young blonde smiled briefly and leaned into the affectionate touch. The woolen mitten was scratchy on her cheek. "With all my heart, Lace," she affirmed softly. "Don't doubt that."

Lacey nodded solemnly, grateful they'd battled this morning and found neutral ground. It hadn't even been a fight really, despite Lacey's best efforts to start one and open herself to angry fire.

Sheriff Railer approached them then, feeling he was interrupting a moment, but knowing he had no choice. He cast Lacey a look she interpreted as anger at her stubbornness the previous night, then he turned his attention to

Rachel, effectively removing the dark woman from the conversation. Lacey bristled, but held her tongue.

"Ms. Wilson, we have the snowmobiles ready and another search crew. We have enough light to go up now if you'd like?"

Rachel nodded, declining to point out that the man was an idiot if he thought she'd sit here all day.

"Good, you can ride with me." He started to take her elbow and lead her away from Lacey but the tall woman interpreted his intentions immediately and cleared her throat.

"A minute, Raich?"

Rachel nodded readily and politely excused herself from her escort. The sheriff glared silently at Lacey's back.

"Baby, he's gonna work you for some info. I didn't give him much last night, just said I thought it was an old business acquaintance bent on revenge."

Rachel nodded and patted her lover's arm. "Don't worry, crony. I understand."

The sheriff did indeed work on Lacey's story during the brief trip up the mountain. Though the ambient temperature was more than bearable for a morning in December, the wind that whipped back Rachel's hair while aboard the vehicle was frigid. She shivered and glanced over her shoulder at her lover who rode on the snowmobile behind them.

"Ms. Wilson? Did you hear the question?" The man tilted his head back so the wind might catch his words and deliver them to his passenger.

"No. Sorry."

"Your friend wasn't being very helpful last night. If you know who's been sending you threats, it could help us to locate your daughter."

"We don't know who it is," Rachel answered honestly. The trick here would be telling them enough information to search intelligently for her daughter without landing her lover in jail. She was pretty sure she was too emotionally and physically exhausted to walk this fine line.

"Ms. Wilson," he said in a disbelieving voice.

She shrugged. "We think it's someone she worked with or against ... someone she met through work."

"What does she do?"

"She's self-employed. A computer security firm or something ... I don't know much about it." So far Rachel was doing fairly well sticking with honesty.

"And this business garners enemies of that nature?" He sounded incredulous.

Well, Rachel mused, *so much for being honest.* "We think it was her previous job. She was doing ... um ... she was a business consultant. Purchasing for a large corporation, investing ... things like that."

"Purchasing what?"

Oops. "Computer parts and stuff." Rachel was incredibly glad the man couldn't see her face as she lied poorly.

"And that inspires that kind of hatred?"

"Competitive market," Rachel mumbled stupidly. "But the list of possibilities is incredibly long. And we were trying to narrow it down."

"Before you got the police involved?"

None of this sounded very plausible the way the sheriff said it. *Sorry, Lace, I'm doing my best.* "You guys are busy." *Jesus, do I suck at this.*

"Are you sure it couldn't be someone you know? Like the girl's father?"

"No." Rachel shook her head. "Positive."

He let it drop, even though he still had questions, because just then they arrived at the spot where Lacey indicated the accident had been. Rachel approached her lover with a meek expression and the taller woman laughed slightly.

"You are a horrible liar."

"I know," she responded softly.

"So is there already a warrant out for my arrest or are you saving that for the trip back down the mountain?"

"Oh, Lace," the blonde moaned. "It's not that bad. I just sound like a moron telling him crap about you buying computer merchandise for Vinnie and how people would kidnap to get revenge."

Lacey laughed. "Oh, yeah. Those memory chips are pretty vital. A lot of people would threaten lives for them."

"Shut up, crony. You didn't prepare me," Rachel growled, only partially joking.

"I know, love." Lacey lost her bantering tone. "I'm sorry."

"Me, too," Rachel sighed, ran a trembling hand through her wind-tangled hair. She met her lover's blue eyes with misty green. "I'm just ... not doin' so good."

"I know," Lacey assured her. "We're going to get through this."

Rachel's eyes filled immediately with tears. "I don't want to get through this without her, Lace. I don't know if I can."

"Shh, baby," the dark woman soothed, stepping forward to envelop her companion in a strong embrace. "I'll find her. I promise you that."

The rest of the group had dismounted their vehicles and now stood around the well-packed-down snow. Everyone was grateful it hadn't snowed the night before.

They made their way as a group lower, towards the section where they imagined Molly had been abducted. Once there, they spread out and began searching further into the woods for any signs of tracks or footprints. They found some snowshoe marks a good twenty yards from the edge and on backtracking spotted where the prints began. Everything to that point had been swept clean, presumably with a branch. The darkness of the night before hadn't allowed them to see it.

Following the prints further up the mountain, they found where they cut across to the slope above where Lacey had been standing. She shivered in the shadow of trees on the edge of the run. They'd walked right past her, carried the little girl within her eyesight, but she'd been so intent on helping the couple.

The sheriff trotted up to Rachel and Lacey as others gathered around. He was wielding his radio as if it were a weapon. "They questioned the person working that lift last night." He pointed across the slope to the lift that stopped in the middle of the mountain before continuing its journey upwards. There was a shack there to shelter the men and women that insured the lift was running properly. "She remembered seeing a little girl and a man right before the lifts went off. Said they went all the way up and the little girl was crying."

Instinctually, Lacey reached a long arm around Rachel's shoulders and pulled her close against her solid body. She could feel the smaller woman shudder. "How about that slope? Where does it go?"

"The lift comes out on top of a blue black. He could have taken it all the way down to the other side of the ski park, by the other lodge. You never would have seen him." He directed this to Rachel, remembering that she'd been sitting at the bottom of the run where they walked now.

"He took her away," Rachel said softly, looking with liquid green eyes from her lover to the sympathetic man in front of her.

Neither one spoke. There was no need to confirm what was obvious.

Finally, it was Lacey who broke the silence. "What about the couple with the injury? Was it a set up?" That thought had been eating at her since Molly's disappearance.

"I don't think so. The hospital released her this morning

and they're back at their hotel room. I think they're legitimate. They agreed to speak with us ... you can come along if you'd like."

Lacey looked to the impossibly blue sky and heaved a huge sigh. Holy shit this whole thing sucked. "Yeah. Let's get off this damn mountain."

After much arguing, Lacey convinced Rachel to go back to the condo where Rico and Mary waited by the phones. The dark woman continued on to talk to Bob and Janet.

The Sheriff was right; she found them perfectly believable. It must have been convenient, is all. The asshole probably watched the girl all day waiting for the right moment.

****

She shifted uncomfortably on the bed and leaned back slightly to look at the window behind her once again. She could see by the cracks around the covering that light was fading. The mean man had visited her once with a cup of water and a peanut butter and jelly sandwich. It was grape jelly and she hated grape, but she was too hungry to care.

Of course, the water had also led to the inevitable need to relieve herself again. She'd waited as long as possible and cried to the mean man to come take her to the restroom. He never responded to her pleas and she gave up in the end, scooting as far as her chains would allow her. She was able to wrestle with her already soiled jeans and pull them part of the way off. She was quite proud of her accomplishment and managed to relieve herself on the floor and not her clothes or the bed. She was grateful anyway to be in dry pants, even if they did still reek.

So now she sat and watched the light fade from the painted walls, leaving shadows in its wake. She wanted so badly to be away from this place. She was afraid of the man and his slitted eyes. She hated the stench of herself and this room. Her belly growled with hunger.

She wanted her mother and Lacey.

The man had never said anything to her except to yell and ridicule her. He'd never explained why she was here or how long she'd have to stay. Molly had asked when he'd come in with the food, but aside from snide comments about her sniveling behavior, he'd remained silent. It had been enough to make her nervous and sick again, vomiting over the side of the bed the remainder of her sandwich. A short time later he'd pounded on the door and yelled at her again, making her sick, making her cry.

She felt better now, not having heard from the mean man in hours. She'd spent the time well, using her mother's advice and remembering good things. She thought fondly of her mother and Lacey, pictured Karma and Jester. She'd remembered playing video games with Rico not very long ago and looked forward to doing it again soon. Lacey would fix this and then it would all be over. She'd come in here and carry her out just as she'd come to the school last week and took her from the principal's office. Just as the dark woman had held her countless times after nightmares, she would hold her when this one was over. She just wanted to be strong until Lacey could get here.

Please let it be soon.

Chapter 13

Rachel was only slightly annoyed at being sent back to the condo with a police escort. She hadn't really wanted to meet the couple, afraid that her anger may be expressed with blame at them and she wasn't really interested in doing that to those poor people. Lacey must have sensed that in her, which would explain her practically forcing the blonde into the squad car.

She sat quietly on the couch in the living room and stared at the wall, holding Karma in her lap. The police officer had stayed, watching Rico's equipment with an interested eye.

The young man had been busy while they were absent that morning, collecting all the bits and pieces he needed to put together a very crude wire tap and recorder. He hoped it was good enough. He had better quality stuff on the way, but didn't want to go without even for a few hours.

The blonde kid was showing his handiwork to the attentive officer when the phone rang. They all looked to each other and Rachel rose slowly and made her way across the floor to pick up the receiver. Karma jingled behind her.

"Hello?"

She was answered by silence as she watched the reels on the small tape recorder begin to spin. She raised her eyes to meet Rico's and then Mary's.

"Hello?" she tried again.

"We have the girl."

The voice wasn't one she recognized, though it wasn't scrambled in any way. Her knees buckled and she leaned heavily on the breakfast bar until Mary came around and pulled a chair up for her.

"Is she okay?"

"For now."

"Can I talk to her?"

The man laughed. "Not yet. But listen." It sounded as if he was moving from one room to another or going up or down stairs. Then there was the faint sound of retching and the man pounded on the door. "You sniveling brat. Cut that out or you ain't ever gonna see your mom again." His outburst was countered by gentle sobs.

"Don't hurt her, please," Rachel pleaded, tears tracking unbidden down her pale cheeks. She felt sick to her stomach and her whole body shook.

"That's not up to me. That's up to you and that cunt you sleep with. I'll call back."

Rachel held the phone silently to her ear long after the dial tone had turned into a relentless annoying beep. It was Mary who finally pried it from her fingers and hung it up. Then the blonde jumped up and ran to the bathroom where she was violently ill. That had escalated into crying sobs and dry heaves until the police officer had called for medical assistance. The sedative was a no-brainer after that.

The doctor had delivered it by needle to Rachel's trembling arm, while the officer called his sheriff.

****

It was late in the afternoon by the time Lacey had survived another round of the sheriff's vicious questioning and walked along the ski town's main street to their rented condo. The entire thing was still so far fetched it was hard to believe. Someone had kidnapped their little girl. She shook her head, dark ponytail bouncing from shoulder to shoulder. She'd left the sheriff's office several hours before, trying to calm herself down before facing her distraught lover.

She could almost smell the impending disaster when she opened the front door. Karma trotted to her with a worried look on her face and there was quite a bit of arguing going on in the kitchen. Lacey made her way past the dog with a gentle pat before emerging in the tiled room.

"Dammit, Rico, one simple job and you can't do it?"

Lacey was shocked to see Mary standing in front of Rico, yelling at him. She'd never heard the woman even raise her voice before.

"Problem?" the dark woman asked huskily, her timbre negating any need to yell.

They both blanched at her word and stood looking at her stupidly.

Lacey glanced around and noticed that nothing seemed out of the ordinary. "Where's Rachel?" she asked slowly, knowing they looked entirely too calm even in this panicked state to be delivering news of that magnitude.

"She's in the bathroom," Rico offered, looking like the cat that ate the canary.

"Okay," Lacey drawled, knowing without a doubt that there was more to the story.

"Being sick," Mary added helpfully.

"Nervous?"

"Maybe that, too." Rico nodded.

"And maybe what else?" Lacey prodded.

"Could be the sedative, don't you think?" He turned his question to Mary, blue eyes pleading with her to help him out a little.

"I thought it was the alcohol, actually," Mary said, hanging him out to dry with a gentle flourish.

Lacey's ice eyes blazed. "What say we start at the beginning?"

While Rico played their copy of the tape for the dark-haired woman, Mary stepped out to check on Rachel. The police officer had already taken another copy to be analyzed.

Lacey guessed it must have all happened after she left the station. She cursed herself for not coming straight back and then cursed the sheriff for not finding her. Rico explained the sedative and why it had been used.

"So tell me about the alcohol?" Lacey said softly.

"Well, I was watching her, ya know," Rico started, inching his way towards the door in case he needed to make a quick getaway. "And she was doing really well, calming down, sitting on the couch. Mary was in the shower. I went into the bedroom to get a book out of my bag and got sidetracked ... sat down in there and started reading it. When I came out, she had that bottle in her hands."

For the first time, Lacey noticed the half-empty bottle sitting on the counter. It was Tequila. Great. "And how full was it before she had it?"

"I don't know, Lace," Rico admitted quietly. "I know you trusted me to watch her and I shouldn't have left her alone. She really did lose it."

Lacey took a deep breath. "And now she's in there puking?"

"Yeah." Mary nodded, coming back into the room.

"What about the sedative?"

"That's the first thing we did," Mary assured the taller woman. "We called the doctor. He said to watch her, but he didn't expect it would be a problem, especially since she was vomiting."

Lacey nodded and started to leave the room without another word. Her lover needed her.

"Lace?" Rico called out to her. "I let you down, I'm sorry."

The dark-haired woman stopped and turned to face him. He really was devastated. He would do anything for Lacey, had even killed for her on more than one occasion. He felt horrible at having done such a bad job at something so important. Lacey teetered on the edge of losing her carefully reined in temper and yelling at him for his stupidity and giving into the soft look in his eyes. She sighed. Loving Rachel had definitely taken the bite out of her bark. "We're all gonna survive this, Rico," she said simply, not ready to forgive him for his transgression, but not willing to leave him broken.

He nodded and Mary stepped closer to him to wrap an arm around his slender waist. Lacey turned and continued to the bathroom to find her lover.

****

Lacey knocked softly on the door to the bathroom and listened. Hearing no sound from inside, she turned the knob and let herself in.

Rachel was draped over the toilet, one arm resting on the rim of the bowl and her head resting on that arm. Her hair was sweaty and stringy and her face was unbelievably pale. She looked up at the sound of Lacey coming in and her somber green eyes registered shame.

"Hey, baby," Lacey whispered, sitting on the floor behind her lover and pulling the smaller woman against her. Rachel struggled. "Easy, I just want to hold you."

"Sick," the blonde muttered, but it seemed to be an

explanation and not a promise of the immediate future, so Lacey held on.

"I know. Lean against me."

Rachel's eyes were droopy from the sedative and after another moment of futile motion, she leaned back into Lacey's chest, her head against her partner's shoulder.

"Had a rough day," Lacey whispered, stroking the wet hair back and kissing Rachel's cheek.

"I heard her."

"I know, baby. They played the tape for me."

"I needed you here," Rachel whispered back and even though there was no malice in her voice, it hurt Lacey just the same.

"I'm so sorry," the dark-haired woman said softly. "So sorry."

"S'okay." The blonde turned to peer at her partner. "Not mad ... just saying it would have been easier."

Lacey nodded.

"Gave me a shot." She gestured to her upper arm with a wrinkled brow. "Hurts."

"From what I hear, honey, they didn't have much a of a choice."

"I heard her," was the blonde's only explanation and it was more than enough.

"Why did you drink that Tequila? You're a lightweight, you should know better," Lacey teased gently, pulling the small body more snugly against her as she leaned back into the white, painted wall behind her.

"Hurts inside."

"Yeah," Lacey said simply.

"Thought the hurt would go away with the sedative and some Tequila."

"Didn't work?"

"Unh unh," she groaned softly. "Just sick and sad and miserable."

Making Strides 159

Lacey nodded silently. Her right hand rested on her lover's T-shirted abdomen and suddenly she felt the rumble of another onslaught. She scooted forward, pulling Rachel's hair away from her face and leaning the smaller woman over the toilet. All that came up was liquid and green bile and then nothing as Rachel suffered dry heaves.

She sobbed, one big gasping breath.

"I know," Lacey whispered, rocking her gently, placing warm lips to her lover's ear. "I know it hurts so much."

"What happens now?"

"She's alive," Lacey said softly, moving and stretching to wet a wash cloth and wipe off her companion's face. "They're going to call back, they want me to be here, probably. They're not likely to hurt her if they're waiting for me."

Rachel nodded, leaning her face into the cool cloth her partner held.

"Rico sent the tape to a specialist in Denver ... recommended by someone Vinnie used to use. The cops have it, too, but I'm not holding my breath for them. That specialist is also trying to get the lines traced, but I'm not sure how that will pan out."

"Rico did good," Rachel murmured.

"Rico is on my hit list for not taking better care of you," Lacey said seriously.

Rachel leaned forward so she could tilt her head and peer at Lacey. Her brow wrinkled gently into a scowl. "Not his fault. I'm not some pet to be watched."

Lacey smiled, hugged the woman closer. "What can I do to make you feel better?"

"Find Molly?" Rachel said softly then hurried to continue speaking when she felt the dark woman tense. "I'm sorry, not fair. I know you're trying."

They sat in silence for a few minutes before Rachel spoke again. "I feel dirty."

Grateful that there was something she could do, Lacey

disentangled herself and moved over to the tub where she began to run warm water. She moved back to her lover to stand the small woman up on unsteady legs and undress her. Then, Lacey helped the smaller woman over the rim and into to the water before guiding her to sit down.

Lacey watched her lover with gentle consideration before shucking her own clothes and climbing in with her. The blonde looked up, startled, as the other woman settled her long frame in front of Rachel, knees bent to her chin.

"You're beautiful," Rachel said softly, wistfulness in her voice.

"Not as beautiful as you, baby." Lacey grinned in response and slowly began to lather up the washcloth she'd picked up again. With gentle hands, she washed her lover's body, sweat-slicked and clammy from her nausea. She turned off the running water, the volume of their bodies in the small space not allowing for a lot of water in the tub. Then she eased Rachel back gently to wet her hair and poured generous amounts of shampoo into large tanned hands, rubbing the suds firmly into blonde tresses.

Rachel's eyes fluttered closed.

"Feel good?"

"Mmmhmm," Rachel murmured, relaxing into the haze of alcohol and sedative and the warm touch of her lover. "Shouldn't have gotten drunk."

"It's okay," Lacey assured her gently. "Honey, I really am impressed with how strong you're being. No one can fault you for a temporary lack of judgment."

"You make me strong," Rachel muttered. "You're so stoic about everything."

Lacey considered the words, not liking how they made her sound. She was slowly falling apart herself. She'd planned on building a life with these two people. She'd left Vinnie in search of a new existence that was peaceful and included Molly and Rachel. She'd struggled through a year of starting a new business, ironing out relationship highs and lows, raising a little girl, only to fail it all in the end. Because without Rachel and Molly, nothing else mattered. And if they didn't find Molly, she wasn't sure how the two of them would survive.

Rachel opened her eyes, blinked fuzzily at her lover. "Bothers you that I said that?"

Lacey shrugged, cradled her lover's head gently as she lowered it into the water to rinse out the suds. "I don't know how much longer I can be strong."

Rachel waited until Lacey righted her and then twisted slowly in the tub to face her lover again. "Baby, I know how much you hurt. I can see it in your eyes and the way you hold yourself. Hurting doesn't make you weak. It's your love and resolve that make you strong. I'm stronger because of your conviction and because I know how much you love us. Together we'll find her."

"And if we don't?" Lacey asked in a strangled voice, immediately regretting the words and wishing she could suck them back in. Rachel needed her confidence, not her doubts.

Rachel smiled gently, pushed Lacey's knees apart so she could scoot forward and wrap the taller woman in a warm embrace. She lifted her own legs over her lover's so her knees rested alongside the dark woman's ribs. At any other time, the delicious feeling of water-slicked skin meeting would have been erotic. Here, in the depths of their shared sadness, it was wholly comforting.

"We will," the blonde whispered. Nuzzling into Lacey's neck and inhaling her scent. It was sweet and musky at the same time, and incredibly familiar. She rested like that for several long moments before she realized she should answer her lover's choked question. It was a valid concern. She suspected Lacey was most worried if their relationship could survive such a horrible blow. "If we don't," she whispered hoarsely, "we can help each other through it, baby. We'll be here for each other."

"You were wrong, you know," the dark woman responded softly. "You give me the strength to survive. You give me the love and dedication to continue. Everything I am and can do is because of you."

"You're being overly dramatic," Rachel chastised gently, kissing the warm skin of her lover's nape.

"Never. I don't do dramatic."

Rachel laughed gently; it was a true enough statement.

They stayed like that for what must have been a very long time, entwined in each other and inhaling the scent of the other as well as the soaps and shampoos surrounding them. Their moment was disturbed by a knock on the door.

"Company." It was Rico's voice.

Lacey pushed away from her lover to determine Rachel's state and found her to still be droopy and quite likely buzzed. "Let's go find our girl."

Rachel nodded, echoing the conviction of her partner.

Chapter 14

The man banged the door open without any sort of preamble, slamming it so hard it bounced off the wall and threatened to close again. He caught it with one large hand and glared at the little girl on the bed.

The sudden motion and noise had caused Molly to jump to her feet on the lumpy mattress. She stood shakily with her back against the wall, watching the man approach with wild blue eyes. They darted momentarily to the still open door causing the man to laugh.

"Not a chance little girl," he growled. "I need you to do something for me."

Molly shook her head mutely, flattened herself into the wall in an effort to escape him.

"Wrong answer."

"You ready down there?" a voice called, startling Molly. Since her abduction the only person she had seen was the meaty man before her. It hadn't crossed her mind that there was someone else.

"We will be," her antagonist called back.

Hollow sounds of feet hitting wooden stairs prefaced the emergence of another man in the room. He was tall and lean with jet black hair and grey eyes. His face was angular, accentuated by a short haircut and a small goatee. Molly watched this new man with terrifying interest. He held something in his hand and stepped closer to the bed.

"What's your name, little girl?" he asked smoothly. Though his voice wasn't soothing, this man was making no obvious attempt to scare her like her abductor had. She watched him warily with wide eyes and closed mouth.

"Name," he cajoled, voice still low but now slightly taunting. A wry smile played at the edge of his lips and he seemed to almost enjoy her terror.

"M-molly," she whispered hoarsely. Aside from crying, she'd not uttered a sound the entire day. Her throat was raw from sobs and from the incessant heaves she'd suffered since the night before.

"Molly what?"

"Wilson. Molly Wilson." Her voice was more sure. She examined the device he held and realized it was a recorder of some kind. She was relieved with that discovery. He must be going to play that for Lacey and her mother. And then they'd pay some money like people do in the movies. And then she'd go home. Always a happy ending ... always.

"Good. Tell your mother that you haven't been harmed."

Molly cocked her head slightly, her hunched posture on the bed reflecting that of a frightened rabbit watching its predator. She considered the question very carefully. She was tired and hungry, her wrists were sore and bloody. She smelled like urine and sweat and vomit. She felt quite harmed and that left her confused as to how to respond to the man's demands.

He took a step nearer. "Tell her." Though his stance

had become more threatening, his voice remained at the same teasing softness. The contradiction of action and voice confused her all the more.

"B-but," she stuttered, trembling again, feeling her stomach churn.

"Tell her."

"I want my mama," she whimpered softly, lacking any other coherent thought at that moment. She glanced to the room's other occupant who had stood silently against the far wall just inside the door since the man with the recorder had entered. He wouldn't meet her gaze, but rather stared straight ahead, so she turned her quivering attention back to the person addressing her.

"Then you'll cooperate you little brat," the lanky man growled.

"I'm not okay," she murmured. "I'm sore and I'm sad. I need my mama and my Lacey." She began crying again and the man grinned evilly. This was going better than he'd planned.

"They're glad to not have you. A worthless kid like you," he said slowly, clearly, making sure his voice was picking up on the recorder. "A brat that does nothing but take up room, cost hard-earned money to keep."

"No," she wailed. "They love me. You don't know! You're just a bad man!"

"Sorry kid. You're not worth love. You're not worth the time of day." He let her sobs be recorded for a few more minutes before he clicked the machine off and angled his head towards the door. Both men left silently and closed the door behind them.

Molly sank to the smelly mattress and cried until she started heaving again. She knew the man was lying. She knew he was trying to hurt her. Still a tiny part of her worried over the words and she prayed that she was right and that Lacey and her mother would want her back.

****

The women changed into clean clothes before coming out into the main part of the condo. Though Rachel appeared plenty green around the gills and more than a touch unsteady on her feet, she followed her lover doggedly down the hard wood of the hallway. In fact, she was following so closely she ran right into the taller woman when Lacey stopped suddenly.

"George?" Lacey said softly.

Rachel tilted her head. "George?" she repeated, peering around her lover's body to see the man in question standing casually in the condo's living room talking to Mary and Rico.

Rachel unceremoniously pushed her partner out of the way and jogged forward for a hug, which was willingly given.

"Hey," George said softly, the tone of his voice soothing and familiar.

Lacey merely stood and watched as he hugged the blonde woman. It had been almost three months since they'd last seen each other and the parting hadn't been on the best of terms. They'd all received the same threats and they'd tried to talk them through, when George had thrown up his hands and said he was leaving. The group had argued for a long time, George and Lacey had exchanged some heated words about being a coward and being too proud to consider the safety of loved ones. The tall black man had stormed out of the offices without so much as a goodbye. Two days later his house had been empty.

He set Rachel aside gently, smoothing her hair back as he did so. He'd always had a tender spot for the young woman, they all did. She'd obviously been blessed by some higher power to be able to walk into Lacey's life and turn the dark woman around. "Lace," he said softly, tentatively, letting his hands drop to his sides.

Even sober, Rachel would have been oblivious to the underlying tension. Until recently, she'd thought George really had left on business issues and had been in too much of a hurry to start a new job out of state to stop by the house and bid farewell. When Lacey had finally brought her young lover up to speed, she'd said that George ran from the threats, never mentioning the anger that had surrounded his departure.

He stepped forward now, dark brown eyes matching the rich hue of his skin, and offered a hand to his former boss. Lacey, Bernard, and George had been the heart of Vinnie's best team for a very long time. They'd been through more deals, more bloody battles, more scenes of death than either wanted to remember right now. But it also gave them an undeniable camaraderie.

"George." Lacey nodded, then her stoic features edged into a small smile. She stepped forward to meet him and hugged him close. "You were right," she whispered, referring to his jabs at her pride causing Rachel pain in the end.

He knew exactly what she meant. "No, Lace. I was wrong. You love them more than anything, I knew that. I was angry. This isn't your fault."

"I wish I could believe you," she whispered as she backed away from him, her hands still clasped on his upper arms. He was the only one on the team taller than she was and she tilted her head to meet his sincere gaze. "How did you know to come?"

"Rico called." He glanced to the young man standing quietly across the room. Rico apparently was waiting to receive Lacey's wrath as he avoided meeting her eyes.

"I thought ... he could help. He always was the best with the technical aspects ..." His voice trailed off.

Lacey grinned. It was true enough. George was a gadget man and built everything from taps to incendiaries to bugs. Before joining Lacey in her work for Vinnie, he'd been a strong part of Vinnie's more legitimate software company. George had been the foundation of their security business once the team had left. "S'okay, Rico," she assured her young friend. "I'm glad we're all here." The dark woman glanced around the room and her eyes landed on her lover who leaned awkwardly against the bar dividing this room from the kitchen.

"Baby." She dropped her grip from George's arm to hold out her hand towards the blonde. "C'mere and sit down."

"M'okay," Rachel protested, but reached for the hand anyway.

"I know you are, love. Come sit with me," Lacey coaxed gently, leading the smaller woman over to the couch.

"Can I get you anything?" Mary asked pointedly, tilting her head in the blonde's direction.

"Water, I think." Lacey nodded. "And maybe put on some coffee."

George watched the exchange with some confusion. Lacey was whispering gentle words to her lover, kneeling in front of her, stroking jean clad thighs. "Should I ask what the story is?" he inquired after a moment's consideration.

Rico gave him the brief rundown and then took the taller man into another room to listen to the tape. Lacey was grateful, being pretty sure her lover wouldn't be able to handle hearing it again.

Hearing the tape sent George to his cell phone to speak with the specialist they'd located in Denver. Then he quietly went to work on the phone lines and confirmed with the police station that records had been requested on any incoming calls.

Lacey and Mary concentrated on getting Rachel coherent while the men went about their business.

It was well after dark when the phone rang again.

****

The caller ID showed the number as unavailable, which was no real surprise. Lacey watched George and waited for his nod before she clicked the speaker button on the phone.

"Hello?"

Immediately the phone crackled and hummed, the connection poor at best. The background noise was loud, making the caller raise his voice.

"Lacey Montgomery?"

"Speaking," she acknowledged shortly. "What do you want?"

Rachel came up slowly and stood next to her tall lover, wrapping a surprisingly strong arm around the dark woman's waist. The several hours since their bath had greatly helped the blonde's level of sobriety.

"I have the girl."

"What do you want?" Lacey growled again, wanting to cut to the chase. Actually, she really wanted to crawl down the phone line and kill this man with her bare hands.

"You."

Lacey nodded slowly. That had been predictable enough. They weren't interested in fortune, that much had been clear from the start. But she wanted the man to talk more, she couldn't recognize his voice from the few words he'd uttered. "What are the terms?"

"No terms. You for the girl. She'll be safe, you'll take her place."

"How do we know you really have her?"

The man laughed darkly at the other end and Lacey felt her partner's body stiffen. She shook her head at Rachel, motioning with her fingers that she should be quiet. "Listen," the voice on the phone replied.

There was silence, followed by a click, and even worse reception as the man apparently juggled the phone and adjusted the volume. It was obvious they were listening to a recording and not the child herself.

"What's your name, little girl?" It was obviously the same man. The question was followed by silence.

"Name."

"M-molly." At the sound of the girl's voice, both women closed their eyes and swallowed hard.

"Molly what?"

"Wilson. Molly Wilson."

"Good. Tell your mother that you haven't been harmed."

Silence.

"Tell her."

"B-but."

"Tell her."

"I want my mama."

Rachel put her hand over her mouth, choking back a sob. Lacey squeezed her close, kissed the blonde's temple.

"Then you'll cooperate, you little brat."

"I'm not okay. I'm sore and I'm sad. I need my mama and my Lacey."

"They're glad to not have you. A worthless kid like you. A brat that does nothing but take up room, cost hard-earned money to keep."

Though the words caused hot red anger to soar through Rachel's body, she felt her lover stiffen and back away. The blonde released the other woman, looking up to see her face pale and her eyes wide. Lacey was shaking her head.

"No," the recording continued. "They love me. You don't know! You're just a bad man!"

"Sorry kid. You're not worth love. You're not worth the time of day."

They listened to her heartbreaking sobs for a moment longer before the recording clicked off and the voice came back. "I have her all right."

Lacey slammed her hands down on the table where the phone rested. The loud crack reverberated through the room. All the occupants watched the dark woman with barely controlled trepidation. Though she'd appeared confused moments before, now the only emotion that could be associated with Lacey was raw, unchecked anger.

"You fucking son of a bitch," she growled. "I'll rip your goddamned worthless tongue out of your fucking mouth!"

Rachel blanched and grabbed her lover's arm. What happened to play it cool? What happened to feeling things out and letting them run their course?

The man laughed, evidently thrilled with the woman's verbal reaction.

"You so much as touch her, you asshole, and I'll break each bone in your body one at a time." It wasn't an idle threat and everyone present realized it. Rachel looked to George with pleading eyes; he merely shook his head and shrugged.

"You'll get the swap information tomorrow by messenger. Sleep well, Lace." The line went dead a second before Lacey swiped the phone off the table and sent it across the room.

"Fuck!" she screamed, her voice hoarse and ragged. She turned to watch her associates with untamed searching eyes.

"Lace? Baby?" Rachel said softly. "You know who it is?"

The dark woman nodded, her expression an odd mixture of rage and sadness.

"Who?" Rachel choked on the single word. She'd never seen her lover so angry and though they hadn't expected good news with the impending phone call, they hadn't anticipated the ex-crony to react with such bald emotion.

Lacey looked to her partner with gently imploring eyes. She asked for love, support, forgiveness in that one blue eyed glance. It was given without question or need for explanation. Lacey nodded, eternally grateful for the unspoken commitment. "Jeremy," she whispered.

Rachel's brow wrinkled in thought and she pursed her lips slightly as she searched her brain for the meaning of the name. No one else in the room seemed to know either until emerald eyes widened with shock. "Holy shit," Rachel muttered. "That's just not right."

Lacey shook her had once before spinning around and storming out of the room.

"Lacey!" Rachel yelled after her.

"It's okay, Raich," the dark woman called over her shoulder. "I'm not going anywhere. I need to beat the shit out of something." Moments later they heard the front door slam.

Rico, George, and Mary all watched Rachel expectantly. They felt like they'd gone to the restroom during an integral part of the plot and were now busily trying to catch up.

"Hope whatever she finds isn't living," George murmured softly. "Care to clue us in, blondie?"

"Jeremy's her brother," Rachel said softly, almost feeling like she was betraying her lover by revealing such information. Without another word she headed out after the dark woman.

Rico glanced to George, confirming it wasn't common knowledge that Lacey even had a brother.

Chapter 15

The stars were more vivid here, dancing and sparkling against the black velvet sky. Lacey even thought for a moment that maybe there were more stars in this part of the country. In the back of her mind, though, she knew it had nothing to do with the number of stars, rather the mountain's altitude and lack of New York City lights allowed for more of them to shine through.

Her mind spun as she recalled her brother's words on the tape. It was almost surreal to hear his voice after so many years. They hadn't spoken in over fifteen years but they'd parted on decent terms. She and her mother had had a battle royale upon her departure to work for Vinnie permanently, but she and Jeremy had hugged and whispered their good-byes.

Confusing the issue more was the unpredictability of the situation. Would he hurt Molly? Had he killed Bernard? At first she'd thought it ironic because Bernie had been like a brother to Lacey. He was a solid friend and a comforting man who'd been with her through thick and thin. It was now she realized that the death of her close friend had very little to do with irony after all.

The dark woman growled and took a gloved swing at a snow bank on the side of the street. The snow was dirty and hard, plowed out of the way of mountain tourists and mixed with gravel from the road. She punched it a few more times, finding the crunch under her knuckles somewhat satisfying, though she would have much preferred the solid contact of a jaw bone and the accompanying bruises to her hand. It had been a long time since she'd wished for the outlet of physical violence against another person.

Completely absorbed in her assault on the hapless snow, she missed the sound of approaching footsteps and only became aware of another's presence when she felt a hand on her shoulder. She spun quickly, ready to swing, stopping her fist inches from Rachel's face. The jade eyes were wide with alarm.

"Go away," Lacey growled, turning on her heel and walking away from the small blonde who meant so much to her. She didn't want her lover to see this uncontrollable rage, the fire that consumed her very being from the inside out.

Rachel had already seen it: the flames licked tauntingly in her partner's ice blue eyes, giving her an overall appearance of cold fury. The anger rolled off of the woman in thick, black waves touching everyone and everything in her path. It was an all-consuming demon that had once ruled Lacey's life, but now only lapped at the edges of her soul...unless something unleashed it as her brother's phone call had done.

"Sorry," Rachel said softly, jogging to catch up. "Not gonna leave you." Her words traveled by way of misty vapor to the striding woman beside her. She found she had to hop every third step just to keep even with the taller woman's pace. Somewhere in the back of her mind, she realized she wouldn't be able to keep this up long, not being acclimated to the poorly oxygenated air at this altitude. She could already feel herself beginning to pant for breath.

"Fuck him," Lacey snarled. "That little two bit nothing. I fucking raised him and this is the thanks I get? He came to my goddamned bed and cried at night when they were screaming at each other downstairs. He found comfort in my arms while we listened to them hit each other."

Rachel followed doggedly, mildly surprised at how much her lover was revealing without careful prompting on her part. She'd never been able to get much out of Lacey concerning her family. Whenever she'd tried, it had seemed like an interrogation with the dark woman squirming as if strapped to a wooden backed chair with a single bare light bulb dangling in her face. Now the words flew out of Lacey. And though Rachel had her own series of questions about Jeremy's possible whereabouts and Molly's potential danger, she chose to keep those to herself for the time being.

"You know how I knew it was him?" Lacey asked her companion. She didn't wait for an answer, which was for the best since Rachel was having trouble catching her breath anyway. "Because of the tape. Because of what he said to Molly. Those words were the same my mother used on me when I walked out the last time. She said she was glad to be rid of me. That I cost too much of her money to keep. Her fucking drug money." Rachel wisely decided not to point out where a large percentage of Lacey's own money originated. "That I wasn't worth love ... wasn't worth the time of day." Suddenly the dark woman stopped and spun on her heel. Rachel gladly stopped beside her, chest heaving.

Lacey watched her lover for a long seeking moment. She knew there were tears in her own eyes, she knew that she likely looked manic to the gentle green gaze before her. But all she saw reflected there was love and understanding. It was much more than she deserved.

"I was fifteen," Lacey said softly, tipping her head up to look at the stars. She felt hot tears leave her eyes at the outside corners and track down into the hair at her temples. "Ya can't say that to a fifteen year old."

"Can't say it to anyone, Lace," Rachel offered softly, her breathing beginning to steady. "It was never your fault they were what they were."

Lacey swallowed hard. "I wanted her to make me stay. I didn't want to go work for Vinnie. I didn't like what he was offering. But I didn't have anywhere else to go. I didn't know what to do."

"Baby, you don't owe me any explanations," the blonde murmured, stepping closer to rest a gloved hand on Lacey's leather clad arm.

"I do!" she groaned, shrugging off her lover's gentle touch. "Goddammit, I do! Look what I've done to you, to Molly."

"No, honey. You didn't do anything but love us and provide for us. None of this is your fault."

Lacey looked down from the sky to the face watching hers. Rachel's blonde hair was pulled back into a tight ponytail, leaving her features open to the dark woman's discerning gaze. The moonlight danced across pale skin and the dark circles under familiar green eyes. Lacey took a steadying breath. "We'll get Molly back and then I'll find somewhere safe for the two of you," she said, nodding her head as if trying to convince her companion. "Somewhere away from me."

Rachel crinkled her brow in confusion, knowing that she was sober enough finally to be hearing things correctly. She shook her head once as if to rattle cobwebs out of her brain. "Crony, I thought we were done playing the push-her-away-for-her-own-good game. I don't much care for the game myself and there is no winner."

Lacey turned as if to storm off again, but Rachel stopped

her this time, wrapping a strong hand around her lover's wrist. "You can't run from me."

The dark woman spun quickly, trying to wrench her arm from her companion's grasp, but the small hands were strong from years of riding and held on with amazing tenacity. Lacey trembled with her rage but Rachel stood there with her, toe to toe, daring the other woman to try to overpower her. It seemed like hours but was actually only minutes that they stood there on a mountain top in Colorado, in the moonlit night, locked in each other's gazes, before Rachel sensed the tension leave her lover.

Lacey snorted and dropped her gaze to the wet pavement at their feet. Then she raised her face skyward to let the stars and moon shine across her sharp features and tanned skin. "You are the best thing in my life, Rachel Wilson," she murmured to the heavens. "The best thing that ever happened to me."

"You know I feel the same way, baby," Rachel responded easily, not letting go of the captured wrist, even though it now dangled benignly at her tall companion's side.

"Everyone else I ever loved pushed me away or kicked me out. But not you ... no matter how much I try." She grinned ruefully, face still tilted towards the night sky.

"Never me," Rachel confirmed.

"I can't shake you." The dark woman held up her arm and jiggled it gently, proving her point when Rachel's grasp was firm. Lacey grinned sadly.

"Nope." The blonde smiled back.

"My mom never loved me."

Rachel swallowed audibly at the muttered words, so child-like in their delivery. She'd always known there was a place in Lacey's past that they'd never uncovered, even during Rachel's own battle with her overbearing relatives and their hateful words. She also knew that, though Lacey presented kevlar skin to the world, counting on her cold exterior and her steely gaze to deflect any wounds, things touched her deeply. She loved with her whole soul, vowing ultimate loyalty to the few she called friends and sheltering that love deep in her heart. The blonde also knew that she was the only one who'd ever been allowed to see so much, know so much. "Lace ... love ... your mother never knew you. She was too wrapped up in drugs and violence to see what you were. What you had the potential to become. She saw you as a means to an end, she didn't see the goodness in you."

Lacey shook her head, refusing to meet the convincing green gaze in front of her. "No goodness. This is what I had the potential to be, nothing more."

"Yes, yes," Rachel agreed readily, placing a warm hand on her lover's taut abdomen. "Exactly! This is what you are, baby. You're a loving partner and a doting mother, a gentle friend. You are the strongest, most beautiful person I have ever met."

Lacey's only response for several long seconds was silence. Her focus concentrated on the evergreen tops towering towards the sky across the street. "Why did Jeremy do this?" she whispered. "I thought he loved me, too."

"Honey, you told me a long time ago that he was fiercely loyal to your mother. Maybe he changed so much once you left. You were the only thing guiding him towards goodness; without that, your mother was able to shape him."

"I made him." Lacey nodded slowly. If only she'd stayed.

"No!" the blonde barked, realizing her mistake the moment the words had left her mouth. "*She* made him. He made himself. We all have control of what we are and what we've become. I'm glad you left them, love. I'm glad you worked for Vinnie and came to Aqueduct last year. I'm glad you saw something in a smart-mouthed exercise girl with a death wish." She grinned gently with her words. "I'm glad you walked away from Jeremy and your mother because it was the path that brought you to me."

"Glad? Even at the cost of your daughter?" Lacey questioned, still refusing to meet Rachel's eyes.

"Don't do that, Lace. Don't you dare try to take the blame for all this. Jeremy is what he is. You could have only guided him, never changed him. The decisions he made were his alone. Just like yours were, and mine. I did some really stupid things and it was you who helped me to see past those. To instead focus on what I was inside and what I had the potential to become. Now do yourself the same favor. Jeremy is not of your making. This catastrophe is not your fault."

Finally, slowly, Lacey did drop her gaze into the eyes of her lover. If only she deserved the devotion she saw there.

"Now, drag yourself out of this dark place you've decided to dwell in, because our little girl is in the custody of a lunatic. And I can't get her back without you."

"It's easy, Raich," Lacey said softly. "He wants me. He gets me, you get Molly. No problem."

"Big problem," Rachel countered. "Huge problem. I'm not handing over one of the two most important things in my life to get the other. Call me selfish, but that is not the answer and I refuse to let you give yourself up that way."

"Selfish." The dark woman grinned gently. She slowly felt her confidence returning as her mind began to truly evaluate the situation. "But I think that's exactly what we're going to do. I have a better chance than Molly."

"No." The blonde shook her head. "Believe it or not, baby, the two of you have about the same chance against a man with a gun."

Lacey shook her head and turned back towards the condo. This time she slowed her pace for her lover who'd dropped her hand from its sure grip to instead tangle with Lacey's gloved fingers. The dark woman knew exactly what she was going to do.

****

Rachel spent most of the evening curled into a soundless ball on the couch in the living room. She watched the fire lick up the flue, touching and scorching as it went. The crackling of the wood was vaguely comforting and the blue in the middle of each flame reminded her of her lover's solemn gaze. It was actually Lacey's quiet voice in the adjoining room that offered her the most comfort and she listened to the familiar rumblings.

Lacey was talking softly with Rico and George, outlining plans for the next day. All they could really do was wait for the messenger to bring the necessary information. But they were planning quietly for possible contingencies and ways to track Lacey once the trade was made. They were talking about this last item when Rachel ventured slowly into the room.

George looked up from the paper they were all making notes on, catching the woman's movement through the threshold of the room. He smiled at her and Lacey spun slightly on her stool to see her partner standing nearby.

"Hey, baby," Lacey murmured, extending a hand. "C'mere." Rachel took the offered hand readily, letting her companion tug her towards the small group. Lacey slid from the stool and wrapped the younger woman into her arms, back against chest. She pressed her face into Rachel's hair, deeply inhaling the familiar scent.

"You can't go," Rachel said softly, resting her arms across the tanned ones holding her.

"It's the only way, honey," Lacey said softly. "We can talk about it a little more in a minute. Right now we're going to give me a tracker. Wanna watch?"

"How are you gonna do it?" Rachel twisted in the dark woman's arms to peer up at ice colored eyes.

George pushed a small plastic box across the breakfast

bar and Lacey disentangled so that she could open the box and show the contents to Rachel.

Moments later, Lacey sat on the stool, her crossed arms on the raised table and her head on her arms. Her dark hair was pushed away to expose her neck. George stood ready with a small syringe of a numbing agent and Rachel thought his hands were trembling.

"Uh, let me do that," the blonde suggested. "Okay, Lace?"

The dark woman was mildly grateful. She knew her lover had experience in delivering shots to her equine patients, which was more than George could claim. "Thank you," Lacey said softly.

"Won't they find it here?" Rachel asked, tapping the syringe. "There'll be a cut."

"He might," Lacey acknowledged.

"Won't that make it worse for you? We should put it somewhere he wouldn't look."

George nodded. "When we worked people over, Lace, where did we never expose?"

"Is he gonna work you over?" Rachel questioned with obvious concern.

"I would if I were him," Lacey murmured to her lover and then turned to her friend with a slight smirk. "The nether regions."

George returned the rueful smile. "Sounds like a good idea to me."

"It would," Lacey growled playfully. "I say that's Rachel's job. We don't need your assistance." The dark woman hopped down from the stool and turned immediately to her young blonde partner, who appeared baffled.

"What did we just agree I'm going to do?" she asked hesitantly.

"You, my love, are going to perform a minor operation," she answered cheerfully, grabbing the small kit and Rachel's empty hand.

"Wait a second, here ... I'm not so sure..."

"Hush, baby. You'll do fine."

Moments later, Lacey sat on the bed in their room. She wore only a nightshirt, which was pooled around her hips, exposing her lower extremities, and sat on a large bath towel to protect the off-white sheets. She leaned quietly against the massive wooden headboard. Rachel knelt between her lover's legs, silently shaving a patch of dark, curly hair.

It was amazingly erotic to both women. The blonde's gentle touch sent chills through Lacey. Rachel was warmed by her lover's obvious trust.

"Won't the shaving give it away?"

"Can't stitch it without shaving," Lacey murmured. "'Sides, I really hope my brother won't be looking there."

Rachel pantomimed a gag and Lacey chuckled dryly.

"Am I hurting you?" Rachel inquired as she finished up the shaving.

"Not at all," the dark woman assured. Rachel used the edge of a towel to wipe away the remaining soap and hair, leaving a square inch bared of kinky hair. The blonde eyed the syringe carefully, raising it up and removing the needle cover. She tapped at it and flushed the bubbles.

"Ready?"

"Mmmhmm." The dark head bobbed in a nod. The blue eyes were amazingly trusting.

"Here goes," Rachel said under her breath. She inserted the needle in several spots over the bare skin and out towards where there was still hair. Her goal was to numb the entire area. "I can't believe I'm hurting this place," the blonde grinned wryly. "Happens to be one of my favorite parts of your body."

Lacey chuckled softly. "Don't worry, doesn't hurt. I couldn't let anyone else touch me there."

"No one else?" Rachel raised her head, green eyes serious. She knew Lacey was committed to their relationship, but liked to be reassured from time to time.

"Nope. Just you. You'll see the scar there when we make love and you'll know why."

Rachel snorted, resuming her task, injecting the syringe into six places before it was empty. "It's the only scar of yours I know the story behind."

"What others do you want to know?" Lacey asked seriously, regarding her lover with tilted head.

"Actually." Rachel capped the syringe and placed it in the small box. She adjusted her rubber gloves again before withdrawing the scalpel. "I don't think I want to know."

"I would tell you anything, Raich."

"I know, baby." The blonde smiled encouragingly, pausing in her actions to give the numbing agent a chance to work. "Maybe we'll reserve the name that scar game for when you come back to me. Are you going to tell me why you have to go?"

"Yeah. We'll talk about it. Do this first."

"Okay," the blonde sighed, absently stroking her lover's exposed thigh while she waited. She could already smell the dark woman's arousal.

"Knock it off, Raich," Lacey growled playfully. Just her young companion's gentle touch was enough to make her yearn for more. "Or we'll have to skip the impromptu surgery."

The smaller woman grinned. "I already numbed you there."

"But not in the right place." Lacey smiled, waggling thin dark eyebrows and causing her partner to laugh.

They regarded each other silently for a few moments, reading more in their exchanged glances than words could have spoken. After a moment, the blonde tapped the shaved skin and surrounding area.

"It's good," Lacey confirmed. "Go ahead."

Rachel took a deep steadying breath and eyed the scalpel before gaining courage and glancing to her lover. She tried to exude confidence, but wasn't sure how well she was doing.

The skin sliced neatly under the slight pressure of the sharpened blade. Rachel felt her stomach roil at the slim line of welling blood and clamped her jaw tightly. Now was not the time to run to the bathroom.

Lacey handed the young woman pads of gauze and watched while she dabbed at the blood. "Now lift up an edge with the scalpel and use the forceps to put the tracker in."

"Does this hurt?"

"Not at all."

"Do I have to turn this thing on?" Rachel squinted at the small device, turning the forceps around in her hand.

Lacey grinned. "No, just put it in."

The blonde did as she was told, finding the procedure easier than she'd imagined. Then she dabbed at the incision again before extracting from the box items she'd need to suture the wound. Reading her young companion's thinly veiled uncertainty, Lacey actually did the stitches since she had experience in suturing. Three tiny sutures finished the job and soon Rachel was applying a dressing, using cloth tape to keep it in place.

"All done," she announced, looking up to meet gentle sapphire eyes.

"You did a good job."

Rachel laughed. "You could have done it yourself, crony."

"Maybe. But you did it for me." She reached a hand out and stroked her lover's cheek. "Do you think you can sleep tonight?"

The blonde shrugged and dropped her eyes to gather up the items she'd used. She hopped from the bed and padded on bare feet into the bathroom.

"Raich, honey?" Lacey called softly.

"I just ... my heart hurts at the thought of losing you," the blonde announced, leaning against the door jamb dividing the two rooms and watching her lover reclining, half-naked, on the bed.

"You're not gonna lose me. Come here." She extended an easily accepted hand and snuggled the blonde securely into her side. Lacey stroked the golden hair with long delicate fingers.

"We have to do the exchange so we can make contact with these guys. We get Molly back to you, they take me. But with this tracker, Rico and George can find them ... and me. End of story."

"Except the killing and bloodshed part," Rachel murmured, placing a kiss on the dark woman's neck.

"Well, I'm hoping to avoid that part."

"Mmm." Rachel nodded, glad to hear that. "Can't we pretend to exchange you and get away with both of you?"

"If we can, we will," Lacey assured her lover. "But we have to kind of play that by ear. We won't know if there's potential for that until we see how things are going to unfold. Me going with them is kind of the basic plan. We can build on it as we go."

"Make improvements."

"Yeah," the dark-haired woman agreed.

"I don't know if I can do this," Rachel said softly, snuggling closer, latching her lips onto the throbbing pulse in her partner's neck. She was comforted by the salty taste and the gentle rhythm. This was proof of Lacey's life, her heart beating, her skin warm and pliant. *Oh God, keep her this way.*

Lacey silently tilted her cheek into the soft, pale hair, knowing that there were no words to calm her lover's fears or her own trepidation. She watched as Rachel's slim muscular fingers trailed patterns on her firm, bare thigh.

For long moments the two women sat like that, entwined with each other, absorbing the warmth and compassion. Lacey glanced to the clock at last. It was nearing midnight. "How about we go tell them the dirty deed is done? Then let's lock ourselves in here for the rest of the night," the dark woman suggested, disentangling herself and climbing to her feet. She gingerly slipped on a pair of flannel pants, stretching the elastic well away from her body over the site of her minor surgery.

Rico and George teased her appropriately before wishing her and Rachel sweet dreams. Both women snorted their obvious disagreement and bade Mary goodnight before going back into the bedroom.

Lacey turned off the light and crawled quietly into the large bed with her lover. Their legs slid together under the sheets.

"You okay?" Rachel queried, obviously indicating the incision.

"No problem," Lacey assured her, but the blonde figured Lacey's arm could be falling off and it would still be no problem.

"How about you?" Lacey asked softly, pulling the smaller woman warmly to her body, making sure they were touching all along their lengths. "I'm sorry I stormed out on you. It must have been hard to hear that tape."

"It was okay," Rachel responded after several moments of consideration. "We know she's alive. We know who has her. It's progress anyway." She paused for awhile. "She sounded really frightened."

"Yeah. She did."

"What do you think she's doing right now?" Rachel whispered into the darkness.

"Probably wishing she were laying here with us. Just like we're wishing it," the dark woman murmured, pulling her lover close and kissing her temple.

"Do you think he's hurting her?" The blonde's voice cracked, obviously on the verge of tears.

Lacey paused for a very long time, torn between reassuring her partner and being brutally honest. She decided honesty would be preferred at this stage in the game. "I don't know. He's no stranger to abuse, and abused people normally make the best abusers. But he has no reason outside of that to hurt her. She doesn't know anything that he needs to find out. Hurting her won't get us to her faster, we're playing on his timeline."

Rachel nodded slightly, her hair rustling against Lacey's broad shoulder. "You had the same treatment as your brother, but you didn't become an abuser."

"Thanks for the vote of confidence, baby, but I'm no stranger to violence," the dark woman reminded her lover.

"But not me and Molly ... you wouldn't hurt your family like your parents did."

"Never you and Molly. I swear that. If there comes a day where I can't control my violence and I hurt either of you ... then we'll have to seriously talk about alternatives."

"Won't happen," Rachel said confidently.

"Hope not." The dark-haired woman nodded. She was quiet for a very long time, watching the moonlight reflect off the snow below the window and play along the floor and wall of the small room. It was peaceful here. The gentle hum of the furnace and the slight rustling of sheets as Rachel quietly shifted were the only sounds to break the silence.

"I have an idea," Lacey said at last, squeezing the familiar body more tightly against her. "When all this is over, you, Molly, and I are going to Hawaii."

"Why Hawaii?" the blonde laughed softly.

"Dunno. Sounds good though, doesn't it? Warm and romantic."

"We'll have to wait until Spring break. Can't take her

out of school."

"Good, it's a plan then," Lacey said cheerfully.

More silence followed for a long time as Lacey trailed gentle fingers over her lover's body, along her skin and through her fair hair. She placed a kiss on the smaller woman's forehead, leaning forward to do so. The blonde's head was tucked neatly into Lacey's shoulder.

"Do you think we," Lacey hesitated, kissed Rachel again before starting her question over. "I want very much to taste you," she admitted softly. "To touch you and smell you."

"In case we don't again?" Rachel asked alarmed.

Not wanting to vocalize that thought, she opted for another truth instead. "I just need it." The admission was harder than she would have thought. The old Lacey wasn't used to needing anything but herself. "Are you up to it?" The last few days had been such an emotional roller coaster. Tomorrow was Christmas, something they'd planned for months previous. She knew Rachel was depressed and making love was probably the farthest thing from her mind.

"Only if I get to treat you to the same," Rachel whispered huskily, moving her body silkily along the lengthy form. Lacey needed no further invitation.

Kisses came easily and caresses, even more so. Lacey pulled off her lover's sleep shirt and tossed it to the side, quickly followed by her own. Her flannel pants came next, allowing her to lay her warm, naked body down on that of her lover.

Rachel raised her knee between Lacey's long legs and felt the taller woman grimace against her neck where she'd been lavishing kisses.

"Oops ... sorry," Rachel husked, lowering her leg again. "How are we gonna do this, gimp?"

Lacey chuckled, the sound dark and dry where it was muffled against pale skin. "Let me."

"Noo," the blonde whined pathetically, even as she was

losing the battle to her lover's coaxing fingers and velvet tongue. "I want to, too."

"Wait your turn," the dark woman instructed, moving down Rachel's smooth body to capture a rigid nipple in gentle teeth. Rachel arched off the bed into the sensation, her small, strong hands tangling into Lacey's hair. The long, black strands tickled the outside of her breasts and down her ribs.

"I never go first," Rachel panted, any attempt at pouting vanquished by her labored breathing and arching back.

"You want me to stop?" Lacey teased, stilling all of her motion to lean back. The moonlight flashed off the pale woman writhing beneath her, illuminating the blonde in muted hues of silver.

"Ungh," Rachel protested vaguely. "Don't stop." She reached up to grip her lover's shoulders, trying to pull their bodies back together.

"Never," Lacey responded with a savage growl. She lowered herself again, taking Rachel's slim thighs and settling them over her shoulders. She stopped like that, reveling in the familiar weight of those legs, the comforting scent of Rachel's arousal. She could already imagine the taste on her tongue, sliding down her throat. Eyes closed, the dark woman savored this moment, wanting always to remember what it was like to be here making love to Rachel, knowing the young woman like no other person could.

"Lace," the blonde moaned, oblivious to the powerful moment her lover was living. She raised her hips off the mattress, pleading, wanting, needing. Her hands clutched at the sheets.

Lacey lay for a while longer, raised on her elbows, stomach on the bed, though her long legs dangled off so her bare feet touched the cold wood floor. Finally, her lover's squirming form brought the dark woman from her melancholy. She grinned. "Can I help you, baby?"

"You'll need help in a minute if you keep laying there doing nothing," Rachel warned, but she was laughing, making her threat futile.

Lacey pursed her lips and blew cool air on the heated area inches in front of her. Rachel jumped slightly, her thigh muscles tensing against the dark woman's ears. Lacey blew again, chuckling, then opened her mouth to breathe hot air on her lover, hovering over the 'blonde's opening and russet curly hair.

"Please." Rachel rocked her hips, knowing what it felt like to have Lacey's lips where she wanted them, unable to wait for that sensation.

"You may have trouble sitting tomorrow," Lacey whispered, leaning forward to emphasize her point with a kiss to Rachel's clitoris. Her nose was nestled in the fragrant patch of hair for just a moment before she backed away again.

All Rachel could do was laugh softly, feeling safe and protected, even as exposed as she was. She reached down and combed her fingers through Lacey's dark bangs. Her hips bucked forward slightly as a pointed tongue swiped gently along her opening. She wasn't sure if Lacey was waiting for her approval, but gave it anyway. "S'okay," she said softly, pressing her heels into the dark woman's muscular back.

It was a night of neediness and clinging, each one wanting so much from the other. Their lovemaking was frantic and exhausting. Through their time together, Rachel had learned a lot from Lacey and had even adopted some of her more interesting character traits, like drowning your emotions in passion. They rivaled each other in their intense need to be lost in the moment.

It seemed to be hours later when they moved against each other slowly, exchanging kisses and running hands up sweaty and salty bodies. Each was exhausted, but reluctant to forego this last crescendo. It was slow and sweet, accompanied by murmured words and rasping tongues. They climaxed together, slicking the other's thigh with shared nectar, tasting the same fluid in each other's mouths from earlier explorations.

They lay quietly, wrapped in arms and legs and scented sheets, each breathing heavily.

"Your incision," Rachel murmured at last, trying to push away to look down to the spot in question. Lacey's tight embrace wouldn't allow her to do so.

"It's okay."

"The bandage came off."

"Help me clean it in a minute. Just stay here for now."

Though inclined to argue for her lover's safety, Rachel just didn't have it in her. She snuggled more deeply into Lacey's warm embrace.

The dark woman's breathing seemed to hitch and the breath that was expelled on Rachel's shoulder was shuddering.

"No, no, baby," the blonde whispered, rubbing her arms up and down Lacey's sweat slicked back. "Don't cry." *Oh God, please don't fall apart. You're all that's holding me together.*

"I'm sorry."

"Merry Christmas, Lace," Rachel whispered, trying so hard not to think of her lonely daughter and her doomed lover. "Our first one together."

"Yeah. It could be better, though, huh?"

"Could be worse, too. We have to be thankful for this." Meaning the two of them, entangled in love.

"How can you comfort me, Raich? I know how much you're hurting."

"So are you," the smaller woman responded gently. It was almost easier to concentrate on her lover's fears and pain than her own. The change in focus allowed her not to cry this dark Christmas morning.

Lacey swallowed hard, consuming her grief with the motion, reaching a hand up to wipe at her moist cheeks. The wetness was a combination of sweat, tears, and Rachel's passion. She thought about that idly as she slipped her tongue out and slid it over her upper lip. She tasted all three.

They didn't speak anymore, instead seeking comfort in supportive arms. Later, they took a quick shower, protecting Lacey's stitches the best they could. Rachel was just applying the dressing again to her somber lover seated on the bed when the morning's orange red rays sought entry into the room through the window blinds.

Chapter 16

The first visit the condo received that morning was Sheriff Railer and a guest. The two walked in without a true introduction, following Rico down the hall into the living room area where the rest of the condo had congregated.

"Ms. Wilson?" the sheriff said, spying the blonde in the kitchen.

Rachel turned and wiped her hands on a tea towel, tossing it back on the counter. She walked forward, leaning her arms on the breakfast bar and eyeing the sheriff and his guest in the adjoining room. "What can I do for you, Sheriff?"

The portly man looked at the young woman quietly for several long moments. She looked worse each day: tired and drawn, dark circles under her eyes. But she smiled for him. "Mrs. Nelson came to my office this morning. She'd seen our signs for Molly and had heard of our search from some of the slope workers."

"Mrs. Nelson." Rachel leaned over the counter and extended her hand. The woman stepped up and took the offering with a firm shake.

"Mrs. Nelson is with social services," the sheriff finished.

Rachel froze and withdrew her hand.

George turned on his heels and went to find Lacey. She'd said she needed a run and had left with Karma nearly an hour ago.

"Pardon me?" Rachel said slowly. "What can I do for you?"

"Maybe we should talk in private?" the woman suggested. She was slightly taller than Rachel, her greying brown hair pulled back into a tight bun. There was no sympathy in her pinched face.

Rachel shook her head. "No. I'd rather have everyone here."

Once they were all situated around the breakfast bar, the social worker cleared her throat. "Whenever a child is missing under abnormal circumstances, it's the job of social services to visit with the family and determine if they've endangered the child. It's important for us to make sure the home is a fit one where the child should be returned."

Rico and Mary turned their attention from the thin nosed social worker to the blonde woman standing next to them. She'd declined a seat, preferring instead to fidget nervously from foot to foot. Rachel remained silent though her mouth was slightly open as if she wanted to say something, but nothing came out.

It was then that the front door opened and Karma came flying down the hallway. The young dog immediately went to the newcomers and sniffed each thoroughly, going so far as to jump up on her hind legs and balance herself with one thin paw on the Sheriff's knee. He brushed her off and it ridiculously angered Rachel.

Breathing hard, George and Lacey rounded the corner into the living room, each stopping as soon as they passed the threshold.

"What's going on here?" Lacey asked darkly, moving around the stomach high counter to her lover's side. Rachel was trembling.

"Uh ... Lace, this is Mrs. Nelson. She's with social services. She's here to determine if we're a fit home for Molly."

"What?!" Lacey spun on the small woman, her eyes bright with anger. Her sweatshirt and shorts were soaked clean through with her sweat, her bangs plastered against her forehead. She looked more than slightly wild and on edge.

The woman raised her hands placatingly. "That's not completely true. I'm just doing a preliminary interview. Social services in New York would have to do follow up work. They would need to visit your home, see Molly's environment, observe how you interact with her. I'm just providing some initial information for the case, since I'm local."

"You're going to take Molly away from us because some asshole kidnapped her?" Lacey growled. It took the gentle pressure of her lover's hand on her forearm to prompt her to take a step back.

"Not me, no," the woman said with a sigh, as if tired of the entire thing already. "I'm just opening the case."

"This is bullshit!"

"Lace, baby," Rachel whispered. "We need to cooperate. The harder we make it on them, the harder they'll be on us."

"You can't take that little girl from us. No one can take better care of her than us. No one loves her more."

"Well, she's not even here to prove that point, is she?" Mrs. Nelson asked bluntly, opening a folder on the counter and spinning a pen in her nimble fingers.

Lacey was on the verge of exploding. Her entire body shook with the effort to control herself. Rachel turned to face her and put both hands on the taller woman's taut stomach, feeling the warmth of Lacey's skin through her soaked shirt. Rachel stepped forward, pushing her lover gently across the kitchen until she was pinning the tall body against the counter. She could feel the anger and darkness in a cloud around them.

"Baby," Rachel murmured. "I can talk to her. They have no reason to take her away from us."

"Let's see," Lacey whispered in a low growl. "We're gay, I'm a killer, the money that supports us is mostly illegal."

"We're gay?" Rachel chided gently. "Whoo. News to me." She poked her lover gently in the ribs. "Courts are more open to that these days. Molly's father isn't in the picture trying to win custody. It's us or the state. They won't be able to argue with her living conditions and they won't want to shell out the bucks to raise her."

"Maybe. What about the rest?"

"How easy is that to find out?"

The dark woman shrugged. She swiped at her wet bangs with a large trembling hand, glancing over at the group across the room, which was trying hard not to stare. "Not very. We were all covered pretty well. Not much good to Vinnie if we're ducking warrants, ya know."

"So let me talk to this lady. You go take a shower."

Lacey looked to her lover, seeing that she'd calmed down quite a bit. Her expression was confident and her green eyes had lost some of the fear that had been there when Lacey'd first come inside. "You sure?"

"Yeah." Rachel nodded.

The dark woman took a deep breath, calming her own rattled nerves. Rachel had some valid points, but the entire thing rubbed her the wrong way. Here it was, Christmas morning, they were waiting for news on how to find their daughter, and this rigid woman strolls in here questioning their worth as Molly's parents.

"Okay," Lacey said at last. "I'll make myself scarce. I'd rather you not speak to her alone, but I'd probably throttle her."

Rachel grinned slightly. "I'm sure Mary will sit with me."

In the end, it had been relatively painless. Mary sat quietly next to Rachel, offering a surprising amount of support for someone who had remained so quiet throughout their entire relationship. She even held Rachel's hand and patted her on the knee from time to time.

The pinched nosed social worker asked questions about their home, their jobs, Molly's school. She asked for a recounting of the events that had led up to Molly's abduction and what had happened that day.

Rachel handled it well, even managed to be evasive about Lacey's history without being too obvious. And, after what seemed forever, Mrs. Nelson announced she had enough preliminary information. Lacey emerged from the shower dressed in jeans and a turtleneck, a white cotton towel draped over her shoulders, her black locks contrasting starkly where they fanned across the fabric. She nodded to the sheriff and the social worker as they departed. The room stood in silence.

"So," George said at last, looking around. "I have a friend coming up from Denver today. She's familiar with the area, I thought that may be useful when the message is delivered."

"Good idea," Lacey acknowledged, crossing to her lover and rubbing the smaller woman's back. "You okay?"

"Yup." The blonde nodded, offering Lacey a smile. "I'm okay. Let's get to work, huh?"

****

The next person to arrive at the condo was George's friend. She introduced herself as Ronnie and strode in purposefully. She was a few inches taller than Rachel, with short cropped blonde hair and round brown eyes. She offered a smile to everyone and a familiar hug to George.

"It's good to see you," she said to him, smiling, sliding her hands down his arms to squeeze his hands. Her cheeks and nose were freckled and tanned, this pattern of bronzed skin across her features and her lithe physique indicating she was a skier.

"Thanks for coming. Especially on Christmas," George replied, applying gentle pressure to her hands before releasing them.

The woman shrugged. "No big deal."

"How's the family?"

She grinned in a way that showed true humor and not just politeness. "Same as always. Ya know how it goes."

George turned her to the group now. "Lacey and Rachel this is my friend Ronnie."

"Thank you," Rachel murmured softly, shaking the proffered hand, guessing the woman before her to be in her early twenties.

"All I can offer is to be a tour guide, really. But I'll do my best at that."

"That may be all we need." Lacey smiled, stepping from behind her lover to shake the other woman's hand also.

George finished out the introductions with Rico and Mary, each shaking the blonde's hand in turn.

"What can I do?" Ronnie asked, looking at the faces around her. They all looked drawn and drained.

George shrugged. "We're mostly just waiting, but when the message comes, we'd like you to take us to the meeting point early so we can check it out."

"If he gives us enough time to do that," Rico interjected.

Lacey nodded. "I think he will. It would be more beneficial for him to do the exchange after dark. Limits how we can respond."

George nodded his agreement.

"So," Rachel said softly, drawing their new guest's attention. "How do you know George?"

Ronnie laughed, looked to George and then took Rachel's arm and dragged her towards the living room where they could sit down.

Mary followed out of curiosity and the others all congregated in the dining room, taking seats at the large oak table there.

"It was just by accident, really. When I was in the military, I worked with a guy that went to school with George. He was here visiting and the guy I worked with had a barbecue of some sort. We met there, started talking geek computer crap, liked each other."

"He's a good man," Rachel observed softly.

Ronnie nodded. "He's helped me quite a few times when I needed it, even mundane things like moving from one apartment to another. He'd always make sure to check on me when he was in town visiting."

"Why do you think he called you instead of that other friend?" Mary asked, more to draw out the conversation than any real need to know.

Ronnie laughed gently, brown eyes sparkling. "Let's just say I'm not as abrasive as he is."

"Do you celebrate Christmas?" Rachel inquired, trying to understand why this woman would come help complete strangers on a holiday.

"I do. But my family is in Denver, too, and always has something bizarre going on. This year my brother's getting divorced from his wife and they were both coming to Christmas dinner. Believe me, I'm glad to be missing it." She shook her head in emphasis, then looked up to meet Rachel's gentle emerald gaze. "I'm very sorry for what happened. I can't imagine what you're going through."

Rachel smiled weakly, trying not to let tears fall. She'd been on the verge of crying all morning. "I'm lucky to have the support of good friends. Lacey's been great."

"Is she really going to trade herself today?" Mary asked softly.

Rachel nodded, unable to talk about it.

"Everything will work out," Rico's girlfriend assured gently, reaching out to rub Rachel on the arm.

"It better," the blonde chuckled faintly. "Cuz I'll have one hell of a bone to pick if I lose either of them."

Ronnie watched the exchange silently, learning a lot from the brief words and expressions. George had given her the basic run down when he'd called last night. The opportunity to see her friend again had been reason enough for Ronnie to come up here, but really she was glad to be helping people that were so important to George. And so obviously distraught.

It was still mid-morning when the ringing of the doorbell announced yet another visitor. This was the one they'd been waiting for. Lacey opened to the door to reveal a teenaged boy in a jester hat and snow pants. He was scruffy and his face red with windburn.

"Yeah?" Lacey said, eyeing the boy up and down. He was eyeing her as well and his cheeks reddened further with a blush as he apparently liked what he saw. He remained silent. "Can I help you?" the dark haired woman prompted.

"Oh." Startled out of his not-so-subtle appreciation, he held out a large manila envelope. "A man gave me this to give to someone at this address."

Lacey took it slowly, glancing behind the boy to the street beyond. It was empty. "Where is he?"

"I don't know. He came up to me on the slopes, said he'd give me two bills if I delivered this."

"Where are you meeting him for the money?"

"I'm not, he gave it to me ahead of time." The kid grinned, his teeth straight and white, thrilled at his good fortune.

"How did he know you wouldn't take the money and run?" Lacey asked, stepping out onto the small front porch and looking around more carefully. They were probably being watched.

"Hey." The teenager looked affronted. "I'm an honest person."

Lacey raised one dark eyebrow into her bangs, letting her ice blue gaze work wonders on the person in front of her. Rachel and George stood quietly in the doorway, watching the scene on the front step.

"Well," he blushed, "guy said he would know and I shouldn't try anything."

The dark woman smiled and nodded. "What did he look like?"

The boy shrugged. "He was pretty tall. Maybe as tall as you are. He had on a hat so I didn't see his hair but he had a black goatee."

"Did you see his eyes? What color were they?"

"He had on shades," the kid said, shaking his head slowly. "Didn't see anything else."

Lacey nodded in response, pursed her lips, and looked around one last time. She heard a vehicle starting and turned towards the main road in time to see a car pull away and begin the journey back into Breckenridge. She watched it quietly through the shroud of pine trees even as George shoved the kid aside and began to run towards the stairs. He stopped mid-stride when the dark woman's hand clasped around his upper arm.

"Unh unh," she said softly. "We play the game the way he wants it played. She'll stay safe that way."

"Lace?" George asked uncertainly, still ready to jump in his rental car and be on his way.

"No," Lacey assured him, looking beyond the tall black man to her lover standing in the doorway hugging herself. Their eyes met. "Let's go inside and check this out." The dark-haired woman held up the envelope and tugged George with her. She remembered to look over her shoulder to the teenager still watching them all. "Thanks."

"Yeah. Sure," he said awkwardly, shoving his hands into his jacket and trotting down the stairs.

****

Ronnie drove silently through Frisco, occasionally glancing at the two women in her back seat. Everyone else had stayed at the condo, Lacey promising to call with a description as to how the trading place looked.

Rachel had wanted to sit in the front seat so Ronnie didn't appear to be a chauffeur but the young woman had insisted. It was obvious how much the two needed to be together, to touch and feel one another, so she insisted that Rachel and Lacey both occupy the back seat.

Lacey held her lover's hand in a sure grip, their fingers intertwined. Occasionally she brought their linked hands to her lips to kiss them. Rachel didn't speak for fear of crying.

"This Castlewood Canyon Park ... you know where that is?" the dark woman asked, leaning forward towards Ronnie. She still held Rachel's hand with one of her own while rubbing the smaller woman's thigh warmly with the other.

"Yeah. It's between Denver and Colorado Springs, on a rural highway."

"Secluded?"

"Very," the driver agreed, nodding.

There were few words exchanged during the journey east on I-70 and through the Eisenhower Tunnel. Lacey watched the passing scenery silently, the mountains white and icy, shrouded with frosted pine trees and jagged rocks.

The grip on her hand was nearing painful, but she accepted it willingly, as it was a way to feel her lover, know that she was there.

Silently they traveled through Idaho Springs, past the Boulder exit, towards Westminster. Ronnie took the 470 loop around the edge of the city and through Englewood until it met with I-25 where they headed south, following the signs for Colorado Springs.

"How much longer?" Lacey asked after nearly an hour of silence.

"Twenty minutes, maybe. We'll get off the highway up here at Castle Rock," she said, pointing towards the sprawled outlet stores just appearing around a bend. "Go east for a little while."

As described, they left the highway, the small sedan turning and going back over the highway, framing the diminishing Rockies in the rear window. Lacey and Rachel both looked over their shoulders at the receding view, astonished by the magnificent sight of snow-draped mountains as far as the eye could see.

"Cool, huh?" Ronnie asked softly.

"Yeah," Rachel agreed.

"It's the best in the morning, with the rising sun reflecting off the snow."

"Sounds beautiful." Rachel nodded slowly.

"Reason enough to stick around, anyway," the driver responded with an easy grin.

State Highway 85 took them directly east of Castle Rock until they met up with an even smaller town that boasted a welcome sign for Franktown. Ronnie stopped at the single light and pointed to her left. "That's where everyone will meet us this afternoon." She indicated a gas station that looked very much like a Mom and Pop operation.

Ronnie turned right onto State Highway 83, picking up speed to the posted limit of 65 and winding through a slight incline where the shoulders of the road met with sheer rocky slopes. The highway had obviously been sliced right through part of the foothills and emerged, around a bend, on a gently sloping plateau. Ronnie slowed her car and indicated right, turning into the entrance of Castlewood Canyon State Park.

It looked like little more than a field with a gate on it. There was nothing but a sign with a brown background to indicate that this rolling prairie belonged to the state. The entrance was barred off with long metal gates and Ronnie stopped in front of them.

The wind was harsh here, whipping down the mountainside and across the plains to actually rock the small vehicle from side to side. The tall yellow grass waved with the wind, winking in the sunlight and dancing to a beat nature provided. It was absolutely quiet and serene, a pasture of horses across the two lane highway and a herd of cattle a little farther up the road. The only house in view was a mile or so distant and placed well back from the road. There wasn't another car in sight.

"Good place," Lacey mused approvingly. "What's in the park?"

"Dunno, never been." Ronnie shrugged her shoulders. "I'm more impressed with the mountains than the windswept plains." She grinned. "I used to work in the Springs and live in Denver with my mom. I traveled this way all the time."

"Is it always quiet like this?" Lacey asked, turning slowly to take in their surroundings.

"Yeah." Ronnie nodded. "What were the instructions?"

"Said a mile south of the park entrance." Lacey pulled out her copy of the neatly typed letter, having to disentangle her hand from Rachel's sure clutch.

"Yeah." Ronnie nodded, remembering. "There's a place up there where the highway widens. Trucks park there sometimes ... I'm not sure what it's really for."

"Is it a good place for this kind of thing?"

"Definitely. This area is so secluded, rarely any vehicles coming one way or the other."

"Other roads?"

"Hmmm." Ronnie shifted her weight to turn and watch the two women in her back seat. Rachel was quiet and pale, rubbing sweaty palms on her jeans. Lacey was cool and self-assured, assessing the situation with professional attention to detail. The dark woman's hair was French braided neatly, leaving the tail to fall under the collar of her leather trench coat. She looked every bit the calmly confident expert as sky blue eyes read over the note yet another time. Ronnie knew the tall woman had already memorized the words. Those eyes looked up and Ronnie realized she hadn't yet answered the question. She blushed, grinned sheepishly. "Highway 85 is the first turnoff north that isn't into a development of some sort. That's the road we took from Castle Rock. Farther east it goes through Elizabeth, another one horse town. Well, actually, they have quite a few horses, but just the one traffic light." She smiled good-naturedly. "South, the first real road is probably a good five miles down, called Lake Gulch. I've never been down that road, but it wraps back around to the highway, I think."

"So both ways go to the highway?"

"Yeah."

"You could go north and double back south?"

"Pretty easily," Ronnie acknowledged.

Lacey pursed her lips and took a deep breath.

"There's just the one road though, Lace," Rachel said softly, surprising both of the other women by joining the conversation. "We could cut him off, get you back."

She shook her head slowly, catching her lover's hand again and squeezing it warmly. "And force a hostage situation. Not a good idea. Best plan is to let him take me, get comfortable, let his guard down. Then George and Rico can use the tracker to come in and get me out while he's not paying attention."

"He has a lot of heat, Lacey. Wherever he takes you will be guarded. Remember all those pictures of people I recognized?"

"Baby," Lacey murmured. "Trust in me? Okay?"

"I do," the blonde sniffled, oblivious to their quiet audience in the front seat.

Lacey framed her lover's pale face in large warm hands. "I'm trying to work out the best way to minimize injuries, including my own. Forcing our hand here is not a brilliant plan. You get Molly and you guys go to someplace safe. Then we work on getting me out and dealing with my brother."

"Are you nervous about seeing him?" Rachel asked suddenly, realizing that Lacey was about to meet her childhood face to face.

Lacey smiled, placing a gentle kiss on her lover's lips. The young woman's sensitivity touched her. "A little bit. But I already know he's not the kid I left behind all those years ago. My Jeremy never would have done something like this."

Rachel nodded and leaned forward to embrace the tall woman. She moved a hand to cup Lacey behind the head, running her fingertips down the tight braid where it hugged her companion's skull. She remembered easily how it had felt to wrap those silken strands into the plait only hours before. She loved to touch her lover like that, accomplish familiar things like brushing her hair or painting her nails. Lacey succumbed to it with just a little protesting, secretly loving the attention, but outwardly scoffing at such lavishness. This morning she'd practically melted into Rachel's gentle touch.

After they parted and resumed holding hands, Lacey requested Ronnie take them to the section of road where the meeting would actually take place. Once there, the tall dark woman unfolded herself from the back seat to stand on the side of the highway. A lone car whizzed past them, easily doing seventy.

Lacey stood silently, hands in pockets, the long tails of her coat whipping in the wind and slapping against her denim-clad legs. She was glad her hair was braided, the restriction preventing anything but a few tendrils from tickling her cheeks and forehead. She spun slowly on her heel, taking in the wide expanse of dried grassland and the mountains behind. The sun was bright and it would actually have been warm if not for the gales that made Lacey squint. Tumbleweeds tangled in barbed wire, fighting for freedom and then rolling quickly across the road into the next fence it met.

Rachel crawled out of the sedan, walking behind it to stand next to her lover. The darker woman looked majestic here, facing the wind, coat billowing. The planes of her face caught the midday sun, highlighting prominent cheekbones and accentuating sapphire eyes. "You're beautiful," Rachel murmured, tucking her arm through Lacey's and joining her perusal of their surroundings.

Her comment was rewarded with a fond look and a warm smile. "Thank you," the dark woman murmured.

"What do you think?" the blonde asked hesitantly.

"I think the plan stays the same. We'll come back here just before five. You'll have Molly with you tonight, baby."

"I want you both," Rachel said petulantly, realizing she sounded like a spoiled child. She glanced apologetically to her lover.

"Soon," Lacey assured her, rubbing the smaller woman's back with a large warm hand. "We have about five hours to kill. What do you want to do?"

Chapter 17

They'd ended up finding a theatre in Castle Rock and seeing a movie. There was little else open on Christmas day. None of them really watched the film: Rachel had clung to her partner desperately, Lacey was deep in thought, and Ronnie was too affected by the two women beside her to concentrate on anything.

They found a King Soopers where they bought some food from the deli section and ate in the car. Lacey'd purchased some candy bars and tucked them away in jeans pockets. It was nearing time to meet the rest of the group and the tension in the vehicle was palpable.

"Let's go," Lacey said at last.

When they met up with George and the others, they were all greeted with hugs. By now Rachel was wiping silently at wet cheeks and Lacey kept constant contact with her even as she caught up Rico and George. The group had decided to leave Sheriff Railer out of this latest development, knowing he would ask questions they couldn't answer and also knowing that he couldn't help them at this point.

Lacey and Rachel crawled into the back of the van. George drove, Rico sat in front. Mary and Ronnie followed in Ronnie's car.

The vehicles parked where the women had stopped earlier in the day, the clicking of guns being loaded and checked made Rachel cringe. The two sat on the floor between the van's first bench seat and the driver's seat, allowing Lacey to settle the blonde between her legs while her back was supported on the wall of the vehicle.

Rachel began to whimper.

"Shhh," Lacey crooned, wrapping her arms and legs around the smaller woman. She rubbed Rachel's stomach with a warm gentle hand, knowing she was probably on the verge of being sick.

"My heart hurts," the blonde woman whispered, turning her head to tuck it under her lover's chin. She took deep breaths of the skin there, wanting the scent of her lover to overwhelm her. The pain was tangible.

"I know, baby."

"I ache inside."

George slid the van door open and stood just outside. As the sun went down, the air chilled dramatically and where before the wind had been cold, now it was downright biting as it whipped into the van and rustled the plastic and papers that lay within. Rachel snuggled more deeply in the warmth of her lover's embrace.

Lacey rocked the small woman, using her right hand to press the blonde head firmly to her upper chest. She dipped her head into the back of Rachel's neck, murmuring words of comfort. They were just streams of thought actually: words about their love and commitment, the time they would share together, how Molly would be home soon.

The pain Rachel felt was beyond sobs. Her chest and throat ached with the soundless sorrow, her face was wet with silent tears. She clutched at the dark woman's lapels, trying to crawl right into her heart, keening softly with her anguish. So consumed were they and so loud the howling wind, they didn't hear the vehicle that stopped opposite them across the highway. George reached in and patted Lacey's knee.

The dark woman looked up and nodded, wiping tears from her face, pushing Rachel away and doing the same to her cheeks. They tumbled out of the van together, the blonde not sure she could even stand on her own and leaning heavily on her tall companion. Dusk was just falling but they could see the vehicle across from them in clear outline. It was a dark Suburban and several people climbed out, all holding weapons. Then Molly was tugged out and stood shakily in the center of the group. Rachel nearly did fall down at the sight of her child.

Lacey's cell phone rang quite unexpectedly and the dark woman answered it.

"You for the girl. Easy enough. Don't do anything stupid."

Lacey looked across the deserted road and saw Jeremy with one hand on Molly's shoulder and the other hand by his ear.

"Not a chance," Lacey assured him, turning off the phone and putting it in her coat pocket. Then she turned to face her lover and shrugged out of her trench coat. She wrapped it around Rachel's shoulders, the length of it brushing the ground. The blonde started to protest.

"No, you wear it," Lacey murmured, tugging the lapels together and pulling her lover closer. "Keep it for me."

Rachel's smile was watery. The coat was very much a part of Lacey, it was a symbol of the dark woman and it was important to her.

The evening was nearing frigid without the protection of leather but Lacey wouldn't have it any other way. She cupped her lover's cheeks, looked deep into liquid emerald eyes. "I love you, Raich. Completely."

The blonde whimpered.

Lacey kissed her deeply, chasing the chill out of her bones with the memories the kiss wrought. Rachel melted into the touch, snaking her arms up to the dark woman's head, holding it still and allowing her to delve deeper. They parted, rested foreheads together. "George will keep an eye on you and Molly, baby. I'll be back soon."

"Okay," Rachel choked.

Lacey kissed her again, hugged her tightly. "Whatever happens, know that you are the best thing in my life, that I love you with all my heart."

"I love you, too," Rachel whispered.

It was hard letting go, but eventually Lacey did, stepping away from the blonde and turning to face the group across the street. She didn't say anything to Rico or George, not being able to speak any more for fear of crumbling. She'd never done anything more difficult in her life than this: walking away from a trembling, crying Rachel. Leaving her family hadn't been this hard. Each step forward was painful as she made her way across the highway. She heard guns cock behind her and in front of her and cringed. Already this wasn't looking good.

Just as the dark woman turned and began to walk away, Rachel saw the van headlights reflect off of something on her lover's hand. Squinting her eyes to see through her tears, she saw that Lacey wore a band on her left ring finger. Despite her hurting heart, the sight made her smile slightly. She recalled vaguely feeling the cold metal against her cheek when the dark woman had cradled her face and kissed her goodbye. She'd not registered the unfamiliar feeling at that moment.

Across from them, Molly was shoved forward and started walking as well, stumbling a few steps and then breaking into a trot.

"Walk!" Jeremy yelled, angered that the meeting would take place closer to Lacey's team.

Molly hesitated.

"Walk, baby," Lacey called gently. "It's okay."

The child consented and slowed her steps again. Their pacing had them meet on the double yellow line, a good twenty-five yards from each group. Lacey scooped the girl up into an embrace, holding her close, unmindful of her stale unclean smell and stringy oily hair. The child sobbed into Lacey's neck, clinging to her tightly.

"Oh, baby," Lacey murmured. "Molly-girl. We missed you so. Did he hurt you?"

"No," Molly replied, voice muffled and choked.

Lacey pushed her away to observe the child's features. Though pale and drawn, she looked unharmed. The dark woman leaned forward to kiss Molly's cheeks and forehead. "I love you, sweetie. You need to take care of your mama for a couple of days until I get back to you. Okay?"

The girl nodded slowly, resisting when Lacey placed her back on her feet. After a long moment she allowed the dark-haired woman to step away. "Go to your mama," Lacey pointed back the way she'd come, "I'll see you soon."

"Lace?"

"Go on, Molly-girl," Lacey prodded. Slowly, the child turned and started on her way. She was no more then five feet from Lacey when Jeremy and his team opened fire.

Lacey froze for just a moment. "Fuck you, Jeremy," she growled. She knew exactly what was going on. He was forcing Lacey to protect Molly. The shots were wild and over their heads, but dangerous regardless. And Lacey's side had answered the fire readily. Lacey dove the short distance to the little girl and bore her to the ground, tucking the small body underneath her larger one.

Molly was crying. "It's okay, baby. Hold on," Lacey said softly.

The sound was nearly deafening between the wind and the gunshots. It was moments later that Lacey realized she heard a vehicle, too. Then she was being dragged to her feet, Molly still in her arms, and tossed into the Suburban. Turning to look over the seat as the vehicle sped northbound, Lacey saw George holding a screaming Rachel in his sure grip. *Fuck. Coulda gone better. I'm sorry, baby, but I'll keep her safe.* She turned her attention back to Molly, cradled in her arms.

She resituated the child, purposefully elbowing the men on either side of her. She recognized both from the pictures Rachel had selected in the office last week. She still hadn't gotten a good look at her brother, who sat in the front passenger seat. Instead she concentrated her attention on the child in her lap.

The little girl's blue eyes seemed wary as they glanced around the interior of the darkening vehicle. When they turned to rest on Lacey's face, she smiled meekly.

"Hey," Lacey murmured, smoothing the girl's tangled hair away from her face. She still wore the clothes she'd been abducted in and smelled dirty and soiled.

Without a word, Molly launched herself at the dark woman again and wrapped thin arms around Lacey's neck.

"I've got you, honey." She tightened her embrace around the child, pressing warm lips against the temple just below her chin.

"Oh, how touching," Jeremy scoffed from his front seat, glancing over his shoulder and meeting Lacey's eyes for the first time.

The dark woman considered him, child still clutched in her arms. She watched his angular profile and those slate grey eyes, realizing she would have recognized him easily even just in passing while walking along the street. He looked very much like the brother she remembered who had snuggled in her bed, tucked against her side. He was almost five years younger than she and she'd taken great pains to raise him when her parents were too busy fighting or dealing, which was most of the time.

His eyes turned cold and his lip curled upwards in a sneer. "How can you care for your whore's daughter? Smelly little thing that she is." He looked forward again as the Suburban stopped. Then he hopped out and removed the roadblock they'd set up, tossing it aside to allow traffic through once more.

Molly trembled at the man's words, pressing herself further into the warmth of Lacey's body.

"Shhh," the woman soothed, rubbing her back. "I love you and your mama, you know that. Whatever that man has said to you, he's only said to be mean."

The little girl nodded, wanting to believe the words. It felt so good to be held in these familiar arms after several days of loneliness and fear she'd endured.

"Hey." Lacey nudged the child away gently as the Suburban started up again. "I have something for you." The woman shifted her weight and stuffed a hand in her pocket to withdraw a slightly smashed Snickers bar. "You hungry?"

Molly's blue eyes flicked from the candy to Lacey and then back. She nodded. Lacey opened the wrapper and placed the chocolate bar in the girl's hands.

The child practically shoved the entire thing in her mouth.

"Easy, baby," Lacey said softly, watching how Molly gripped the bar with both hands and chewed on one end voraciously. It was this close observation that allowed her to see the raw rings around the child's wrists. She thought she might explode from anger.

Lacey recognized the man to her right as Lionel from the pictures Rachel had identified. He appeared agitated by the girl or the candy bar, or maybe both. The large man eyed them as if debating whether to deny the food to the child and to Lacey he looked like he might move to do just that.

Lacey raised a slim dark eyebrow, clearing her throat and getting the man's attention. "Lay one goddamned finger on her and I'll kill you with my bare hands," she growled softly, sending chills into everyone in the vehicle.

Jeremy chuckled after a prolonged silence. "Big words considering the situation the two of you are in."

"The deal was me for the girl, you bastard. I see you're even less honest than you were as a kid. Part of this job is morals and ethics, Jeremy. You fucking blew that right out of the water."

"Tell ya what, Mary Poppins, you can lecture me on proper etiquette some other time. Right now I suggest you shut up and keep the brat quiet. We all have a better chance of getting along that way."

Though she desperately wanted to leap into the front seat and pound some sense into her brother, Lacey restrained herself. She looked down into Molly's trusting face and saw that she'd finished the candy. Lacey wiped her face off with large gentle hands, smiling warmly and kissing the pale cheeks.

Her touch was reassuring and incredibly welcome. Even with these men around, Molly was able to soak in the woman's warmth and love, snuggle more deeply into her lap and arms, and find a peaceful sleep that had evaded her for days.

Now that Lacey was here and protecting her, she knew everything would be okay.

Chapter 18

George sat silently in the darkened bedroom. He'd pulled the not-so-comfortable chair up to the bedside and held Rachel's hand in his, smoothing his thumb across the back of it, feeling the fine bones there. Even in the near darkness, his chocolate skin contrasted starkly with silvery pale hue of her skin.

The young blonde had been alternately sick, hysterical, and quietly pensive. Now she sniffled softly into the pillow.

They'd had to bodily drag her into the van to leave the scene before the gunfire attracted legal interest. She'd begged from the backseat for them to follow the Suburban but Rico and George were nothing, if not loyal to Lacey and they knew her plan should be followed. Tonight, late, they'd activate the tracker and pinpoint the location. Deciding not to drive all the way back to Breckenridge, they found themselves at Ronnie's parents, taking over the lower level with many apologies.

Her parents had been surprisingly calm about the whole thing, as if this was nothing, causing George to tease his friend about the hellion she must have been growing up, since this catastrophe didn't faze them. Ronnie'd taken the ribbing easily and had immediately left with Mary to go back to the condo and get Karma. In between whimpering for her lover and her child, Rachel had voiced concern for her pet.

"George?" the blonde murmured, bringing her guardian's attention back to the present.

"Hmm?" he responded gently.

"I'm sorry I was so difficult tonight."

"Oh, honey." George scooted to the end of his chair so he could lean over Rachel's head and shoulders. "You weren't." He stroked her back tenderly. He spoke the truth. She'd been distraught and argumentative at first, turning to devastated as the evening wore on. But she'd been responsive and understanding, allowing the others to handle arrangements and discuss their plans for the evening. Even when she was kneeling in front of the toilet, suffering retching and dry heaves, she'd been quiet and receptive to George's solicitous attentions.

"We met a year ago two weeks from tomorrow," Rachel murmured, opening glittering eyes to study her friend in the gentle moonlight.

"You're the best thing that ever happened to her," George said honestly. "I've known her for a very long time, but you bring out a different person in her."

"I don't see her like you do. I never have. I know that she was cold and violent and did horrible things ... but to me she's warm and gentle and kind."

The black man nodded, squeezing the hand he held. "She is those things. I think she always had it in her, which is why she was already questioning what she was doing. When she met you, you were the beginning of her leaving. She had the will, she needed the motivation."

"She'll be back," the small woman whispered with honest conviction.

George nodded, having no doubt in his mind that Lacey would move the world to come back to this woman and bring her daughter. "Yeah. Tomorrow at this time, the three of you will be sleeping soundly."

They heard the front door open and moments later the bedroom door was pushed open to allow Karma entrance. The dog loped into the room and jumped on the bed, washing Rachel's face with a warm tongue.

The blonde pushed the licking beast's face away, but pulled her closer into an embrace. The dog settled on the bed next to her mistress, tucked gently into her arms. Ronnie stood at the doorway and watched them.

"How are you?" The other woman's voice traveled easily across the silent room.

"M'okay," Rachel muttered. "Thank you for driving all the way back for her."

Ronnie shrugged, moved quietly into the room. "Coupla hours, no big deal." She looked to George and rested a hand on his broad shoulder. "You want a break? I'll chat with Rachel for awhile."

George looked from the standing woman to the prone one, getting a barely perceptible nod from the latter. He rose to his feet and reached down to pat Rachel's hip. "I'll be back in a bit."

Ronnie claimed his seat and leaned back quietly, moving her feet to rest them on the bed. "This okay?" she asked the small woman, indicating her stockinged feet.

Rachel nodded.

They were silent for a very long time, soaking in the darkness of the room and the varying emotions of the day. "I know we don't really know each other," Ronnie said softly after a while. "I just ... I wanted to say that I really feel, inside, that everything's gonna be fine. Because what you have is too special to end any other way."

"Thank you," Rachel murmured. "I appreciate that.

And I appreciate you keeping me company. I'm not sure I can be alone right now."

"I'm glad to be here, Rachel."

****

Lacey was only aware that they'd gone north before cutting across to the highway and doubling south. After they exited from the freeway, there was too much darkness to be able to discern much more than trees.

She'd been dragged out of the vehicle, the motion causing Molly to stir and awaken. Lacey shifted her weight gently and kissed her temple, causing the little girl to wrap the woman tightly in an embrace. For the first time, she got a look at the driver of the vehicle and realized it was Peter Grazier, the man Rachel had recognized at the student union and quite possibly the muscle behind the entire operation. She studied him as best she could before Lionel shoved her none-too-gently away from the Suburban.

The driveway was gravel and as Lacey pivoted quietly, she saw nothing but moonlight and trees. They were in a very secluded area. The house before them opened as Jeremy slipped inside and disappeared. Lacey and her charge were ushered into the house, through the kitchen, and then down narrow stairs into the basement. Molly whimpered when she blinked open weary eyes and recognized her surroundings.

Lacey wrinkled her nose as she took in the room. It was small and smelled badly of excrement and sweat. Obviously, this is where the girl had been kept for her stay and hadn't been allowed facilities or any means to wash herself. Lacey's eyes landed on the chains and cuffs and she trembled with anger.

"Tell that fucker brother of mine to get his ass down here," she forced out between gritted teeth. She hugged

Molly to her, rocking her slightly.

Lionel looked at her stunned, surprised that she'd be demanding anything.

"Fine." Lacey turned on her heels and started back up the stairs herself. The men who'd accompanied her to the basement followed, startled.

She found Jeremy in the back of the house in the dining room with Grazier. Her brother was flipping through some papers and glanced up at her when she came in. He stood up and began to berate his men for their lack of skill.

"Shut up, Jeremy," Lacey barked. "Listen to me. I'm really not in the mood to figure out why the hell you're doing what you're doing. I'm not going to ask you how you forgot what we were, how much we meant to each other, how we turned to each other when our parents beat the shit out of us. Why you hired someone like Peter Grazier," she purposefully used his name so the two would know she was well informed, "and his thugs to pull off such an idiotic stunt. I am, however, very much in the mood to beat the shit out of you myself, right here, right now, if you don't improve our conditions a bit."

Jeremy stood silently for several beats, something close to shame may have flashed across his face. He noticed how the girl clung to his sister with infinite faith and trust, vaguely remembered a time when he'd done the same. He found, here in the end of the execution of his plan, it wasn't nearly as fulfilling as he'd hoped. He glanced to the burly man at his side, a man hired to complete a job. The other man's obligation would be up by morning, when Lacey and the girl were delivered. Jeremy turned back to his sister.

"What do you want?" he said at last, wearily.

Lacey accepted the change in demeanor and gentled her tone. "We need a clean room. And some time in a bathroom with a shower. She needs some clean clothes, even a clean T-shirt or a sweatshirt or something. She needs a decent meal and water."

Jeremy met his sister's eyes for a long time before tilting his head in consideration. "Fine." He turned to Lionel. "Take them to the upstairs bathroom. They can have the room at the end of the hall, nail the window closed, guard the door." Without another word he turned to his files again.

Lionel checked the medium-sized bathroom over completely before exiting and using a quick jerk of his head to indicate that Lacey should go in. She did, closing and locking the door behind her. Then she knelt down, steadying Molly on her feet in front of her.

"No," the girl cried, clutching at her, not wanting to lose the connection.

"Shhh, I'm right here," Lacey crooned, gently undoing the girl's pants and pulling them down. Molly clutched at Lacey's shoulder and cried. With distaste, the woman tossed the soiled pants aside.

"Don't be mad," Molly sobbed.

"Honey? What are you talking about? I'm not mad." Lacey looked to the child, greatly confused.

"I wet my pants," the girl choked out, pressing her face into Lacey's neck.

Lacey shook her head slowly, amazed that Molly would be focusing on that. "Shhh, it's no big deal, Molly-girl. We'll just get you cleaned up, is all. Accidents happen."

"Embarrassed," the child whimpered.

"I know, honey. But it's okay. Here." She pushed Molly away gently to pull off her shirt and toss it across the room as well. Then she removed the soiled underwear, adding them to the pile. Molly stood naked before her, trembling and still clutching at Lacey, loathe to break the contact.

Lacey took the opportunity to examine her. Aside from the chafing on her wrists and her jutting ribs, she really did look unharmed. Satisfied, Lacey stood, picking up Molly as well when it was obvious the girl wasn't going to give her any other choice. She brought them over to the tub and knelt again, turning on the water and checking the temperature. Molly remained attached to her, leaning heavily on the dark woman.

"Ready?"

Molly shook her head, still crying.

"Baby, you'll feel better clean. I promise."

The child was sobbing too hard to speak, trying to scale the woman's body to get back into her arms.

Lacey sighed, picked Molly up and rocked her. "I know it was horrible. We were so worried about you. But I'm here now, and I won't let anything happen to you. You don't have to be frightened anymore."

"He called me bad names. And you and Mama. Said I was worthless."

"I know," Lacey murmured. "But they were all lies, just words to make you sad, Molly. Nothing more." She rocked her silently for several long moments, waiting for the tears to subside. Molly was weary and exhausted, overwhelmed by her own emotions as well as the events of the last several days. Lacey knew that they'd be dealing with the repercussions of this for a long time to come.

"I have an idea," Lacey said at last, still rocking the small naked form. "How about if we shower together? Would that be okay?"

Molly nodded, finding this an acceptable solution. She released her death grip from Lacey, though she retained some form of contact even after the woman set her on her feet in order to take off her own clothes.

Though Lacey and Rachel had changed in front of Molly without thought and Rachel had showered with the little girl before, Lacey felt mildly awkward as she stepped into the shower with Molly's small form. Any uneasiness vanished when they began the task of washing. Lacey shampooed the girl's hair twice, using long fingers to massage Molly's scalp and lather her hair.

The girl accepted the attention easily, swaying on her feet as she leaned into the touch and absorbed the tenderness. She blinked open blue eyes once her hair was rinsed, glad to be sheltered from the blinding spray of the water by Lacey's tall body. She noticed the bandage at the top of Lacey's pubic hair and reached out to touch it very gently.

"Are you hurt?" she whispered, looking up the long body in front of her.

Lacey knelt down and grinned, smoothing back Molly's wet hair. "Unh unh. That's how Rico and George are gonna find us. Shhh." She raised a finger to her lips. "Our secret."

Though Molly returned the smile with a small one of her own, she was obviously confused. "By a cut?"

"There's a little machine in there that will let them know where we are. Your mama put it in for me."

Blue eyes twinkled with the prospect of getting out of this horrible place and back to her mama. "Really?"

"Yup."

"And Rico and George will find us?"

"Yup." She kissed the child's forehead and repeated her earlier request. "Our secret."

"Okay." She nodded, enjoying the conspiracy. "George is back?" she asked, suddenly realizing what both of them had said.

"He came out here to help us find you."

She nodded silently, apparently pleased with this information.

"Let's finish cleaning up so we can eat and go to sleep."

Molly nodded again, taking the bar of soap Lacey offered her.

While Lacey was toweling the child dry, there was a knock on the door. Molly nearly jumped out of her skin.

"Yeah?" the dark-haired woman called.

"Clothes," came the gruff reply.

"Stay here, baby." Lacey steered the little girl between the toilet and the tub. She wrapped the towel around her and kissed her head. Then she donned a towel as well.

Looking over her shoulder to be sure the child was where she'd left her, Lacey unlocked the door and opened it a crack. The outside air was cool compared to the steamy heat of the bathroom and she took a deep breath of it, collecting the stack of clothing Lionel offered.

"Great. Thanks," Lacey said sarcastically, closing and locking the door again.

Then she tugged Molly out of her corner and back into the middle of the room. "Let's see what we have, here," the dark woman murmured, rifling through the clothes.

There was a T-shirt that was an adult size small so she pulled it out. Then she found some sweatpants that were also small, but would be ridiculously big on the child. It was better than nothing and luckily the pants had a drawstring.

She pulled the T-shirt over the little girl's head and noticed it fell to her mid-thighs. Lacey smiled and Molly leaned forward to kiss the dark woman, wrapping her arms around the broad shoulders. "I love you."

"I love you, too, baby," Lacey whispered back, pulling the pants onto her willing subject. Then she disentangled herself so she could tighten the waist and fold up the legs. She leaned back to look at the results.

Molly stood before her, drowning in the borrowed clothes, still holding onto Lacey's arm. But she was clean and much calmer than she had been before.

"Give me a minute to get dressed?" Lacey requested gently, unhooking the child's fingers and backing away. Molly agreed reluctantly, watching as the dark woman changed back into the clothes she'd been wearing before. She pressed the towel against her wet but still braided hair before hanging the damp towels over the shower curtain rod.

"Ready?" She turned to Molly, who looked at her with big, round eyes. "Sure you are. C'mere." She extended a hand and Molly stepped forward to take it. Lacey unlocked the bathroom door with her free hand and they stepped out into the hallway together.

Lionel glanced at them, nodded shortly. "Follow me." He stepped down the hallway. Lacey glanced at the other guard before stepping behind Lionel and heading towards their room. Lionel opened a door at the end of the hall, sweeping his hand toward the room beyond.

Lacey stopped just outside the threshold, still holding Molly's hand. "What about her dinner?"

"I'll check on it," he growled. The dark woman offered him her most feral grin. He seemed surprised.

"You do that," she snarled back, raising a slim eyebrow.

Lionel gained some courage from somewhere and leaned forward, towering over the child, but not Lacey. "You talk pretty big for a prisoner."

Molly whimpered, uncomfortable in the big man's shadow. She pressed back into Lacey and turned around, trying to scale the tall body. Lacey picked her up with no evidence of exertion and held her close, rocking her gently. "Prisoner implies I'm here against my will." Lacey grinned evilly. "Let me assure you that I'm not." She passed the man and went into the room, pulling the door out of his hand and slamming it behind her.

The words were true enough, she'd come here of her own free will.

Dinner was delivered shortly in the form of grilled cheese sandwiches and vegetable soup. It was better than the child had been receiving and she ate it greedily, small body pressed tightly to her mother's lover while she ate.

Lacey didn't have much of an appetite, but made sure the child ate all of her own food and then some of Lacey's as well.

"Can you sleep?" Lacey asked gently, taking the tray and carrying it over to the dresser by the door. This room was larger and better furnished than the hole in the basement. There was a queen-sized bed with a comforter and several pillows. The dressers were all a light oak, matching the end tables and the woodwork surrounding the door and window. Overall, it was a comfortable surrounding and Molly had relaxed quite a bit since being closed in here with just Lacey.

Molly shrugged, watching the door warily.

"What is it, baby?"

"I need to go to the bathroom," Molly whispered shyly.

"Ah," Lacey nodded, "good idea." She took the few extra steps to the door and knocked on it. She heard the outside bolt being pulled back.

"What now?" Lionel growled, thinking watching his small charge had been much easier before the bitch came along.

"We need to go to the bathroom."

"Great," he sighed, pulling the door wider.

Lacey went back to the bed and took Molly's hand, tugging her gently. The girl followed willingly, though she was practically attached to Lacey's leg.

It wasn't much later that Lacey crawled into bed with the little girl. Molly curled against her warmly, wrapping the dark woman tightly in small arms and legs. Lacey hugged her as well, stroking the still damp hair with gentle fingers. She didn't plan on sleeping at all, wanting to be completely awake when Rico and George made their appearance.

"You're wearing the ring," Molly whispered. "Did you give Mama hers?"

"Kind of." Lacey smiled, kissing the top of Molly's head.

"Kind of? Did she like it?"

"I dunno. We'll ask her when we see her."

Molly was quiet for a few seconds. She snuggled even closer. "Does this mean you're married?"

"Mmm." Lacey considered the best way to answer. "More like we're committed to each other. We can't get married because we're both women."

The child pushed away to seek Lacey's light eyes in the darkness. "If you could marry her, would you?"

"If she'd have me." Lacey smiled.

The little girl chuckled. "Of course she'd have you. What does it mean to be committed?"

Lacey pursed her lips in thought. "It means that your mama and I will be together always. That we'll work through the hard parts and cherish the good parts. That we want to be together for our lives."

Molly appeared to consider this. "Mama said that?"

"Not exactly." Lacey grinned at her own evasiveness. "But I feel that way, so I think she does, too."

"The rings give you that?" Molly asked incredulously, thinking those were some pretty magic rings.

Lacey laughed softly, bouncing the child with her body. She leaned over and kissed Molly's head again. "No. We give each other that. The rings are a symbol of it so when we're not together, we can touch the ring and know. And it's so other people know that we're committed to each other." She raised her hand to examine the band in question. It glittered in the moonlight, catching each beam and sending it back with fractured elegance.

Molly fell into silence, finding the explanation acceptable. Slowly the silence faded into a deep sleep.

Chapter 19

When George came back into the room, it appeared that both women were sleeping. Rachel had kicked off the covers and partially laid on them so instead of waking her up, he took Lacey's leather trench coat and settled it over the small woman. His motions woke Ronnie.

"George," she murmured, wiping at sleepy eyes.

"Hey, how are ya?"

"Okay. She fell asleep?"

"Looks that way." George nodded. "You look like you could use a bed, too."

"Did the tracker work?"

"Yeah." The black man grinned. "We have her pinpointed. She's on the north edge of the Springs, east of Monument."

"Just land out there. Pretty secluded."

"That's what we figured from the maps." George nodded. "We'll be leaving here in a couple of hours to get her."

"I hope it works."

"It will," George said softly. "Lacey has a way of making most anything work. Come on, let's find you a place to crash." He gently guided his friend from the room, closing the door behind them.

Rachel rolled over after they'd gone, blinking emerald eyes into darkness. She took a deep breath, inhaling the scent of her lover surrounding her in the form of the leather coat draped across her. She hugged it to her and noticed a hard object. Slowly, the blonde reached her hand into the pocket of the jacket, finding Lacey's cell phone. While she was pulling the phone out to sit it on the nightstand, her hand brushed against something soft. Setting the phone down, she reached back into the pocket. Her fist closed around the object she'd felt, withdrawing a small velvet box.

Her heart pounded in her ears as she scooted to a sitting position and reached over to flick on the small lamp on the bedside table. It cast a ring of light at the head of the bed. Holding her breath, Rachel flipped the top of the box open, revealing a silver hued band with intricate etchings across its surface. It was simple yet complex, much like her dark lover. Though there were no stones in the design, the detail of the etchings, entwining and circling in on themselves, was astounding. There was a folded paper crammed into the top of the box and Rachel extracted it, unfolding it with trembling fingers.

Raich,
  I bought matching rings not long before
  Christmas, Molly helped'me pick them out. I
  wanted them to be a symbol of our love and
  commitment, our lives together, our future as
  yet untold. I love you, Merry Christmas, and
  see you soon.
          All my love,
                Lace

Silently, Rachel slipped the platinum band onto her finger, enjoying the weight of it there. She felt her lover near, felt their love bubbling warmly inside of her. She tucked the box back into the pocket where she'd found it, turned the light off, and snuggled into the pillow where she cried tears of grief, loneliness, and love, the ring pressed solidly against her lips.

****

The door creaked open quietly and Lacey watched as the silhouette moved from the lit hallway into the darkened room. The bedroom door stayed open, allowing the dark woman to see that the profile approaching was her brother.

Molly shifted slightly in her sleep, holding the tall body more tightly.

Lacey murmured reassurances and kissed the blonde head until the child settled again.

Jeremy took a seat in the chair by the bed. "Lacey," he acknowledged softly.

"Jeremy," she responded.

He was quiet for a very long time before he indicated with his hand the sleeping child. "You used to hold me like that, too."

"Yes," the dark-haired woman agreed.

"I missed you so much when you left."

Lacey snorted, tucked the blankets more firmly around her sleeping child. "Yeah. Great. You missed me so much you killed my best friend and kidnapped my lover's child. That's just charming, Jeremy."

"Lace—"

"And what about the car? Trying to kill Rachel and Molly? Hiring a killer and his cronies to follow her around? You're so damn compassionate. I don't give a fuck what you want."

"I was wrong."

"Damn right you were, you little bastard. I raised you." Lacey was furious though the extent of it was muted here in the darkness. Her words were whispered hoarsely in an effort not to disturb the small form sleeping against her.

"You did," he acknowledged softly. "I thought that Mom was a victim. I always did, even after you left. So when she came to me—"

"What?!" Lacey snarled. Molly mewled and shifted in her sleep so the dark woman settled back down. "This is her doing?"

The man shrugged weakly, flashing grey eyes everywhere except on his sister. "She said breaking you was the answer."

"The answer to what, Jeremy?"

"To breaking Vinnie."

"Oh, you're fucking brilliant, shit head," the dark woman growled, her voice low and rumbling. "I left Vinnie a year ago. I didn't even have contact with him again until you and your fucking stupidity forced me to consult him."

"She said—"

"Shut up, Jeremy. You were always an idiot when it came to her. You dealt her drugs and did her jail time. She tells you to jump, you ask how high. She tells you to ruin my life, you agree without question."

"I thought it was a ruse ... you not working for Vinnie anymore," the man said weakly, dropping his gaze to study his clasped hands.

"What the hell did she want with Vinnie anyway? She's chump change compared to him."

Jeremy sighed, ran a large hand through his close-cropped hair. "I ... I was looking through the files tonight ... the information she'd given me to get to you. And I realized that it had nothing to do with Vinnie after all. She was trying to get back at you."

"Get back at me? For what? I never did a damn thing to

the two of you. I walked away and I never looked back."

"And you became successful and independent and self-sufficient without her."

"In spite of her," Lacey corrected. Molly moved again and Lacey resituated the child, kissing her forehead.

"She wants to destroy you, Lace. She wants me to bring you to her so she can break you."

The dark woman snorted, shook her head. "She's an amateur, Jeremy. She couldn't break me with all the money in the world. You wanna know why?"

Jeremy looked up for the first time in a long time, able to catch the glinting sapphire eyes of the sister he'd loved and lost so many long years ago.

"Because I understand now. It took me most of my life to figure it out. But life isn't about money and drugs and who has power and who doesn't. It's not about working for the winning side and playing an advantage. Life's about this." She hugged Molly. "It's about having people who love you regardless of who you are and what you've done. People who want to wake up next to you for the rest of your life. I never knew that before. Lord knows Mom and Dad didn't teach us that."

The man remained silent.

"That's why she won't break me. I always have them. I have them in my heart and my soul. She can never touch that because she doesn't understand it."

"She tried to take them away from you."

"And I would have hunted her down and killed her. You too, Jeremy. Because I guarantee they mean more to me than either of you do. They never tried to make me something I wasn't."

Jeremy swallowed and nodded, knowing his older sibling spoke absolute truth. Knowing, for the first time in his life, that he'd chosen the wrong team all those years ago. "I don't know what to do, Lace," he whispered.

"You dig your own holes, Jeremy. You killed my best friend, you tried to kill my lover and her child. There's no haven for you with me."

He nodded; he'd known that. But during the night, after seeing his sister's obvious tender devotion to the child, he'd begun to question his loyalties. And he wished, more than anything, that he'd never been a part of this atrocity. "You made your own decision fifteen years ago, Lace. I think it's about time I made mine."

Lacey took a deep breath, tilting her head and observing her brother. "Just tell me one thing, Jeremy. How did she convince you to do this to me?"

He snorted, averted his gaze. "She told me the horrible person you were. She showed me evidence of your work for Vinnie and pictures of Molly. Told me that you were hurting the little girl and abusing the woman."

"I would never..." she growled but was interrupted by Jeremy's raised hand.

"I suspected that when I met Molly yesterday. She cried for you, wanting to be with you. I never felt that way about our parents. I know you didn't either. And when I see her with you now ... I know our mother was lying."

"Why did you even think it was the truth, Jeremy?" Lacey asked softly. "You knew me ... you knew how I felt about what they did to us."

Jeremy laughed quietly, turned his head away from her. "Because I became them. I had a son and a wife. I was too wrapped up in the business to pay attention to them. I was drunk and high, she made me angry."

Lacey's glare was icy. "You killed them?"

"She threatened to turn Mom and me in," he choked. "Mom took care of it. Four years ago. She told me you were like that, but hadn't had a reason to sober up like I had. That you were going to kill the girl and her mother in a drunken rage and we needed to stop you and get to Vinnie."

"If that were true, why did she count on me trading myself for Molly? If I didn't care about them, how would that part of the plan have worked?" Lacey asked reasonably.

After a long silence, he shrugged into the darkness. "It sounded good at the time, I didn't really think it through. I wanted it to be true. I wanted you to be the same monster I was because it would give me an excuse. It would have taken my fate out of my hands."

Lacey sighed, stroked Molly's soft hair. "I was that monster. Mom was right. Until about a year ago when I met Rachel and Molly. They're my salvation."

Jeremy was quiet for a very long time and Lacey thought they may be done talking, until the man cleared his throat. "I think maybe they're my salvation as well," he murmured. "I promise you'll be safe, Lacey."

The dark woman watched him silently. She tilted her head in consideration, seeing the boy she loved in the man before her, wanting very much for him to be telling the truth and not trying to find more weak spots. She sighed, decided to go for broke. "You'd better bring me a phone, Jeremy, because they'll be coming in here with blazing guns before the night is over."

The man looked at his sister with slight startlement before breaking a grin and nodding. "Shouldn't have expected any less, huh?"

She grinned without comment then slowly began the process of disentangling herself from Molly. The girl moaned her protests so Lacey leaned over her and smoothed her hair back, humming a soft tune, until Molly settled again. She considered taking the child with her, decided instead to let her sleep, guessing correctly that she hadn't had good sleep in days.

Jeremy led the way out the door and down the hall. He took her downstairs to the room where Lacey'd seen him earlier. There were still files scattered about and Grazier sat quietly in the corner.

The hired henchman eyed her with concern until Jeremy spoke up.

"You're done, Peter," he said softly.

"I thought tomorrow?" the gruff voice responded.

"I can handle it from here. Thank you for your services, you'll be paid in full."

Grazier stood and pursed his lips, watching his boss. Then, with a shrug, glad for the finished job, he left the room. "We'll be out in a few minutes," he tossed over his shoulder.

After the man's departure, Jeremy indicated a cordless phone sitting on the table atop the files. Lacey hesitated.

"What?" Jeremy asked, sensing his sister's indecision.

"I can't just forgive you, Jeremy. You tried to take my family from me." Her heart hurt. She wanted everything to be okay. She wanted to go home and still have a relationship with her brother, but she didn't know how. Not after what he'd done.

"You've done worse," the man pointed out slowly.

She pursed her lips and turned away, looking into the darkness beyond the window. That was true enough. But this was Rachel and Molly he'd tried to hurt. And he'd been behind Bernard's death. How do you walk away from that? She sighed, the weight of the world on her shoulders. She'd killed many people, without heart, without regret. She'd left women as widows, children without fathers, how could she judge the man before her? Her only answer was because this was personal. With that brand of logic, there were a lot of people who hated her and probably wished her dead.

"Yeah," she murmured at last. "I have."

He watched his sister's tense back with melancholy. She was very much as he remembered her: strong, responsible, self-reliant. She carried herself with an atmosphere of arrogant confidence, yet shrouded herself with brooding self-hate for what she considered her shortcomings. "Can I get you a drink, Lace?" he asked softly, letting the silence stretch between them as long as he dared.

"No thanks," she replied, rolling stiff shoulders. She was about to turn back for the phone when she heard a blood curdling child's scream from upstairs. *Oh, fuck.* She turned and ran as fast as she could, taking the stairs three at a time, shoving Grazier out of the way on the landing. She slid to a halt in front of the open bedroom door and glared at Lionel who stood just inside.

"What did you do?" she snarled.

He held up his hands in conciliation. "Nothing. She was screaming, I opened the door."

Lacey's blue glare softened as she turned her gaze to the sniveling child. Molly was curled in a ball at the head of the bed, trembling, rocking back and forth. "Baby," Lacey whispered, stepping forward.

Molly looked up at the sound of the dark woman's voice and propelled herself across the bed and into Lacey's arms.

"Lace," she whimpered.

"Right here, Molly-girl," Lacey soothed, rocking the girl in a tight embrace.

"Thought they took you away," she sobbed. "Alone ... missed you." Her words were expelled on panicked shallow breaths and Lacey knew where this would be going shortly.

"It's okay. Calm down or you're gonna be sick, baby," the dark woman crooned. "Shhh. I've got you. I went downstairs and I didn't want to wake you."

"Don't leave me again," Molly wailed.

"No, I promise. It was silly of me. I should have brought you with me. I'm sorry." She rubbed the girl's back with strong strokes, her large hand nearly covering the width of Molly's thin back. "Okay? Forgive me?"

Molly nodded, her sniffling slowing. "I was afraid it was a dream," she whispered.

"No dream. I'm right here."

"Don't leave," Molly repeated.

"I won't," Lacey assured her. "Come on. I have a surprise for you." Lacey carried the little girl out of the room and towards the stairs where Grazier glared at her. She shrugged at him, not apologizing for her hasty flight minutes earlier. Jeremy followed them back into the room with the files and phone.

The dark woman sat on the couch, child still in her grasp. She waited several minutes for Molly to calm completely. In that time, Grazier rounded up his team, spoke with Jeremy, and made their retreat. Now Lacey and Molly were alone in the house with Jeremy. It was a sign that he'd been honest with her earlier.

"We're gonna call your mama," Lacey said softly, picking up the phone and dialing her cell phone number. Molly shifted slightly so she could lean her head against the dark-haired woman's shoulder and watch the room at the same time.

****

George was fighting sleep, his chin resting in the palm of his hand, elbow on the arm of the chair. He blinked into the darkness, the only light provided by silver streaks of moonlight that fell across the small blonde woman and the dog she hugged.

The silence was interrupted by a shrill ring and it took George several long seconds to figure out it was the cell phone on the nightstand. He reached over and answered it, assuming it to be more demands from Lacey's asshole brother.

"Yeah," he said softly, trying not to disturb the woman on the bed just a foot away.

"Hey."

The voice startled him, recognizing it immediately as Lacey's husky undertones. "What's going on?" he asked carefully.

"I think we've reached an agreement, George. You don't need to send in the cavalry."

"Help me out here," George said slowly, not believing that Lacey was calling off the rescue attempt.

"You know where we are?"

"Yeah."

"Come get us. Jeremy and I talked some stuff out. He sent the goons home and Molly and I need a ride."

George shook his head, not sure he was hearing any of this correctly. "Just like that?"

"Not exactly. But I'm telling you the truth." Lacey paused. "How is everyone? Was anyone hurt in the gunfire?"

"Nah. But I hope to hell you added insurance to your vehicle rental."

Lacey's smile was evident in her voice. "Put Rachel on the phone."

"She's asleep," George replied.

The dark woman snorted. "My ass, she's asleep. I know her better than that."

Giving into his friend's demands, he leaned forward towards the bed. "Raich."

Rachel rolled over, her green eyes reflecting moonlight. "I don't want to talk to those assholes," she murmured. "Tell 'em to fuck themselves."

Lacey heard the other woman's words and she chuckled.

"It's Lacey," George explained, extending the phone.

Rachel sat up slowly, taking the offered phone and looking quite bewildered. "Yeah," she choked, then tried again. "Yeah?"

"Hey, baby," the dark voice purred.

Not believing her ears, a sob caught in Rachel's throat.

"Where are you? Are you okay? Oh God, Lace—"

"Shhh," the husky voice on the other end of the line interrupted. "I'm okay. Molly's okay. You need to roust those guys to come get us because we're ready to come home."

"What about Jeremy?"

"We talked. I think he's willing to let us walk away."

"Didja knock any heads together?" Rachel asked gently, some of her good humor returning just at hearing the familiar voice of her lover.

"No. But I'm not done yet," Lacey chuckled softly. "Hold on a sec." There was silence and then some murmuring.

"Mama?"

"Oh, Molly," Rachel whispered, wiping at her wet cheeks. Karma stood and stretched beside her then leaned forward to lick at salty tears. Rachel pushed her away gently. "I miss you."

"I miss you, too, Mama," the child's voice responded. "I think I've had enough of Colorado."

Rachel laughed. "You and me both, kiddo. Are you and Lacey okay?"

"We're fine, Mama. Lacey protected me."

"She's good at that," Rachel agreed. "I think we're going to come get you pretty soon."

George had left the room and come back with Rico and Ronnie in tow. He flipped the lights on when he entered the room and Rachel and Karma both squinted at him. He mouthed a silent apology.

"Lacey wants to talk to you again," Molly said. "I love you, Mama."

"Love you, too, baby," Rachel whispered, gratefully accepting some tissues from Ronnie.

"How are ya?" Lacey's voice was gentle with concern.

"M'okay," Rachel responded, not able to hide the crack

in her voice.

"It's almost over, Raich. We're all okay. And we're gonna walk out of this together."

"I don't know how to thank you," the blonde murmured, words failing to express the gratitude she felt.

"Don't be silly, love," Lacey replied. "You don't need to thank me. Now give those guys a kick in the ass and get out here. Because I need to hug you so badly."

Rachel laughed at her lover's growled tone. "I need it, too. Here's George. I love you, Lace."

"I love you, baby. See you soon."

Rachel stood and handed the phone back for them to work out the logistics and was immediately pulled into a warm hug by Ronnie. She cried softly on the other woman's shoulder for several long moments before pushing away. "I'm sorry." She wiped at her cheeks, casting her eyes to the carpeted floor.

"Don't be sorry," Ronnie chided gently. "Get ready to go. We're probably over an hour from where they are."

Rachel nodded and headed towards the restroom to clean up.

Chapter 20

It truly did appear to be darkest before the dawn. Rachel looked silently through the sedan window into the darkness beyond. Out here, on Highway 83, the only lights were from very occasional oncoming traffic. There were no streetlights and the clouds had obscured the moon shortly before the small entourage had headed out.

Now Ronnie and Rachel sat together in the back seat of Ronnie's car. The van would have only drawn attention with its bullet-riddled side panel. Tucked behind the larger vehicle, the little sedan hadn't been harmed in the gunfire.

George drove, Rico sat beside him. It was a tense atmosphere, all worried about what might meet them at the end of their journey. Though Lacey had sounded positive, they couldn't help think they may be walking into a lion's den.

Jeremy had even gotten on the phone and delivered succinct directions, allowing the group to get there more quickly than they would have using maps and the transmitter. They'd brought all of the hardware along, just in case.

They'd passed the scene of the earlier exchange nearly a

half-hour before. There were a couple cop cars and some floodlights highlighting the uniformed officers who walked around marking the scene and collecting shells. They'd stopped the sedan and asked some questions but George's story about leaving a friend's house late after a long Christmas day held and the patrolman waved them on.

"I think it's up here," Rico said in a hushed voice, interrupting the silence. He leaned forward and squinted at the road sign as George slowed down. "Yeah. Hodgen. This is it."

George took the left turn and started down yet another endless road lined by darkness and pine trees. They'd been in the vehicle for close to an hour and a half. Rachel fidgeted.

"We're almost there," Ronnie offered, smiling at the woman and patting her arm gently.

Rachel smiled nervously and wiped her sweaty palms on her jeans.

They turned a short while later, heading south on Bar X Road further into the trees. George drove at a snail's pace, not wanting to miss the driveway in the poor lighting.

"Here we go, Raich," the black man called over his shoulder. "Stay in the car until we figure out the situation."

Though it would be difficult, Rachel knew he was right and nodded her agreement. "I will."

He drove up the gravel driveway to a larger parking area in front of the house. He put the sedan in park but left it running. George leaned over the seat, patting Rachel's knee, smiling at Ronnie, then he and Rico checked their weapons and slipped out of the vehicle.

Lacey had been sitting by a front window, Molly snoozing again in her embrace. She heard the car and stood up. "Wake up, sleepy," she whispered into the child's hair. "Mama's here."

Molly struggled to full wakefulness, blinking bright

blue eyes open and grinning slightly.

Lacey moved to the door slowly, carrying Molly with her. She eyed Jeremy, who stood across the room, leaning against the ecru painted wall, arms crossed in front of him. Naturally suspicious, the dark woman couldn't help but wait for the other shoe to drop. This was too simple. And then what? Would they come after her again? Would she spend the rest of their lives looking over her shoulder? She took a deep breath, unsure of what to do. Two years ago she would have shot them all and called it over with.

Lacey opened the door as George came up to it, letting the man come inside. Across the dark front yard she saw Rachel's blonde head in the car and Rico standing next to the running vehicle. George stepped in and grinned widely at Molly who was absolutely beaming.

"George," the child murmured sleepily, leaning from Lacey into the man's arms. He handed his drawn weapon to Lacey and took the child, hugging her fiercely.

"The Molly-meister," he crooned. "It's good to see you! You've gotten so big."

Lacey checked the automatic pistol quickly and efficiently, then set it on the small stand just inside the door, slipping the safety on. She patted George's back. "It's good to see you, too. How's Raich?"

"She's good. Worried, scared ... but okay."

"Can I see my mama?" Molly whispered, struggling out of George's arms to slide to her feet and stand at his side. Lacey looked from the girl, to George, to her brother still standing across the room.

Jeremy nodded slightly so Lacey took advantage of it, determined to at least get the little girl out of the house. She still wanted to talk to her brother about the future. The dark woman opened the glass storm door, not stepping out herself but leaning down and hugging Molly to her with one strong arm.

"Your mama's in the car. Go on to Rico and he'll help you out."

"Come with me?" she asked plaintively.

Lacey shook her head slightly. "Not yet, baby. Go on, now." With a kiss and a gentle shove, she sent the little girl on her way.

Molly turned once to look over her shoulder before trotting ahead to Rico who swooped her up and hugged her close, his own weapon still drawn. *Guns and kids*, Lacey grimaced. How she hated to see the two together.

She watched a moment longer, until Rico opened the car door and handed Molly over to her mother. Then Lacey closed the door and turned back to the group inside.

****

Rachel practically crawled over Ronnie to reach her child. For her part, the other woman pressed herself against the back of the seat and helped the small girl climb to her mother. Then Ronnie scooted over, giving the two most of the backseat of the sedan for their long awaited reunion.

Both were sobbing and clutching at each other, the child glued to her mother, Rachel's face buried in Molly's soft hair.

"Mama," the girl murmured between tears. It was a statement of confirmation more than anything else.

"I've got you, baby. We're gonna go home," her mother assured, rocking the child, smoothing her back with affectionate hands. "I love you, sweetie. I missed you so much."

"Missed you too." Molly nodded her agreement.

Rachel pushed the little girl away so that she could look at her face and wipe at wet cheeks. "You okay?"

She nodded, leaning back to her mother for more hugging. Unable to deny the request, Rachel pulled her close again: hugging, rocking, whispering her words of love even as she tried to staunch her own tears of relief.

****

The group in the house stood watching each other civilly, the gentle overhead lighting of the room affording them a comfortable view of each other.

"Okay, Jeremy," Lacey said at last, reaching up to extend long fingers through her braid and scratch at her scalp. "This has been your damn game from the start. Where do we go from here?" Blunt was good. She liked blunt.

Jeremy looked from his sister to the tall black man at her side. He sighed. "It's just us. Grazier and his crew are gone. You can walk for all I care."

"What about her?" She couldn't bring herself to claim her as 'Mom'. "She'll send more goons after us. I'm not going to run from her the rest of our lives."

He snorted, pushed himself away from the wall. He was as tall as Lacey and had the same lean muscle body type. But his grey eyes held none of the humor and very little good will. "Just kill her. Right?"

Lacey bristled angrily, since those thoughts had flitted through her mind only minutes before. "Any ideas, Jeremy? You got us into this mess."

"I'm also letting you live. What else do you think I owe you."

"A lot," Lacey snarled. Jeremy seemed more on edge than before, less certain of his decision and his mannerisms lacked that earlier conviction. Lacey felt herself stand taller, shift her weight to the balls of her feet. She was ready for anything. Anything except the one thing that happened.

Rachel walked into the house.

"Get in the car," Lacey growled, not wasting time on pleasantries, barely glancing at her partner.

"Not without you," the blonde woman said softly, stepping forward to slide her arms around her lover. "God, it's good to see you. How are you? You look okay. Molly said you saved her..." She let her babbling trail off when she finally became conscious of the tension in the room. Something wasn't going right.

Rachel turned her attention to the man standing opposite them and offered him a heartfelt grin, forgetting for the moment that this was the man behind her daughter's abduction. Rather she was just grateful to him for turning them loose. "You must be Jeremy," she stated with a tilt of her head.

He nodded solemnly. Rachel saw some of her lover in him. Then Jeremy stepped forward and held out his right hand to her for a shake.

Without hesitation, Rachel stepped forward to accept.

Lacey felt tingles all up and down her spine, knowing this was wrong, all of it. She reached a hand out and wrapped strong fingers around her lover's bicep but the smaller woman was already a full stride ahead of her, already grasping Jeremy's hand in a firm shake. The click of a gun cocking echoed through the room and Rachel's whole body jerked as the barrel was pressed into her forehead with Jeremy's left hand.

Silence.

They all watched each other, Rachel trembling but otherwise standing very still. George had reclaimed the gun by the door and placed it into Lacey's grip, the dark woman's left hand was still grasping her partner's arm.

Jeremy stood stock-still, grey eyes cold and emotionless. Lacey knew that look well, had used it herself many times.

"Let her go. I'll fucking kill you and you know it."

"You can't do it before I kill her. And it's more important for you to see her alive than see me dead."

Lacey growled, deep and primal, the sound more felt than heard. This could have gone a lot better. *Oh, Raich. Why did you come in here?*

"What do you want?" the dark woman managed to grit out between clenched teeth.

"I'm thinking I'm in a no win situation. I let you walk, I die. Mom gave me a job, I couldn't pull it off."

"What happened to your word? What happened to keeping us safe?"

"Sometimes you have to look after yourself, Lace. Isn't that why you left so long ago? You finally had to look out for yourself." He was so calm and collected. Lacey didn't see any of the compassion she'd seen earlier. She cursed herself for letting the situation get this far out of hand.

"I'll go with you to see her, Jer. Let them go. All of them. They can drive away and you and I will go see her."

He seemed to consider this for just a moment before he tugged hard on Rachel's arm, nearly pulling her off her feet. The blonde woman stood stretched between the two like some ludicrous dog tug toy. She would have resented the treatment if she weren't scared to death.

Jeremy moved the gun slightly to jam it into the young blonde's cheek. "Let her go, Lace, or I'll kill her. I'm dead either way."

George watched the battle of wills before him, cursing Rico out for letting Rachel get in the house, knowing he wasn't in a position to do a damn thing.

Finally, slowly, the dark woman uncurled her fingers. She was unsure. If it were anyone but Rachel she would have called the bluff, but she wouldn't risk her young lover for stupid machismo. Rachel was ripped from her grasp and spun so her back was solidly against the lanky man's chest. His arm was across her neck, the barrel at her temple.

Not an improvement, Lacey surmised.

"Now what?" she snapped. "You're calling the shots,

you bastard."

"That's not very lady like."

Lacey grinned, forming an idea. She changed her tactics. "I never was, Jer," she said softly. "Remember how hard Mom used to try to get me to wear dresses? Curl my hair?"

His grip seemed to lessen. He smiled slightly. "Yeah. And you had me sneak into the house for jeans and a T-shirt so you could change on the way to school."

She nodded, lowered her weapon, realizing it was only adding to the tension. "You always did for me, Jeremy. You always helped me."

"You held me at night when I cried myself to sleep," the man murmured.

Lacey nodded again, meeting her lover's mist green eyes. *Hang in there, baby, it'll all work out.* "You used to distract Mom so I could sneak out at night to go to the movies."

He seemed torn, teetering between a long-lost loyalty and one ingrained in him for many years. He loved his sister dearly, always had. But it was his mother who had formed him, taught him, made him what he was. He was a drunken murderer, a man who would kidnap his sister's family, threaten to kill them, to please a wicked old hag who never had a heart to start with. How would he face his mother? What would he do?

The pieces seemed to click into place for him and the peace that filled his gaze was obvious to both George and Lacey, though neither could interpret it. His gun hand had been wavering a moment before but now the grip became sure again as he raised the weapon.

"No, Jeremy," Lacey whispered, all the previous bravado and harsh words melting away. "Give me this. Give me her. Everything we did, all we shared ... all I want is Rachel and Molly to go away from here. Is that too much to ask?"

"I don't think so," the young man agreed softly, continuing to raise the weapon. It took a brief second for Lacey to realize what he was doing, but even that bare moment in time was too much. It was already too late. She tried to lunge across the room, close the distance between them even as she heard the report and watched emerald eyes go wide with fear and shock.

Jeremy's grip on Rachel brought her down with him as he fell to the floor, lifeless and broken. Lacey arrived a moment later, pulling her lover up into her arms.

The blonde was frantic: trembling and whimpering. Her hair and back were splattered with Jeremy's brains and skull fragments. Lacey embraced the small form tightly, rocking the slight frame, closing her own eyes to the scene at her feet.

"Shhh, it was him, baby. You're safe. It's okay. It's okay." Unable to keep her eyes averted, Lacey blinked them open and watched her brother's dark blood pool on the beige carpet. Hard to believe twenty-five years of being a big sister would end like this. She knew she was crying, couldn't help it. So was the woman she held.

Lacey felt hands on her, knew that George was tugging her gently away from the room. In the back of her mind she heard Rico's familiar voice muttering something. Then they were out of the room, in the bathroom, falling to the floor to wrap each other more firmly in desperate, clutching arms. George closed the door and left them to their privacy.

Silent sobs became racking chokes as they held each other dearly. The choking became hiccups and then, finally, murmured words of love and affection and lifelong commitment. Until the two women were peering into each other's eyes, emerald and sapphire awash with tears.

"I missed you so much," Rachel murmured.

Lacey chuckled, kissed the fair woman's wet cheeks. "It

was only one night."

"One night too many. I thought I'd never see you again."

"I'm right here," the dark woman assured. "Always with you."

Rachel's face scrunched with immense sadness. "He killed himself," she said simply.

"Yeah, baby," Lacey agreed, trying to smooth the lines of grief with her thumbs. She didn't want to dwell on that now. She knew it would hit her hard soon, that the previous moments of tears and embracing were merely the tip of the iceberg.

"I feel him ... on me."

Lacey nodded. She'd wondered how long it would take her weak-stomached partner to reach that conclusion. "Let me clean you up."

Moments later, Rachel was bent over the sink with her blonde locks darkening under running water. Her lover's strong gentle fingers worked lather through the tresses, her touch confirming and comforting at the same time.

The dark woman tried hard not to notice the pinkish colored suds and the tainted water that swirled in the sink. She tried not to think about how she was washing away the remnants of her very own brother. He'd been such an affectionate, gregarious kid but always frightened and needing support and guidance. He'd tried so hard to please his mother and his big sister. He'd failed them both in the end and taken his own life instead of facing that shame.

There was a knock on the door.

"Yeah?" Lacey called hoarsely, rinsing out the last of the suds, searching in vain for some kind of conditioner in the mirrored cabinets.

"I called Vinnie. He's sending someone. We need to get out of here."

"I'm gonna owe that man my damned first born," Lacey

grumbled. Then, more loudly, she called, "Thanks, George. Can you find a T-shirt or sweatshirt or something?" She'd tossed aside Rachel's blood stained shirt and bra. There were some slight splattering stains on the woman's jeans, but it would have to do for now.

"Be back," George agreed.

Lacey pulled her lover to a standing position and grabbed a towel from the rack to rub through the woman's hair. "Gonna tangle," she said apologetically. Rachel nodded from within her terry cloth shroud.

"I love you," the blonde murmured impulsively.

Lacey smiled sadly, hugged the half-naked body to her. With the towel still over her head, Rachel leaned her cheek against her lover's broad shoulder.

"Hey," Lacey said into the silence. "That ring looks pretty good on your finger."

Rachel laughed despite herself. "You are so damn romantic, crony."

"C'mon now, I wrote you a nice little note," Lacey whispered, pretending to be hurt.

"I'll keep the note always," Rachel swore, her voice muffled by the terry cloth but her seriousness quite clear.

"And the ring?"

"MmHmm."

"And me?"

"MmHmm."

"You're not much for romance, either, babe," Lacey pointed out dryly.

Rachel leaned back, reaching up her hands to tug the towel away. Her hair was wet and wild, falling at all angles around her gently planed face. Her jade eyes were earnest and affectionate. Lacey thought she'd never looked more beautiful.

"I love you more and more each day, baby. I love to wake up beside you, fall asleep in your arms, look in your eyes and see the kind of devotion and love I never deserved. The only thing that makes me happier than remembering all of those moments in the past is looking forward to every one yet to come. There's nothing I want more in this life than to share it with you."

Lacey's chin sagged in astonishment, her blue eyes watered with emotion. For several heartbeats she just watched her young lover, studying the earnest eyes puffy from weeping. Finally, quietly, a grin tugged at the edge of her mouth and she simply said, "Ditto."

Rachel laughed out loud. It was the first time she had done that in nearly a week. She laughed so hard she cried, clutching to the tall woman before her, muffling the sounds of her mirth in Lacey's turtleneck. "Oh God," she said at last. "I love you so much."

The dying laughter was interrupted by a knock at the door. Lacey tucked the blonde's half-clad body behind her and opened the door to accept the sweatshirt George offered. The dark man turned caramel-colored eyes, deep with concern, to his friends.

"Thank you," Lacey said softly. "We're okay. We'll be out in a minute."

When George had left, Lacey turned to tug the shirt over her lover's wet head. She settled the collar and sleeves with firm, affectionate hands and then tugged out the golden wet tresses. "Turn around," she murmured. With gentle fingers, she combed through Rachel's tangled hair and fashioned it into a loose braid, taking the band from her own hair to tie it off.

"Now, let's go get Molly-girl and get the hell out of here."

****

It was far from a comfortable ride. George glanced in

the rearview mirror, smiling warmly at what he saw there: Rachel and Lacey were pressed solidly against each other, the small girl sprawled across their laps. Ronnie sat against the other window, idly scratching at the denim over her knee.

The first twenty minutes of the ride had been punctuated with whispers and whimpers, gentle touches and silent kisses. When Molly had fallen asleep, tucked securely against both women, Rachel and Lacey relaxed as well, entwining fingers together.

Now, they listened to the gentle strains on the radio and watched the sun rise across the plains. The bright rays shot across the road in front of them to bounce off the mountains on the west. The snow fractured the light apart, sparkling in brilliant pinks, oranges and reds as dawn become day, ending the longest night of all their lives.

Chapter 21

It was nearly dusk when Lacey blinked weary blue eyes open and flashed them around the bedroom of the condo. Light was trickling onto the hardwood floor, dancing with the dust particles that floated around the room, resting on the end of the bed. Karma twitched her ear, the hair glistening in the sunlight. She yawned and stretched, opened one eye to look at Lacey, then settled more deeply onto the covers.

Lacey poked her affectionately with her toe and Karma let out a gentle moan of protest so Lacey did it again with the same response.

"Stop torturing that dog," Rachel murmured, scooting herself closer to the lanky body of her lover. She blinked her eyes open briefly, only to confirm her daughter was still soundly tucked against Lacey's other side. The blonde woman grinned weakly, turned her head to kiss Lacey's shoulder.

"But it's fun," Lacey whispered with a grin, snickering slightly and doing it again. Still absolutely unmovable, Karma groaned, flicking velvety soft ears.

"Stop," Rachel moaned, sounding almost like her protesting dog and rubbing the taut abdomen under her hand.

"What are you gonna do about it?" Lacey teased gently. She was completely and absolutely relaxed, lying here in the fading sunlight with her lover on one side, their child on the other, and their dog snoozing at their feet. She would worry about her mother tomorrow. Tonight she would embrace the emotions tangible in this room.

"Ask me again later. When we're alone," Rachel growled playfully. The body she was wrapped around jiggled with a dry chuckle.

"Promises, promises." Lacey grinned, kissing her lover's temple.

"I'll keep 'em." Rachel leered, sliding up to kiss the dark woman's lips.

"I know you will, baby," Lacey replied warmly. She tilted her head to the other side to look at Molly's face.

The child's face was tense, not slack in sleep as it should have been. Her eyes twitched under pale lids.

"Nightmares?" Lacey asked softly.

Rachel reached a hand over to smooth her daughter's hair back. She rubbed her thumb along the creases in the child's forehead. "Maybe," she murmured at last.

"I think when we get back to New York we should find a doctor for her. Someone she could talk to."

Rachel flicked green eyes from her daughter to her partner. "A therapist?"

Lacey thought for a long moment, unsure if she was overstepping boundaries. As much as Rachel talked about their joint efforts in raising this little girl, the dark woman couldn't help but wonder how true that was. She suspected some day she would push the boundaries and be accused of meddling. The honest green gaze assured her differently. "I think so, baby. With us ... or by herself. Whichever the doctor thinks is better. Jeremy didn't hurt her physically, but to be kept away from us, chained by herself in a room for days ... I think it's a good idea."

"I do, too, Lace. Thank you," Rachel whispered. She was rewarded with a heartfelt smile that startled her with its intensity.

Molly started to murmur then, her small hand clutching and releasing its grip on Lacey's shirt. The dark woman raised a hand to cradle the child's head. "Easy, Molly-girl," she muttered. The whimpering intensified. "Wake up, honey."

Rachel reached across her lover to grip the child's shoulder. She shook it gently until blue eyes popped open. Both women watched the fear flash across the child's irises before recognition settled in. Then Molly's eyes filled with tears and she scrambled on top of Lacey's body, throwing one arm over her mother and wrapping the other behind Lacey's neck. She buried her head next to Rachel's, her body shaking with sobs.

"Don't leave me, don't leave me," the child chanted over and over again. This same scene or one very much like it had been enacted several times throughout the day.

"Never," Rachel assured, kissing Molly's forehead, rubbing her back firmly.

"We love you," Lacey whispered, combing through the child's blonde hair with long fingers.

"MmHmm," Molly murmured, knowing this to be true, warmed by the presence of both of her mothers.

They remained silent for awhile longer, waiting for Molly to calm down, for her grasp to relax.

"You hungry, baby?" Rachel asked at last. "I sure am."

"Yes," Lacey and Molly said at the same time and Molly giggled.

"Let's go out to eat," Lacey suggested, starting to disentangle herself from woman, child, and sheets. "You can give Rico more Zelda pointers."

****

New Years Eve, the group stepped off the plane at La Guardia, met by vaguely familiar faces. Vinnie's henchmen. Lacey grimaced and cast a look to Rico, seeing the recognition flash across his features as well.

Lacey greeted the men with a silent nod, squeezing Rachel's hand when the smaller woman glanced at her with a questioning glance. The henchmen fell into step behind them as they made their way through the throng of holiday travelers towards baggage claim. Rico dropped back to walk beside Mary. They'd said goodbye to George in Denver.

Once they had their luggage and Karma, Lacey ushered them all to the doors where they could wait for the parking shuttle.

"We have cars," Henchman Number One said softly. "One to take them home, one for you to go see Vinnie."

"I don't want to see Vinnie right now," Lacey said softly. "I want to go home with my family."

"It's urgent," he supplied. Silence fell hard and cold across the group. The same henchman sighed, took a deep breath, and pulled out his trump card. "It's about your mother."

Ice blue eyes flashed to him with anger, but she had to admit her curiosity was piqued. She looked to her lover.

Rachel nodded silently, knowing this was something Lacey needed to do. She wouldn't hold her back.

"You sure?" the dark woman murmured, bending her head lower to speak into Rachel's delicate ear.

"Yeah," the blonde nodded, placing a gentle hand on Lacey's stomach. "We'll go on home and get settled. Come as soon as you can."

"Okay." She kissed her soundly in the middle of the bustling crowd, unconcerned about the looks flashed their direction. "I love you." Then she knelt down to hug Molly close. "Love you, too, Molly-girl. Take care of your mama. I'll be home in time to tuck you in."

Molly nodded bravely, but it was obvious to both women that she was on the verge of breaking. She couldn't bear to be separated from either of them.

"Go on," Lacey urged, giving them a gentle push to follow Henchman Number Two. She blew them both kisses and watched them settle into the waiting limousine with Rico and Mary.

****

Rachel paced the upstairs hallway, Karma hot on her heels. Molly had fallen asleep in the master bedroom while they watched the Times Square countdown. She was too exhausted to wait for Lacey's promise. The young blonde, however, was having a hard time calming her nerves enough to relax. Where was Lacey? Why was she so late?

As if in answer to her question, the door from the garage to the kitchen slammed hard and Rachel heard the mute beeping of Lacey disarming and resetting the alarm. She flew down the spiral staircase and into the kitchen, sliding across the tiled floor on stocking feet and wrapping her lover in a warm embrace.

"Hey, hey," Lacey murmured, returning the hug. The previous feelings of anger and frustration slowly dissipated while captured in these familiar arms. "It's okay."

Rachel merely nodded. She could feel the tension in the taller woman's body and toyed with the idea of questioning her lover. She was still considering this approach when Lacey actually offered information herself.

"Let's put some coffee on and chat? Okay?" she suggested, pulling away from Rachel. "How's Molly?"

"She's asleep in our bed."

"Our sex life is gonna suffer," Lacey joked weakly.

Rachel smiled.

"C'mon, crony. Coffee sounds great."

They sat in the winterized screened-in porch. It seemed a familiar place for these heart-to-hearts. It was calm and quiet and they watched the stars flicker in the clear night sky while they sat in darkness.

"So he told me that he ... took care of my problem," Lacey muttered after giving a brief overview of her car ride to Vinnie's.

"Do I wanna know what that means?" Rachel asked hesitantly.

The dark woman took a deep breath, reaching across the glass patio table to clutch Rachel's small hand. "He killed her and most of the idiots working for her. She was running a small drug ring out of South Jersey and he tracked her down ..."

Rachel was shocked into silence for a very long time. "Why?"

"Because he knew I was in a corner. He knew I wouldn't be able to take care of it myself." She sighed, looking to her lover, seeing pale moonlight reflect off her gentle face. "Vinnie has a soft spot for me, I guess."

"So he kills your mother?!" Rachel barked, astounded.

"Oh, Raich," Lacey groaned. "It's so complicated. He was right. I would have done the same thing to protect you and Molly. But I can't anymore. That ruthless part of me is gone."

Rachel was silent for several heartbeats, trying not to judge her lover or the woman's previous life. She'd promised herself she'd never do that. "What did you say to him?" she asked at last.

"I screamed at him. Yelled, ranted, raved. Told him to go to hell, I didn't need his fucking charity."

"What did he say?"

Lacey snorted, rubbed her face with her free hand. "He

just sat there and took my bullshit. Then he asked me if I was ready to go home."

"That was hours ago."

"I wasn't. We talked for a long time. Vinnie ... he's an interesting man, Raich. Family is important in the business, but it usually only goes as far as loyalty. When I turned my back, he should have, too. But ... we've spent a lot of time together, we know each other well. I watched his children grow up and had worked for his father. He wanted to give me the way out I needed. He saved us all."

"He killed your mother," Rachel said, exasperated.

The dark woman shrugged. "Wasn't my mother. Just some lady I never knew."

Rachel sighed, relaxed back into her chair. "When you're ready to talk about it, Lace, I'm here."

"I know." the ex-mafia woman nodded. She squeezed Rachel's hand again, twisting the ring she found there with nimble fingers.

"So we're safe?" Rachel said after a long time.

"For now," Lacey confirmed. She felt none of the passionate anger she'd felt before. In its place rested quiet acceptance and resigned confidence. "Let's go to bed." The dark woman stood, pulling her lover up beside her. She grinned gently, looking into emerald eyes and pulling her lover close. She bent and captured willing lips, hungrily tasting and searching.

Rachel snaked her hands up and around Lacey's neck, tangling fingers in dark hair, pulling them closer. She kissed her lover deeply, plunging her tongue into the familiar depths. She felt her knees turn to jelly and collapsed against her tall partner.

Lacey nipped the small woman's lower lip then laved it with her tongue. "C'mon, baby."

"You tease," Rachel laughed softly, tugging the dark woman's hand and leading the way upstairs.

Epilogue

July was hot and unbearably humid in the best of places and New York wasn't one of the better places to be during the month of independence. Lacey groaned, adjusted her tank top and wiped her brow with a sweat-slicked forearm. Leaning against the rail, her eyes never left the youngster in the arena.

The place was packed, horses and riders everywhere. The dark woman figured it a miracle that no one had been hurt yet, but it was all the more reason to keep her eyes glued to the young blonde rider.

"How's she doing?" a familiar voice asked behind her. Lacey glanced over her shoulder to smile at Mary.

"She looks good. Jester's behaving."

"Good to hear." The smaller woman leaned against the rail as well, glanced to her left and right to see all the other nervous parents doing the same. "How are the nightmares?" she asked at last.

Lacey shrugged. It had been seven months and though the episodes had lessened, they were still there. She twirled her ring nervously, a habit she'd picked up since first putting the jewelry on Christmas day. Just two nights ago, Molly's screaming had forced a sleepy Lacey to stumble through the upstairs hall to fall into the child's bed and comfort her there.

Somehow the pattern had settled easily. Rachel slept like a damn log and though she did hear her child and went willingly to comfort her, it was Lacey who best provided the midnight conversations and gentle reassurances. As a result, she was the one who got up with Molly. She held her while she cried, kissed her and comforted her. It was Lacey who either slept in Molly's bed or carried the child to the master bedroom to sleep. It was a natural routine, which she could never begrudge and on some level even treasured. The trust her lover exhibited in handing her that duty was greatly cherished.

Unsurprisingly, Molly's nightmares had lessened drastically once social services backed off. For the first part of the year it had seemed there were endless visits and interviews, stressing the small family nearly to shattering. Then, finally, with the help of Molly's therapist and trustworthy Aunt Helen, the judgment had resulted favorably. Molly was found to be in a loving home and a safe environment and social services stopped knocking on their door.

From across the arena, Molly waved, a big white grin presented beneath the bill of her hard hat. Lacey and Mary both waved back.

Rico announced his arrival with an arm around Mary's shoulder. A young redheaded girl stood at his hip and held up two sodas. Lacey took one with a grin and a gentle ruffle of the little girl's hair.

"Thanks, Lauren." She smiled fondly. The youngster had become somewhat of a fixture in their lives since Christmas. She and Molly were best of friends and absolutely inseparable. It was only right that she be here at Molly's first show.

"Rachel's class is going in," Rico announced. "Go

ahead, I'll stay with Molly."

Lacey grinned her thanks, eager to watch her young lover and Sunny.

"Can I come with you?" Lauren asked quietly.

"Of course, kiddo. Come on." Lacey took the child's hand with her free one and together they left the practice ring to walk across the fairgrounds to the main arena. She easily spotted her lover atop the lanky bay colt.

Sunny was quiet and accepting, big round eyes taking in all that was around him. Being a schooling show, Rachel'd had a hell of a time convincing the stewards to admit a stallion. She'd had to get waivers and approvals and had even brought him early this morning so the stewards and judges could see the horse's attitude. Satisfied with the good manners the stallion possessed, they permitted him entry.

It was a hunter over fences class. Rachel'd thought she was probably pushing the horse too much but he'd excelled in all of his training and had shown great skill over low fences. She knew he would perform well over the higher jumps as well but, at four, he was too young for the physical stress that involved.

The blonde beamed from ear to ear when she saw her lover and the little redhead approach. Lacey was dressed comfortably in a white tank top and denim shorts. Her dark hair was pulled back into a long ponytail and her ice blue eyes were shaded with sunglasses. She also wore low top hiking boots to protect her feet from stomping hooves. All in all, to the blonde's discerning gaze she was absolutely gorgeous. Rachel leaned over Sunny's shoulder to kiss her partner.

"Hey, gorgeous," the dark woman purred, releasing Lauren's hand to rest a warm palm on her lover's thigh. "How do you feel?"

"Good." Rachel nodded. "Can you check his boots?"

Lacey nodded, she'd been well trained to be a show

mom. It was all Molly had talked about the entire spring. They'd missed the first three schooling shows for various reasons, so everyone had been more than eager to come to this one. Lacey bent over and slid her fingers between Sunny's cannon bone and splint boots. She checked the tightness and security of the velcro straps of each one before straightening and nodding. Being a schooling show, aids and protective gear were allowed. Lacey had learned this from Molly just last night.

"How's your number?" Lacey asked.

Rachel turned in the saddle so her lover could inspect the pinning job of the paper number. The dark woman nodded her approval, resting her hand again on the lycra of Rachel's breeches. She offered up the soda from which Rachel took a long drink gratefully.

"How's Molly doing?"

"She looks great," Lacey assured. "Jester's doing well." It had been bad luck that their classes were too close for Rachel to participate much in Molly's preparation. She'd decided not to enter until Molly and Lacey had worked her over, encouraging her and assuring her they could handle Jester quite well.

"Thirty in the ring, five on deck, twenty-seven in the hole," the loudspeaker blasted. Lacey walked towards the deck with Rachel and Sunny. Lauren followed them, sipping from her soda.

When Rachel went on deck just a few minutes later, Lacey gave her the best smile she could manage and kissed the blonde's gloved hand, feeling the solid metal of the commitment ring. She could tell her lover was nervous. Secretly, so was she.

Lauren and Lacey found themselves spots near the gate and watched silently from ring side as the tall bay colt cantered perfectly into the ring. He stopped squarely and stood calmly while Rachel nodded to the judges. Then she gathered her reins and turned Sunny towards the rail, nudging him into an easy canter, loosening his joints. She took him the long way around to the starting jump, giving him the extra time to eye most of the jumps on the way by. He seemed absolutely unperturbed.

    Lacey watched with some trepidation when horse and rider hit the first fence. It wasn't as neat as it could have been. Lacey'd learned what to look for after hours of watching them practice. Rachel was slightly behind the jump, the colt's legs were slightly loose beneath the knee, but he landed well and both gathered themselves for the next jump, which was executed perfectly. There were eight fences in all, none were complicated since this was a simple class, and their confidence grew with each until they cleared the last, completing the course without faults. Rachel gently pulled her mount back to a walk then a halt in the center. She nodded to the judges and then turned searching green eyes to find Lacey. The grin that flashed across her face was absolutely blinding in its intensity. Lacey could only return it with equal wattage.

    When the class was over and everyone was called back into the ring, Rachel and Sunny were honored with the red of second place. The blonde patted the colt's shoulder with obvious affection, then leaned forward to hug him. He sedately shook his head and neck in disgust at the display, causing Lacey and Lauren to laugh.

    As that class exited the ring, Molly's class was lining up at the entrance gate. Stewards and ring assistants were scurrying around to take down the poles and supporting standards, making way for the junior rider English Equitation class. Lacey found Molly and Jester in the middle of the milling group of people and horses. She thanked Rico for his solicitous attention before clasping the little girl's knee.

    Molly grinned. "Mama got a second place."

    "Yeah, she did. They were great. Coke?" She raised

the cup to Molly and the girl willingly grasped the straw between her lips without letting go of her reins.

"We're just gonna do our best."

"That's right, baby." Lacey nodded, squeezing the child's thigh. The announcer started preparing the class to enter, so the dark woman stood on her toes and Molly leaned down for better accessibility. Lacey kissed the child's cheek and murmured encouraging words in her ear.

Molly beamed. "I love you."

"You, too, honey. Go on." She patted the gelding's shoulder. "Be good, Jester, or you'll have me to answer to."

The loud speaker crackled to life and then blared across the grounds. "Class number twenty-six, Junior English Equitation, is now entering the ring. Riders please cross the arena at a trot and turn right along the rail."

Molly nudged Jester forward, lifting her hands into the saddle seat position her mother had shown her countless times before. Right before she passed through the gate she looked back over her shoulder to flash a toothy grin at Lacey. It was so much like her mother's, it tugged at the dark woman's heartstrings. She offered the child a thumbs up and then the small entourage went to claim a place on the rail.

Lacey watched the girl and gelding cross the ring as instructed and find their spot on the rail. She felt a hand at her back and turned to see Rachel standing behind her, long blonde hair tucked up into a bun. The wisps were wet with perspiration from being tucked under the hunt cap. Looking past her blonde lover, she saw Mary standing beyond the spectators holding Sunny's reins, giving Rachel the freedom to watch her daughter ride. Lacey smiled her thanks before pulling Rachel in front of her and wrapping the blonde in a tight embrace. She leaned forward to whisper her congratulations into the smaller woman's ear.

Rachel leaned back against the sturdy form of her lover

and watched Molly trot around the ring. Though it was swelteringly hot and miserably humid, and the sun beat down on them with relentlessly bright rays, causing them all to squint even through the lenses of their sunglasses, Rachel smiled and gripped the arms that held her. With her lover behind her and their daughter in front of her, this was quite possibly the most beautiful day she had ever witnessed.

Coming next from
Yellow Rose Books

Seasons: Book One
By Anne Azel

Roberta "Robbie" Williams is a successful playwrite, actor, and director - a remarkable testament to her parentage. She has it all - wealth, fame, respect - or does she? Her facade of being happy in her life is shredded to pieces by the entrance of her deceased brother's wife, Janet, and their daughter, Rebecca, at his funeral. Janet is a strong willed small town principal of a school for the gifted and talented and Rebecca undeniably bonds with Robbie the moment she holds her. Under the pretense of "protecting the sole Williams' heir", Robbie escorts the young widow home and ends up unrepentantly gaining an education in the true meaning of life, living, and love. Seasons: Book 1 entails the frustration and tribulation of a new found love compounded with the daily trials of living in a small town, drastically differing careers and the choices required of them, and the strength and courage needed to survive a life-threatening disease. Seasons: Book 1 is about the courage of being professional gay women in today's society.

Available – September 2000.

Available soon from
Yellow Rose Books

Mended Hearts
By Alix Stokes

Two little girls meet at a hospital and become best friends. One of them undergoes open-heart surgery. They are separated, but meet again 24 years later. By now, the older girl, Dr. Alexandra Morgan, is a brilliant Pediatric Heart Surgeon. The younger girl, Bryn O'Neill, is a warm and loving Pediatric Intensive Care nurse. When they meet, they feel an instant connection. Will Dr. Morgan's tortured past keep her from remembering their childhood friendship?

Bar Girls
By Jules Kurre

Keagan Donovan is a taciturn English major. Keeping control of her emotions has always been second nature until the aspiring writer meets Rudy, a fellow English major, in a local bar. Keagan and Rudy find they have a lot in common but as they spend more time together, Keagan's insecurities contiune to keep them at arm's length. Will Rudy have the patience to deal with Keagan's inconsistent behavior? Will Keagan be able to overcome her fears and accept Rudy unconditionally into her life?

Encounters
By Anne Azel

Encounters is a series of five stories: Amazon Encounter, Turkish Encounter, P.N.G. Encounter, Egyptian Encounter, and Peruvian Encounter. The stories are interrelated by the characters who all share a common ancestor. A loop in the space/time continium allows the couples of today to help their ancestors find their own troubled path to happiness.

Tumbleweed Fever
By L. J. Maas

In the Oklahoma Territory of the old west Devlin Brown is trying to redeem herself for her past as an outlaw, now working as a rider on a cattle ranch. Sarah Tolliver is a widow with two children and a successful ranch, but no way to protect it from the ruthless men who would rather see her fail. When the two come together sparks fly, as a former outlaw loses her heart to a beautiful yet headstrong young woman.

Other titles to look for in the
coming months from
Yellow Rose Books

Tiopa Ki Lakota By D. Jordan Redhawk
(Fall 2000)

Seasons: Book Two By Anne Azel
(Winter 2000)

Prairie Fire By L. J. Maas
(Winter 2000)

Dr. Livingston, I Presume By T. Novan
(Winter 2001)

None So Blind By L. J. Maas
(Winter 2001)

Daredevil Hearts By Francine Quesnel
(Winter 2001)

Safe Harbor By Radclyffe
(Spring 2001)

Storm Front By Belle Reilly
(Summer 2001)

Tonya Muir lives in Colorado with her husband, 3 dogs, 2 horses, and 3 cats. She graduated from the University of Pittsburgh with a degree in Computer Science. She spent some time in the Air Force being a programmer analyst and handling worldwide installations, but was stationed in Oklahoma City and Colorado Springs. After separating from the military, Tonya took a job as a personnel manager for a telecommunications company in Denver, which eventually became a Program Management position. She is currently on medical disability leave from that same company due to a cancer diagnosis (adenocarcinoma of unknown primary).

Tonya greatly appreciates your purchase of this book and the generosity of the publisher in donating proceeds to the research of this cancer.

Printed in the United States
3108